D0168585

stonekiller

stonekiller

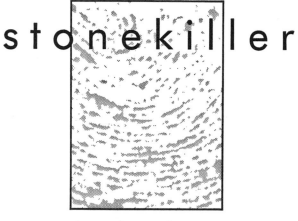

j. robert janes

First published in Great Britain by Constable & Company Ltd.

Published by
Soho Press, Inc.
853 Broadway
New York, NY 10003

Library of Congress Cataloging in Publication Data

Janes, J. Robert (Joseph Robert), 1935–
Stonekiller / J. Robert Janes.
p.   cm.
ISBN 1-56947-107-X (alk. paper)
I. Title.
PR9199.3.J3777S   1996
813'.54—dc21   96-48522
                                CIP

10 9 8 7 6 5 4 3 2 1

To each a stone to mark the beginning and the end.

author's note

Stonekiller is a work of fiction in which actual places and times are used but altered as appropriate. Occasionally the name of a real person appears for historical authenticity, though all are deceased and the story makes of them what it demands. I do not condone what happened during these times, I abhor it. But during the Occupation of France the everyday crimes of murder and arson continued to be committed, and I merely ask, by whom and how were they solved?

acknowledgement

All the novels in the St-Cyr-Kohler series incorporate a few words and brief passages of French or German. Dr Dennis Essar of Brock University very kindly assisted with the French, as did the artist Pierrette Laroche, while Ms Bodil Little of the German Department at Brock helped with the German. Should there be any errors, they are my own and for these I apologize but hope there are none.

This is for Maurice and Pierrette Laroche
with whom I share a love of prehistory.

stonekiller

Among the broken saplings in the centre of the glade, sunlight trapped the blowflies. Now they rose above the corpse which was still hidden from view, now they settled on it. And in the stillness of an early summer's afternoon, their sound was constant.

Alarmed, St-Cyr held his breath. Nothing stirred but those damned flies. 'Hermann, a moment,' he breathed.

'Be my guest,' softly grunted the Bavarian in guttural French that was still improving. 'She's all yours.'

'She?'

'It's just a thought. Rape and then silence, eh? That hangdog truffle hunter who reported this should have taken a closer look.'

'Perhaps he did but was afraid to admit it.'

'Perhaps that sow he uses to find his truffles stuck her snout into something she shouldn't have.'

Ah *merde*, must Hermann? 'In the Dordogne, as elsewhere, my friend, the fall is the time for truffles. Don't tempt the pig before the fungus is ripe. That hunter might just have been checking the ground but *not* with his pig!'

The forest canopy had opened, ferns giving way to saxifrage and vetch whose soft blue and pale purple flowers were tangled among the tall grass, swaths of which had been beaten down. Burdock grew here too, and goldenrod, fly honeysuckle and elder. But everywhere the ferns had crowded closely, holding to the shade of limestone shelves beneath dark humus, holm oak, walnut and chestnut, one of which had fallen many years ago to open up the glade.

St-Cyr stopped suddenly and said, sadly, 'Ah no.'

Kohler heard the flies as they rose in a dense blue cloud to shimmer in the sunlight and give pause to their egg-laying. The wounds, the lacerations and punctures were all puffed up, dark and oozing. Dried blood was glued to blades of grass and broken wild flowers. The pale and flaccid buttocks were blotched by putrefaction. The stench hit him and he turned suddenly away.

'*I warned you!*' hissed St-Cyr. 'Piss off now. *Vite, vite, dummkopf!* Go and have a cigarette *if* you have any left!'

'I haven't,' came the whispered confession. 'I gave the last of them to that girl I met on the train.'

Ah yes, the one with the nice calves she kept trying to hide. 'She *knew* you were Gestapo, idiot. She was terrified.'

'I told her I was a salesman of polished gemstones and ashtrays from Idar-Oberstein. She was convinced.'

'*You were old enough to have been her grandfather!* Just because there are so few young Frenchmen around doesn't mean you can take advantage of their absence.' Furiously a crumpled packet of Gauloises Bleues, the national curse if one could get them — *if* — was snatched from a slightly ragged jacket pocket and thrust into the Bavarian's hands.

Shaking, Kohler lit up and inhaled deeply. Retreating quickly across the glade into shade, he shut his eyes and silently cursed the French. Why did they always have to kill each other in such horrible ways?

It was Friday 21 June 1942. Jean-Louis St. Cyr—Louis—the Sûreté's Chief Inspector, was now firmly planted just outside the cloud of blowflies. A cinematographer at heart—such a lover of the cinema he would take time out if possible to see again a film he had already seen nine times—Louis would memorize every detail. A gardener, a reader of books when time allowed, he was fifty-one years of age, married and with a little son he seldom saw. The wife, too, and she was pretty and all alone in Paris. A worry, ah yes. Sooner or later there'd be trouble, and who could blame her if she wanted a little something on the side?

Unaware of his partner's thoughts, St-Cyr let his gaze move slowly over the victim's back. The dress had been one of her best, if not the best—he was certain of this. It was of a vivid dark blue seersucker, pre-war, and must have been very chic for these parts. It was belted at the waist but the fabric had been torn and cut to shreds. There were no undergarments. The legs were spread and slack and at odd angles—clumsy looking but that was common enough in death. Had she family? he wondered. There'd been no missing-persons report. Not one word, a puzzle.

The wounds were many and, though most were shallow, some were far deeper and had been worked at. The flies descended *en masse* and began to worry the flesh. Bruises that might have lightened had she lived were everywhere but hard to define due to the discolouration. Often the weapon had struck her bluntly, not breaking the skin until the second or third attempt. Had her killer been unfamiliar with it? Could it have been a jagged stone? Were there still traces of rigor?

He crouched over the corpse. Disturbed, the flies rose up, buzzing unhappily at the intrusion of dispersing hands.

'Married,' he said. The wedding band was wide and at least of eighteen carat gold, and it caught the sunlight and glowed warmly from between its puffy edgings. Perhaps some well-off relative had donated the ring—this was often done in the country. Life was closer, more solid, more meaningful than in the large cities where a girl from the country would only feel out of place. But the dress was at odds with the country. It really was. Ripped to shreds as if hated.

The finger was slack. 'Dead at least three days,' he murmured. 'Maybe four or five, Hermann,' he called out.

'Four, you idiot! *Four!* I could have told you that hours ago. I'm going to take a look around. I'm going to leave the details to you.'

'Good! Look for little things, eh? Things our truffle hunter might not have touched.'

'Or taken.'

Ah yes. These days, especially, one could never tell what had been removed to be saved for later use or sold on the black market. A lipstick, a compact, a pair of underpants, even a set of keys to a flat someone else would briefly go through.

She had worn matching gloves but these had been taken off and folded neatly over the belt—he could just see them. The belt was tight and the gloves didn't appear to have been disturbed. Few if any signs of a struggle then—yes, yes, but her strand of pearls had been broken. The pearls were scattered in the grass about her head. Good ones too and old, yes, old.

A woman, then, who had dressed as if to meet someone, a lover perhaps, but had found death instead.

She must have worn a slip, underpants and a brassière but of these there was still no sign. A disturbing puzzle. Had she taken them off elsewhere and then come on here? Where were her shoes, her hat?

Questions ... there were always questions, but he didn't think she had snatched up the gloves at the last moment. No, they must have been intentional. The dress, the belt, the pearls and the gloves but nothing else.

Instinctively St-Cyr looked up and across the glade, realizing that he was still not alone. Hermann was a big man, a giant with the pugnacious nose, lower jaw and jutting chin of an ageing storm-trooper, though he swore he was but three or was it really four years older than St Cyr. Shrapnel scars glistened about the ragged, dissipated countenance whose puffy eyelids drooped and bagged from faded blue and often expressionless eyes.

The shrapnel scars were from that other war. They'd been enemies then, in 1914. God did things like that to detectives, this one in particular. Ah yes, of course. Necessity and nearly two years of fighting crime together—arson, murder, extortion and kidnapping, et cetera, et cetera—had welded their partnership so that now, though they were still discovering things about each other, they each knew how the other thought and worked. Hermann was wanting to walk through the woods. He hated death. He was afraid of it always though he'd been a Munich detective long before this lousy war, long before Berlin and his ascendancy to Paris, and had seen lots of similar things. Well, not like this. No, not quite like this.

He was standing among the ferns, reading the woodcraft signs. The big, strong, stumpy fingers were delicately touching a broken leaf as if it was a tripwire or the timer of a bomb he had to defuse.

'Louis. . . .'

'Yes, I know. Follow her trail. See where she came from but don't go too far and *don't* get lost.'

'Sarlat isn't too far. The Dordogne is close.'

'Yes, yes, and the woods and valleys are thick and many.'

'I'll shout.'

'You do that.'

'I'll find the railway line and follow it out to the road, *dummkopf*. She must have come along it. She can't have gone far in her bare feet.'

Somewhat chubby, somewhat diffident, the Sûreté's *détective* was broad-shouldered, not tall but not short either, a solid trunk of a man whose dark brown hair was thick and carelessly brushed to the right. Unlike so many of his contemporaries who tarted themselves up in ersatz cloth of human hair or cellulose or in black-market suits and shoes of good quality, Louis depended on things from before the Defeat, from before the Occupation.

The dark brown moustache was thick and wider than the Führer's and had been grown long before that ranting little corporal had ever wet his pants over Czechoslovakia. The bushy eyebrows and large, brown ox-eyes sought Kohler out again.

'Ah *mon Dieu*, Hermann, why hang around? You know I need to be alone with her. It's always best, isn't that so?'

'Was she raped?'

'How could I possibly tell?'

St-Cyr watched as his partner and friend slowly picked his way through the woods until, at last, he had disappeared from view.

'He desperately needs a holiday,' he said apologetically to the corpse. 'He's got a new girlfriend in Paris but she's playing hard to get and he hasn't yet introduced us or said much about her. If you ask me, I think he's planning to set up house even though he has a wife back home on her father's farm near Wasserburg, and when he is forced to see someone like yourself, this causes him much concern.'

Though he could not yet prove it, St-Cyr felt the woman had bathed and then had calmly put on the dress. The pale, light brown hair was loose and it must have fallen to her shoulders but was now matted forward over the back of her head and caked with dried blood through which, among the hairs, there were bits of grass and torn wild flowers. Some yellow, some pale blue among the amber strands of what he felt must surely have been her pride and joy.

The killer had even hacked at the back of her neck—had he tried to saw off her head with that thing? Ah *merde, merde,* what the weapon been?

'Both sharp and ragged but pointed too and blunt also,' he said aloud.

He knew he had to turn her over but had best wait until a photographer could be summoned and then the district coroner. It could and would take ages and time . . . time was a luxury they did not have.

The Sturmbannführer Walter Boemelburg, Head of the Gestapo in France and Hermann's Chief, had telegraphed to say he wanted to see them immediately on their return to Paris. *Immediately.*

A mere stop for boiler water at a small station and they'd been pulled off the train from Bergerac. Two 'free' detectives on the run back to Paris with nothing else to do but try to read a train novel—a paperback—or chat up some pretty girl. God did things like that—yanked them out of the doldrums and threw them into the woods without even the benefit of a glass of Vichy water. Ah *merde*, this Occupation, this blitzkrieg pursuit of crime and its perpetrators. It was no life for Marianne and the boy. There was never enough to eat in Paris and she was always wanting to take Philippe home to her parents' farm in Brittany. 'He'll have milk, Jean-Louis, and meat sometimes. He'll have bread and potatoes and be warm in winter. Paris is so lonely.' She had said it with such feeling and so often. 'I am a stranger. The house, it is too empty.'

This woman would have understood Marianne. Though he felt odd at the thought, instinct told him it was true but had Paris ever figured in the victim's life? That, too, was a thought, and suddenly, though he still wanted to be alone with her, he wanted to be with Hermann.

'Find the place where she bathed, *mon vieux*,' he whispered. 'Find her other things but do not touch them until I've had a look.'

The valley was secluded and well wooded, and when he had gone up it a few hundred metres, Kohler heard the waterfall in the distance and then he found the cave. It was high up beneath a thick limestone ledge and from its darkened mouth, the sun-drenched slope below glared with the tumbled grey-white rubble of the ages until this progressed into brush and then into trees. He let his eyes linger on the cave. He couldn't understand why its presence frightened him. Christ, it was just a cave. The Dordogne was riddled with them.

On 12 September 1940, cave paintings far better than any others had been discovered at Lascaux by four boys searching for a lost dog a mere twenty kilometres to the north, which just showed a person what boys could find when hunting for something else. But those paintings were only twenty thousand or so years old, which was long enough to make one wonder why the clergy had taken such an interest in them. Rumour had it that some local abbot was now calling that cave the Sistine Chapel of the Périgord!

Had the abbot found any crosses, any fish symbols among the paintings? A staunch non-believer, not a conscientious doubter like Louis, Kohler had little time or patience for religion, let alone that of the Nazi ideologists who fabricated to suit themselves. But being alone in the shade, and standing on two flat stones in the bed of the nicest stream he had seen in ages, he was deeply troubled by the sight of this cave. He had the sudden thought that he could not possibly know what it might mean to the murder, yet it must mean something. She would have been only too aware of it.

The sound of the waterfall came to him. There was leafy shade along the banks of the stream, now dark and cool, now light and warm. The pungent scent of moss and decaying vegetation reminded him of a graveyard, which was stupid really, but he couldn't shake the thought. It was that kind of place.

The stream-course took a small bend. There were blocks of light grey to dark grey limestone among the trees, and everywhere there was moss growing green on grey and still, so still. Ferns and King Solomon's seal, May lilies after their flowering, bluebells too, probably.

High above the little valley a honey buzzard soared against the sun-hammered sky.

When he found her shoes, he found the blanket she had spread under the arms of a giant chestnut tree. There was a picnic hamper lying broken open, its contents scattered by badgers, the leftovers foraged by mice and squirrels. Her clothes were neatly folded to one side of where the hamper must have once rested. A rough beige skirt, serviceable white blouse, pale yellow cardigan, kerchief, raincoat, knee-length stockings with elastic bands, slip and underwear and sturdy shoes . . . the handbag in which she had brought the dress she had then put on. The truffle hunter had touched nothing.

A sliver of pre-war soap lay on a modest towel. Beside these, there was a pair of glasses in their leather case, a sandpaper board for the nails, a pair of clippers, and a blue velvet-lined box for a strand of pearls.

From the picnic site beside the stream it was but a short walk through the woods to the waterfall, and along the way, in the dark humus and in clean sand, he found faint traces of her footprints. Bare feet, no other prints but hers. She had stripped off at the blanket and had come this way and then had gone back.

There was a small ledge of limestone, a pavement broken by rectilinear cracks. This ledge led to the base of the waterfall, to large rectangular blocks of limestone that, through time, had collapsed from above. Though the water fell among them, some thoughtful soul, 20,000 years ago perhaps, had cleared a place for bathing.

When he found, in the undergrowth near the blanket, a basket of mushrooms and the worn but razor-sharp paring knife she had used to gather them, he saw she had covered them with a thick layer of once dampened moss. There were puffballs and edible morels—any farmboy, such as he had been, could have identified them. Sweet-chestnut boletus too and parasols, others too. Others.

He removed the moss completely, noting that she had placed a pair of thin cloth work gloves between the mushrooms in a small canvas collecting bag. The gloves were worn through at the thumbs and fingers and stained not by humus as he had thought, but by ochrous fine sand, grey ash and some sort of very black powder.

There were also tiny bits of black flint no longer than a few millimetres at most.

When he opened the collecting bag, he saw very quickly that she had been up to mischief. Death cap and fly agaric lay side by side and there were several specimens of each.

If she had intended to kill someone, she had been prepared to make a damned good job of it. An omelette, monsieur? A little more of the *pâté* or the *champignons à la crème*?

The French were always killing themselves with such mistakes—there were always warnings posted in prominent places—but this was intent. Why else would she have gathered them, seeing as she damned well knew her mushrooms?

The identity card in her purse gave the name of Madame Ernestine Fillioux, born 15 March 1896 in the village of Beaulieu-sur-Dordogne, upriver a piece.

Her height was 167 centimetres (5'7"). *Hair: light brown; eyes: brown; nose: normal; face: oval; complexion: pale; special signs: small brown mole on the right cheekbone; freckles over the bridge of the nose; a three-centimetre scar on the left forehead.*

There were the usual two fingerprints, the thumbs, below the 13-franc stamp, and over these and the signatures of herself and a witness, the stamp of the Commissariat de Police in Périgueux. The thing had only recently been renewed and was dated 17 August 1941.

Her occupation was listed as shopkeeper and postmistress, her marital status as war widow.

Kohler searched the photograph for answers but all he found was a forty-six-year-old woman with a proud chin, rather strongly boned, sharply featured face, good firm lips, steadfast eyes, a high forehead and hair that was pulled back into a chignon which did little but add severity to what might otherwise have been attractiveness.

'What happened?' he asked. 'Why the special dress, and why the mushrooms? Why the walk through the woods to that glade when this little valley is so much nicer?'

No matter how hard he tried, he could still see her lying face down in the grass with her arms and legs flung apart and the flies crawling all over her.

Had the blue of them not matched that of her dress?

The seersucker was finely crinkled, the cotton both cool in the heat and so easily crushed it was like a caress. It had the feel of money and class. 'Paris . . .' murmured St-Cyr. 'The rue du Faubourg Saint-Honoré, the avenue de l'Opéra.'

Naked beneath it, she would have felt so very good. Proud of herself, yes—what woman wouldn't have been? He was certain she was from the Dordogne, had felt this all along but could not yet put a finger on the reason. Perhaps Hermann had found something by now.

Gingerly he used a pair of tweezers to pry the collar free of caked blood and read the label with a sigh, 'Barclay, 18 to 20 avenue de l'Opéra, Paris.'

Barclay's had had shops in Vichy, Nice, Cannes and Deauville, too, before the war but now operated under a name he had deliberately forgotten in protest.

1937 or '38, he thought. By '39 tensions would have been too high for such extravagance and it was extravagance, this dress. 'A hat from Yvette Delort, madame, to please your lover? Was he the one who did this?'

He was certain she had either gone to Paris to buy the dress before the war or had ordered it especially and had waited the days or weeks until it had arrived.

A woman, then, who had known exactly what she had wanted.

She had not been surprised by her assailant and this made her killing and defilement all the more puzzling. She had apparently come to the glade unaware of any danger and had paused at its edge, among the ferns where Hermann had picked up her trail. She had said, '_____, is it really you?' or perhaps, 'I am so sorry. Am I a little late? My watch . . . I must have left it where I bathed.'

She had then gone forward to stand facing her assailant who

had come to the glade as they had, from the opposite direction—he was certain of this. She could not have known of his or her intentions since she *had not run,* had not even backed away.

She had stood facing that person, in awe, in tears, perhaps—how could one possibly know now if there had been tears or only soft words of hesitation and relief? She had been struck hard between the eyes. A stone? he wondered. It had split the skin badly. Now stained as if by some horrible accident of birth, the wound's livid dark plum-violet to greenish-yellow putridness marred her brow forever.

She had fallen back, had tried to get up—one hand had perhaps been placed behind her, the other stretched out towards her assailant, he could see it happening so clearly. She had then been struck at least twice more on the head. After this, while still on her back, she had been stabbed repeatedly and slashed with that thing, then flipped over.

Grim at the thought of what must have happened, he stood and, carefully folding a bit of fabric, tucked it away in an envelope, then cleaned the tweezers on some grass.

Fortunately his other jacket pocket, the one with the loose thread that had been carefully coiled and saved at the end of its freely dangling leader, held a pair of ancient rubber gloves.

He put them on and, finding some inner strength of will, turned her over with much difficulty, scattering the flies and finally stepping back to gasp, 'Ah *nom de Jésus-Christ!'*

She had been partially disembowelled—butchered. Opened to the groin. The oozing, stinking mess of dark, sticky offal was ripe with violet and yellow. The flies . . . the flies . . . they descended. They worried. They fought with one another to get at her and dig deeper.

Her throat had been hacked at. The jugular, the carotid arteries, the windpipe. . . . Her tongue was black. Both breasts had been crudely parted lengthwise down the middle and peeled aside so that now, as he watched, the left half of the left breast slowly slipped away until it hung by a strap of rotting skin.

When he found Hermann, a bottle of champagne, discovered in the stream, was all but gone. 'I saved the other one for you, Louis. Come and sit a while. You look like you need it.'

'I told you not to touch a thing!'

'Hey, it's a Moët-et-Chandon 1889, *mein Kamerad*. That's definitely not the year of her birth.'

A Moët-et-Chandon, the 1889 . . . How had she come by it?

They sat with their feet cooling. They didn't say a thing for quite some time. The champagne was absolutely magnificent, a real treat in which they silently toasted the victim at impromptu moments.

'Jesus, Louis, why the hell does it always have to be us?'

'Murder doesn't choose. God works in mysterious ways. Frankly, I don't think He has ever forgiven me for having looked up my Cousin Denise's skirts. I was ten at the time and didn't know any better. She was eating the strawberries I had stolen for her and said I could do as I pleased, but my Aunt Sophie thought otherwise.'

Louis was always being called to account for childhood misdemeanours and for others as well, ah yes. 'Don't worry about Marianne's birthday. Your big Bavarian brother's taken care of everything. Roses, Louis, and if not them, then masses of petunias and ox-eye daisies. I asked a girl I met at Madame Chabot's on the rue Danton to look after things if we didn't get back in time. Giselle will do her best. You can count on her. She's very reliable—I like that in a girl. She'll steal them if she can't find any to buy.'

Ah *merde*, the wife's birthday and theft from the Occupier? Hermann had no scruples about stealing from his confrères, just as he had none when it came to choosing his women. Another prostitute. Marianne would have a fit. 'You ought to mind your own business!'

'I am. I have to live with you, right? Admit it, you forgot and a man can't forget things like that. He really can't. Not with a skirt like her. She'll leave you just like the other one did.'

The first wife. 'Spare me the lecture. Go and talk to that corpse as I have. Hey, from now on I am going to leave the "details" to you.'

'Not before I give you the grand tour to open your eyes and get the fly-eggs out of them. Come on, relax. Here, have some more. Our woman was really something.'

From the scattered, foraged contents of the picnic hamper, St-Cyr reassembled the menu. '*Pâté de foie gras truffé* in a stone crock with a tight seal, alas now broken, radishes and bread. *Confit d'oie* in another stone crock, this time still in one piece. After the *pâté*, the remaining meat of the goose is cooked in its own fat and preserved under it.' He held up the crock. 'The contents would have been carefully taken out with a dinner-knife and placed on one of the plates to be exclaimed over and admired before being grilled and eaten with a little more of the bread perhaps.' He tossed a hand. 'The shells of the six eggs the badgers have eaten indicate an unrationed omelette was to follow.' He held up a small copper skillet. 'A little of the leftover goose fat to cook the eggs and the mushrooms, but did she plan to kill her fellow diner?'

Kohler knew Louis was enjoying himself and let him continue.

The withered remains of some lettuce and endive were plucked from the grass along with those of several green onions and cloves of garlic, only bits of which remained. He found a small bottle of oil, unlabelled, the container saved to be used time and again. '*Salade à l'huile de noix* (with walnut oil). Then cheese, probably, with grandjean walnuts—they're very meaty—and fresh, sweet cherries. Afterwards, coffee from her thermos. It's no longer hot but it's real. She has even added a little cognac.'

The wines included a fine red Château Bonnecoste and the *vin paille de Beaulieu,* in addition to the champagne. There were glasses, plates, cups and cutlery for two with linen napkins. 'Fantastic china, Hermann. Old like the pearls. Sèvres and quite expensive.'

She had thought of everything, even to uncorking the red to let it breathe and sinking the white in the stream to cool, but had she intended to poison the person she had gone to meet?

'Or did she intend to kill herself as well, Louis, and take down the two of them?'

'Or merely use the specimens to show someone else what not to collect?' That, too, was often done.

'Then why collect so many?'

'Ah yes, that is a problem most certainly.' The poisonous mushrooms were one thing, however, the work gloves that separated them from the others in her basket, quite another.

Gingerly St-Cyr teased the gloves out and prised them open, showering a little rain of fine yellowish sand and tiny shards of black to dark brown flint. 'These gloves haven't been used in years,' he said.

'Then where did she find them?'

'Or why did she bring them?'

'That cave?' asked Kohler hesitantly.

'Perhaps, but then . . .'

'There's a black powder, a pigment of some sort.'

'Manganese dioxide—the mineral, pyrolusite. It's quite common in the Dordogne. The ancients used it to. . . .'

'To paint their caves,' breathed Kohler.

Both of them knew they would have to make the climb. The cave was nearly seventy metres above the stream. Sweat blurred the vision and stung the eyes. Twice they had to pause for breath. The talus of angular, slab-like blocks of grey-white limestone was difficult to traverse and blinding in its glare. Impatiently St-Cyr yanked at a collar that was too tight. The button, its thread frayed, popped off and he saw it bounce from a rock, blinked and said, 'Ah no. It has disappeared.'

Such little losses were devastating these days, thought Kohler. Replacements were so difficult to find. 'Tough luck. I'll tell Boemelburg you lost it in a whorehouse.'

'You would. Save it for Pharand.'

'That little fart? He'd love it.' Pharand was Louis's boss, a file-mined, officious, insidiously jealous, territorial twit who was dangerous. Very dangerous. Ah yes. 'That champagne wasn't such a good idea, Louis. I think I'm feeling dizzy.'

Mopping his brow, the Sûreté's little Frog dropped his suit jacket onto a slab of rock and took time out to use his necktie as a bandanna. 'There, that is better. Now you also.'

They continued on and up beneath the soaring of the honey buzzard, two fly specks in a bleached and broken land to which scattered scrub, a *maquis* of sorts, gave absolutely no comfort. Had they the vision of the hawk, they would have seen a well-treed plateau on high with an oak and chestnut forest and a stream that flowed to the head of a once much larger valley before leaping off its limestone cap to fall in a spray that glistened in the sunlight. They would have seen the railway line, a little to the south of them as it followed the flats along the north bank of the Dordogne. They would have seen that line turn to the north-west towards Sarlat. There was a road and a viaduct, a railway overpass. They had come in from the west. The woman had come in from the east, gathering her mushrooms until, at last, she had reached the valley and gone up it to the waterfall.

'Louis, I'm going to have a bathe when we get back down there.'

'Me also, but first, a moment, please, Hermann, for the quiet contemplation of what is now before us.'

The cave entrance was perhaps four metres wide by two in height but it had, originally, been much larger. In medieval times the cave could quite possibly have been used by shepherds to pen their flocks at night. More recently the layered deposits at its entrance, a hard breccia of broken bones, flints, sand, and rocky debris that had fallen from the roof, had been excavated. These dull reddish to pale yellowish deposits—some with sandy layers and some more bouldery—had a depth of about three metres. Down through the ages rubbish had been piled up at the cave mouth. These deposits had been cut into platform benches about a metre and a half high and perhaps three metres in depth and two in width. A trench ran through them to the darker recesses of the cave.

Spoil from the excavations had been thrown to the right and now lay behind a low retaining wall of dry-stone flags that extended out from the cave mouth and a little along that side of the valley. Rusting sardine cans, some so riddled with holes they must have been left before that other war, lay with shattered bits of wine bottle, nails and other trash. 'Two-legged badgers,' commented the Sûreté tartly. 'Artefact plunderers. Why can't people show respect and leave places like this to be studied? A prehistorian dug this excavation, Hermann, but that was years ago. They have even pulled the nails he used to mark the layers!'

Across a cleared span of the original cave floor, there was a ladder leaning against the innermost bench. The floor was littered with broken black flints, yellowish to reddish sand, ashes both grey and black, rock from the roof above, and broken, charred animal bones. Bones everywhere.

In one instant, standing at the entrance, how much history could they see? 'Perhaps a hundred thousand years, Hermann. Perhaps more. From deep within the Pleistocene Ice Age to the present, from the severe cold of a world gripped by continental glaciation whose ice-front lay to the north near London, Rotterdam, Köln and elsewhere through countless cycles of cold and warm, the not-so-cold and not-so-warm, to what we have today. But always there was life here and a place to live. Sometimes permanently frozen ground and tundra vegetation, sometimes fir forests, grasslands or deciduous trees. Many of the flints show signs of having been worked. The bones . . . the bones are from animals some of which no longer roam these parts or, in some cases, even exist.'

Kohler stepped into the shade and at once the coolness of the cave beckoned. 'A broken femur, Louis.'

Wolf, cave bear, Merck's rhinoceros, woolly mammoth, reindeer and wild boar came quickly to mind, a smattering from across the ages.

'A deer, I think. It's a bit charred,' said Kohler.

'The red deer, a preferred food, as was the horse of those days, though it looked more like the Mongolian horse of the present or a large and shaggy pony.' Reverently the Sûreté took it from him and ran a finger over its length. 'Our victim,' he said, and Kohler could detect the sadness in his partner's voice. 'These three, parallel incisions just above the knuckle.' He held the bone upright with the knuckle down. 'These are the marks made by a stone chopper as the meat was removed.'

Oh-oh. 'Was she butchered that way?'

'Yes, I think so.'

'The bone was smashed after a brief roasting, Louis, and . . . and the marrow sucked out.'

'But when? Thirty thousand years ago, or one hundred thousand?'

It was only when they began to examine the walls of the innermost benches that they saw that some layers contained worked flints, ashes and bones, while others contained none of these but were of sand that had been blown or washed in or debris that had fallen from the roof of the cave. All of the layers had been cemented by lime that had been deposited from percolating groundwaters.

Beyond the benches, the floor of the cave remained littered with broken bones, flints, ashes, sand and bits of stone but this litter was shallow and lessened as the floor extended into deeper darkness. Lights would be needed to probe it further. Lights and ropes.

The roof was perhaps three or, in places, even four metres high, the walls curved outwards and perhaps ten metres apart. A cave of long but not always continuous habitation then, thought St-Cyr, one that would have formed the home base for several people at a time. Neanderthals first and then, more recently, Cro-Magnons.

They shared a cigarette as they stood in the cool darkness looking out towards the entrance. They began, as they so often did in such instances, a rapid exchange of thoughts. 'Madame

Fillioux leaves Beaulieu-sur-Dordogne by train, Hermann, perhaps four or five days ago. Let us give putrefaction its chance but concede that the heat of summer would have speeded things up.'

'She gets off at a siding, dressed in everyday clothes and with stout walking shoes, her coat, picnic hamper and basket in hand. She must have been seen by several people yet no one has thought to mention this nor has anyone reported her missing.'

'Madame Fillioux then walks along the tracks following the departing train but soon turns into the woods and begins to climb. She knows her way—she has done this before many times.'

'She must have, mustn't she?' The cigarette was passed back.

'Yes, yes, of course. She collects mushrooms, becomes completely absorbed in the task—ah, some edible morels are deep in the refuse of a rotting stump.'

'Fly agaric and death cap go into the collecting bag. She feels a sense of what, Louis? Relief at finding them—she'd been so worried there wouldn't be any—guilt, fear, you tell me.'

St-Cyr inhaled deeply. 'It's too early for such things. She reaches the valley, had stopped collecting at some point distant from it.'

'She lays things out for the picnic, has a bathe and puts on the dress.'

'And the pearls. Pearls that are really quite valuable but were ignored by her killer. Hey, it's your turn with the cigarette. Don't take all of it.'

'I won't. You can trust me. She crosses the stream and follows it downstream a little, Louis, then goes into the woods, leaving the valley, climbing its gentler slope. She passes through the woods and up a little hill, then down into a shallow hollow and through the forest to another hill. There are trees and underbrush all the way until she comes at last to that glade.'

'To find her assailant waiting for her, Hermann. She pauses. She does not retreat in fear.'

The cigarette was handed back. 'Did he watch her having a

bathe? Did he follow her but reach the glade from the other direction?'

'Apparently she knows this person and suspects nothing. *Nothing!* She advances towards the assailant, is hit hard and goes down. She is hit again and again, and then ... then is crudely butchered with ... with one of these, I think, though I cannot yet say for certain nor can I yet fully come to grips with the horror of it.'

Plucking at his partner's sleeve, St-Cyr pulled him forward until they had reached the innermost bench. There he knelt and ran a forefinger over one of the layers of habitation. 'A stone tool, Hermann. A handaxe, perhaps. Something with both sharp and ragged edges, a point as well but also blunt.'

Kohler swallowed dryly. Champagne always did that to him. Louis found his pocket-knife and, opening it, began to pick at the layer but all he got were little bits of flint, ash and sand.

The cigarette clung to his lower lip until it had burned down to all but nothing and had finally gone out. A half hour of struggling ensued before he had what he wanted. 'Ah *nom de Dieu, de Dieu*, Hermann, it's magnificent.'

Almond shaped and showing clearly the shallow, conchoidal hollows where the flint had been spalled away when struck hard by a hammer stone, the handaxe was no more than seven centimetres in length, perhaps four or five in width and two or three in thickness.

With it there had lain a smaller flint, much more finely worked and with a convex cutting edge that was serrated. There was also a scraper that had once been used to clean the flesh from animal hides. 'Pressure flaking,' mused the Sûreté, 'with a bone or wooden stylus that had first been hardened by fire. This handaxe is far too small for what I want. It's of too recent an origin—perhaps only twenty thousand years. For our murder weapon, we must go back in time to those lower layers where the tools are simpler, the handaxes far chunkier, yet still very effective.'

From the cave entrance they looked down over the valley and

off towards the site of the murder. Shadows now cooled the lower slopes. Night was coming but would take its time. At peace with the world and left largely to itself, the little valley exuded only the gentle hush of its waterfall and then the sound of birds awakening after the heat.

Kohler sensed his partner needed this moment. They were standing in the footsteps of ancestors who would have looked out on a quite different valley, yet it was the same. Pristine.

Louis heaved a sigh. Kohler held his breath. It was at times like this that the bond between them only grew stronger, more welcome, more. . . .

A scream shattered the silence. Long and hard and high pitched, it was ripped right out of the person who uttered it. Again and again it came, shrill as it raced across the trees to them.

For perhaps ten seconds there was a pause. Eyes riveted on the distant spot, their whole attention focused, they waited. Then again it came. Again! Anguish and despair and then . . . then . . . 'MAMAN! MAMAN! AH NO! NO!'

They leapt off the edge and went down the talus flinging their arms out for balance, racing . . . racing . . . No time . . . no time . . . Got to find her. Got to stop her. Got to get her away from that thing. That thing. . . .

DAWN CAME AT LAST, AND FROM THE RIVER FAR below the ancient fortified town of Domme, mist in tendrils hugged the lowlands along the Dordogne.

St-Cyr heaved a sigh. The view, among the finest in France, was fantastic, yet try as he did, he could not keep from hearing that poor woman's screams and feel, as he had yesterday, the profoundness of the encompassing silence. Had screams like that echoed in that little valley one hundred thousand years ago?

The mist lay in a whitish-grey gossamer over the deep, dark shadowy blue of the river and the green of ordered fields and poplars. Not a swastika showed, not a Wehrmacht convoy or patrol, not even the open touring car of some SS bigwig or Gestapo 'trade commissioner'. He was in the Free Zone, in Vichy-controlled territory, yet conditioned by the Occupied Zone in the North, one always had to look for such things, one always had to ask, How long can this last?

In the distance, the same bare escarpment rocks as those

beneath his shoes boldly faced the sun to glow a soft yellow-grey under forest cover. Behind them, the wooded hills, valleys and plateaus of the Périgord Noir continued on to Sarlat and east-wards to the site of the murder and well beyond. Mist would cloak that little valley too, even as at the dawn of prehistory.

They had found the victim's daughter on her knees hugging herself and rocking back and forth in grief beside that corpse. They had dragged her from it even as she had fought with them to be left alone until, in compassion only, he had clipped her under the chin and into oblivion.

Juliette Jouvet née Fillioux, born Beaulieu-sur-Dordogne, 3 April 1914, age now twenty-eight, and only child of the victim. Married and with two children of her own, a boy of seven years and a girl of five. A schoolteacher. Husband, a former colleague and now a disabled veteran of the Russian Campaign, one of the LVF, the *Légion des volontaires français contre le bolchévisme*. A sworn enemy of Russia and a member of the PPF, the Parti Populaire Français, violently anti-Communist, anti-de Gaulle, anti-Jewish, anti-everything including the police, and now . . . why now a very bitter man. Ah yes. The war in Russia had not been kind. Few acknowl-edged the bravery of the wreckage that had returned. Most simply ignored him and felt uncomfortable in his presence.

Jouvet had not been co-operative nor had there been one word or gesture of compassion for his wife.

Sedated by the cognac Hermann had forced her to drink and had found God knows where, the woman had slept. Sour on *vin ordinaire*, the husband had retreated into a brooding, surly silence. The children had watched their father in alarm before casting warning glances at each other and retreating to bed.

It was not good. Ah no, it wasn't. Murder and domestic prob-lems so often went hand in hand. Madame Jouvet had had a painful welt and bruise from a fist high on her left cheek—now her lower jaw might well be swollen, a worry. The skin had also been yellow and dark around the half-closed eye, a massive shiner that was at least five days old.

How had she borne the shame of it, a teacher in a little place like this? Had the argument, preceding the death of the mother-in-law, signalled trouble?

Fortunately transport had arrived with two *flics* from Sarlat. They had soon got the woman home and it was then that Hermann and he had discovered what had transpired.

Word had reached Domme that a body had been found but that its identity was still unknown. Abruptly she had left her students without explanation, had run frantically outside to grab her bicycle and pedal the twenty-five or so kilometres. First downhill to the bridge across the river, then on to Vitrac, Montfort and Carsac-Aillac before turning northwards towards Sarlat and then east. Tears, prayers, perhaps exhortations of remorse and then ... then the dropping of her bicycle on the railway track, the running through the woods. They had found one of her shoes. She had known exactly where to find her mother. *Exactly.*

Longing for his pipe and tobacco, he studied the distant terrain noting every little nuance as his mind probed the murder until a stick whacked a tombstone behind him, a throat was cleared. Spittle darted to one side. 'Monsieur ... ?' he began. The set of his lips was grim.

'It's *Captain*,' spat Jouvet. Hammered by the early-morning light, the veteran stood stock-still in the graveyard. There was a stout walking-stick in his left hand and he leaned heavily on this to relieve the constant pain of the bullet-wasted leg the Russian partisans had given him. Once handsome, now grey with fatigue and unshaven, he wiped his nose with the back of a right hand that was far from good. 'So, you have some questions. Why not start asking them, eh? She's still sleeping it off but will have to do her duty. No replacement can be found and I cannot be expected to fill in for her. Not yet. We need the money.'

'The money, ah yes.'

The grey-green trousers the Germans had given the husband in lieu of the promised French Army uniform, were unpatched in places, the wooden sabots and faded blue denim jacket with open-collared dress shirt disrespectful of his former status as a teacher who had once had students to command. An Iron Cross Second-Class clung defiantly to the left breast. A frayed rope had replaced the belt whose buckle would have borne the words *Gott mit uns*, God with us. The black beret was filthy.

He made no move to come closer. The no man's land of the esplanade separated them.

'Captain, was your mother-in-law to visit with you and your family after first going to that valley?'

'To the cave, Inspector. Why not say it?'

'All right, the cave.'

'Madame Fillioux could well have been on her way here afterwards. I would not have known. Lies . . . all I get from that wife of mine is lies. I'm not well. I can't get around easily.'

'Then why bother to convince me of it?'

The smile was crooked, the stick was waved. 'Only that I could not possibly have killed her.'

There, does that satisfy you? St-Cyr could see this clearly written in the man's expression but he calmed his voice and kept control. 'Tell me about her then. She was a shopkeeper.'

'Her papers will have told you that. Why waste my time?'

'Yes, but what kind of a shop?'

'An *auberge-épicerie*, what else in a lousy little dump like Beaulieu-sur-Dordogne? With the PTT of course—she couldn't have survived without it. Half our rural shopkeepers couldn't.'

The post office, telephone and telegraph exchange. An inn and a grocery shop—tinned and dry goods mainly, and half-empty shelves for there were shortages here, too, in the South. Extreme shortages.

'She was always bitching about the parcels. Meat stinks after a few days,' taunted Jouvet.

No letters were allowed to cross the Demarcation Line between the Occupied and Unoccupied zones. Only postcards with minimum words now instead of gaps to fill in within the printed message that had had to serve everyone no matter what.

But in one of those quirks of Germanic control, parcels had been overlooked in the Defeat of 1940 and postal clerks the country over had simply shrugged and carried on. Forgotten relatives had suddenly been remembered, especially if they had a farm or access to one. Deals had been struck: the tobacco ration every two weeks in exchange for a chicken, a bit of goose liver, some fish perhaps or butter. . . .

The meat and other perishables often stayed in the post offices for days on end. Months in several cases, for the second-class postal service paled against that of the postcards which wasn't all that good either but could sometimes be very efficient.

St-Cyr crossed the esplanade and went in among the tombstones to face the man and stand in danger of his walking stick.

Disdainfully, Jouvet shook his head at the offer of a cigarette. 'I've already had mine. I'll wait until noon, if I can stand it. One has to do such things because of people like you.'

To contain oneself was often the supreme test not just of an honest detective in these troubled times, but of a patriot. Everyone questioned those who had something they didn't have. 'The cave, then, and the site of the murder, Captain? Let us concentrate on them.'

The Sûreté's gaze must be returned measure for measure as with the partisans one had had to question before stringing them up. 'Each year that stupid woman took her little trip. Always on the same date, a Monday, a Sunday, it did not matter. Always to the same place—you'd think she would have got tired of it. First the mushrooms, then the climb up to that hole in the rock and afterwards, after rooting around in there, the bathe in the buff, the dress—ah, I see that you have discovered it. The size of the dress changed over the years as her weight increased but always it was of the same cloth. The strand of pearls, then the little walk through the forest.'

Ah *nom de Dieu, de Dieu*, why was he enjoying the telling of it so much? The dark brown eyes smouldered under puffy eyelids. A man perhaps a good dozen years senior to his wife. 'Monsieur . . .'

'It's *Captain*, damn you!'

One must remain unruffled. 'Captain, you had best tell me what you know of this affair. The ritual of its repetition?'

Jouvet stank of urine and the thought of its splashes made the Sûreté glance questioningly at the veteran's right hand and ask himself, Could it have held a stone?

'A ritual, yes. Call it what you will.' Jouvet tossed the hand for emphasis and clenched it tightly until he winced with pain just to prove he hadn't missed a thing. 'If you ask me, that woman was crazy. *Revering* her dead lover like that. Her *lover*. Ah yes, Inspector, you people from Paris, you come here, you ask the questions but you do not stop to dig beneath the pus to clean the wound. You did not know she had spread her legs in the woods and had conceived without a proper marriage.'

'Pardon?'

Was it so impossible to comprehend? 'I married a bastard, Inspector. A *bastard*. Everyone thinks it of my wife, no matter what that mother of hers tried to do to cover things up.'

'Now listen, cut the vitriol and tell me things plainly. Each year she made the same visit on exactly the same date?'

'*Yes*! The 17th of June.'

Five days ago, on Monday. 'Was she planning to meet some-one this time?'

The veteran's eyes swept anxiously over him. 'Only her dead lover. A captain like myself but from that other war. He died on the Marne with his face deep in the shit probably but she was still able to obtain the *mariage in extremis après décès* to make legal the thing she had carried in her belly. After four years of her trying, the authorities finally listened and gave in—who could blame them with a woman like that? She became Madame Fillioux at last!' He flicked a vindictive glance at his wife who approached.

'Mother raised me on her own, Inspector. No one helped her—not even the Church. She was a very strong-willed person but I adored her as she adored me. We were very close. My heart is broken.'

Grief was held in check by some fantastic strength of will. The daughter's feet, shod in rough espadrilles, were firmly planted, her hands jammed into the pockets of a knitted soft yellow cardigan. A kerchief covered the light brown hair. Some flour or clay had been used in an attempt to lessen the severity of the welt. The black eye was looking a little better. A redness lay under her chin but it was not too swollen. Hermann was right behind her.

'That place. . . . The cave, Inspector, it's very old, very precious. The bones and stone tools go back far into the distant past, far beyond the Cro-Magnons and well into the earliest days of the Neanderthals. My father was a prehistorian, an assistant at the Sorbonne while studying for his final degree. He . . . he spent all of his waking moments patiently excavating the deposits at the mouth of that cave. His hands would always be cut, the skin worn right through—even the gloves *maman* took to him were never enough. That site was to have been the making of him.'

Louis waited. Kohler knew his partner was giving her time.

'She . . . she found the cave for my father, using an old diary from the trunk of artefacts the Abbé Brûlé had left but . . . but then my father, he went away like so many, never to return.'

A diary and a collection of stone tools probably gathered in the early 1800s. There'd be time to dig into that. 'Please, I know this must be very difficult for you, madame, but it was a yearly visit?'

She threw her husband a dark look. 'The visit was her expression of a love that never left her, Inspector. Though there were many offers to take my father's place, *maman* refused all of them. I know. I saw the disappointment in their eyes as they said good-bye to her. She was very pretty and very good with things, very businesslike—she had to be, isn't that correct? Dependable yet . . . yet tender when needed. A real catch.'

The walking-stick jerked. 'Juliette, don't be so stupid. Control yourself.'

'Control? Why should I control anything now that she's

gone? I only did it for her sake, André. On my own I would never have married you, not in a thousand years. Mother wanted things to be better for me. A teacher . . . a teacher married to another and living here in Domme, a step up in the world. Ah yes. God forgive me. I should have listened to my heart!'

'You bitch!' The stick threatened.

'Monsieur,' began St-Cyr.

'It's Captain, damn you!'

'Please don't touch her. Please. My partner, he is right behind you now and if I give the nod, he will flatten you or worse still, cram that foul-tempered mouth of yours into the ground!'

Louis seldom lost his composure. A born diplomat. Fumbling in a pocket, Kohler suddenly remembered a cigarette tucked away for a rainy day and, straightening it, offered it to her.

With a quiet calm that only threw its acid into the husband's face, she accepted and when she inhaled, she stood there looking at Jouvet as if all the bitterness of an unhappy marriage had suddenly been lifted from her.

'You're enjoying his tobacco, aren't you?' seethed the husband.

She tossed her head and shrugged. 'It's not often I get the chance. Since women are denied a ration, you forced me to steal what little I could or barter for it when your back was turned.'

St-Cyr sucked in his breath impatiently. These two would kill each other if they could. 'Madame, let us walk a little. Hermann, please accompany this one back to his command post behind his wife's school. Pry what you can from him and remind him that the Sûreté and the Gestapo require full and accurate answers.'

Namely, when and where was he on the day of the murder. Kohler knew this was what Louis meant and grinned. But when he had the man alone, he, too, tried to make peace. 'My two sons are in Russia. They've told me how it really is.'

'Have they? Then did they tell you, please, that it was we of the LVF who were always given the task of guarding the rear and facing the partisans? One could not take a crap or a piss for fear of having his balls shot off or the organ removed with a knife and fed to him as his throat was slit!'

'I thought it was freezing? I thought it was too cold to . . . well, wave the wand,' shrugged Kohler.

'*It was!*'

For a man with a bad leg, Jouvet could ignore pain when he wanted. Deft with his stick, and by throwing his right side forward, he adopted a twisting gait that soon took them through the graveyard to ruined walls and beyond. Domme had lots of open spaces, the houses often being situated around irregularly shaped quadrangles, and everywhere behind them there were gardens that had been turned over to sustenance. Pigs, goats, beans, potatoes, artichokes. . . . Mentally the farmboy in Kohler ticked them off with appreciation, giving credit where due.

Jouvet knew the town well, knew every wall and bolt hole. Each house, most of one storey with attic dormers, was of that same soft honey-coloured limestone but often with steeply pitched roofs that were shingled with *lauzes*—slabs of flat grey limestone. Where the roofs were far less steep, they were covered with the thick flat reddish tiles so common in the Périgord and the South.

Not on Berlin Time like the Occupied Zone, where 8 a.m. meant 6 a.m., nevertheless the town had long since been up and about. The house, both school and home, was but a stone's throw from the rampart walk but separated from it by a single row of houses. Here on this side of the street, there was only the school and the gardens; the other three sides of the quadrangle held distant rows of houses. Again there were tethered goats, geese, ducks, rabbits in cages, chickens, people working, men, women, boys and girls. . . .

A small schoolyard was to the left of the building. Jouvet went through the boys' door like a rocket to shriek the kids into silence. No one dared look up from his or her desk. All hands were folded in front—perhaps thirty pairs. A portrait of Pétain hung on the wall dead centre and just below a clock with Roman numerals. There was a stove which, in winter, would always have a pot of water with sweet-smelling herbs simmering in it. A small blackboard, a stack of slates brought back into use due to the shortages, some tired exercise books with a few empty pages . . . little else met the eye until Kohler noticed the cut-outs rescued from ancient magazines. Fish swam across the imaginary sea of one wall. Pages of sheet music with pictures of symphony orchestras competed to broaden young minds but there were also things from their own world, though everything extra was probably dead against the regulations of the Ministry of Education. A taste of honey in a world of rote memory and annual examinations.

The silence was penetrating, the wait an agony.

'*Bon*. That is how it should be,' said Jouvet. 'There has been a murder, yes, and the Inspector here has come all the way from Paris seeking answers. Your continued silence is mandatory even if it has to last for the next ten days.'

Christ!

These students were the little ones from the ages of four to seven or eight, but it was exactly the same in the upstairs room. Not a whisper.

'They aren't just afraid of you,' breathed Kohler. 'They're terrified.'

'As they should be.'

The view from the promenade des Falaises was lovely, a Lilliputian landscape with distant rows of tall, spindly poplars along the roadsides and boundaries but St-Cyr had no time for it. 'Madame, I must ask you some difficult questions. Please, if at any time you feel it is too much, simply say so.'

A nod would suffice, for he was trying to be kind. The Inspector fiddled with his pipe, deciding to ration himself, but when she asked for another cigarette, he readily gave it up as if he had plenty.

'Your husband, madame . . .' he began and she thought, Yes, he would start with André and she would have to tell him something, though suddenly *maman* was no longer here to advise her, to direct, to say, You must give him only a little.

'André was not always like this,' she hazarded softly.

She did not avoid his gaze. He must be gentle. 'But things have never been good?'

Her shrug said, Why should you care? Life's like that sometimes.

'My husband always felt he had married beneath him, Inspector.'

'But was your mother aware of this?'

Why must he ask it? *Why?* What had he found at the cave or in that valley? '*Maman* believed each married couple should stay together, no matter what.'

'That is not what I asked.'

Her look was one of instant betrayal. 'Have you found something?' she asked sharply and turned away to seek the distant scarps and wooded hills where the murder had occurred. Ash was irritably flicked from her cigarette. 'Mother didn't know of it. There, does that satisfy you?'

She clenched a fist. He waited. He never took his eyes from her. She could feel him memorizing every last feature, the tears and how they could not stop, the chin—was it not a little proud? The bruise . . . the throat as she swallowed. 'We . . . we exchanged letters every week, Inspector. Sometimes twice and even three times. Sometimes mother would telephone the post office here and . . . and Monsieur Coudinec, the *facteur*, would send his son to fetch me.'

He hated himself for pressing her. 'And these letters, madame, these telephone calls, was your husband aware of them?'

Behind the tears, her smile, though crooked, was soft and forgiving. 'There are no secrets, are there, in a little place like this? André often knew of the calls and intercepted her letters and read them. He knew *maman* hated him for what he was doing to me but also he knew she despised him for having proved her judgement so wrong in the choice of a husband for me.'

'And the letters you wrote to your mother?'

'He did not read them. That was not possible but . . . but mother kept them just as she kept everything I ever did. The notice of my first communion, the little cards of greeting I made for her at Christmas and for her birthday and that of my father—my dear father, Inspector. The letters *maman* made me write to him at least once a week!'

Ah *merde*, the poor child. . . .

'It was her way of not only keeping me in touch with the father I would never meet, but of making sure I could read and write at a very early age. She was like that, Inspector. She always had to have two or three good reasons for doing something. Now, please, let us walk a little more. People will see us here. There will be enough talk as it is. I've left the children again without their teacher.'

From the promenade des Falaises, the walk passed below the public gardens which, in spite of the war and the hardships, held masses of flowers. 'It's our mayor,' said the woman, welcoming the digression. 'Monsieur Pialat insists pride of place is important particularly in hard times. The mill is just along here a little. Please, it is not far now.'

About seven hundred metres separated them from the grave-yard at the other end of the esplanade. The windmill drew them to its soft yellow stone walls and he could see that it must have been a refuge for her when the troubles at home had become too much. Not used in years, its ancient walls had been left to the quiet dignity of decay.

She sat before him on the worn steps with her knees together and her arms wrapped tightly about them. She was, in that slender moment, like a woman who has suddenly been relieved of a tremendous burden but is still afraid to admit it to herself.

'Madame, did your mother plan to visit you afterwards?'

Instantly the knees were released. 'Not to stay with us. We . . .'

we haven't room and André . . . well, we've already discussed him. *Maman* would take a room . . . Ah no, I must cancel it, mustn't I? A room at the Hotel Esplanade. She . . . she always liked to stay in a good place when she came to see us. She always said the sacrifice, it . . . it was worth it for my sake, and for the children's.'

The pretence of being well-off had been important to her mother—she could see the detective thinking this. There would always have been those who criticized such foolishness—she could see him thinking this too. André most especially. André. . . . But there would be those who, on seeing her mother so well dressed and spending her money like that, would think well of the daughter she had raised. Ah yes, the detective, he thought this too.

'We shared our meals. The children loved her visits. Dinner at her hotel, supper at the Auberge de la Truffe Noire, afterwards a drink in the Café de Bon Père under moonlight with the sounds of the cicadas in the trees. Before this war, a *poulet en croute aux truffes, fonds d'artichauts au foie gras, champignons à la sarladaise, ragout d'écrivisses, clafoutis aux cerises* or perhaps if it was a really special occasion, a *génoise à l'abricot avec les noix pilées.*'

Chicken in a pastry shell, with slices of truffles under the skin; artichoke hearts with *foie gras*; mushrooms cooked in goose fat; a stew of crayfish; fruit pastry with cherries, or an apricot Genoese cake with crushed walnuts. Ah *mon Dieu, mon Dieu*, the very mention of such things made the juices run.

'Mother would always insist Monsieur Aubré, the chef and owner of the Truffe Noire, should cook some of the mushrooms she'd gathered to her specifications and afterwards would exclaim how perfect they were. The children used to make a little joke of it by saying he could just as well have burnt them to a crisp, *maman*, she would still have said they were perfect. They were her little treat. We . . . we always went to stay with her during the summer holiday, but now. . . .'

Nervously, she drew on the last of the cigarette and for a time said nothing. When he sat down beside her, their shoulders touched. She flinched and moved away a little, then abruptly stood as if she had had enough.

Pressing the cigarette against the stone wall, she extinguished it then took the trouble to carefully brush the ash mark from the stone before thrusting the butt at him. 'For your little tin, yes?' she said. 'It's the least I can do.'

'My tin, ah yes. *Merci.*' People from all walks of life collected cigarette butts openly and without shame, the old, the wealthy, the priest, the poor. Never had the streets and cafés been more empty of them.

The *mégot* tin was dented and old, a specimen of raspberry throat lozenge that was no longer available and hadn't been seen in the shops since that other war.

He carefully tucked the butt in among the others. Some had lipstick on them.

They looked at each other and she knew he saw doubt in her. She waited. She let him study her. She forced herself to stand before him.

He saw her blue eyes blink at last in fear. He saw the high cheekbones, the high forehead, clear skin, long lashes, wide lips, the proud chin he himself had hit.

In anger, she unbuttoned her cardigan and pulled it off. 'It's getting hot,' she said tightly.

A pretty woman. 'Tell me about the meals your mother prepared at your house.'

Ah damn him. 'Did André partake of them, is this what you are asking?'

'If you wish.'

'Then, *yes*, he ate them without comment just as he has all the thousands I have had to cook for him. He never said a thing unless it was to find fault. Mother never let it bother her. She was here to be with me and the children.'

He was not going to say anything about the mushrooms he

must have found. She realized this and turned abruptly away. Her shoulders tightened. A fist was clenched, the sweater purposefully folded.

'Madame, at about what time would your mother have reached that little valley?'

She flinched. 'What time? Ah . . . no later than two o'clock, so as to have everything ready.'

'The picnic.'

'Yes. The *vin paille de Beaulieu* always had to be at the temperature of the stream and this took about three-quarters of an hour perhaps, so she would hurry a little to be early if possible. The Château Bonnecoste had to breathe. She liked to warm it in the sun, but not too much.'

He must go carefully now, she thought. He would sense this in the way she was standing with her back to him. He would know she was thinking of those last few moments.

When he said nothing further, when he just let her pull away the webs of memory to see herself with *maman* in years gone by, she bowed her head and tearfully blurted, *'He was a monster.'*

'Who?'

'The man who killed her.'

St-Cyr could still hear her screams echoing in that little valley, but even so he cautioned, 'We are not certain it was a man, madame.'

She clenched her fists and stamped a foot. *'No woman would have done such a thing!* To use a . . .'

She choked. She buried her face in a hand. 'I . . . I didn't mean to say that. You . . . you must not listen to me. I'm not myself.'

'A stone tool?'

He was right behind her now and if she moved away, she knew he would force her to stand still.

When she nodded, the Inspector let go of her. He did not take chances, not this one, she told herself. He will force me to tell him everything.

Taking a deep breath, she wiped her eyes and nose with her hands and fingers. 'We ... that is, *maman* and I, knew the ancients used such tools to butcher their kills. We talked of it while skinning a rabbit or cleaning a chicken for the pot. Mother was very curious about such things. She experimented—people knew of this, much to my discomfort. She ... she showed me how it must have been done and made me do it, Inspector. *Me*. I was only five years old that first time. Five!'

She calmed herself and went on, could not keep the sadness from her voice. 'The flint knife for carefully splitting the skin as the surgeon's scalpel does, the scraper for removing the fat and flesh from the hide, the handaxe chopper for ... for ....'

St-Cyr leapt. She tried to run from him. She fought to get away and started to scream, to kick, to ...

'*Stop!*' he said into her ear. 'Be brave. Please, I am sorry. Let us start back. Your classes ... someone will be asking for you.'

'I *can't* go in there any more. I can't! It isn't fair. Mother butchered like that, me with my bruises and my black eye. I'm going away. I'm leaving this little place. Now that I'm free of her, I'm free of him.'

Jouvet and family lived in two rooms and the attic of the school. From where he sat at the kitchen table across from the husband, Kohler could see right through the open doorways to the senior students. Girls and boys were segregated, the girls in view. Those directly in line with him could not help but see him if they raised their eyes.

They didn't. The oldest was about fourteen. Several silently wept for madame's sake. Some worked their lips in prayer, others worried their fingernails or simply filled in the time by stolidly waiting. Perhaps twenty students in all and Madame Jouvet teaching both upstairs and downstairs under the critical eye of her husband and run off her feet, what with the household chores, the hunt for food and things, the rationing.

'So, okay,' he said, deliberately lowering his voice. 'Let's go over it again. You went to Sarlat to see about your leg and to find out if your request for a pension had been finally considered.'

The dark brown eyes faced him as they had faced the Russian winter. Gaunt and empty of all feeling.

'I have nothing to hide.'

'Then don't be so stubborn. Just give me the names of those who saw you there. Monday, right? Remember it was Monday and you took the *gazogène* autobus to Carsac-Aillac to catch the train to Sarlat at about what? 11:00 a.m.? Yes, that ought to suit. Bang on for a walk up the tracks and into the woods, my friend, with plenty of time to spare on the return journey and no one the wiser.'

The day of the murder. The detective was just trying to rattle him. Kohler could know nothing. 'Our mayor gave the driver of that bus a letter and some papers to deliver to the mayor of Sarlat. Old Pialat will have seen me sitting right up front because of my leg. Why not ask him? He'll tell you I was on the bus. He's full of wind, that mayor of ours, but sometimes what he says is true.'

'I will, but first I want to hear from yourself the names of those who can prove you were in Sarlat. That mother-in-law of yours may have known her killer.'

'Known her killer? Oh come now, Inspector. Ernestine did not put up a fight—is this what you are saying?'

It was.

The Russian winter returned, causing Kohler to think of his two sons, a pang of worry, was it really so terrible there?

Jouvet gave a shrug, a toss of his crippled hand. 'All right, I went to Sarlat for a meeting of the LVF. We are planning to take part in the Bastille Day parade. My comrades in arms, Lieutenant Henri Chevalier and Sergeant Hervé Prunet will vouch for me. They will also tell you I made an enquiry into my pension and found my request had not yet been considered by those bastards in Vichy.'

'Those two would swear to anything. You knew that mother-in-law of yours was coming for a visit.'

'So I buggered off to Sarlat, what of it? Her visits weren't exactly pleasant.'

'Don't get smug with me, my friend. You walked up that railway line and went into the woods. Maybe you spied on her bathing in the buff, maybe not. God only knows what kind of a figure she had before you started hacking at her with that. . . .'

'That stone chopper . . . is this what I used, Inspector? Come, come, be a little more forthcoming, eh? Don't stint yourself. The flint handaxe? The stone knife—one can shave with flint. Hah! I should tell you, my fine *Detektiv* from Paris, me—yes, me—I have shaved the cunt hair of several partisan bitches with flints I had carried in my pockets all that way. I know it works.'

Ah *nom de Jésus-Christ!* 'Find paper and pencil. Set out the times, the names and addresses of everyone you met or who might even have seen you in Sarlat or on that train or at the station. Let it be for your *certificat d'études primaires,* my sick friend. Now I'm going to dismiss the school. Please maintain silence here while the kids rejoice in the fact I've got your number.'

Kohler got up. He started for the doorway. He knew he ought to ask if the rucksack on the floor was the husband's. It had the look of the Russian Front. There were things in it. A stone hammer, a pick, a flint knife . . . ?

Without another word, he went into the classroom and without a sound the students left.

'Monsieur. . . .'

'It's Inspector to you.'

Caught in the doorway, Jouvet looked like death. He wiped his brow with that crippled hand. 'Please, I did not kill her. Ernestine, she . . . she always made a circuit of that little valley so as to see if it was free of others. If not, she would wait. Sometimes she would not even unpack the picnic hamper and lay things out or put the wine in the stream to cool and uncork the red to breathe.'

The man swallowed. Feeling lost at what he was saying, and

calling himself an utter fool, Jouvet knew he had trapped himself into continuing. 'Sometimes there were others in the cave, rooting around for things. Usually they left when she told them it was forbidden, though it wasn't of course. Sometimes they drove her from it and she would come to us in tears saying they were ruining the site, taking everything her husband had wanted so much to record and preserve. Any one of them could have killed her. I . . . I have thought I should tell you. It could have been a rapist, a. . . . Well, you know what I mean.'

Kohler turned away to find the daughter facing him.

'Mother would always be most distressed, Inspector. Before the war she would telephone the Museum of Culture and the Sorbonne, demanding that they listen to her. She would write letters to them, so many letters. They . . . they thought she was crazy. A shopkeeper, a postmistress from a little place like ours talking about things only they could know about but refusing always to give them the exact location until they agreed to excavate the deposits properly and give credit to my father. Her requests all fell on deaf ears. Money was always too difficult to find, the time too short, the staff too small and overworked, ours but one cave among so many.'

A tow-haired, skinny girl with freckles and reddened blue eyes, peeked uncertainly out at him from under the left arm of her mother. A hank of black hair hung down over the boy's forehead. He had the dark brown eyes of Jouvet, a steady, searching look that asked, Is he really guilty?

Louis quietly slid in to one side of them to lean against the rear wall and remain as unobtrusive as possible.

'My father was going to write a series of scientific papers about the site, Inspector.'

'To startle his colleagues with his discovery. *His*, Juliette? Tell them that, please,' demanded the husband.

She must remain calm. 'André, let us be at peace for the moment. Mother is dead and we must help them find her killer. That site, as I have told you, is very special, Inspectors. An almost continuous record exists there from earliest Neanderthal times. A book was to follow and was to contain all his detailed notes and sketches. The discovery was to have been the making of his reputation as a prehistorian, that cave, his life's work.'

'And your mother found it for him?' asked Louis gently.

She would not turn to look at him. She would keep her eyes on Herr Kohler and André. 'Mother found the location in the diary of the Abbé Brûlé. The ink had run with the dampness. Some of the words, in the dialect of the Périgord, were unfamiliar to my father. Monsieur l'abbé came across the cave in 1856 and found some astounding pieces. Stone figurines, incised bits of bone, an amulet. . . . These and other artefacts were in the trunk he left in the safekeeping of my grandfather. The artefacts were all carefully labelled as to the levels from which they had come, locations my father was then able to confirm.'

A trunk . . . all Kohler could think of was the penchant of Paris trunk murderers to send their victims to Lyon with no traceable return address. 'And this trunk . . .' he began only to hear her take a deep breath and give a worried sigh.

'The trunk had rested in the cellars of my grandfather's house in Beaulieu-sur-Dordogne for all those years, Inspector. It was covered with mildew when my mother showed it to my father in the early spring of 1912.'

The mother would have just turned sixteen.

'Father had the trunk shipped to Paris, to the house of his parents. He . . . he forbade them and my mother to say anything of it because of the amulet and the figurines. Nothing so old had ever been found.'

'The figurines?' asked Louis, digging out his pipe and tobacco pouch only to realize he was on harsh rations.

'Beautiful carvings in the soft yellow stone of these parts. Very primitive. An Adam and Eve, the abbé called them. Exquisitely executed but simplistically so, without details of the faces, the hands or feet.'

'A bulge for the testicles and penis,' snorted Jouvet, causing Kohler to turn on him and breathe, 'Speak only when spoken to.'

It was Louis who quietly said, 'That cave was not a religious site, madame—at least I do not think it was from the little we have seen. It was an *abri*, a shelter that was used for daily living and whose layers of refuse had been built up over the millennia.'

This time she turned to face him. 'An *abri*, yes, and not a *grotte*, not a religious site which would seldom contain the refuse layers, the *gisement* at its entrance.'

She released the children and urged them to have a wash. 'We will eat in a moment,' she said. 'Jean-Guy, help your sister to set the table, please? The special dishes, yes? We . . . we must make it just as *grand-mère* would have wished. Please set a place for her, too, so as to remind us.'

Louis gave that nod his partner had come to know so well, but as the boy passed him, Kohler said, 'Bring me your father's rucksack. I want to have a look in it.'

Incensed, Jouvet darted into the kitchen and came out with the thing. 'Then look, idiot! Look! It is not mine. It is *hers*.'

They took it with them. They promised to return it but a little of her died then, for they would begin to question things now. Ah yes. They would want to know more.

When André hit her, she fell back against the stove but did not cry out or try to defend herself.

Blood ran from her battered lips. The children raced upstairs to the attic. Some dishes fell.

He stood over her with his stick. He let her have one on the shoulder for good measure. 'Kill me then,' she spat. 'Kill me too.'

'Not before you have suffered.'

From the school to the Porte del Bos was not far, yet they could not make the journey unnoticed. Children whispered to their elders. Some tossed their heads. One boy was brazen enough to point.

A cartful of manure trundled by, its axle complaining in the noonday heat. Flies rose to worry the tail of the donkey. The driver did not even acknowledge the presence of the two visitors. They had *flic* written all over them, Paris too. A priest hurried past.

Kohler grinned. 'I like it, Louis. We're already famous.'

'Let us find some shade.'

'It's good to be free of those two for a little. Marital strife gets to me.'

Louis hurried on ahead, tossing a hand. 'Oh for sure, you ought to know, eh? Your wife Gerda's going to dump you. You watch, my fine Bavarian papa, she'll turn to someone else. When was it you last went home?'

Must Louis remind him? 'After Holland, I think, and before Paris.'

The summer of 1940! August perhaps. Had Hermann really been in Holland? He had never said so before. 'Admit it, you're on holiday.'

'*Ja, ja,* some holiday. She'll just have to understand there's a war on.'

'And a pretty little whore in your bed.'

'Quit having a guilt complex over your own wife. Stop playing God.'

'It's God I'm worried about because He's frowning at us again. Did Madame Jouvet and that mother of hers cook up a little plan to poison that husband of hers, or did our victim plan it all by herself?'

Louis was really serious. They had stopped in the middle of the street just before the gate.

'Did Madame Jouvet let slip their intentions, Hermann? During a beating perhaps? If so, our veteran would have killed his mother-in-law with relish.'

'And with a stone chopper. He told me he could shave the female partisans with flint. The water must have been ice.'

Trees crowded the base of the ramparts. A *bastide,* a fortified town which dated from 1283, Domme had three gates. This one was the most easterly and it was from here that the road

Madame Jouvet had ridden her bicycle down took a tight S-bend before continuing eastward along the heights just out-side and below the walls.

There were walnut trees to the left and below the promenade des Remparts, holm oak, chestnut, lime and mulberry. It was lovely in the shade and one had to think how nice it would be to live in a little place like this. Yet could one ever do so after Paris? asked St-Cyr of himself, heaving that sigh not just of a man whose holidays were long overdue—five years at least—but one who recognized his soul belonged to the countryside, his heart to the city.

The pungent scent of walnut leaves came instantly as he broke a leaf and brought it to a nostril. 'So, *bon*,' he said, drop-ping the leaf before moving into deeper shade. 'Let's have a look at her rucksack.'

Kohler undid the straps and dumped everything on the ground. 'A towel, no soap, trousers, a work shirt . . . gloves . . . a short-handled pick, chisel and hammer, a knife. Eight small lumps of black stone and one flat rock. Pale yellow, Chief. Limestone, I think. The local stuff.'

'A mortar stone, Hermann. No thicker than a normal *lauze* and a little longer than my hand. Its edges have been worked but not perhaps in twenty thousand years.'

'There's that sooty black stuff again.'

'Yes, yes. The mortar was used to grind the pyrolusite. Our teacher has been collecting lumps of a mineral her ancient forebears used to paint the walls of their caves.'

Kohler took up the mortar and ran a thumb over it. The stuff was not slippery like graphite or shiny. 'So, what's she been up to? Painting that cave?'

'Hiding something from us. She mentioned the mushrooms but only in memories too dear to lose. The mother always brought them. Always one of the local chefs would be required to cook some under her directions but Madame Fillioux also cooked them herself at the house of the daughter. The hus-band, along with the rest of the family, ate them.'

'A half of the omelette, eh? and an end to the bastard.'

'Madame Jouvet made no mention of the champagne, Hermann. Surely if it was a part of the ritual, she would have included it.'

The sound of a well-tuned engine came to them. Cars were so few these days, one had to be curious. Even here in the *zone libre*, gasoline was all but impossible to obtain.

The car took the grade easily. Its engine hummed then throbbed as it sped uphill. An open touring car. Grey. A Mercedes-Benz.

'Four men and one woman, Louis. No uniforms.'

'The sous-préfet of the Périgord Noir.'

'Is the woman his mistress?'

'Idiot, you're slipping.'

'And the other three?'

'They don't all look like SS or Gestapo with false papers but then . . . ah then, Hermann, it is often so hard to tell with those, is it not, and they would need false papers to venture into the Free Zone under cover.'

'Piss off! They're just friends along for the ride.'

'Then let us see what they want.'

3 SUNLIGHT STRUCK THE PLACE DE LA HALLE AND glared from the tiled roof of the town's seventeenth-century covered market. It made the air above the car's bonnet vibrate and brought the smell of vaporizing gasoline.

The only shade was under the timbered balcony of the market or within its expanse, the only sound, that of a flight of homing pigeons. Perhaps one hundred and sixty people were gathered. Shopkeepers, café owners, waiters and chefs stood in aprons at the doors of their premises. Mayor Pialat, florid and in a hurry in a black homburg, heavy black woollen suit, black tie, vest, gold watch chain and stomach, paused half-way between the Governor's House, with its shuttered first-storey windows and its second- and third-storey side turret, to stare up at his precious pigeons and wet his lips in apprehension.

Mopping his brow and grey bush of a moustache, he continued on across the stony square where tufts of weeds and wedges of stunted grass had suffered the ravages of drought and tethered goats.

He disappeared into the shady recesses of the market. Not a word was said. Though the crowd listened intently, all they could hear were those damned pigeons.

No swastika flew from the grey-roofed turret of that lovely sixteenth-century house. No German sentries stood on either side of its french doors, no patrols tainted the air with the smell of sweat and saddlesoap or the sound of their rifles as they fired at a post and white-targeted 'terrorist' or hostage and saw him suddenly slump.

No swastika pennant flew from the front left wing of the car yet it could just as well have done so, such was the mood of the crowd. The South was haven to far too many the Germans wanted. Homing pigeons such as those might carry secret messages and were forbidden in the North.

Like tourists from the other side of the moon, the five visitors waited impatiently for the mayor to unlock the old iron gates to the stone staircase that led down into the warren of caves and tunnels beneath the town. Used as a hiding place during the Hundred Years' War and then in the Wars of Religion, the caves would be pleasantly cool.

But why the interest? wondered St-Cyr. Why the impatience? And why the hell was sous-préfet Deveaux playing tour guide and host when he knew very well there was a murder to attend to?

The visitors were swallowed up, the woman going first in that hip-clinging white silk dress of hers and a big, floppily-brimmed and beribboned *chapeau*, the mayor bringing up the rear and bleating, 'The lamps, madame et messieurs. You must each take one so as not to get lost.'

'Toto, darling,' came the earnest female voice up from the darkness, rich and deep and musical, the accent exquisite and one hundred per cent of the salons along the rue Royale. 'Toto, light one for me. There's a good boy. Willi . . . Willi, how can we possibly get a crew in here?' The switch to *deutsch* maintained the richness. 'Franz, it's fascinating—were the English slaughtered or did they hide in these caves?'

'Baroness, I believe the Huguenots captured the town in 1588.'

'Did they slaughter the French Catholics or did they, too, escape into these caves? It's marvellous what holes in the ground can tell us about history. Willi . . . Willi, make a note of that. Oo, darling, there's such a lovely breeze. It's blowing right up my dress. It's like the bathe I had under that little waterfall. It's delightful.'

A short, stocky *Périgourdin* of sixty years, sous-préfet Odilon Deveaux returned from the depths and as he came up the stone steps in his banker's suit, he was caught in the half-light by the two from Paris Central and shrugged. 'Jean-Louis . . . ah, a moment. Yourself also, Haupsturmführer. Please.' A stumpy forefinger touched the grim-set lips of a cop who had seen it all and had just lost patience. The gaze was hooded, the nose massive, the warts, moles, scars and clefts pronounced, the eyebrows a bushy, unclipped iron-grey.

Out of breath, he had to pause at the top of the stairs. 'The asthma,' he managed. 'The pollen and the dampness. Cats . . . she has a cat. Her perfume . . . ah, it may be marvellous but it's giving my lungs a seizure! A moment.' And then, 'Come . . . come away for a little privacy. Give me a cigarette, please.'

Gathering them in, he guided them across the covered market to a line of benches against the far wall where a helmeted Wehrmacht corporal held a carbine in poster-paper over the words, *Give your labour in the fight against Bolshevism*. 'Paris . . . ,' he wheezed in again. 'Only one of them is Parisian—an ex-waiter, ex-boot-black, I think. The rest are originally from Berlin and Vienna. Very famous, very connected and very demanding. The cigarette?' he repeated.

Kohler shrugged, I'm fresh out. Louis found his *mégot* tin. Consternation registered. 'But . . . but what is this?' managed Deveaux. 'No tobacco but those? I would have thought. . . .'

'It's the way things are,' shrugged Louis apologetically. 'We beg, we borrow, we pick up like everyone else but we cannot steal.'

'Or be caught doing so,' offered Kohler, the chief tobacco thief whenever possible.

Hermann chose five of the butts and began that painful process of first trying to free the tobacco and then of finding paper and spittle enough to roll one. Though a former bomb-disposal expert and prisoner of war, he could not roll a cigarette. It was God's little irony. 'Here, Louis, you do it. I'm all thumbs. It's that dress and a bathe under that waterfall. Our princess must have paid the valley a visit.'

'Baroness ... she's a baroness and Austrian. That site, my friends. . . . That site has to be "cleaned".'

'Pardon?' managed Louis.

' "Cleaned", as I have said. The film crew, they are shooting at Lascaux but are to descend on the valley in a matter of days. Two perhaps or three. It depends on the weather and the shooting.'

'A film crew?'

The cigarette was handed over. Deveaux couldn't wait for a match and hauled out a battered lighter with a flame-thrower's torch. 'Ah!' he said, narrowly missing his eyebrows. 'Fucking gasoline. One has to be careful, eh? These days one has to make do in so many ways. It's desperate. I once took my eyelashes off.'

He coughed. He inhaled again and rested his back against the wall. 'They are shooting a film, yes. A docu-drama—please don't try my patience with questions. Let them tell you themselves. I will give you the essence of it.'

Another moment passed. The rise and fall of his chest began to lessen, though God knows why, thought Kohler. That 'tobacco' could be anything. Sweepings of manure and herbs, dried linden blossoms or carrot tops.

'It's about a cave, a trunk of artefacts that was found in a Paris antique shop, and a woman—please don't ask me to explain how their minds work, these creative people. The film is to be called *Moment of Discovery*. She's the female lead. The boy from Paris is just an assistant on the "dig".'

'And the archaeologist, the prehistorian?' asked Louis quite pleasantly.

Deveaux was quick to sense trouble and eased his crotch with a massive heave. 'These fucking trousers . . . ah, the crap they make these days. Always pinching in the wrong places, always splitting up the ass when you don't want them to and causing the balls to sweat.'

So much for the shortages.

'The archaeologist, yes,' said Deveaux. 'That one flubbed his lines the other day. He's being shot again—yes, yes, that is what they have said. Shot for being nervous, eh? Stage-struck perhaps, who's to say. The male lead in the thing. The woman, the Baroness, found the cave for him by deciphering the hieroglyphics of some abbé. The Church . . . must the Church always stick its nose in things?'

They waited. They did not dare to say a thing, these two from Paris Central. So, good, yes, good, let it be a lesson to them. Jean-Louis was more than an acquaintance but would not understand why the matter was very delicate, very difficult. Ah yes.

Deveaux hauled at his crotch again and let his stomach relax. 'There are two prehistorians on the staff. Advisers, yes. One is from Paris and is French so as to give our side of the story perhaps. The other is German, a professor from Hamburg, but they are not actors. The one who flubbed his lines is the cock of those ancient times perhaps, though if you ask me, my friends, I would have split his skull long ago and dined happily on the brains and heart! These others, they are also at Lascaux, each ranting in his own way about possible damage to the cave paintings. They're purists.'

'A film,' said Louis, throwing Kohler a worried glance.

Clouds of smoke poured from the hairy grottoes of the souspréfet's nostrils. 'Yes. A joint production of Continentale and the Institut des Filmes Internationales de Paris. Lights, cameras and action, and slate boards to tell us which scene they are shooting. Without those boards, no one would know which end was up. At least I wouldn't.'

Kohler let Louis ask it. 'And they want the site of the murder *cleaned?*'

'Yes.'

'That's not possible.'

Deveaux gave the sigh of a father whose patience has just been sorely tried. 'Jean-Louis, it was I who had you pulled off that train. A stroke of luck, I thought. Ah, I cannot tell you how relieved I was to learn that you and the Haupsturmführer were available, but,' he tossed the hand with the cigarette, 'but I will let these feelings I have for you be set aside in honour of saving your hides. Herr Goebbels, the Reichsminister of Propaganda, has personally sunk 50,000 marks of his own money into the project.'

'Goebbels . . . Ah *nom de Jésus-Christ!*' exploded Kohler. 'I knew we should have stayed on that train. This is all your fault, Louis.'

'It can't be his own money, can it?' hazarded the Sûreté. 'Besides, a delay of a few days cannot matter.'

'Perhaps you should personally ask him,' countered Deveaux. 'Perhaps, as the Baroness von Strade has said, the Reichsminister will pay the site a little visit.'

Oh-oh . . . 'A propaganda film?' bleated Kohler.

'The dawn of prehistory. *Moment of Discovery.*'

Kohler tramped on the accelerator to cool things off. The touring car, big and heavy, shot along the narrow street and out through the Porte del Bos, to rip down the cliffside and hit the bridge across the river. Ninety . . . one hundred and twenty kilometres an hour . . . one hundred and ninety . . . a great set of wheels.

'*Hermann—horses!*' cried the only passenger, hastily crossing himself.

The horses were all over the road ahead. Twenty . . .

thirty. . . . Rumps and tails and lonely brown dumps on the stones. . . .

The brakes were hit. The car slewed. The horses, on frayed tethers, bolted heavily into the surrounding fields, dragging their dealer with them.

Dust rose and settled. The smell of burning rubber was unpleasant.

'I warned you,' seethed St-Cyr. 'I have tried to tell you to expect the unexpected on our roads but ah no, no, the Gestapo are invincible. They know everything. They *steal* a car so as to hurry to a murder scene before everything is removed, and all but kill its only passenger. *Grâce à Dieu*, I have not soiled my trousers. Excuse me, Inspector, while I relieve the bladder.'

Kohler could hear him pissing against a rear tyre, a favourite French trick, since it gave the lie of big, proud, brave dogs in a nation defeated.

The horse-dealer, a member of the *nouveau riche*, was not so pleasant. Having recaptured two of his nags and burned the skin off both palms, he approached the car in a hurry. '*Imbécile! Salaud!* Did your mother have the syphilis, eh? Did she not obtain the *certificat sanitaire* before conceiving you?'

There was more. Age, some fifty-six years perhaps, did not interfere. Barnyard bootscrapings were referred to. Horse shit was furiously flung at the car.

At last the dust settled. The nags snorted and tossed their wild-eyed heads. The moon face of the dealer began to lose its colour. The dark brown eyes under that cap and thatch of grey hair, began to worry. The half-smile was crooked.

'Your name?' breathed Kohler, still from behind the wheel of the car. He had the sun above and the world at his feet.

St-Cyr did up his flies. The engine cooled.

'My name . . . ? *What has that to do with things? Are you so stupid you cannot see what you have done? Those horses—all thirty-six of them—were for the Russian Front!*'

'Louis, check his licence.'

'My licence . . . ?'

'Illegal dealers, a lack of labour, and enforced shipments of produce to the Reich are the curse of French agriculture,' mused the Gestapo whose only proffered identification was a wallet badge that was held up in the palm of a giant's hand. 'Production has fallen drastically and since there are so few horses left in the *zone occupée*, the farmers there are forced to plough using the wife and kids while here in the South, the Reich employs whatever means it can to get what remains.'

'But . . . but you're one of them?'

'Hermann, we have work to do.'

'The fact that I'm "one" of them does not matter.' One of the few good things Vichy had tried desperately to do was to save what few horses remained.

Kohler calmed the two horses and from a shabby pocket, found the stray carrot he had picked up in the market—a piece of good fortune, a future snack. 'We're waiting,' he said, giving each of the horses a half-carrot.

The man winced and tossed the wounded hand of inconsequence. 'My licence . . . oh, well certainly, it is . . .'

'Not so good, right? Then you're under arrest, my friend. Climb in the back. You can help the boys in blue remove the corpse we found. Maybe they'll let you ride with her.'

'Hermann, *please*. He will only be an inconvenience. Let us tear up his licence. Let us remove his boots and make him walk down this road as his horses will eventually do.'

There was a nod the Sûreté understood only too well. The man's undershirt and drawers were used to clean the bonnet and windscreen, the tweed cap gave a nice shine. Water was no problem for the river was close and the labour free.

The current caught the jodhpurs and other things. It took the jacket and the bits of an identity card that would be very hard to replace. It took the torn scraps of a dubious licence.

They left the man without a stitch, to bathe his hands and think about breaking the law for profit, no matter for whom.

Hermann had a thing about horses. 'Those poor old nags wouldn't have come home from Russia, Louis. I had to do it.'

'Of course.'

When they reached the glade, the body had already been removed. The grass and wild flowers had been cut and raked so hard, the place all but looked like a lawn, albeit damp from several washings, and smelling like a brothel sprinkled with cheap perfume. There was no sign of the picnic under the chestnut tree by that little stream, no sign of anyone. Even the empty champagne bottles had been taken, even their corks and wires. It was as if the murder had never happened. Even the honey buzzard had buggered off.

'Sarlat . . . they will have taken her there,' managed Louis. It was not far. Perhaps seven kilometres at most.

'Death caps and fly agaric.'

'Ah *merde* . . .'

Nightmare visions of some undernourished *flic* came to them, those of the family also. Seven children perhaps and the wife and both sets of grandparents.

'With the phalline poisoning of the death cap, Hermann, induced vomiting, even immediately after eating, is often of little use, since the poison, it is so readily absorbed.'

They were moving now—thrashing their way through the underbrush. They could not travel fast enough.

'Though the symptoms are delayed from twelve to twenty-four hours,' sang out the Sûreté anxiously, 'they consist of violent pains and burning sensations in the stomach, fainting fits, cramps, unstoppable diarrhoea, bloody stools, vomiting, cold sweats, shivering and an enlarged liver. These things can last up to ten days. *Ten!*'

Breathlessly he finally broke free of the woods to slide down to the railway embankment. Kohler followed and they ran along the track. 'At the end, the pulse slows, the victim turns yellow, the breathing becomes very laboured. There is collapse and then death.'

A not-so-speedy release. End of mushrooms, end of lecture. 'Hey, since you know the way, I'm going to let you drive,' said Kohler. 'Don't hit anything. My nerves won't take it.'

* * *

The telephone calls were made, the panic had subsided. Mathieu Vaudable, in his forty-third year as coroner of the Périgord Noir, removed his gold-rimmed pince-nez. He cleared his throat and the sound of this, caught in dank medieval cellars off the rue de Siège in one of the oldest parts of Sarlat, was harsh.

'These cellars,' he said by way of apology. 'Jean-Louis, I regret the apprehensions you and Herr Kohler have suffered on account of the mushrooms. I myself was shown the basket and took immediate possession of it.'

In specimen after specimen, *Amanita phalloides* (death cap) and *Amanita muscaria* (fly agaric) lay among the stone tools Vaudable had had sent over from the local museum. He had not yet taken time out for his dinner and probably wouldn't.

He picked up a death cap with his tweezers. 'The flat but round cap and dirty green shade which fades to brownish-yellow,' he said, 'but is sometimes pale yellow or bluish, yes? The most deadly of our mushrooms, messieurs.'

There were white gills but on some specimens these had acquired a greenish cast. Each specimen had a swollen base, and a cup that was enclosed in a sheath. The presence of this indicated that the mushrooms had been dug out.

'The *Amanita muscaria* is not nearly so poisonous. The cap, though similar to its little friend, is a brilliant vermilion to orange red. The gills are white or yellowish and the stem underground is covered with white scales. These specimens have also been dug out by our victim.'

'And the stone tools?' managed Kohler.

'Ah, yes. A mid-Acheulian handaxe, three cores which have been made into knives and scrapers but could be further worked as the need arose, and a smaller, more perfect knife with a pressure-flaked, serrated edge. All are of the black flint and bear the patina of great age.'

'The wounds . . .' began Louis.

Vaudable sadly shook his head. 'Never have I seen such a

thing. Passion, yes, but was it only that? To open the victim? To partially disembowel her? To split the breasts—such things took some doing with tools such as those. Her assailant must have straddled her during the butchering. Blood would have covered his hands and arms, his face, chest and thighs—it was a man, wasn't it? Was he naked? Did he remove his clothes first and then bathe in the stream afterwards? Ah, these things I have to ask myself because his clothes, they would have been ruined.'

'Perhaps it was a man, but,' said Louis, 'this we really do not know.'

'The time of death was last Monday, or perhaps the day before it.'

'And the primary blow, was it struck with a tool such as this?'

Louis picked up the handaxe and, gripping it firmly so that it filled his hand, brought it down broadside and hard only to stop just above the desk. 'The nodule of flint, the boulder, Hermann, it is worked by striking the edge so that the flint spalls inwards and upwards away from the edge you want. This then causes the spalls to radiate out from a summit near the centre of each side so that you have points there that are useful as a hammerstone.'

The complete tool, then. Axe, chopper, cutter and hammer all in one. Kohler hefted the thing. It weighed about three-quarters of a kilogram, was perhaps at most twelve centimetres by ten by three in thickness. In some places a crude flaking gave a coarsely serrated edge. Other edges were even more crudely worked but all around the top of the tool, where it would have been gripped, there was unworked original nodule, with a white, calcareous encrustation.

'The wound to the forehead,' said the coroner. 'Let us examine it.'

'Louis. . . .'

'Stay here. Examine the tools. Try to figure out if our assailant knew she planned to poison him.'

'If it was a man.'

'Yes, yes, of course.'

Deft with the scalpel and tweezers, Vaudable had managed to peel back the skin of the forehead to reveal the bone beneath. 'Though the fractures radiate from all around the area of impact, some are longer towards the scalp and chin.'

The smell was terrible but he paid it no mind.

'Was it a handaxe or perhaps the vicious downward slash of a walking stick?' asked St-Cyr, peering closely at the fractures.

'A walking stick? Ah, no. No. That could have been set aside in any case. No, I think the handaxe just as you have held it. One savage, sudden blow caught her right above the eyes. She fell back. Again she was hit on the head and again. He then fell on her. First the sharp edge of that thing to her throat, then the point of it, the multiple stabbings with the full weight behind them—a right-handed assailant. Material from the dress has been caught in many of the wounds. Then the butchering with other stone tools. Did he have them in a little bag he carried around his loins as a savage might? Did he pause, I ask myself, to select or attempt to select the tool best suited to his purpose? The skin of the left half of the left breast, Jean-Louis, I feel certain a scraper was used to remove the flesh and that is why that portion of the breast hangs only by a flap.'

Blue-black, green and yellow with tinges of wine red, and suppurating, Madame Ernestine Fillioux lay on her back on the raised stone pallet with the drain at her feet. Maggots had had to be scraped away. Legions of them still fed on her.

'The sexual organs?' asked St-Cyr—one had to ask.

'Violated with a razor-sharp stone. All of the tenderest of places. Pubic hairs have been scraped away. A savage attack, but as I have said, one, I think, of experimentation. It is as if whoever did this needed to try out the tools. Perhaps she knew of them herself and perhaps he laughed as he used them—the mind seeks answers as it probes for truth.'

'A stonekiller,' breathed St-Cyr. 'A film . . . *Moment of Discovery*, whose story line follows the life and times of our victim.'

The life and times. . . . Now what was this? wondered Vaudable but thought better of asking. 'Ah yes, a film. I am sorry about the need for haste. These days it is difficult to raise an objection. Oh by the way, the muscarine poisoning of the fly agaric is quite different from that of the phalline of the death cap. To choose such two poisons is a puzzle. The fly agaric's poisoning resembles very closely that of the deadly nightshade. Within one to four hours—not the twelve to twenty-four hours of the death cap—the victim feels ill but cannot quite define the problem. The throat is dry. One has trouble swallowing. It is something they ate, perhaps the mushrooms, but let us wait to see, eh? Then there are the stomach cramps, the vomiting and the diarrhoea, the dilation of the pupils, the fainting, the hallu-cinations, the rapid acceleration of the pulse, delirium and prostration.'

'Ether should be inhaled. The patient must be kept warm.'

'And given frictions—rubbing to stimulate the circulation. Recovery is often in two days but death can occur.'

'Alcohol must not be consumed because it dissolves the poison.'

'And there was alcohol. A flask of cognac in addition to the wine and champagne.'

'Cognac?'

'Yes. It was found in the underbrush along the stream near the picnic site. Its contents had been consumed, but then the cap had been replaced and the flask washed.'

'Ah *merde*, after the killing.'

At 4:00 in the afternoon the heat began to lessen but still the back streets of Domme were silent. Carrying the daughter's rucksack, St-Cyr walked alone, and when he found her, Madame Jouvet was behind the school. Her light brown hair was pinned up, her skirt hitched into her belt, the flowered print housedress clinging to her thighs and buttocks with dampness.

Painfully she hung the last of the laundry, but had not yet noticed him for the clothes-lines ran away from the school. 'Madame . . . ,' he began. She stiffened. She would not turn to face him. Tugging at the legs of the short pants her son would wear to church tomorrow, she tried to unrumple them. 'Madame, please, a few more questions. Also I must ask you to identify some things. It's important.'

She gripped the clothes-line and waited for the blows of his words to strike her. 'Madame, the things in your rucksack . . . the nodules of pyrolusite and the stone mortar, where and when did you get them?'

She shut her eyes and though he still could not see her face, he would know she was praying. 'At the cave. I . . . I went there the . . . the day before mother's visit. André . . . André hated her complaining so much when things went wrong, I . . . I had to see that the site was all right. A year had passed. I . . . I was not certain if vandals had visited the cave. I *needed* to know ahead of time what to expect of her.'

'Last Sunday, the day before she was killed.'

'Yes.'

Compassion all but overwhelmed him and for a moment he could do nothing more than set the rucksack down. He wished she would turn to look at him but knew she wouldn't, that he would have to force her to do so.

'And that is when you gathered the lumps of pyrolusite,' he said more harshly than intended. She dropped her hands, tugged the skirt from her belt and tried to free it from clinging to her thighs.

'The stones for the cave painting, Inspector—you know this is what they were for. Why is it, then, that you demand it of me?'

She was facing him now and saw him draw in a breath in shock. She tried to smile self-consciously and this split her battered lips and made her wince. Blood trickled down her chin and she wiped it away with the back of a hand. 'The sooty black dust of another era, Inspector. The children . . . my students. I was preparing for a little lesson in our history. I thought if I had some of the black, a little of the ochre, some grease— dear God there is now so little of it here and it is hoarded as never before and always priced too high.' She stopped herself, touched her hair, felt suddenly at such a loss to appear so poorly, and tucked strands of her hair up under the tight diadem of braids.

'Some oil, yes, or melted fat—*foie gras*, isn't it possible that the ancients might also have loved the fat of goose livers?' she asked. 'Some clay to mix with the colours if needed. I could let the children see for themselves why Lascaux, it . . .' Ah no, why had she said it? she wondered.

'Lascaux?' he reminded her.

Her hands fell to her sides in defeat. 'Yes, the cave paintings everyone still talks of. The Sistine Chapel of the Périgord.'

And a cave *painter*, madame, was that it? he wondered but did not ask. She had been badly beaten by her husband. Blood had seeped through to stain the left shoulder of the housedress but she was, as yet, unaware of this. Perhaps five metres separated them. The rabbits slept, the chickens took little interest. The smells of both mingled with that of the vegetables and earth she had watered with the leavings of the laundry.

'How did you find the cave on that Sunday?' he asked.

'Disturbed. I knew someone had been there very recently to look it over—matches . . . I have found some burnt ones. Ah, I thought,' she shrugged and winced and clutched her left shoulder only to drop her bloodied fingers and stare at them in dismay. 'I . . . I sensed it, Inspector. Right away I felt the presence of another—yes, yes, that was how it was. It made me uncomfortable. I hesitated to go into the cave but mother was coming and I had to be warned ahead of time of any trouble. I went in only to the *gisement*, not into the darkest parts behind. I kept my hammer ready.'

'Madame, your shoulder . . . ?'

'It is nothing. It will stop.'

Damn you, *don't* interfere in something that doesn't concern you! was written all over her. So, okay, he would have to leave the shoulder for a moment. 'But . . . but you collected the pyrolusite lumps?'

She had him now; he could not know the truth. 'Yes. Mother and I had a cache of them. From time to time when others came to the cave, they uncovered pieces from the *gisement* but thinking them of no value, left them. These lumps we hid, the little mortar also.'

'And you met no one?'

'No one.'

Ah *merde*, why must she be so wary? 'Did you know of the filming?'

She blanched. 'The filming . . . ? Please, what is this?'

She was lying and he knew it but there was nothing she could do about it, she said to herself. Nothing yet.

'The story of your mother and father, madame. The trunk of artefacts you spoke of, the diary, her finding the cave and leading your father to it, their visits in the spring and summer of 1912 and again in 1913. The beginning of the ritual, madame, that would eventually lead your mother to her death.'

He gave her a moment. She knew she had betrayed herself by lying.

'Now come, please,' he said. 'It's unforgivable of me to press so hard. There must be a doctor. That shoulder had best be attended to.'

'Then come into the kitchen. Fix it if you must and let me change. I will not walk with you or anyone through this town, not now, not until my lips have healed at least a little.'

Once bared, the shoulder revealed the skin had been broken in several places. The slash from the walking-stick had left a welt perhaps as long as the width of his hand. He bathed it and changed the dressing she had applied herself. His touch was very tender and all the time he worked, he muttered things to her and to himself. 'Our attitudes must change. No man has the right to do this to any woman. Sutures . . . you had best have them.'

She shook her head. 'It will heal. I can't have talk.' He dabbed at the skin to dry it but did he notice how fine her skin was? Did he think it a shoulder worth caressing, and not of her mother's but of her father's family, of wealth and good breeding? Did he wish the dress would drop so that he might see her as she had been under the waterfall on that Sunday? That Sunday. . . .

He would have found the towel in her rucksack, would have discovered the change into work clothes but had yet to say anything of them. 'Where is your partner?' she asked tightly.

'With the others. Returning the car we borrowed. Asking questions of them.'

'The others?'

He was noticing the older welts on her back. He would be dropping his eyes slowly down the gap in her dress.

'Yes. An actress, a film producer and a young man of twenty perhaps. He is an assistant on the archaeological dig in the film. Two others also. One from the Propaganda Abteilung at 52 Champs-Elysées, Paris. The other is the sous-préfet of the Périgord Noir.'

She didn't say a thing. She only looked at the wall in front of her.

'My partner, madame, he's very good. He's from the Gestapo but is not like any of those types. We're simply Common Crime, the two of us. The Kripo for him, the Sûreté Nationale for me and no Gestapo brutality so do not worry yourself. If you find my fingers gentle, his would also be.'

We aren't here to hurt you, we are here to help. This was what he implied, but how could anyone help her now?

'There,' he said at last and let her pull up the shoulder of her dress. 'I will wait outside while you change.'

'No . . . no, it's all right. I will go upstairs to the attic.'

There was no sign of her two children and he knew she must have sent them off to that old mill perhaps, or to gather clover and dandelions for the rabbits. There was no sign of Jouvet.

The school was quiet and far hotter than before. He wondered how Hermann was doing. He knew he had to ask her about the champagne and the flask that had been found—the initials HGF engraved in dull grey, dented silver. A flask that had seen some use—how many had he seen himself among the officers of that other war?

HGF, the letters overlapping. 'Henri-Georges Fillioux,' he muttered to himself, seeing any one of the so many plain brown, waxed cardboard boxes that had come back with the last effects, the boots perhaps, the belt and webbing, the tunic and cap, the bloodstains—how heartless of the army. The last letters too.

Knowing that he had best not confront her with her father's flask, not just yet, he waited but she did not come down from the attic and he heard himself saying to himself, Hermann . . . Hermann, I think I need you.

Kohler wasn't sure but thought the Auberge de la truffe noire was in what had once been a small monastery. Languidly the Baroness strolled arm in arm with her Toto. And in her white dress she was like a fluid wraith passing through sunlight and shade, tall and graceful along the little paths that fell away from the inn to where the monks had prayed or gone about their humble chores in what had once been a *potager*. Herbs, vegetables and fruit trees.

No one was inclined to effort. The meal he had not partaken of had been too large, the wine excellent, the cognac superb.

Dreamily the Baron Willi von Strade, age sixty if a day, watched his actress-wife of thirty-five hold in close and serious discussion her latest lover, a boy of twenty, one Gérald 'Toto' Lemieux of Paris, on contract to the Institut des Filmes Internationales. Did the former boot-black have promise? Was she planning his future or merely going over a minor scene to save him from a life of shining shoes or waiting on tables?

Lemieux was handsome, straight and tall, but no match for the Baron who could, Kohler surmised, simultaneously pluck the eyes and cock from a cobra unharmed. *Verdammt*, what was he to make of them?

Franz Oelmann of the Paris Propaganda Staffel was bemused by the little tête-à-tête and the Baron's apparent complaisance. Perhaps he knew what went on between the Baron's sheets, perhaps he even watched the fun. Stamped with that blue-eyed, closely trimmed blond print of the Master Race, he would no doubt carry double duty, working both for Goebbels and for Heinrich Himmler. Frankly, he stank of the SS and that only made one uncomfortable since von Strade and his wife would be certain to know of it while saying nothing and indicating absolute innocence of even such a thought.

Sous-préfet Odilon Deveaux, his chair tilted well back against the wall, propped by a foot that was jammed against a stone pillar, dozed as he should with half an eye open.

Only Mayor Pialat seemed anxious. Flustered—florid from too much wine and *foie gras*—he continually stole little glances at his pocket-watch and muttered about the urgency of things to himself. His pigeons were gone and might now have been plucked and eaten, but he could not leave. After all, the visitors were paying guests and the assistant chief of police was among them. Poor Pialat mopped his brow and wiped his lips, held up the flat of a hand at the refill Kohler offered, and said, 'Ah no. No, *merci*, monsieur. A splendid meal. Magnificent. Exactly as in the years before everything was taken from us.'

Oelmann and the Baron let him say it unchallenged. Embarrassed at the stupidity of his tongue, Pialat tried to tuck the watch away. He couldn't understand more than three words of German. Exhausted from smiling and nodding, he again retreated into worry. With watery large brown eyes he searched the skies above the line of distant trees until, at last, Deveaux took pity on him to smile reassuringly and shrug as if to say, *Les Allemands*, my friend, we can do nothing but await their pleasure.

But all the time things had been going on in the Baron's cranium beneath the immaculately brushed grey locks whose growing bald spot shone. As if on cue, he spoke. 'What will it take, Herr Deveaux? 25,000 each to get them off our backs?' The cops, the two detectives.

'Marks or francs?' asked Franz Oelmann.

'Marks, of course. *Reichskassenscheine*, Herr Kohler, because that's the way it has to be.'

And they can't be sent home but must be spent in the occupied country. 'This is still the Free Zone, isn't it?' said the sous-préfet. 'I merely ask so as to be aware of things.'

The Baron overlooked the slight. 'Even so, at twenty to one, that is still 500,000 francs, a substantial sum but worth it.'

'But,' sighed Deveaux, 'Herr Kohler is subordinate to Gestapo Boemelburg in Paris who is, himself, subordinate to Gestapo Mueller in Berlin, is this not so? Correct me, please, Baron. If Herr Boemelburg insists, as he has by telephone this morning, that his two detectives continue their investigation with the utmost urgency, who are we to question such as him?'

'We need the woman's house,' said Franz Oelmann flatly. 'It is crucial to the story. The trunk will be taken there and Marina will find it.'

'The Baroness. . . . Ah yes, of course,' enthused Deveaux expansively, 'but let our two detectives from Paris Central first examine the contents of the house. Letters, papers, little things—there may be something that will tell them where to look for the one who did the killing.'

Verdammt, the insolence of the French! 'It's someone local,' snapped Oelmann. 'A voyeur. He will have followed her, seen her bathe—watched her—good *Gott im Himmel*, idiot, use your brains. Excited by her nakedness, he went crazy and attacked her. Surely you have dossiers on all such types? You do, don't you?'

Deveaux said nothing. He was like a man who quite willingly would give his worm to the fish who had stolen it, knowing well that little fish would soon be eaten by another.

Kohler thought he'd best say something. 'That's interesting. A voyeur?'

The Baroness and her Toto had disappeared behind a stone wall.

'Look, this is serious,' insisted Oelmann. 'We have a very tight schedule. Shooting at Lascaux will be done in a day at most. Then it's upriver to the house of that woman to find the trunk of artefacts and the diary of the abbé. Then we're on location at the Discovery Cave, damn it, for whatever it takes.'

Kohler refilled the Propaganda Staffel's glass and nodded for him to continue. The Baron let him and Oelmann, irritably taking out his cigarette case, lit up to decide how best to proceed. 'Look, it's unfortunate the woman was murdered but we can't let it interfere. *Moment of Discovery* is to be previewed by the Reichsminister Goebbels in Berlin on the 15th of November. The Führer is to see it on the 5th of December at Berchtesgaden, after which it will be shown simultaneously in eighteen cities. Köln, Düsseldorf, Munich, Essen. . . . It's crucial to the war effort that the people see it. Here, too, in France as well.'

He really meant it. He believed, as so many of the Nazis did, in the invincibility of the Reich and in their mission. 'We'll need transport,' offered Kohler. 'Louis and me, to check out the victim's house tomorrow. Have the trunk there. We'll want to take a look at it. Oh by the way, how did you come by it?'

Von Strade decided to intervene. 'An antique shop in Paris last spring. An archaeologist, one of their leading prehistorians came upon it. We've hired him as an adviser and script consultant but have, of course, brought in our own expert to verify both the contents of the trunk and the cave. Make no mistake, we're on to something with this.'

'The very dawn of history,' offered the sous-préfet.

'And in our very own cave,' said Pialat. 'Who would have thought it possible.'

Canny suspicion, awe and pride were mingled so well in the voices of the two Frenchmen only Kohler noted it and rejoiced again in the French. *Verdammt* but they always surprised and amused, even if they were often troublesome.

A hand fell lightly on his shoulder and he felt the softly perfumed caress of fingers in the short hairs behind his left ear. 'I play the part of the Frenchwoman who is ignorant of all these things, Herr Kohler, but whose very psyche is awakened by the Herr Dr Professor of our film who sees, as only the expert prehistorian can, the true meaning of what she has stumbled upon in the mouldy trunk of a long dead monk.'

The Baron gave her a brief smile of encouragement. Rather than use a meaty forefinger to extricate a few drunken fruit flies from his glass, he swished the cognac around and tossed it out.

More than fifty years of patient history hit the ground. Any sensible Frenchman would have downed it with pleasure. Deveaux wore the pained expression of the wounded who could say nothing. Pialat was so flabbergasted, he could not pull his gaze from the stained cobblestones.

The glass was refilled by Franz Oelmann. The fingertips continued to curl the hairs at the back of Kohler's head. 'You smell nice,' he grinned. The Baroness pressed a hip against him and her sea-green eyes came down to look more closely into the faded blue depths of his. The thick, soft mass of strawberry blonde hair floated all around him. Her breath was warm.

'At the cave we dig, we strip away the layers of the past, Herr Kohler.' Her eyes widened to emphasize this. 'It is all done very carefully, very correctly. We encounter stone tools quite different from the more recent, we dig deeper ... deeper.' Her chest swelled. 'I find an Eve, the Professor finds an Adam. We see each other as at the very dawn of time. Love blossoms—isn't it so when a woman works alongside a man in such a place? But we are pure, we are driven by a far higher ideal. The discovery.'

Of *what*, precisely? he wondered. Tomfoolery of the highest order, straight from the High Priest of Propaganda himself in Berlin, or. . . .

She fingered the white, cloth-covered button at the top of her dress. She had nice fingers, nice nails.

'An amulet of deerhorn, *mein lieber Detektiv*. A species of deer not seen perhaps since time began.'

'It has beautiful incisions,' offered Franz Oelmann earnestly. 'The first hole ever drilled, the very first ornament or piece of jewellery but not,' he emphasized, 'to be worn as frivolous finery but as something far deeper. A divine right.'

Oelmann's steel-blue eyes registered the intensity of his belief in what they had come across.

'We're talking about the Neanderthals,' said von Strade firmly. 'Not the Cro-Magnons.'

'So, I find the piece, the amulet,' said the actress, 'and I show it to the Herr Doktor Professor and we both kneel on the floor of the cave to gaze up at the paintings on the roof and walls as if in supplication before their god and ours, both one and united over the span of the millennia.'

She really believed it too. Emotion filled her eyes with moisture. She was an absolutely stunning woman. 'But . . . but there aren't any paintings in that cave.' he managed. 'Louis and I didn't . . .'

A meaty hand fell on his to grip him with the urgency of a film producer who had much to lose and wasn't about to let it go. 'Oh but there *are*, Herr Kohler. Paintings of such extraordinary import as to be priceless and far beyond the value of those even at Lascaux. Our cave will become an international shrine when we're done with it. People from all over Europe will come to witness what our film has shown them.'

Deveaux's chest rattled as he heaved the sigh of a sous-préfet from whose hands the matter had fallen into those of another. Well, two others: Louis and his partner. Kohler threw him a glance that was ignored as, waistcoat unbuttoned, Deveaux's thumbs were slid behind the broad suspenders and his chest eased a little.

Pialat searched the skies for his pigeons. Franz Oelmann's gaze had lost none of its intensity.

The Baroness smiled excitedly. A hole in the ground . . . wasn't that what she had said about the caves beneath the town? 'Willi, it's marvellous what holes in the ground can tell us about history.'

And then, of the breeze down there and with hands perhaps clasped, 'It's like the bathe I had under that little waterfall. It's delightful.'

Pialat didn't waste time. A bachelor all his life, the mayor had worries of his own now that the visitors had departed. Kohler found him in the turreted sixteenth-century dovecote of the Governor's House. As he went up the tightly spiralled staircase, he realized the tower had been modernized so that now a dark and heavily timbered floor above hid the roof. Formerly the droppings had just collected on the walls and at the bottom as a rich and much coveted source of phosphate for the garden. Now they would still be saved. Ah yes.

When he reached the open trap door, he could hear Pialat's voice among the cooings of his little charges. 'Oh my pretties, my precious ones, I have warned you. I have pleaded.'

From cage to cage he went with water and feed. Each pan of droppings was scraped into a bucket and then carefully brushed. 'It was old Vivan again, and that son of his,' said the mayor, grinding his teeth and still unaware of the visitor. 'The adhesive on the limbs of their cherry trees, the scattered grain and the gossamer of their nets . . . . Those bastards. Three . . . is it three or four I have lost to their table this time?'

He noticed the visitor. His mouth fell open and for a moment, he couldn't decide what to say. Then he shrugged and reached for a pigeon to calm himself. 'Those two I mentioned, Inspector, they are always waiting, especially now with the shortages but . . . ah *grâce à Dieu*, I have not lost more of them this time. Jean-Guy, he was supposed to come and shut them in but . . . but the boy and his sister, they have not come today.'

'Jean-Guy . . . ?'

The bird relieved itself into the mayor's hand. Droppings spattered a knee of the black suit. Feathers stuck to the front of the waistcoat and jacket lapels.

Pialat released the bird and let it fly around them until it finally settled on one of the ancient stone roosts above. 'Yes, the children of Madame Jouvet. Very reliable, very polite—always dutiful. It is a little job I give them from time to time to help the family out.'

Three more pigeons were released and he let their feathers and bird shit damage his best suit. He seemed to need their closeness as they perched on his shoulders and hat, and he fed them little titbits he had scrounged from dinner.

'Even with such a tragedy, Madame Jouvet would not have kept her son from his duties. She's so conscientious, that one. A husband like that. Who would have thought he would do such a thing? He did it, didn't he?'

'He says he was in Sarlat.'

The hand with the pigeon was automatically lifted. 'Ah! Sarlat. Of course. It's to be expected. The ironclad alibi while the blood, it still cools. Those friends of his aren't to be trusted. Volunteers for Russia. Hah! they hated their jobs and wanted adventure and they got it. Rape, pillage, murder and wounds to boast about. That poor woman should leave him. I myself would sign the divorce papers and go to Rome to plead with the Pope!'

Pialat handed him the pigeon. 'She's pretty, isn't she?' Kohler had to ask himself did the mayor mean the actress, the schoolteacher or the pigeon.

'Beautiful,' he said and only realized, as he gently caressed the head and neck, that Pialat had used it to test him.

'We are of one mind with such as these, Inspector,' he said, 'but you did not come here to see my birds.'

Kohler met the steadiness of his gaze. 'What was the mother worth?'

So that was it, and one might have known. 'Talk—there is always talk in a little place like this. Some said 500,000 francs, some said no more than 5,000. Certainly there is the shop and post office, the telephone but. . . .' He took the pigeon from him to kiss it and return it to its cage. 'But in a little place like Beaulieu-sur-Dordogne, those are nothing. It's a poor village and they don't keep it very clean. The citizens need a better mayor. Always if there is good leadership, pride of place and that sense of community, hard times can be withstood. The well of human endurance is deep and best tapped when brother helps brother with no thought of profit.'

He should have been mayor of Berlin! 'Tell me about the film people. I gather they have already visited the cave?'

This, too, was something that should have been anticipated. 'Yes, they were there on the Thursday and the Friday before the killing. Two visits—all of our visitors on the Friday, that actress and her young friend on the. . . . Why is it, please, that the boy is not in a prisoner-of-war camp with all the others or under the earth?'

Like so many, the mayor had a right to be indignant. More than two million French soldiers languished behind barbed wire in the Reich. 'Maybe his family didn't want him killed?'

'And bought his freedom from duty—a pauper? Ah! let us leave the matter to Saint Peter. The actress and her young friend went there on Thursday by themselves. It is the half-holiday.'

The last pigeon was locked up. The mayor waited for him to say something. He even took out a pocket comb and went to work on his walrus moustache just to make sure there wasn't any bird shit in it.

'You'd best tell me,' said Kohler cautiously. 'Only the schools get Thursday afternoon off.'

'Ah! may God forgive me, I had better, hadn't I? Early on that Thursday afternoon Madame Jouvet took her bicycle and left by the Porte del Bos. That husband of hers saw his wife even as I did myself. The rucksack on her back, the kerchief on her head, the haste, Inspector, to get away unseen if possible. She had received an urgent telephone call that morning from her mother.'

'Ah *merde*, so she was there on Thursday too. The film . . . the cave paintings. . . .'

'Inspector, what has happened to her children? It really is not like her. That old mill. . . . She might have gone there. The beams in the floor above, they are still sound. There are ropes— I myself keep taking them down for fear the boys who swing from them and climb too high might have an accident but a woman in great distress . . . a woman who was so close to the mother who directed her life, a mother who would know all about painting caves . . . ?'

'I'll go there now.'

'No, I will go with you. If she has hanged herself, I will never forgive myself. I shall resign as mayor and take the blame for not having put a stop to that husband of hers.'

He would probably kill his pigeons too. He had that look about him.

St-Cyr tried to open the door to the mill but it wouldn't budge. He threw a shoulder against it—nearly knocking the wind out of himself. He ran around to the side to gaze up at the gaping hole of a once-glazed window.

Lazily a heavily knotted rope swung from an ancient timber inside. 'Madame . . .' he began, desperate now. 'Madame, you had nothing to fear from me.' Thoughts of the two children came. What would they do without their mother? Relatives . . . would there be someone to take them in?

It was Hermann who hoisted him up and by degrees got him through the window, but Louis paused up there.

Pialat threw Kohler a frantically questioning look.

The Sûreté's hand earnestly motioned to them for silence. 'Leave him,' croaked Kohler. 'Let him have a look.' The cinematographer had taken over. *Verdammt* another killing!

The rope swung gently, and in the shaft of sunlight from the opposite window, it hung from the centre of the timber and stretched all but to the floor. Mill dust stirred and eddied. The inside of the door had been braced with the heavy cross-timber once used to secure it in earlier times of strife.

There was rubbish—the broken machinery of past times, what could not be reused elsewhere. A few pulley wheels, some old straw . . . a few of the baskets that had been used to collect walnuts but were now beyond repair. . . .

Alone in the centre of the floor, at the end of that rope, she sat on a small tier of wooden blocks and every time the rope she gripped so tightly came towards her, she rhythmically sent it back but maintained a tension on it that greatly troubled the detective in him.

If ever a woman had sat in debate over killing herself, it was this one.

'Madame,' he said, as gently as he could. 'There is no need. We are here now and will protect you.'

Somehow she awoke to his presence but said nothing, only gazed up at him as if still not sure there was anyone there. 'The door, madame. Please open it.'

Pialat called out, 'Juliette, *ma chère*, it's me, Alain. Please, you must open the door and tell them what you know. The children . . . where are they?'

'Monsieur *le maire* . . . ?' she blurted and searched desperately for words. 'But . . . but I know nothing, Monsieur *le maire*. Nothing.'

'The children?' he repeated earnestly.

'The children,' she echoed. 'Ah . . . Getting clover for the rabbits, I think. Your pigeons . . . I have forgotten. Forgive me.'

Pialat did not turn away. He shook himself and clenched his fists. Suddenly he gripped his mouth to stop himself from vomiting, shed tears of relief for her and could not help but let them fall.

Verdammt, thought Kohler, what have we here?

 IN THE COOL HALF-LIGHT OF HIS GRAND SALON, Pialat put a glass of cognac into her hands. Gruff with embarrassment, he made excuses so as to leave them but as he went towards the door, she had to say something. 'Alain, I . . . I did not know how you felt about me. I should have. Forgive me.'

'It does not matter.'

'But it does. You know it does. Perhaps when this is over and they have . . . have found the killer, we can again speak of such things?'

A compromise. 'The killer . . . Of course. Yes. Yes, that would be fine.'

He closed the panelled doors leaving her to face the two detectives all alone. 'I . . . I really didn't realize, Inspectors. It's stupid to have been so blind but things . . . things haven't been good. He's more than twice my age.'

She shrugged at the futility of it and sat down again in a sofa that was both elegant and of that severe though simple beauty of sixteenth-century Dordogne. A tapestry covered it.

St-Cyr let her take a hesitant sip. Kohler offered one of the mayor's cigarettes from a carved wooden box that must predate the very use of tobacco.

'*Merci,*' she said, subdued and, trembling, accepted his offer of a light. They would want to know everything, these two from Paris. Why she had thought of killing herself. *Why, please, madame?*

Why she had gone to that cave not just on the Sunday before the murder but also on the Thursday, ah yes, that Thursday, messieurs.

'My husband,' she began. Again there was that shrug. 'I cannot live with him any more. It's impossible.'

'But to take your life is to leave your children in his hands?' said the one called St-Cyr. He was so earnest. There was compassion in the look he gave.

'That is why I have not used the rope. An intense inner struggle, yes, which love and duty overcame.'

'And now?' asked the one called Kohler. 'Are we to keep an eye on you always lest you seize the next opportunity?'

They were really very worried about her and not without good reason. Dead, she could tell them nothing.

Instinctively her smile was faint and self-effacing. She lowered her eyes and let the smoke curl up from her cigarette as she whispered, 'Forgive me. It . . . it was a moment of weakness. I . . . I shall try not to succumb.'

Ah *merde*, thought St-Cyr, is she threatening us with the possibility? 'Madame,' he began. Her answered, 'Yes?' was much too quick and startled. 'Madame, a flask was found near the stream. I have it here.'

She waited but he did not hurry. At last she had it in her hands and it was cold and worn and dented but engraved sharply with letters. . . .

They were both watching her intently. '*HGF,*' she whispered. 'Henri-Georges Fillioux . . . but . . . but, please, messieurs, what has my father's flask to do with *maman's* murder?' She set it aside as if afraid to touch it.

Ah *nom de Dieu, de Dieu,* wondered St-Cyr, has she suddenly realized that she herself may well be in danger?

'There was some champagne, madame,' said Kohler gruffly so as to let her know he had had about enough of her evasiveness. 'A Moët-et-Chandon. The 1889.'

She blanched. 'The . . . the 1889? But . . . but mother never took champagne to the picnic. Always the *vin paille de Beaulieu* because once my father had said he liked it very much and she never forgot for a moment every word he ever said; the Château Bonnecoste also but. . . .'

'But, *what,* madame?' he insisted, reaching for the flask to remind her of it.

She straightened her back and shoulders. 'But champagne, that . . . that was only once and my father brought it. A day in the early summer of 1913. In June. The . . . the 17th.'

The same date as that of the murder. 'Two bottles?' hazarded Kohler.

The faintness of her smile was again instinctively self-effacing. Blood beaded on her battered lips and she tried to hide this but gave it up. 'They loved each other and I am the result, and yes, my father probably got my mother a little drunk and very receptive to his advances if you wish to look at things that way—I don't. It . . . it was a moment of weakness *maman* refused ever to regret; myself also. Is it so terrible a thing?'

The flask was making her nervous.

'No, no, of course not,' muttered St-Cyr uncomfortably. 'Such things, they happen all the time between those who truly love each other.'

You hypocrite! A girl of seventeen, Inspector, and a man of twenty-six? she said silently, giving them a moment to think of it themselves.

Satisfied, she said, 'But if the truth were known, Inspectors, they shared each other's bodies more than once that summer and well into the fall, well past the time of her knowing. At least, this is what I have since come to believe but not,' she held up a hand, 'because of the words of my husband who has constantly reminded me of it.'

'The cave,' breathed Kohler. 'The waterfall and that little glade.'

Places André knew only too well—she could see them thinking this. My husband, she said silently. He . . . he did it, didn't he, but why the flask? she asked herself. The flask . . . ?

'Tell us about that Thursday,' said St-Cyr. 'Begin by revealing why you tried to hide this visit from me.'

'You received an urgent telephone call from your mother that morning, madame,' said Kohler. 'You left the school that afternoon—the half-holiday. You were in a hurry and didn't want to be seen leaving town.'

André must have told them. André . . . 'I . . . All right, I did go to the cave on that Thursday. Mother was very agitated. She spoke of a mortar and some lumps of the black pigment. She wanted me to get them before it . . . it was too late. They . . . they were too precious to leave to chance.'

'Too late for what, please?' asked Kohler.

'This . . . this she did not say.'

'But how did she know of them,' asked St-Cyr, 'if she only went to the cave once a year?'

'They were in a cache of ours from the years before, as I have already told you. Mother had her reasons. I . . . I did not question her. One seldom did.'

But you are afraid, madame, thought St-Cyr. Either you have done something you fear we will soon discover, or you are aware that your mother intended to poison your husband perhaps, and someone else, the one she thought she would meet. Your father. 'And on the Sunday, madame, the day before her death? When you were hanging out the laundry, you said you had removed the things then.'

He would not leave it now. 'For the lessons in cave painting, yes. That . . . that part was a lie for which I apologize, but I did remove them then. It . . . it was not possible on the Thursday afternoon as she had insisted.'

They let her finish the cognac. They let her fiddle with the last of a forgotten cigarette. They would see that her face was flushed beneath the bruises but would not understand the reason for her embarrassment. 'I . . . I could not get to the cave on that Thursday afternoon. Others were there and they . . .' she shrugged and tossed her hands, 'they interfered. Please, I don't know who they were. I saw only a couple exploring the cave. Strangers. A boy of twenty and a woman—wealthy . . . well-off in any case and from Paris, I thought.'

'And?' asked the one called Kohler. Were his eyes always so empty of feeling?

'I . . . She . . . They . . . they made love in the cave. Love and . . . and I . . . I listened. *There* . . . there, now you know the reason why I could not recover the things nor tell you of it.'

'What did you hear?' asked Kohler severely.

'*What do you think?*' she countered hotly.

'So you went back on the Sunday to get them?' said St-Cyr, seemingly oblivious to the fuss.

'*Yes!*'

'But . . . but, madame, you have already told me you thought there was someone else there then?'

'He . . . he watched me but . . . but I could not see him.'

'Could it have been your husband?' asked Kohler.

'André . . . ? This . . . this I do not know, Inspector.'

Or your father? wondered St-Cyr but did not ask it. 'You went into the cave but only to the *gisement*. You changed into your work clothes knowing there was someone else around?'

'I kept my hammer ready.'

'You bathed afterwards under the waterfall?'

'Yes, but . . . but by then I was certain he had left the valley.'

'A man and not a woman?'

'Yes, but . . . but I cannot be sure, of course. It was only a feeling I had. I often got those feelings even as a child. It's that kind of place.'

And you have now countered all our questions by saying the feeling was common to you. She could see them thinking this.

They were silent, these two from Paris. Perhaps they thought she was lying—she really couldn't tell. Perhaps in their imaginations they saw her naked under the waterfall knowing someone was watching her and that this might also account for her embarrassment since she had done it willingly.

'Your father's family, madame,' said the one from the Sûreté, reaching for the flask. 'Please tell us what you know of them.'

'A house in Monfort-l'Amaury,' she said stonily.

'About forty-five kilometres to the west of Paris,' acknowledged the one called St-Cyr. There was no hint in his voice of the wealth involved.

'A villa in Paris, in Neuilly on the boulevard Richard Wallace overlooking the Bois de Boulogne. Mother always had the address, since she and my father had sent the trunk there in the late fall of 1912.'

A trunk that would then reappear in an antique shop in Paris thirty years later to spawn a film. A trunk that had since come back to the Dordogne and would soon be opened in the very house where the abbé had left it so long ago.

'Madame, could your father have come back?' asked St-Cyr.

'To kill my mother? Why . . . why, please, would he do such a thing if . . . if he was alive? He's dead. He died on the Marne.'

'Then why, please, was his flask discovered lying in the bushes near the stream?'

'I . . . I don't know. How could I?' She blanched.

'And the cave paintings, madame?' asked Kohler.

'The lumps of pyrolusite. Pigments. . . .'

'Please, I. . . .'

'A film?' demanded Kohler. 'Cave art like no other?'

'You are afraid, madame. Is it that you have done something you now regret or is it that you fear for your life at the hands of another?'

What the hell had she been up to? wondered Kohler. Ah damn, why would she not answer?

'Messieurs, she has had enough. She needs to rest,' urged Pialat who had come silently into the room. 'Please, until

tomorrow, yes? It is not much to ask. Rooms have been provided at the hotel where her mother used to stay. She'll go there
with the children. You will each be on one side or the other
of her.'

'Good,' said St-Cyr testily. 'That's perfect.'

'Louis, we can't watch her all the time.'

'Of course not, but at least the word will get out that we are
doing so.'

'Did the champagne come from one of the family's cellars?'

'Perhaps, but then was Henri-Georges Fillioux only listed as
missing in action and presumed dead? Did he return to Paris
but never tell our victim of it?'

'The poisonous mushrooms,' breathed Kohler. 'Madame Fillioux found out he had lied to her. She was about to pay him
back for all those years of loneliness and privation.'

'But why, please, did it take her four years of constant harass-
ment to obtain the *mariage in extremis après décès*?'

'Maybe the family didn't want her demanding her rightful
share? Maybe there were others he hadn't told her about? A
son, a daughter, a wife who, accepting his death, had then
remarried and didn't want a fuss.'

There were always so many questions and always there was so
little time. 'Monfort-l'Amaury is extremely pleasant, Hermann,
because money makes it so. The house in Paris must be worth a
tidy fortune even if it has been requisitioned for the Duration.'

'Von Strade said there were cave paintings far better than at
Lascaux. An international shrine.'

'Yet the daughter is sent to retrieve a mortar and some lumps
of pigment? Was the telephone call the first she knew of those
things?'

'Was our victim a cave-painter, Louis? A forger?'

'Ah *merde*, I wish I knew. The Baroness visits the cave with
her Toto on the Thursday afternoon. The daughter, who has
always held that little valley in respectful awe, hears a woman
cry out in ecstasy.'

'And cannot help but think of her mother and father.'

'Was Madame Fillioux aware of the plans to make a film of the discovery?'

'Did she object and the film people not want her interfering?'

'An amulet, Hermann. Incisions—scratches on a bit of deer-horn. A thong-hole, the first such one in history.'

'Two primitive figurines in stone. An Adam and an Eve.'

'Goebbels invests 50,000 marks.'

'The film is a matter of great urgency. There's a very tight schedule.'

'*Moment of Discovery* is crucial to the war effort.'

'Why would the daughter bathe in the buff without first having thoroughly checked that valley?'

'You're improving. Working with me is good for you.'

'Did she see him leave, Louis? Is this what she's afraid to tell us?'

'Or is it simply what her mother really intended to do with the mushrooms?'

'Poison the daughter's husband and poison her own.'

'Only to be killed herself.'

It was a land of castles where beauty leapt to meet the eye in towering cliffs whose ancient ramparts hugged a treed and placid river, warm yet cool in the early morning light. Franz Oelmann knew the road well and was an excellent driver. Hermann, seemingly content to play the man on holiday, lounged affably on the seat beside him making idle chatter or pointing out some feature far more worthy of the Rhine!

In the back seat of the big touring car, Madame Jouvet had shrunk into a far corner to stare blankly at the front seat. Knees primly together, hands in the lap of a pale blue dress, her fingers were tightly knitted. Now a sudden, nervous twisting of her wedding ring, now the gripping of a clenched fist.

St-Cyr sat opposite her across the barren no man's land of leather that gave her no comfort. She knew she was trapped. He knew that if she got through the day, she might well try to kill herself.

What has she done? he demanded harshly of himself. Helped that mother of hers to paint the inner recesses of that cave? Helped to pull the wool over everyone's eyes?

The repercussions of such a fraud would cause heads to roll. His own, his partner's, others too. Ah *merde*.

She dreaded what they would discover in the house of her mother. She hated every kilometre of this magnificent route, the ancient traverse of traders and pilgrims, monks and their abbots, Cro-Magnon, too, and Neanderthal. As the crow flies, it was not far. Perhaps some fifty-five kilometres to the east-north-east. By road, perhaps eighty or ninety. And Franz Oel-mann, who knows all the short cuts, has been looking at you, hasn't he, madame? he asked himself, seeing her turn swiftly away to stare bleakly at a stone farmhouse and seek its every detail as if she, too, was aware of his thoughts.

He sees you as a threat he cannot tolerate, madame. Of all the heads to roll, his must surely be the first. He *won't* let you do that to him.

A Nazi, a jackbooted boy out of one of the Ordensburgen, the Order Castles, and now a man specializing in propaganda and covert operations, Herr Oelmann had marked her down but she was not yet completely aware of this.

You poor thing, said St-Cyr to himself. We must not let it happen no matter how guilty you are.

At Souillac they left the river. Frightened by its absence, she tried to ignore the wooded hills and plateaus. And when a valley appeared, incised and cradling an ancient village, she shud-dered as distance collapsed and the house drew nearer.

A narrow side road forced Oelmann to slow down. A cart, pulled by an old woman in sabots and black sackcloth, caused them to pause. The woman took her time and when the cart, with its load of sticks and manure, drew alongside she set the shafts down and paused to wipe a runny nose on a tattered sleeve. 'Juliette . . . is it true?'

Deep wrinkles screwed that ancient face into the ripe olives of dark eyes that missed nothing. 'Attend to me, my dear. It's your Aunt Liline who is speaking, is it not? The same whose name you took for your very own daughter.'

'It's true.'

The woman pinched her nose and flung the rheum aside. 'Then we must prepare for the burial and that fine husband of yours can kiss the blade before the guillotine falls.'

'Must you?' cried the daughter. 'You know how hard this is for me. Can you not give me a moment's peace? Always you are criticizing *maman*. She *wanted* me to marry André. I couldn't say no. I *couldn't!*'

'It's as I've always said. He was no good and the marks you bear on that pretty face your father's family gave you are proof enough.'

'Madame, please explain yourself,' said St-Cyr. 'We're detectives from Paris.'

She stooped to take up the shafts. For one split second she gave him the benefit of a scathing glance and the finality of a curt nod. 'Ernestine was a good woman whose only fault sits beside you, the result of her attempt to find a better life and lift herself from among us. The *vin paille de Beaulieu*, eh, messieurs? The sweet wine of the virgin sun-dried on a bed of straw.' She clucked her tongue and tossed her head in salute. 'The legs must never be spread to the moment of hope's foolish passion nor should the years ever be given to its fleeting memory and futile prayers for its return. Now I will leave you to your murder and to this Paris you speak of.'

Ah *nom de Dieu, de Dieu,* the walnut had shed its husk. Now only the hard dark shell remained.

For as long as she dared, Juliette Jouvet looked tearfully at the cloud of yellowish dust that enveloped her aunt. At last the niece faced the back of the front seat again to knit and unknit her fingers, captive to the car. And all who saw it pass, paused in their labours to stare at her.

The house was not in the centre of the village but down by the river in the midst of a cluster of Renaissance buildings whose tiled roofs rippled orange-brown in the sunlight. There were three arched double doors at street level—former entrances to what had once been stables and pens for livestock. A simple set of wooden stairs led up to a door at the side—the shop entrance. Above the shop and post office, a covered balcony ran the width of the house with timbered, stuccoed walls behind. One french window was to the far left, a solid oak door off-centre to the right. Posters of some sort clung to the walls—the *auberge* was on this floor. Above it, the steeply-pitched roof rose to two garret dormers, one wide open to the elements and without the benefit of even a shutter, the other with its broken shutters closed.

There was a square tower to the right, set awkwardly into the corner of the roof, making the place look lop-sided. Here small shutters all but closed off a meagre window. Stucco and lath were being constantly shed from the tower's base.

Madame Fillioux had left her son-in-law and family a costly bill for repairs.

Signs targeted the place. A drunken telegraph and telephone pole, barren of the ivy that sought to climb it, stood nakedly just off the front right corner. Grapevines did climb the walls but only to the balcony railing for ease of harvesting. Not a tree stood nearby to give the place a modicum of shade or grace. Not a flowerpot of geraniums. Madame Fillioux had had no time for such things. It would be cold in winter and insufferably damp.

'Messieurs, could I . . . could I have a moment in there to be alone with my thoughts. It's a very difficult time for me.'

Oelmann grinned. Kohler said nothing. Louis had to tell her. 'It's impossible, madame. I'm sorry but we have to see everything.'

'And you do not trust me, do you?'

Had it been clever of her to ask, a last desperate attempt to find out exactly where she stood?

'Please, as soon as we can, my partner and I will leave you with your memories for as long as you wish.'

She could only try. That was all she could do, she said to herself, and hope they wouldn't be able to keep their eyes on her all the time.

Light from the double doors filtered into the shop where worm-eaten beams were festooned with hanging pots, straw hats, brushes, coils of wire, coal scuttles no one would buy these days because there was so little coal, laundry baskets, coat hangers, ah so many things. Row on row of them above a long counter, cash desk and weighing scale where space was at a premium and glass display cases competed with a few dried beans and lentils, a little brown rice, split peas, cracked wheat and rolled oats. Toilet water, bleach—bleach for the hair also—pins, needles and ribbons, thread, bunting and buttonhooks, Madame Fillioux had carried the centuries. Poverty and isolation had combined to allow much of the pre-war stock to remain. Suspenders, eyeglasses, corsets and lisle stockings, ladies' shoes with long laces. Lye and camphor. Spices . . . spices such as were no longer seen in the *zone occupée*. Cloves in tall glass jars, cinnamon sticks and whole black peppers. She must have kept a rigid control over those.

Beyond the produce shelving, a wide doorway led to the post office and it was from there, most likely, that the stench of rotting meat and rancid butter came.

'Madame,' hazarded St-Cyr, not realizing the four of them were in a cluster. 'How is it that for almost a week now the village has gone without service?'

'Monsieur Auger usually fills in when mother is away. He delivers the mail throughout the *commune*. He's very good, very reliable—she would not have employed him otherwise—but. . . .'

'But he has not filled in.'

'Louis, I'll check upstairs.'

The stench was everywhere. 'Hermann, you know I'm better at it. Madame, does the sous-facteur live alone?'

'Alone . . . ? Why, yes. Yes, he lives on his farm and . . . and comes in each day.'

'And the *garde champêtre*?' The village constable.

'There . . . there isn't one.'

Ah *merde*, no *flic* and two murders, was that it then? St-Cyr looked questioningly up at the ceiling but could see no stains. Could they leave it for a little? A half-hour, an hour, would it matter?

Franz Oelmann's clipped voice broke the thoughts. 'I'll go. Madame, please accompany me.'

The Sûreté threw out a hand. 'Not if he's lying up there. No. . . . No, she will stay with us,' he said sharply. 'We'll leave the upstairs until later. We will take things as they come and that is final.'

'Then get on with it. We haven't all day. The Baroness and the others will soon be here with the trunk.'

'Ah yes, the trunk.'

Juliette felt Herr Oelmann brush against her left arm. She knew he wanted to be alone with her. The one called Kohler grinned and said, 'Will we need a key to the cage?' He missed nothing, even to seeing how flustered she was.

'It . . . it will be in the drawer under the counter. Please, I will get it for you.'

She moved away but when she went to pull out the drawer, Herr Oelmann's hand closed over hers. 'Let me,' he said.

Kohler saw her wince. Oelmann held her that way a moment. The drawer came open. She could not take her eyes from its contents. Old ledgers, tidy bundles of receipts bound with elastic bands or bits of string. . . . A tin of dress pins, another of drawing pins . . . a stamp pad, ink, pens and pencils, a carving knife. . . .

'Mother . . . mother always kept that handy in case of robbers. The key is there, at the back, on its little hook.'

Herr Oelmann nodded, forcing her to awkwardly bend down while he stood over her so closely his left leg was pressed against her hip. Kohler watched from the other side of the counter—

she knew this. And when he rained a handful of beans onto the wood, this startled her and she found him grinning like a small boy who knew there was mischief afoot. 'The key,' she said, colouring rapidly as she thrust it into his hand.

Behind the cramped cage, whose wire mesh would have withstood a battering ram, the parcels in stained brown paper wrappings, string and cancelled postage stamps filled one narrow set of shelves to the ceiling. Big, small, what did it matter? Most oozed rancid butter, dribbled maggots, leaked and stank to high heaven.

She didn't know what to do.

'Parcels for the *zone occupée*, Hermann. Food, warm clothing, thread, black pepper, salt, sugar perhaps and potatoes.'

'Hams and geese, *foie gras*, two chickens by their look, a roast of lamb, a side of bacon—*verdammt*, three trout! Their tail fins have broken through.'

'Walnuts and walnut oil. Some sweet cherries that should have been dried and would have been mouldy on arrival even *if* the service had been excellent!'

'The French,' said Oelmann sarcastically.

'The shortages, including that of the railway rolling stock that has gone to the Reich,' breathed Kohler. 'Not all are for Paris, but like them, Paris has no milk, no cheese for Louis's little boy, no flour, sugar, meat and bread or too little of them. Potatoes also.'

'And it's all our fault, is it?' shot Oelmann.

St-Cyr knew he had best intercede. 'Hermann, please check the postmistress's parcel book. All parcels are listed with their destinations, weights and postage paid. See if one of the family's addresses crops up. It's just a thought.'

A thought ... *Le numéro* 26 boulevard Richard Wallace, messieurs? she cried inwardly. Again the one from the Sûreté looked questioningly up at the ceiling. Again she shuddered inwardly at what they might find.

Herr Oelmann examined the malleted rubber stamp with which her mother had cancelled the postage stamps. He fingered the little silver lever of the telephone and she saw *maman* firmly thrusting it in to ring a distant operator and urgently call into the speaker. But now the crowd was no longer present. Now, but for the probings of the detectives and Herr Oelmann, the place could give up its ghosts and she could hear the hubbub of each girlhood day, the exhortations, the complaints about the long line-ups, the pleas for credit justly refused.

Bang, bang—she heard the stamps being furiously cancelled. *Maman* had been at the very centre of village life. The one called St-Cyr would be only too aware of this. He would know her mother had kept a secret drawer, a hidden cache that, like so many others in her position, was for a rainy day or for memory's sake.

A handful of louis d'or, the little diamond pin father had given *maman*, the thin silver necklace whose links were so delicately interwoven they were like a spider's web.

The letters from the battlefields . . . letters she had later used as proof of his undying love. Had the things been stolen? Had the murderer found them? Had he killed Monsieur Auger who could not possibly have known of that little hiding-place?

Blank identity cards were purchasable from each PTT but still Herr Oelmann fingered these.

When he found a bundle of postcards—the ones with the printed messages whose blanks were to be filled in that were no longer in use—her heart stopped.

She heard the dry sound as he riffled through them. From time to time he paused as if suspicious of something and she knew he was watching her out of a corner of his eye. 'Madame,' he began, and she heard his voice against the clamour of the past. 'Madame, these cards. . . .'

A car horn sounded. Someone leaned impatiently on it. The detectives stopped their searching, Herr Oelmann swore beneath his breath, 'Marina. . . .'

He left them then and she went to close the drawer only to see that the postcards did not contain those urgent pleas for help her mother had received from Paris. Pleas that had been steadfastly refused. Yes, refused!

St-Cyr noticed her furtively glance up at them. Four greasy, putrid parcels had been selected to lie waiting on the sorting table. 'All are for the parents' address in Paris, madame. Two fat geese, a loin of pork, some butter and cheese.'

'Ah no . . .'

'Did your mother not tell you she was sending food to your father's family?' he demanded.

'*No!* No, she didn't!'

And now there are tears and you feel betrayed, he said silently to himself, because she didn't tell you everything.

The stamps had been cancelled on Saturday, the 15th of June, two days before the murder. A last gesture of reconciliation?

The detectives were upstairs now, in the *auberge* where heavy floorboards complained even from beneath carpets that had hidden them for ages. The halls were dark, the ceilings low, the hanging iron lamps extinguished, the rooms shut in by heavy drapes *maman* had refused to replace. 'Some day,' she would say—and Juliette could hear her mother's voice so clearly— 'some day these things will be worth a fortune.' The heavy oak chests and massive armoires, the dressers and canopied beds whose carvings a timid girl had secretively traced when opening a room to a visitor who had looked and searched and inevitably found it wanting.

There had never been many of these visitors. Travelling salesmen and produce buyers mostly, sometimes an estate agent or notary. Often *maman* had argued with herself about living down here but always the possibility of lodgers had presented a moral and economic dilemma particularly when she, herself, had grown old enough for men to look at in that way men did. Yes, yes, she said, remembering suddenly a heavy door that had closed behind her, an unwanted, terrifying hand and panic . . . panic like she had never known before.

Maman had called up the stairs to save her. *Maman* . . . Why had she not told her about the food parcels directed to that address in Paris when she had sworn never to send the parents Fillioux a single morsel? *"Never, so long as I live!"*

Suddenly finding herself alone, Juliette blinked and tried to remember which of the rooms the detectives had just entered. Herr Oelmann was downstairs with the Baroness and the others. Perhaps the film people had gone to look at the river, perhaps they simply waited in silence. With him, as with the detectives, she would never know if she was alone until it was too late, but she had to try or else the one called St-Cyr would only find the secret drawer and take from it the postcards *maman* would have saved. The postcards . . .

The room she wanted was behind her, at the head of the stairs. The floorboards sighed. She felt a draught—Herr Kohler? she asked herself but heard only the board as her weight was released.

From the head of the stairs, whose dark railing she had polished countless times, she chanced a look down to the entrance of the shop.

No one was there so that was good. The ancient latch was stiff as always. The armoire was to her left, the bed to the right. Only a small, shuttered window could be opened in this room.

Closing the door behind her, she tried to calm herself but it was no use. The bed was old and high up off the floor and she remembered it so clearly. There were also two heavy armchairs she had never liked, a simple washstand with stone basin, a jug, a mirror, a towel. . . .

These things were all to one side of the armoire whose severe dark oak was so forbidding she had to remind herself St-Cyr had already opened it in search of Monsieur Auger's body.

Kneeling on the carpet, she threw a glance behind her as she felt deeply under the right side of the armoire for the little pewter pin one had to pull down before the spring-activated drawer would automatically open.

Maman had chosen to hide her most valuable things in the

poorest and least expensive of the rooms, the room in which Henri-Georges Fillioux had first come to stay in the early spring of 1912, the room in which his daughter would now. . . .

No one walked along the corridor outside, no one called out to her. There was not a sound yet her fingers shook so hard they could not find the pin and she had to ask, Is this not the same armoire, the same room?

The drawer popped open. It slid so easily it was like magic. Relief flooded through her and for a moment she shut her eyes and pressed her forehead against the carpet but then instinct drove her to silently close the drawer and to hesitantly stand with her back to whomever had come so stealthily into the room.

He did not move. He made no sound. She felt her skin begin to crawl. She knew he would make her tell him everything. He'd make her open the secret drawer.

'Henri-Georges Fillioux,' muttered St-Cyr, standing in the attic beside the victim's bed, 'have you come back from the dead to murder the woman who never stopped loving you or did Jouvet, the husband of that daughter your parents ignored, do it to save himself?'

Like so many such photographs from that other war, this one could not help but evoke poignant memories of fallen comrades. Fillioux wore his captain's uniform well. The high cheekbones of the daughter were there, the long lashes, wide lips, proud chin and serious gaze. He had even given her the blue eyes—all these things were stamped on her as if by the insistent mallet of the mother.

But what would Fillioux look like today at the age of fifty-five? Almost certainly heavier about the face, with sagging jowls and pouches under the eyes, the skin far less smooth, the cheeks less cleanly-shaven due to that ever-present shadow most men develop with age. Grey-haired too, perhaps, but suave and aristocratic—yes, yes, unless so battered by the war, all such things had become totally meaningless to him.

There'd been no sign of the sous-facteur Auger, no sign of a break-in either. Though he felt the attic had been thoroughly searched, St-Cyr could find no evidence of this. Even so, he used the point of his pocket-knife to open the drawer of the bed-side table.

Unlike so many, Madame Fillioux had not kept a rosary beside her at all times. There was no handkerchief, no alarm clock for one who would hear the cock crow anyway. No lurid train novels or books of romantic poetry.

The handaxe was beautiful, the scrapers, knives, burins and awls so perfect on their bed of towelling, they evoked instant images of the cave and that little valley, and he knew then that before she went to sleep each night, she had used these talismans to keep in touch with her dead husband.

'Ah *merde*,' he said of the handaxe, 'was this used to kill you? Was one of those scrapers used to remove the flesh, that knife to open it?'

The tools were all carefully numbered and he knew she would have a record of the locations where they had been found in the layers of the *gisement*.

A small, suede-covered book of photographs, patiently picked through with the aid of the knife-point, revealed that the girl of seventeen had learned well how to use a camera. There were several shots of Fillioux, lithe and handsome but so very serious. In one he was removing encrustations of lime from the arte-facts, in another, diligently writing up his journal. Some photos recorded their own little moments of discovery—a blade of flint, a knife with a deliberately fashioned place for a forefinger to rest as the tool was held between the thumb and middle finger, a handaxe, a lump of pyrolusite, a mortar, the grinding of pigments of various sorts, the mixing of them with grease and sometimes clay on a rough pallet of stone with a spatula of flint.

A blowing tube of bird bone was being used to spray ochre onto a flat rock—handprints were being recorded. Charcoal had been ground.

Cave art was known in those summers of 1912 and '13. As

the couple had worked at excavating, so had they developed their ideas of the life of those times. Fillioux had been far ahead of the traditionalists, a renegade no doubt among academic circles. A heretic perhaps but he had grasped the truth in the only way one really can, by doing each task as his forebears had.

A pile of flint chips revealed the art of cleaving a usable tool from a nodule by sharply striking the cutting edge one wanted in the finished tool and splitting the larger fragments away from it. Too often his fingers had been cut and she had had to bandage them as best she could. In one photograph the lace of a torn petticoat was inadvertently revealed.

Fillioux seldom smiled but when he looked at the camera, did he see a girl so suited to his needs he wanted her by his side always or did he simply see someone he could use to advance himself?

Only at the last was that handsome frame uncluttered by clothes. In one shot, the naked savage held a handaxe and a flaming torch at the mouth of that cave. In another, disembowelled, a piglet lay ready for the spit. Blood covered the prehistorian's hands and forearms. Blood was spattered on his chest and face, his thighs and groin.

The smashing of the roasted bones to free their marrow was recorded, the eating of it.

Wearing nothing but a skin pouch of stone tools, Fillioux gazed at her as she must have at him, their own Adam and Eve, but had he really loved her?

There were no photographs of the girl she had once been, none of the picnics beneath the chestnut tree or of the wine, the champagne. Perhaps he kept these photographs from her and took them away with him to the Marne, perhaps he didn't bother recording her at all. But he had written letters to her and these she had used to establish her claim.

There was no sign of these letters or of the marriage certificate. Though he searched, St-Cyr could not find them but thought again that she would only have left such things in a very special place.

* * *

Alone, Kohler could hear the Baroness and the boy at the foot of the stairs. 'Toto, darling, please go up to find out what is taking the detectives and everyone else so long. Ask Franz to come down and see me. Ask Professor Courtet or the woman's daughter. Janine ... or was it Juliette—yes, yes, that was it. *Someone* must know what is going on.'

'Why must you always order me around?' blurted Lemieux.

There was a pause. Perhaps she touched the boy's cheek or traced a fingertip down the open neck of his shirt front, perhaps she gave him a whiff of that perfume the sous-préfet's asthma had rebelled at.

'Darling, you know I love to do it with you. Isn't that enough? Here, then, take me by the hand. Together we will mount the stairs to discover the secrets of this little place.'

'You know the Professor and then Herr Oelmann told us to stay with the trunk. You know the detectives will only start asking questions if they find us up there.'

'But, darling, how can *we* possibly know anything?'

'We were at the cave on that Thursday before the murder.'

'But no one saw us. We were quite alone. You excelled yourself. You were very much the savage. It ... it was really quite remarkable and exquisite, isn't that so? Sex in the coolness of a primitive hole in the ground whose walls and roof hauntingly reflected the light from our candles and evoked the trampling herds of the past.'

'Damn you, Marina, why must you do this to me?'

'Because it pleases me.'

'Courtet won't like it if I leave his precious trunk outside.'

'Then let the Professor come downstairs to protect it himself.'

The Professor, ah yes, thought Kohler. The French half of the scientific team that was to vet every little aspect of prehistory in the film. An intense, wiry little man, very academic, very serious and with gold-rimmed spectacles, a sharp nose, thin, angular face and lips that seldom smiled. The one who had come from Lascaux with the trunk, not letting it out of his sight for a moment until the temptation to be alone with Madame Jouvet had proved too much for him.

Grey-haired, immaculate in a dark suit, vest and tie, and in his mid-fifties, Courtet had known exactly which room the woman would be in. Perhaps he had read the father's diary, the record of a first visit to a tiny *auberge* in an insignificant little riverside village. Perhaps he had simply guessed correctly, but Franz Oelmann had been right on his heels and the good professor should have known a hawk like Oelmann would hunt for every mouse.

Kohler let the couple pass by. He gave them time to find a room of their own, then stepped along the corridor silently to ease the door open a crack.

The voices were muffled if insistent but clearly the daughter was on the defensive. She stood with her back to a tall armoire and Kohler could just catch a glimpse of her in the mirror above the washstand.

Oelmann was standing nearest the bed, the Professor on the carpet in front of the woman.

'Madame, I wrote to your mother requesting permission to use the story of your parents in the film. All I want is the return of my letters,' said Courtet.

'I don't have your letters, monsieur. *Maman* must have destroyed them. She seldom kept such things.'

'Letters of such importance?' demanded the Professor, irritably tossing a hand. 'Oh come now, madame, your mother was far too astute. She wrote back to state that the payment of 10,000 francs was more than adequate.'

'10,000 francs, it is not so much.'

'Letters?' said Oelmann. 'Surely you mean postcards?'

'Postcards then,' swore Courtet hotly. 'Eight of them since only so many words are allowed each time. Letters still cannot be sent across the Demarcation Line even if they deal with something so crucial to science and the war effort.'

'She has them,' breathed Oelmann.

'I don't. Mother never told me of them. *Never!*'

'Look, madame, I need the postcards only to justify the payment that was made.'

'But, please, Monsieur le Professeur, how was the money sent when one cannot wire funds from the *zone occupée* or from here to there?'

'I . . . I delivered it. I had to go over a few things with her—your father's journals, the contents of the trunk, the cave. . . . She and I visited it last year in . . . in the late fall before . . . before the opening of the second chamber, before its discovery.'

'And now you regret having to tell me of this visit, monsieur?' she taunted angrily. 'Why is it, please, that only now is anyone paying attention when, for all those years, *maman* could get no help?'

Courtet shrugged dismissively. 'It was not up to me. Others made the decisions.'

'Admit it, you all thought she was crazy. A postmistress from a little place like this? A woman who spoke of the Neanderthal and the Acheulian as though she not only knew them well, monsieur, but had *lived* their history. Can you fashion one simple stone tool, please?'

'How dare you? I do not have to answer that.'

'I dare because that is all I have and when I was a child, *maman* told me all about your hatred of my father, your constant jealousy and ridicule. He was an expert, damn you. An expert!' She tossed her hands and head. 'Ah! if you will allow me, I will gladly reveal to you the art of pressure flaking or the crafting of a Cro-Magnon spear point.'

Ah *Gott im Himmel*, thought Kohler, go carefully, madame.

It was Oelmann who said, 'Your mother must have kept a few things. She would not have left you to find that little hiding-place all by yourself.'

Defiantly she stood her ground and folded her arms across her chest. 'I know of no such place. We were too poor, monsieur, or is that simple fact not evident enough?'

'Please,' said Courtet, 'the postcards. That is all I ask.'

He was not happy, this professor of prehistory. He did not like the inconvenience of her refusal or what she had said to him. 'Is it that the postcards, they are incriminating, Professor?' she asked.

His fists were doubled in anger but he did not even realize it, though Herr Oelmann did.

'How is it, please, that you discovered the trunk?' she demanded. 'My father forbade his family to say anything of it.'

He shrugged. He silently cursed her probably, then snapped acidly, 'Time passes, things change. The parents Fillioux are both in their final years, or did you not know this, eh, madame? Needs unimagined became paramount. The trunk was put up for sale in a shop I frequent. One day it was there—oh *bien sûr,* I had heard whispers of your father's preliminary investigation before his tragic death in the war—a great loss, madame. Please, I assure you. Who of us hadn't heard of those whispers? But until that day last year in June, I and my colleagues had never seen the trunk let alone any of its contents.'

And now you hate me, she said to herself but asked, 'What day, please?'

'The 17th of June.'

Their anniversary.... 'A shop where, please?' she asked harshly.

Kohler noted how quickly moisture rushed into her eyes. Mollified, the Professor said, 'The Marché aux Puces. The Biron stalls.'

Paris, Saint-Ouen and the flea markets.

'Its contents are priceless, madame. Your mother was absolutely right.'

Was it an offer of conciliation? wondered Kohler.

'All mother ever wanted was to place my father's name amongst you and see that he received proper recognition. Why did she have to die?

'Your mother's efforts will not have been in vain, madame, I assure you. When the film is complete, it will carry her name and that of your father among its credits. The cave will bear a suitable bronze plaque. A tribute to her dedication and resolve, to the memory of your father also.'

Lips were pressed against Kohler's left ear. Fingers tickled the short hairs. 'How touching of him,' breathed Marina von Strade. 'Left alone with her, would our professor be so kind, or Herr Oelmann? Our Franz who is so watchful, Inspector, he sees so many things, doesn't he, Toto darling, but says so little. That's what makes him so very dangerous.'

Kohler nudged the door open but by then Louis was right behind him.

Juliette Jouvet withdrew into herself. They were all in the shop now and gathered about the trunk which the professor was opening. The one called St-Cyr stood next to the far end, while Herr Kohler stood back a little so as to watch the others and herself.

She had a good view from behind the actress and her lover. She had thought it the very best of positions, for it gave a chance to think and to try to calm herself though Herr Kohler could see her clearly enough. He knew she had been terrified up there in that room. He knew she was hiding something.

They had not forced her to reveal where her mother's hiding-place was, not yet. For that Herr Oelmann would have to wait and so would the Professor but now each would compete with the other to get her alone and she did not know which to fear the most.

The Professor was pale from being indoors a lot. Indeed, now that she could examine him more clearly, she felt that the stories *maman* had told her as a child had been absolutely true. Like so many of his colleagues, Professor Courtet had always had others to do the work of excavating for him. The skin of his hands was smooth and soft-looking, the nails fastidiously trimmed. An expert, yes, of course, but one who preferred to keep his distance from the things he studied whereas her father, unlike most other prehistorians, had been just the opposite.

The last strap came undone, the lid was opened. Nearer to her, an arm swung down, a hand was pressed flat. The fabric of the Baroness's zebra-striped dress rippled as it was smoothed.

At the opening of the trunk, Toto Lemieux had chosen to comfort the Baroness in the only way he knew. By fondling her seat while everyone else was distracted! Everyone but herself, the daughter, who had watched the two of them as they had kissed and played with each other under the waterfall and then had climbed naked to the cave, to enter it and each other.

Wrapped in a brown chamois and tied with stout white cord, the figurines lay in a bundle on the partitioned upper tray of the Abbé Brûlé's trunk. His leather-bound journal was there beside that bundle, and next to these things were her father's journals, all twelve of them. Five from that first season's work, seven from the second, just as *maman* had said.

There were handaxes and other specimens of stone tools in the several compartments which varied in size so as to accommodate everything, even the extra nails and twine the good abbé had used to peg out his layers, the measuring tape too—a dressmaker's tape. Again, it was just as *maman* had always said.

The cord around the chamois was being untied.

'Professor, a moment, please,' said the Sûreté, his pipe cupped in a hand—ah, she had not seen him even light it! The one called Kohler was no longer where he had been standing. Herr Oelmann was looking at her. What does he see? she asked herself and silently wept.

'Professor, you were a contemporary of Henri-Georges Fillioux,' said St-Cyr with a little toss of his pipe-hand. 'What was he like?'

Ah damn the Sûreté! thought Courtet acidly, his glasses winking in the light. 'Jealous. Insidiously private and secretive. Very possessive of his research. Young to the point of being arrogant beyond his years. We were both assistants under Mouton at the Sorbonne. Henri-Georges went to war and I stayed on. It was a toss-up. Old Mouton said that even though our families might think to shield us from the cannon, he would see that the nation at least got a half-measure of our powder. A fifty-centime piece was tossed.'

'And he won,' breathed Herr Kohler who was now standing directly behind her—why . . . why had he moved himself so close? wondered Juliette.

'Yes, he won, if you wish to put it that way.'

'I do,'—she heard Herr Kohler saying this even as the Professor's dark brown eyes fell from looking at him to momentarily settle on herself with a coldness that hurt so much she could not meet his gaze.

She let her eyes settle on Lemieux's hand to watch the lover brazenly caress the Baroness.

A hush fell on the gathering as, side by side and perhaps no taller than the length of her hand, the soft yellow stone figurines lay revealed on their little rumpled bed of brown suede as if in the exhaustion of having just made love fifty thousand years ago. The arms were cut off almost at the shoulders so that they, with the bodies and the very simply crafted heads, formed the two crosses the Abbé Brûlé had been so excited about.

The legs were long and straight—rigid from their loving. The hips of the woman were somewhat broader than those of the man. Only at his waist had the ancient sculptor carved a girdle from which to hang a pouch of stone tools.

'Adam and Eve,' said Courtet.

'Cro-Magnon,' said Louis. 'Upper Palaeolithic and no older than about 20,000 years, as are similar things from other sites.'

'It is as I have thought myself, Inspector,' acknowledged Courtet reluctantly. 'But the abbé's notes position the figurines much lower in the *gisement*. Henri-Georges was most thorough in pin-pointing the exact stratum. Those, he said, were found with the chunky, flint tools of Neanderthal and are Mousterian in age, so far, far older. Perhaps fifty thousand years.'

'But those are not all that was found,' said the Baroness softly. 'Show them the amulet. Here, let me.' She moved away from her friend.

'Ah no, madame. No. Not even if my life is to be forfeited,' seethed Courtet.

'But I'm going to wear it in the film?'

'*No, you're not!*' hissed Courtet quivering. 'We are having a replica made. Did you think for one minute I would let you handle them again?'

You fool, swore Kohler. You don't know what you're saying to that woman.

'Baroness, it's all right. It's all being taken care of,' soothed Franz Oelmann. 'The Reich's prehistorian, Herr Eisner, has okayed everything, Professor. The replicas are to be used *after* the Baroness has first opened the trunk to reveal the figurines. She will put on the amulet then as that one's mother did.'

'The amulet . . . ?' began Juliette only to stop herself and ask inwardly, *Maman . . . Maman*, what is this he is saying about your wearing it?

A knotted thong had been thoughtfully provided and yes, the tongue-shaped bauble of deerhorn had probably been polished thousands of years ago, and yes, it had been engraved with the primitive incisions of some ancient scribe but was it any more than twenty thousand years old? wondered St-Cyr, and concluded, no.

The cluster of sharp, short incisions gave no pattern. Some were parallel to the length of the piece, some at right angles to it. Some had a short barb at one end, either slanting to the left or right. Clearly they had been cut by working the point of a flint burin back and forth. The shavings would have been blown out from time to time but did the markings mean anything? Were they the first sign of written language?

Only when Courtet had taken a small, marked disc of tracing paper from his wallet and had slid this over the scratches, did they see the swastika among them.

'At least fifty thousand years old,' he said. 'Henri-Georges was always an advocate of greater age than anyone else, but I have to conclude that he was correct.'

'Fifty thousand years,' said someone.

'Perhaps far more,' whispered Juliette. *Maman,* she cried inwardly. *Maman,* what is this?

'A swastika,' breathed Kohler.

'Yes,' said Courtet. 'I do not doubt it for a moment and neither does my colleague from the Reich, the Herr Dr Professor Eisner.'

'The greatest discovery of all time,' said the Baroness. 'Now you see why the filming of *Moment of Discovery* is so important and why the Reichsminister Dr Goebbels is urging us to keep to the schedule.'

St-Cyr drew on his pipe in quiet contemplation. The amulet was certainly very old, the figurines also. And true, one could sometimes make unexpected patterns out of primitive scratches but *nom de Dieu,* was this not going too far?

Hermann seemed to think so too, but still gazed on the objects with the rapt attention of a small boy at a carnival.

The Sûreté had best clear the throat and the air. 'Professor, upstairs in the room my partner overheard you saying something about another chamber?'

'Ah, the *grotte,* yes. After I had visited the cave with Madame Fillioux, I went back to study it alone. I had the journals of your father madame, and that of the abbé. I felt certain though that they both had missed something. Henri-Georges ... your father, madame, he was always too intense, too patient with his little investigations. Every grain of sand had to be examined and accounted for. The *gisement* was there at the mouth of the cave and, yes, this suggested a place of lengthy habitation, not a *grotte* for the worship of creatures of the hunt. But the cave, it has two entrances, yes? A much smaller one to the east, one not much used since it is barely large enough to slither through. A ventilation conduit for the smoke of their fires perhaps. This entrance suggested to me that there might possibly be further openings and I persisted.'

Good for you, was that it, eh? snorted Kohler inwardly.

Courtet went on. 'I found a fissure and rocks that, on close examination, revealed lime had been redeposited to cement the

gaps. Clays washed in from the plateau above had contributed
to the hiding of the opening of this new chamber. Believe me,
the paintings are magnificent, Inspectors. For an hour or more
I walked along the ancient channel beneath them, looking
up always and aided only by the beam of my torch. Then I
could no longer help myself. Ah, I could not. I knelt, as those
early hunters must have done, in abject prayer. My moment of
discovery.'

'Dr. Goebbels should see them then,' said Kohler firmly. 'I'll
let Sturmbannführer Boemelburg know of it. He and Gestapo
Mueller are old friends. They'll impress upon the Reichminister
the importance of his coming here to consecrate the site.'

'After he's seen the film,' said Oelmann tightly. 'Do we have
clearance to shoot the initial scenes here at the house?'

'Clearance . . . ? Ah no. No, I'm afraid not,' said the Sûreté.
'Not until the victim's living quarters have been dusted for
fingerprints.'

'But there was no body, no murder here?' objected Courtet.
'Surely there is now no need for further delays?'

'Well?' demanded Oelmann.

'Yes, please tell us,' insisted the Baroness.

The hand with its pipe was given that little toss Kohler had
come to know so well. 'A day, two days . . . perhaps a week.
Until I am certain no one has searched through Madame Fillioux's personal belongings, that attic is sealed.'

'But that's impossible,' swore Oelmann, darting an accusing
glance at the professor. 'Filming is to begin up there.'

'But the trunk, it had lain in the cellars, had it not?' said
Louis.

'They lived up there,' countered Oelmann harshly. 'We want
to record the poverty. It's important to show how she lived. She
did not realize the true meaning of what she had stumbled
upon.'

Ah, the wonder of celluloid, thought Kohler. An ignorant sixteen-year-old peasant girl portrayed by a thirty-five-year-old Austrian baroness with a bottom that liked to be polished.

* * *

The heat was on, the noonday silence of the village seemingly impenetrable. As St-Cyr and Kohler shared a cigarette, Franz Oelmann tinkered with the car's engine while Courtet, morose and silent, sat on his precious trunk refusing to budge until Lemieux came back to guard it. Not wanting to return to Lascaux just yet, the Baroness and her Toto had gone to find the village's only café. Juliette Jouvet had retreated to the river to avoid Herr Oelmann and seek solace in her loneliness.

'Louis, this thing . . . ,' began Kohler, and St-Cyr could tell his partner was really worried. 'A fucking swastika on a bit of deer-horn fifty thousand or even twenty thousand years old. Goebbels and Himmler—*der Führer*, for Christ's sake. Ah *verdammt*, what are we to do? Take the Baron's offer of 250,000 apiece to look the other way or get stubborn?'

Hermann had never looked the other way. 'Remain calm. Try to think as Madame Fillioux would have done.'

Kohler took a deep drag before handing the cigarette over. 'Postcards from the father's parents in Paris.'

'Pleas for food Madame Fillioux ignored until two days before her death.'

'Postcards from the Professor he absolutely has to have returned. 10,000 francs and a visit to that cave with her.'

'Then miraculously he finds the paintings in another part of the cave, having already come into possession of the trunk.'

'A cave she must have known only too well,' grumbled the Bavarian. 'Our schoolteacher receives a frantic telephone call from the mother and pays the cave two visits before successfully retrieving the mortar and lumps of pyrolusite. She lies about the first visit. She thinks someone was watching her on the second. Could it have been that husband of hers?'

'Our veteran. . . . Perhaps, but are there postcards from her father, Hermann? Postcards her mother didn't tell her of? Is this not what she is now worrying about? Everything suggests Madame Fillioux thought her long-dead husband had returned but our victim also knew Professor Courtet.'

'Yet she laid out the picnic as for the husband,' said Kohler, exhaling smoke through his nostrils in exasperation. 'Champagne was left at the site. She didn't bring it but did the husband? His flask is found—she couldn't have had that, could she? Christ, so many went AWOL in that last war, who could blame them.'

St-Cyr took the cigarette from him to savour it. 'Henri-Georges was very skilled in the use and making of stone tools but is Professor Courtet?'

'Not according to the daughter. She even challenged him to make one. When she was a child, the mother told her Courtet and her father hated each other.'

'And now the Professor has everything Henri-Georges once had.'

A cave, a trunk and now a film and fame. 'Oelmann must be Himmler's man on location, Louis. If that cave really is a forgery, our friend from the SS will do everything necessary to keep it quiet. They're in too deep.'

Everything including killing the woman? But what of the sous-facteur Auger, wondered St-Cyr. What of the daughter's husband?

Only time would tell, and time was something they did not have.

5 BEYOND THE DIRT TRACK THAT LED TO THE VIL-
lage, the road climbed tortuously into the hills.
Oak woods crowded closely, sweet chestnut
grew near each habitation, and where sufficient land could be
cleared and the soil was right, walnut plantations had been set
out. But after nearly ten kilometres, they knew they had to turn
back, knew also that they had been deliberately led astray.

Subdued and pale in the back seat beside Louis, Madame
Jouvet had been giving herself time to think and had let them
pass the turn-off.

'Well? snapped Oelmann.

She was sickened by the little smile he gave. 'The lane is very
difficult to see. Monsieur Auger lives alone and uses a bicycle,
so does not often need the fullness of an *Autobahn*.'

Touché, was that it? wondered St-Cyr, wishing she hadn't let
Oelmann get the better of her. 'Madame, is it that you are afraid
the sous-facteur has also been murdered?'

She dropped her eyes so swiftly it startled him. She turned
away to stare at a fine old tree. The car crept along through

woods where raspberries grew in summer and the voices of her mother and those of her children on holiday would come to her.

When they found it, the lane pitched downhill and, rather than chance the wash-outs, Oelmann said he would stay with the car.

Kohler didn't like it one bit. Oelmann was only stalling. The bastard was going to follow at a distance.

They walked in silence. The wash-outs deepened. On the steepest slope, the lane became a scree of pale yellow boulders among the trees, and it was alongside this that a rope had been placed.

'Auger would have had to carry the bicycle,' breathed Kohler, shaking his head. Rather than fix the bloody road, the sous-facteur had probably written to the authorities and, having heard nothing, had got his back up and refused to do a thing. A stubborn man.

'Madame,' hazarded St-Cyr still looking at the scree, 'would your husband and his friends in the LVF know of this farm?'

'André . . . ? But . . . but with his leg, monsieur? Surely you don't think. . . .'

'I am merely asking about his friends, madame. They are to march in the Bastille Day parade. To do so, implies a certain mobility.'

'André would . . . would not have killed Monsieur Auger, Inspector. He had no reason to.'

She waited for him to ask, But what about killing your mother? She knew this was what he really wanted to say but he let the silence do its work.

Using the rope, they picked their way down the hill and when, at last, they had reached the bottom-lands, they saw the farm beside a bend in the river. The stone cottage with its tiled roof was all but hidden in a grove of walnut trees on the far side of a small pasture where a russet mare paused in grazing to flick her tail and stare at them. The sound of geese came from behind the cottage. There were no cows to milk.

'He's not alive,' she said desperately. 'No smoke comes from the chimney.'

The place was too quiet. 'It's summer. He'd only need the fire just before dawn and maybe in the evening,' breathed Kohler. 'Why'd he live alone like this?'

'Why? Because it is the land of his father and when his older brother was killed in the last war, the farm fell to him.'

'A bachelor,' said St-Cyr, carefully searching the landscape for every last detail.

'My mother was the only woman he ever loved, Inspectors. Though she refused him, she needed him and in her need, there was a kind of contentment for him. He never gave up trying and I was always the daughter he had never had. I loved him as a father.'

'Ah *merde*, stay here, then, with Hermann.'

'Try down by the river if . . . if he is not in the cottage. He . . . he liked to go fishing and would have spent all his time doing so if it had been possible.'

'But only on a Sunday would he have had the time,' sighed St-Cyr.

The Sunday before her mother was killed. The day she herself had returned to the cave to retrieve the lumps of pyrolusite and the mortar before it was too late.

'Oelmann has a pistol, Louis. I left our guns in my other bag, the one that stayed on the train.'

'Idiot! If you don't have your bags chained to your wrists these days, they are stolen!'

'I checked it through. It went into the luggage lock-up.'

'Destined for the Gare d'Austerlitz? Hah! a *perfectionniste*!'

It was Hermann's responsibility to look after their guns when not in use.

'*Befehl ist Befehl,* Frau Jouvet,' seethed St-Cyr. '*Ist wirklich ganz einfach.* An order is an order. It's really quite simple. I leave you with him and trust that God will not ensure yet another blunder!'

'He speaks *deutsch*. It helps,' offered Kohler lamely after

Louis had left them. 'Now why don't you tell me about the post-cards? Oelmann will only find out, then where will you be? He's SS, madame—he has to be. They teach them how to deal with recalcitrant tongues. Men, women and children, it makes no difference.'

'This is not the *zone occupée*, monsieur. Here there are still laws against such things.'

But for how long? he wondered sadly. 'They'll strip you naked so as to humiliate you. Then they'll make you sit before them under the lights or they'll hang you up from a meat-hook and make what that lousy husband of yours does seem like a picnic. Guys like Oelmann can always get help, madame, even here in the *zone libre*. All he has to do is make a phone call. If not a *Sonderkommando*, a special commando, then the Vichy Security Police who work hand in glove with them in spite of your laws. He won't even lay a finger on you unless he gets a kick out of it, but we'll find you in some field with the flies buzzing.'

'*Stop it! Please stop it!*'

'Hey, I'm really sorry I had to do that but you have to have the truth. Louis and I can't be with you all the time. Not if we're to deal with this thing.'

Sweat stung his eyes and St-Cyr cursed it. The geese were worried. Perhaps forty of them disinterestedly pecked at the stubble about the door but on seeing him the whole flock rushed to a tiny shed at the side of the cottage. There they beat their wings and stretched their necks as they complained loudly.

'All right, all right,' he said. 'A moment, please. Ah *nom de Jésus-Christ!*'

They fretted. They rushed him again. They pecked at his shoes and ankles. One worked on the turn-up of a trouser leg, another at a sock until he slipped and went down hard to scramble up as they fluttered about and he flicked his hands to clean them and roared, '*Is Auger in there, eh? Bloated, butchered, festering among the wooden rakes?* Ah *merde,* look what I've done to my clothes.'

He was glad Hermann hadn't seen him fall. He would never have lived it down.

The shed was primitive, the feed-bin half empty. Seizing the wooden bucket, he dug it fiercely into the cracked corn and tried to repel the invasion. 'Now, now,' he said. 'Don't be greedy. There's enough for all.'

A pump in the yard gave salvation, a towel on the line was used. Wiping his shoes off as best he could, he lifted the latch and went into the cottage. The soot-stained fireplace held cold ashes; the bare, plank table and benches had seen years of use. There was nothing out of the ordinary. The place was clean and simple and elementally perfect once one had got used to the geese. A box bed, with big drawers beneath it, was near a plain armoire. Heavy log beams were above. A small attic was through a trap door to which a ladder of peeled poles rose steeply. Again there was nothing much but again, as in Madame Fillioux's attic, he had to ask, Has the place been carefully searched?

Several of last year's walnuts lay in a bowl in the centre of the table, the large grandjeans still in their shells. . . .

Down by the river, the grass and wild flowers were tall. The sun was high overhead.

Auger's lacquered, split-bamboo fishing rod protruded from the ample lawn chair he must have purchased at auction or been given years ago. Solid comfort. Cushions even. A pipe and small tin of tobacco were nearby, some matches—the matches destroyed by the rain on that Sunday . . . that Sunday.

The fishing line had been cut. No hook, worm, sinker or fly trailed in the water. There was no sign of a body, only the mocking laughter of a river which joyfully tumbled over clean white gravel.

'*Merde,* where is he?' It was not nice, this isolation. Though everyone would have missed the sous-facteur, had none bothered to search?

Looking back towards the cottage, he could just see the crown of its roof above the walnut trees. There was no sign whatsoever of Hermann and Madame Jouvet. It was as if he was all alone.

There were no stones nearby large enough to crush an unsuspecting skull. No hat had tumbled aside. 'Then why cut the line?' he asked.

There were no worms in the earth of the bait tin beneath its cover of moss. Deliberately they had been freed from their little prison. 'Hermann,' he said. 'Hermann, we have a problem.'

Kohler didn't like it. Oelmann could have made a detour down the bluff, but had he seen the two of them step through the shoulder-high bushes into tall grass? Not a lark stirred, not a sparrow. Instinct warned. It was as if a hunter stalked. Everything else had gone to ground. Everything but the bees and butterflies.

'Stay here. I won't be a moment,' he breathed.

'Ah no, please don't leave me.'

She was terrified. 'I have to. I can't have him getting the jump on us, madame. It'll be all right. I'm used to this.'

He moved away. The bushes hardly stirred. For a big man, Herr Kohler was quiet but it was not nice, sitting here alone, half hidden by the grass and wild flowers. It made her think of *maman* in her lovely dress. It made her think of blood rushing up past the blade of a flint knife to wet the fingers and then the chest. The smell of it, the stench, the sound of blowflies. . . .

'Ah! . . .'

Torn from her thoughts, she was grabbed by the hair and mouth and lifted up so suddenly her bladder emptied as she fought to get away . . . away. Bushes . . . bushes . . . she screamed at herself, her face hitting them. My hair . . . my hair. . . .

Oelmann rushed her through the brush. He took her far enough, then slammed her down hard on the ground.

Winded, in agony for breath, she tried to move, tried to fight him off.

All but smothering her, he let her pass out. 'So, *gut*,' he caught a breath. '*Gut*. Now we vanish for a while.'

He waited. He looked slowly around. Kohler must have heard them but there was no sign of him. *Verdammt*, where was he?

Dragging the woman behind a nearby copse, he used it as cover as he hoisted her over a shoulder. Thirty metres later, he re-entered the woods and began to climb to the car but at a point half-way up the slope, in a wooded hollow, he again paused.

Kohler was out there somewhere. The woman lay slackly on the ground. Eyes shut, mouth partly open, she was breathing normally. Could he leave her for a few minutes? Could he circle round and put a stop to Kohler? He had to find out what she was hiding. Nothing must jeopardize the film, not now, not when the Reichsführer-SS Himmler, the Reichsminister Goebbels and the Führer himself were so excited and had placed so much confidence in him.

With her shoelaces, he tied her wrists behind her back. With the belt from her dress, he tied her ankles. Yanked up, her dress was jammed into her mouth.

Kohler heard him leave the hollow. The gun in Oelmann's hand was a Polish Radom 9-millimetre semiautomatic. Mean, dark and lethal, it was one of the most durable pistols known. But what its presence, and the way it was held, said more than anything else was that Franz Oelmann wasn't just SS. He was a veteran of the Polish Campaign and of the blitzkrieg in the West.

Ah *merde*, the Totenkopf, *mein herr?* The Leibstandart Adolf Hitler, or the Verfügungstruppe, the forerunners of the Waffen-SS?

Brutal, fanatically ruthless and determined to the point of being suicidal, they had more than satisfied the Oberkommando der Wehrmacht that the SS should have their own fighting units in the regular army. Hitler had been pleased. Himmler had said, 'I told you so, Mein Führer.' Goebbels, as

Minister of Propaganda, had let the world know and must have seen in one or several of the newsreels that had come back from the front, just how useful Herr Oelmann could be. An Obersturmführer-SS, was that it? A lieutenant, wondered Kohler. A Standartenführer? A colonel.

Himmler had teams of prehistorians digging at sites all over the occupied territories—in Poland, the former Czechoslovakia, the Lowlands, Norway, Denmark even, and Russia. Anywhere proof could be found to justify the conquest and historic reclamation of ancient lands by their Aryan, Indo-Germanic former and rightful owners.

It was all bullshit but serious and funded by the Friends of Himmler, the Society for Cultural Exchange—bankers, lawyers, industrialists and businessmen. Never had so many prehistorians from the Reich's universities had it so good or caved in to warping history so much.

But the Führer must be complaining that all the Reichsführer-SS ever dug up was a lot of old broken pots and rusty ironwork no one would want to look at.

Proof was desperately needed and proof they now had in a cave deep in the heart of France and in the simple story of a sixteen-year-old peasant girl, a musty old trunk, and the young prehistorian who had shown her the light. Never mind that the cave was in the *zone libre*—such minor details were insignificant. But this time round, the Führer had used his head and had entrusted the matter not just to the prehistorians of Heinrich Himmler, but to the arts of Dr Goebbels himself.

It was all so simple when one was forced to think about it, a real moment of discovery. But Oelmann had vanished. Now only Madame Jouvet lay there with her eyes open at last.

The hay rick was in the centre of a stone-fenced field. A wooden-tined fork and rake leaned against it and, with the sunlight, the scene was like a painting by Monet. But had Auger run out there? wondered St-Cyr. Had he been chased by a fleet-footed stonekiller?

Nothing untoward presented itself. Butterflies sought nectar where stubborn chicory and clover bloomed again. A week . . . at least a week of new growth. The sides of the rick were perfectly round. Thatch covered its roof. The softness of a breeze was at his back as he started out. A few flies buzzed—just a few. But as he drew nearer, the sound of them increased.

There were hundreds among the hay. They fought with one another, crawling over each other and buzzing . . . buzzing. Putrid and swollen and crawling with maggots, the corpse became visible. Fluids oozed from the nostrils, mouth and eyes. The top of the sous-facteur's head had caved in. One blow perhaps. Had he tripped as he had run from his assailant? Had the stonekiller used a boulder?

Naked . . . had he or she been stark naked as they had run across this field in pursuit of their quarry?

Taking a deep breath, St-Cyr removed more of the hay. There were apparently no other wounds, no stab-marks from a handaxe, no slashes with a flint knife, no experiments with such primitive tools.

Auger's skull had simply been crushed. 'But the murder,' he said, standing back, 'must have been done on the Sunday, perhaps in the afternoon. If so, the killing was but a prelude to that of Madame Fillioux on the Monday.'

There was no sign of the boulder that must have been used, and he had the thought then that the stonekiller must have carried it well out into the river when he or she had gone there to wash away the blood.

'Naked still,' he said. 'A savage. Ah *mon Dieu, mon Dieu*, but strong and fleet-footed, capable and able to remain so detached afterwards that the fishing line could be cut, the worms freed and the rick rebuilt.'

Sickened by what lay before him, Kohler silently cursed their luck. Oelmann had doubled back. The son of a bitch had used the woman to lure him into following only to return.

Forgotten in haste, her belt lay among dead leaves. There

wasn't a sound. The woods were too quiet. Was she softly weeping? Was she begging for her life?

The bluff sloped upwards steeply through the trees. Knowing he had no other choice, he started out and when, at last he broke through to the road, the car waited some fifty metres from him. No sign of anyone behind the wheel. No screams of terror, nothing but the heat of the afternoon and that damned car.

Cutting across the road, he picked his way through the brambles. Sweat beaded on his forehead. Irritably he wiped it away with the back of a hand. Where . . . where the hell were they?

When he found them, the woman, still with her hands bound behind her back, was awkwardly lying on the ground and the point of fifteen centimetres of razor-sharp chrome-nickel steel had dug itself into the nipple of her left breast. Her chin was up and back, her head half hidden by the brambles. Tears poured from her.

Oelmann had slit open her dress, shift and brassière so swiftly, she had been too startled to even cry out.

'Now talk,' he said softly. *'Talk!'*

Stealthily Kohler started forward only to stop himself when he saw the gun.

'The . . . the . . . ,' she began. 'The drawer, it is . . .'

Blood trickled down her breast. 'Please,' she begged. 'Please don't hurt me. I . . . I will tell you all I know.'

'Good. That's good. The drawer?'

'It . . . it is under the armoire. There is a pin you must remove. I . . . I do not know if the postcards are there.'

'Why does Courtet want them back?'

The knife was hurting her. 'I . . . I really don't know. *Maman*, she must have exchanged a few with him. She . . . she has told me so little, I . . . I really know nothing, monsieur. *Nothing!* Ahh, my breast. My breast.'

Laying the knife on her chest so that it pointed at her throat, Oelmann cocked the pistol and looked around.

Ah *merde*, thought Kohler sadly, he intends not only to kill her if necessary but me as well.

'Are there postcards from anyone else?' demanded Oelmann so suddenly her body arched. His voice was hardly audible.

'The . . . the parents of my father, since . . . since *maman*, she has sent food parcels to them.' Herr Kohler, she silently begged. Herr Kohler, where are you?

'Was there anyone else who might have sent them to her?' asked Oelmann with a finality that shattered her completely.

'*Maman*,' she blurted through her tears. '*Maman, he is going to kill me!*'

He gave her a moment to silence such childish pleas.

'Mother said only that . . . that she would deal with them.'

'When?'

'When she . . . she came for her little visit.'

'To the cave and then to your house?'

'Yes . . . *Yes!* Ahh my ear . . . my ear . . .'

'So, she would take care of them, madame. Who did she mean?'

'I do not know! *"Them"*, that is all she said! My . . . my husband and . . . and someone else, someone she was going to meet.'

'At the cave?'

'In . . . in that little glade where . . . where she and my father had . . . had first made love.'

There it is then, thought Kohler. The mother was definitely going to poison Fillioux and the son-in-law.

'There . . . there may be postcards from this other person. I . . . I was so afraid the detectives would find out what mother intended. I knew about André—yes, yes, but I . . . I did not know about the other one. It . . . it might have been my father.'

'He's dead. He died on the Marne.'

Ah yes, said Kohler to himself, but can the dead not walk again if listed only as missing in action?

* * *

Furious with himself at taking so long, St-Cyr glanced at the sun and then at his watch. The rick had been perfectly rebuilt, a puzzle for it suggested strongly that the killer knew something of farming. 'The summer holidays perhaps,' he said, for he, himself, had often done such work not only in his student days but as a boy. But to rearrange the hay so carefully also implied an extreme eye for detail, one every bit as good as his own, and a detachment that was crucial.

Beyond the stone wall, on the opposite side of the field, bushes hid a clearing no more than two meters in diameter. A sandy floor, some dried leaves and sticks, a few paper-thin snail shells and white pebbles were all that readily came to view but through a gap in the leaves, he could just see Auger's chair in the distance.

'Ah *grâce à Dieu*,' he said, 'someone stood here as I am now standing.'

Two thin dogwood branches had been broken to clear the line of sight and now hung dead with their leaves, forgotten in haste. Soft, shallow dents in the sand had not quite been removed. The bare feet, he told himself and nodded grimly.

Combing the sand with his fingers, he came upon two walnut half-shells. Like ships caught in a storm, they now rode a turbulent sea.

Five scattered, tiny shards of deep cobalt-blue grass and two grains of the same were nearby. Were they merely the remnants of a laudanum or iodine bottle swept downstream years ago?

'Then why, please, are they not frosted and rounded?'

It wasn't much to go on but animals sometimes hunted in packs. Cro-Magnon and Neanderthal would have done so. The latter had often resorted to cannibalism, or so some prehistorians maintained.

But had the person who had waited here gone out to stand naked behind the rick until Auger had run towards it? Were the arms then thrown about to frighten the quarry and cause it to change direction thus slowing it down for someone else to kill?

Try as he did, he could find no evidence of this. 'Has it all been so carefully removed?' he asked, and stood looking first towards the path, to the bend in the river and the fishing-place, and then back towards the hiding-place. Two assailants, not one. Had the stonekiller, having first gone over the ground, then hidden to remove his clothes and prepare for the hunt?

When he reached the cottage, there was no sign of Hermann and Madame Jouvet who should have been there long ago. When he looked out over the pasture, he realized right away that the mare was gone and the gate wide open.

Having been led up through the woods, the mare now thundered down the lane. Branches swatted at her russet flanks and at her rider. Sweat poured from them both as, wild-eyed and in a lather, she finally broke through to the road to Beaulieu-sur-Dordogne.

'Come on, my sweet,' urged Kohler, clinging to her shaggy mane. Her hooves threw up the gravel. Startled peasants gaped. There was no sign of Oelmann yet. None at all. Ah *Gott im Himmel*, it was hopeless.

Oelmann had taken the woman with him in the car and had left some time ago. By now he would be in that room with the contents of the drawer spread before him. Postcards . . . postcards, and Madame Jouvet still every bit his prisoner. And never mind the Baroness and the others. They wouldn't say a thing or lift a finger if they were still around.

A bend in the road drew near. No traffic. Clean as a whistle and not far now. Would Oelmann torture her again or would the drawer give him what he needed—proof of the cave's authenticity or fraud and if the last, would he say a thing about it? Of course not. He'd simply kill Madame Jouvet to shut her up and then would destroy all evidence even torching the mother's house.

It was not pleasant to think of such things. Louis should be with him but Louis was nowhere near.

When he saw the car ahead, Kohler tried to rein in the mare

but she would have none of it. Madame Jouvet, freed at last, stood to one side of the road clutching the front of her dress closed and still terrified, poor thing. An overturned cart blocked the road. Chickens were everywhere and the front left wheel of the car was dead flat, its fender crumpled. Oelmann was in a rage and trying to get the owner of the cart to change the tire.

'Run,' cried Kohler. '*Run, madame. I'll try to stop her.*'

The wind was in his hair. As its hooves threw up clods, the mare left the road to scatter the chickens. A shot was fired. This only produced a further burst of speed.

The damned thing headed straight for the river and a drink. Oelmann had caught up with Madame Jouvet. There was only one thing to do and quickly. 'Come on, my beauty. Build a fire in your lungs again.'

The mare's chest was heaving. She tossed her head, flicked her tail and refused to co-operate. Wading out a little farther in the shallows, she again began to drink.

Oelmann fired at them twice and that was enough. Thundering through the shallows, the mare broke back up onto the road and then in among the cluster of Renaissance houses. Her hooves clattered on the ancient cobbles. Marina von Strade stepped out from the shade of the café. Courtet reached for his hat.

The mare raced past them down the lane between the houses to finally pull up sharply at the post office. 'Ah *nom de Dieu*,' swore Kohler. 'You *knew* exactly where we were headed!'

Standing on her back, he pulled himself up onto the balcony and once within the inn, went along the hall to the room at the head of the stairs.

'Louis . . . Louis, we've done it!' he cried breathlessly as the drawer popped open.

There wasn't a damned thing in it, not even a speck of dust.

Hands folded in her lap, her dress pinned in places, Juliette Jouvet sat on the edge of the bed with eyes downcast in despair. There was the loss of everything—the postcards, yes, yes! The silver necklace and diamond pin, the few louis d'or, the savings of a lifetime, the 10,000 francs also.

There was the presence of Herr Oelmann too, and she could still feel the nearness of him, the knife at her breast.

Herr Kohler reached out to her from the chair he had drawn up. 'Is this the only place your mother would have hidden things?' he asked.

His voice was very gentle and she knew he regretted terribly what had happened to her. The emptiness that was usually in his eyes was gone but her heart was hard. 'This is the only place,' she said stonily. 'Search the rest of the house if you wish. It will do no good.'

Kohler nodded. He understood only too well that she would find it very difficult, if not impossible, to forgive him, that he, too, as one of the Occupiers from the North, was as much to blame for what had happened to her as was Oelmann.

'Madame,' he said, and again there was a sincerity and concern that only made her want to scream at him to leave her alone. He asked about *maman's* telephone call on that Thursday morning, and she had to repeat what she had told Herr Oelmann. ' *"Them"*, that is all mother said. She would "take care of them"! She ... she could not tell me who she meant, could she? Monsieur Coudinec, the *facteur* in Domme, he always listens in. André could well have found out that ... that mother intended to poison him. This ... this is what I have thought.'

There, now they knew for sure she herself had wanted André dead and that she felt he had killed *maman*.

'The mushrooms,' said Oelmann. 'But "them" means someone else.'

'The one Madame Fillioux went to meet,' sighed Kohler evasively. 'Someone from Paris perhaps.'

'The father?' asked Oelmann sharply.

Ah *merde* ... 'Perhaps. Look, I really don't know, do I?'

'Mother ... Mother must have been trying to keep me out of things,' said Juliette. 'After she said she would take care of them, she begged me to go to the cave to remove the mortar and the lumps of pyrolusite. She did not tell me specifically what it was she wanted taken from the cave, only that I was to remove the things from our little cache. "I put them there some time ago," she said.'

'When?' demanded Oelmann only to see her shrug and hear her say, 'Hurt me if you like. It will gain you nothing.'

'Either before or after she visited the cave with Professor Courtet,' offered Kohler. 'Look, there's no sense in questioning madame further. She doesn't know anything else.'

Could he leave it? wondered Oelmann. Kohler wouldn't tell him everything unless he felt the fear of repercussions.

The Bavarian said, 'Don't be asking the SS of the avenue Foch to put the squeeze on me, my friend. All they'll do is start asking questions of their own and thinking those paintings in that little cave of yours are a fraud and the film a bust. Egg on the Führer's face and in Technicolor—is that what you want? Don't be a *dummkopf*.'

'There is always the *Sonderkommando*-SS we have in the Périgord,' said Oelmann quietly. 'I have only to call them.'

'For help? Ah *Gott im Himmel*, Herr Obersturmführer or whatever your rank is, you know only too well each undercover special commando in the *zone libre* reports daily to the avenue Foch.'

Up close, the threatening muzzle of the Radom pistol felt just like any other. 'It's simple,' shrugged Kohler. 'Their little grapevines are everywhere and each of them runs right back to Berlin as well and the ears of the Führer. Let Louis and me handle this. We'll fill you in. No problem.'

'Even after what I did to that one and my shooting at you?'

Oelmann couldn't be such a fool as to believe they'd co-operate, but there was no harm in pretending. 'Hey, it's all in a day's work. Louis and I don't ever want trouble with the SS.'

Kohler was just gassing about. The SS of the avenue Foch and Gestapo Paris Central had little good to say about him but could he and his partner be used?

Oelmann cocked the pistol and gave the Bavarian's temple a nudge. 'Perhaps what you say is true, perhaps not. We shall have to see.'

The bastard curtly nodded at Madame Jouvet, causing her to shudder. He would now rejoin the world of film and be as smooth and charming as ever, if a trifle silent.

The door closed. They waited and when, finally, they heard Herr Oelmann's car start up, the detective heaved such a grateful sigh, she had to look questioningly at him.

The smile he gave was warm and conspiratorial. 'For now he's satisfied, madame. If it helps, I think he'll leave you alone and seek his answers elsewhere.'

'Are they all like that, the SS?'

She'd go to pieces if he didn't offer hope but she had to hear the truth. 'Most of them. The only good ones are the dead ones.'

Tears began again. Her lower lip quivered. 'But . . . but are you not also of the Gestapo and the SS, monsieur?'

'Only under duress and only as a detective, and not SS. Louis and me, we hate the very thought of what they do and are just itching to get back at bastards like that.'

Once more she could see that what had happened to her was a great sadness to him but so, too, was his connection to those agents of terror. When his hand was extended, she found she had to accept it. He had a way with him and that was good. He did not accuse or blame her for having kept to herself that *maman* had intended to poison André, even though she had also meant to kill someone else, someone whose name might well have been on one of those postcards. Her father's. 'All right,' she said and found the will to smile. 'Let us help each other.'

The cavalry were down in the river in shirt sleeves, bare feet and rolled-up trouser legs, laughing and tossing water from a wooden bucket over a horse that loved it. A tattered crowd of children had gathered and now squatted on their haunches or stood along the bank amused and passing judgment as the giant with the Fritz haircut shouted sweet endearments to a plough-horse.

'You've found a friend, I see,' said St-Cyr, having walked in from the farm.

'She's a beauty, eh, Louis? What took you so long?'

One had best remove the shoes and socks and give the feet a little cooling. 'Another murder,' he confided discreetly so as not to set the village abuzz too soon. 'The possibility of two assailants, one to divert, the other to make the kill—it's just a notion. I must ring up Deveaux and ask for the troops and a photographer. If possible, I will wait here for them.'

'Good. Yes, that's good, Chief. You can catch a meal and a glass of the *vin paille* at the café of the beautiful walnut, or whatever they call it. I've bummed a ride to Domme for Juliette with Marina and friends. I'm not just sure which of those gorgeous creatures is going to have to sit on my lap, but I'll be sure to behave myself.'

'You do that. Now inform me, please, of what has transpired.'

'An empty drawer, no postcards. Nothing. Sautéed mushrooms for two but not for herself. No, Madame Fillioux would have wanted to see the results of her little plan and would have gone to prison and the guillotine quite gladly.'

'She meant to poison the one she was to meet in the glade as well as her son-in-law,' sighed St-Cyr, wetting a handkerchief to bathe his face and neck.

'A visitor from Paris, Louis? A recipient of some of the good madame's parcels? The father perhaps?'

'Yes, yes, the father. Then it is as we have thought, Madame Fillioux expected to meet him.'

Kohler pulled off his shirt, handed it and the halter rope over, then took to dry land to remove the rest. With a bellow, he ran joyfully into the water to splash about and seek depth.

As naked as at the dawn of time, his voice filled the valley and broke the children up until they laughed and cried and clapped so hard their sides were cramped. The giant finally lay down in the shallows and let the water pour over him. 'He's like that sometimes,' said St-Cyr to one of the littlest. 'He has had a hard day and is trying to forget it, if only for a moment.'

Marina von Strade was ecstatic. 'Oo, he should be in our film,' she said with bright green eyes still hungering after the savage, her hands clasped beneath her chin. 'Next to him, I could really play the part I have been given. Toto? Toto, darling, don't you think so too?'

Gérard Lemieux only grunted disparagingly as a jealous and lonely young Neanderthal buck might have done in a darkened cave.

'He's magnificent,' enthused the woman. 'He's exactly what we need.'

Later they sat alone on the bank and shared another cigarette. 'To chase with a boulder requires strength and speed,' offered Kohler.

'Unless the boulder had been placed at the site of the killing ahead of time and a handaxe first used. The footprints, I believe, were those of a woman.'

'Why cut the fishing line and free the worms?'

'A last touch. An act of supreme detachment and defiance perhaps but done after the hiding of the body, after the killer had carried the boulder well out into the river and had bathed.'

'A straight stalk, chase and kill.'

'But perhaps with two assailants. The father and ... and someone else, a woman. Auger must have known too much. Perhaps he could have identified one of them.'

'No one's stayed in that inn of hers for ages, Louis. I took a look through her register.'

'And what of Herr Oelmann?'

'Forgery is a bad word and Berlin has ears. Russia's too cold but so is the concentration camp at Dachau.'

'And our Madame Jouvet?'

'Scared out of her wits yet still not telling us everything. Has no immediate plans for suicide. Will see it through if friend Oelmann will let her.'

'She's the third one, then. She's the next victim.'

'Hey, I think maybe you're right, Chief. I'll try to keep it in mind.'

**6** Ruefully St-Cyr surveyed the greasy parcels they had laid out on the sorting table. Three kilos of unsalted butter—could it be derancified? he wondered. The same of cheese that had gone so mouldy in the heat, the mice had had a feast. Two fat geese and, lastly, a loin of pork—perhaps five kilos of it and worth a fortune in Paris on the black market but never seen in the *boucheries* these days.

Every one of the parcels had been destined for the family's address in Paris. Running a fingertip back through the ledger, he could find no other record of Madame Fillioux's ever having sent parcels to that Paris address or to the one in Monfort-l'Amaury. Perhaps a few postcards, yes of course. Negative responses to the earnest pleas of her dead husband's parents for help. Negative until the Saturday before she died.

Again he went through the ledger. It was infuriating not to find a thing. The stench was getting to him. He was tired. He needed time to think things through.

When he saw an entry from Auger, he stopped cold and held his breath.

The sous-facteur had sent a parcel of seven kilos on the 15th of April of this year to place des Vosges, number seven, apartment five. Rundown, but still one of the loveliest and certainly the oldest square in Paris. Its symmetrical two-storeyed houses of soft rose-coloured brick with white stone arcades had formerly been the town houses of the fashionable but had long since lost out to the Palais Royal, the place Vendôme and, yes, streets like the boulevard Richard Wallace overlooking the Bois de Boulogne. Now it was the address of those who wished to rise above such a station but could not yet find the wherewithal to do so.

A Mademoiselle Danielle Arthaud, a niece? he wondered. A goose perhaps, judging by the weight.

Search as he did, he could find no other instance where sous-facteur Auger had sent anything to Paris, let alone to this Danielle Arthaud. Though he would perhaps never be able to prove it, he was certain Madame Fillioux had done the sending but if so, why had she not used her own name since she had used it on the other parcels?

Perhaps to let others know she was not alone—it was a thought most certainly. And Auger would have seen that his name had been used. It would have appeared on the return address, so she must have asked him if he would not mind.

'*Bitte*, everyone,' announced the Baroness. 'Please, Madame Jouvet has escaped from her dreary life as a teacher. Has anyone a spare dress that would fit her? Something a little dangerous but not too much. The timid awakening, yes? The freeing of the dove if only for an evening. She has two children, has just left a husband who beats her terribly. It is the story of her mother and father we are filming.'

Work at Lascaux had been completed. It was time for a little rest and recreation. A hush fell over the baronial hall of the

château that housed the film crew and cast in their off moments. Perhaps some two hundred were crowded at long tables,
all eating, drinking and until now, engaged in umpteen conver-
sations or simply brooding and wanting to kill a latest rival over
some trifling slight.

'Please,' said the Baroness, 'her dress has been torn—a little
accident. She will only be embarrassed when we want her to be
happy and welcomed as one of our own.'

'Hey, it's okay, eh?' whispered Kohler to Madame Jouvet.
'She means to be kind. I'll see you get home.'

Concerned blue eyes flashed up at him. 'Where is Herr Oelmann? I do not see him among all these. . . .' She was at a loss
as to what to call them. 'Men, women, girls of fourteen and boys
of the same age, younger ones too.'

'Gone elsewhere, I think.'

'Back to the house of my mother perhaps?'

'Ah *merde* . . . Don't worry. Louis can take care of himself.
The sous-préfet and his men will soon be there.'

Instead of taking her to Domme, the Baroness had insisted
they come here 'at least for a bit of supper.' A slender arm,
bronzed by the sun and bare to a finely moulded shoulder,
gracefully waved from the back of the hall, electrifying those
around it.

'Ah! Danielle,' sang out the Baroness. '*Merci, ma petite.* You
are very kind, very beautiful and exactly the twin of Madame
Jouvet.'

The twin . . . Ah *nom de Jésus-Christ*, what was this? wondered Kohler. Svelte, fluid, and wrapped in a clinging white
halter-sheath with finely pleated skirt, dark blue beads, bangles,
ear-rings and high heels, the actress made her way among the
crowded tables evoking strident cheers, hand-clappings and
whistles and not just from the men.

She was about thirty or so but looked one hell of a lot
younger, had thick, wavy auburn hair that fell to soft curls over
coyly half-hidden ears, had large, deep dark brown eyes—

stunning eyes—long lashes, beautiful eyebrows, high cheek-bones and, up close, a generously wide, very engaging, very brave and open smile.

'Danielle.'

She and the Baroness kissed. A hand was extended. Kohler felt the silk of fingers as they slipped into his own. 'Inspector,' she said and her voice, her accent was like a caress, like a salutation.

'Madame,' she said. 'You poor thing. These people—oh they are such creatures,' she tossed a dismissive hand. 'Everything, it is a spectacle to them, isn't that so, Marina? Everything but their little lives which are only spectacles to others. Come . . . let me find you something to wear. It is not nice what has happened. Two murders. Your mother . . . you must be in shock but you must also eat, yes, to regain your strength.'

As if the chosen one of a very large family, Danielle Arthaud leaned over the head table to a stack of dinner plates and gathered the necessities, then went from dish to dish with complete self-assurance. '*Les truffes sous la cendre?*' she asked. 'They're so good, so fantastic I have discovered a passion for them and will take another two for myself.'

Spiced truffles wrapped in thin slices of pork, heavy brown paper and roasted under the ashes, the truffles first seasoned and then sprinkled with brandy, and to hell with rationing.

'A few oysters, a little of the *ballotine de dinde*, or would you prefer the *rillettes de porc*? The *ballotine*? Ah yes, I thought so.'

The white meat of turkey stuffed with *foie gras*.

Just a spoonful of the eggs *en cocotte à la périgourdine* was taken, eggs on a layer of *foie gras* baked in a saucepan with a rich brown sauce in which there were thick, round slices of truffles. Some salad was added from one of several bowls. 'And yes, a bottle of the Monbazillac, you do not mind? It is my favourite since I have come to this marvellous *département* of yours.'

A golden dessert wine, an apéritif too, perhaps.

'Sweet, fragrant and heady,' confided the Baroness to Kohler.

'Our *petite Parisienne* has acquired a taste for it also. It owes its special fragrance to the *pourriture noble*, the noble rot which reduces the acid of the raisin.'

'A Renaissance wine to go with this house,' indicated Danielle with such a generous grin it banished all thought of spite. 'It keeps for thirty years but this one, ah it is not so old, I think.'

Ah *Gott im Himmel*, she was electrifying. Beautiful, exciting and very, very sure of herself.

She and Juliette moved away from the table to pass below a tapestry and coat of arms high on the ancient stone wall. They went up the staircase, and as all eyes watched, she turned at the balcony to give them the briefest of glances as if she owned the whole damned place. The perfect exit.

'Come,' said Marina von Strade, taking him by the arm. 'You must be tired and hungry. We will eat and then we will view the rushes and afterwards you can meet everyone. For tonight you are mine.'

'Who was that?' asked Kohler.

'Danielle? Ah, you are interested? You find her attractive? Until the war came, she was a nothing actress. Impoverished, struggling, always trying to meet the rent—you know the type. Now she has blossomed so much, she can toss away promising work in two other very good films to accept a far lesser part with us. But she is clever. She knows that *this* is the film that will be her moment of discovery.'

'No boyfriends?'

'Don't be so curious. Ah! what is a woman to do? *Strip* before you? She has lots of boyfriends. They sniff at her heels. She picks, she chooses. It's her privilege but . . . ah but she has only one love.'

'Your Willi?'

'Don't be silly. Willi is a businessman. To him sex is just a function like any other and everything can be settled with cash. It's only a matter of the price.'

*   *   *

'A litre of the *vin paille de Beaulieu*, please,' said St-Cyr.

'And for dinner, monsieur?' asked madame *la patronne*. The place was absolutely quiet, though several of the village regulars were seated at their customary tables. There were also two guests, salesmen by the look of them.

'Dinner . . . ah, I have no ration tickets. Give me whatever you can.'

'But . . . but that is impossible. Without the tickets, one is lost.'

'Even in a little place like this and in the *zone libre*, madame?'

The generous waist drew in, the aproned bosom swelled. 'An officer of the law and you demand the black-market meal? Ah no, no, monsieur. Here in Beaulieu-sur-Dordogne we do things *legally* or not at all!'

'A police officer, ah yes, of course one has to be careful but . . .'

'Marie . . . Marie . . . what is all this commotion? My cooking, my customers, *chérie* . . .'

'All right, all right. Forgive me,' motioned the Sûreté. 'It is only that I have had a long day and no sustenance and still have much work to do. When sous-préfet Deveaux arrives with his men at first light, he will give you all the tickets you require.'

'Deveaux?'

Was it such a calamity? 'Yes. Your sous-facteur has been murdered but the sous-préfet cannot come until dawn.'

The couple went into a huddle, the others cautiously laid down their knives and forks or set their glasses aside.

Florid, round-faced and perplexed, the *patron* blurted, 'Murdered? But that is not possible, monsieur.'

'Possible or not he has had his head bashed in a week ago. Late in the afternoon, I think, but of course I cannot yet be positive.'

'Last Sunday?'

'Did anyone not from this area pass through the village? At dawn perhaps, or at any time up to, let us say, noon.'

The hotel, in a big provincial house, was on the place du

Champ-de-Mars right in the heart of the village and well above the river and the streets around Madame Fillioux's house.

Both shook their heads, an automatic response. The woman hesitantly smoothed her apron. 'The *vin paille*,' she said warily, '*l'omelette aux champignons, salade à l'huile de noix*, grand-jeans, sweet cherries and the ersatz coffee since no other is available these days. The *prix fixe*, monsieur.'

The chef's special if incomplete but the very same meal as Madame Fillioux had planned. A meal that had, no doubt, been one of several stand-bys for the past thirty or more years until the Defeat and had captivated the young prehistorian so much, Madame Fillioux had repeated it every year since then.

'No mushrooms, please,' he said, giving the woman a suitably pained look. 'The stomach, madame, the ulcers perhaps. A detective's life. . . .'

'No mushrooms,' she said tartly. 'You offend the chef.'

The husband had vanished to his frying pan. 'All right, then, the omelette too.' He was in God's hands.

So, thought the woman sharply, Ernestine, she has picked her harvest a little differently this time and the detective, he is only too aware of this and is squeamish. It could only mean she had intended to kill her son-in-law.

'Our mushrooms are not poisonous, monsieur,' she said sweetly.

They exchanged a look so knowing he winced. 'Tell me about Madame Fillioux. What was she like?'

Suspiciously she looked at him. 'As facteur, shop owner and innkeeper?' she asked.

'As a girl, madame. One of sixteen or seventeen.'

The chest swelled. The lips were compressed. 'Far too ambitious for a little place like this. That father of hers should not have been tempted by the few miserly francs her future "husband" offered for her . . . her services. Letting her stay at the farm of a relative nearby the cave so that those two could spend every waking moment without supervision? Pah! what did the imbecile think he was doing but putting the teat into the lamb's mouth?'

'Had she no friends in the village?' Everyone was listening.

'Not after throwing herself away like that and being so stubborn and proud. Paris . . . an intellectual, a student-assistant to some professor at the Sorbonne. It only goes to show what schooling like that does to a young man. Handsome . . . oh yes, Inspector. Henri-Georges Fillioux was very handsome.'

Several of the regulars nodded agreement.

'Already married, if you ask me,' she went on tartly, 'and keeping that choice little bonbon to himself. This hotel was too expensive for the likes of him. Hah! he was only after something else and had an eye for it.'

'The trunk.'

'Those old stones, yes, and whatever her little capital was worth to him.' Her virginity. 'She . . . she used to be my dearest friend, Inspector. We shared our every confidence until that one came along and now . . . now she has been *murdered*!'

Everyone in the place could hear Madame weeping as she went into the kitchens. Giving a futile but apologetic shrug to the other diners, St-Cyr took to fussing with his napkin and to self-consciously rearranging the cutlery. These little villages . . . one had always to be so careful.

When the stoneware jug of wine was thumped down, a little of it spilled out to stain the cloth. 'All right, then,' said the *patron* fiercely. 'What has really happened to Ernestine, eh? For years I have had to put up with those two not speaking a word unless necessary and now, suddenly, we may all have to launch a boat to escape the flood.'

'Dead of multiple stab wounds from a flint handaxe and repeated slashes with a flint knife or some other such tool. Disembowelled and left to rot in the little glade where love was first consummated.'

Ah *nom de Dieu*, how terrible! 'He's come back then, has he, that "husband" of hers?' stormed the *patron*. 'A coward, if you ask me. "No soldier," she said and meant it too. "Amnesia," she would say. *Amnesia!* Shell-shocked, eh, and wandering about for nearly thirty years? A deserter! A weakling who crumpled under the first barrage!' He thumped the table, sloshing more of the wine. 'She waited only for his return. She always swore he would come back. She was very pretty, monsieur, but far too intelligent and ambitious for her own good—he did that to her. "He frees my mind," she used to say.' A hand was tossed, the puffy eyelids were narrowed fiercely and then widened with sincerity. 'But the interest she had in those old things, ah let me tell you, never have I heard one speak of them so convincingly and with such passion. And speak we did, at times.'

'*Antoine, get in here!*'

'Marie, she's gone! Can you *not* find it in your heart to forget and forgive what I once felt for her?'

Ah *merde*, a full public disclosure with more tears and a scorched omelette!

The *patron* hunkered down over the table. 'No one came through the village on that Sunday, Inspector, but I will ask around just to be certain. Perhaps one of the children saw something. Perhaps whoever murdered Monsieur Auger knew only too well the places where one can pass unseen. Nothing has changed much in these past thirty years. Nothing.'

Henri-Georges Fillioux did it, so okay, we've got that firmly, said St-Cyr to himself. 'Did no one question the sous-facteur's absence?'

A shrug was given. 'Several of us tried to find him but without success. It was not a pleasant feeling. The incoming mail was piling up. We were all very alarmed, especially when Ernestine did not return from her little holiday. Two days, three at the most were usual, never more.'

'And the PTT, why was it left locked up for a week? No telephone, no mail service?'

'We were afraid to break in. Ernestine. . . .'

St-Cyr gave an audible sigh. 'She would have pressed charges.'

Ah, trust the Sûreté! 'Her hatred was only the result of our blaming her for something that, had the young man been from these parts, would have soon been taken care of and forgotten.'

'But Fillioux was from Paris and of good family. One of the little aristocracy.'

'He made us feel inferior, Inspector. When Ernestine got pregnant, we rejoiced, to our shame. She was a good woman in spite of what everyone thinks.'

'And her daughter?'

The large brown eyes filled with moisture. 'Blamed for everything though it was no fault of hers, poor thing. It was wrong, though, of Ernestine to force that girl into a marriage Juliette did not want. My son, he was killed in the Ardennes, in the invasion of 1940, but Juliette and he, they were always in love. Even after she went to Domme to teach, they would write to each other in secret at least once a week, and when she and her children came home for the summer holidays, they would walk along the river bank with the children. Nothing . . . nothing ever happened to stain their relationship. Nothing. It was pure.'

A nod would be best to indicate he understood. 'Was there anything to suggest that this most recent trip of Madame Fillioux's was any different than all the others?'

'Nothing. Ernestine kept to herself about such things. Her private life was her fortress.'

'But you have said the two of you spoke of the past?'

'Years ago and never of her private life.'

'Then was there anything unusual about last year's visit?'

'Last year's . . . ? But . . . but she made two visits, Inspector. One at the usual time and the other in mid-October, the 15th, I think.'

The visit with Courtet. The payment of 10,000 francs.

'Did Juliette know of this second visit?' asked St-Cyr calmly.

The shoulders were shrugged. The *patron* simply didn't know.

'And the visit of 17th June of last year?' The day the trunk had turned up in an antique shop in Saint-Ouen.

'For several days after her visit Ernestine was preoccupied and forgetting things she would not normally have forgotten. Little things, you understand. It was as if she had either done or seen something she regretted, something she could tell no one, not even Juliette.'

'When, please, did the husband leave for Russia?'

'Ah! not until September of last year. Ernestine was so happy when she heard the news, she forgot the past and tried to mend all fences. "It is a gift from Heaven," she said. "He won't come back. They will kill him for us." '

"And when *did* he come back?'

'In the third week of March.'

The rushes were being shown in the *grand salon* of the château where magnificent crystal chandeliers, gilded mirrors and deep blue velvet drapes rose to elegantly formal soft blue swirls and cream mouldings of plasterwork. Louis XIV sofas, settees and armchairs were lined up together with much-used wooden and canvas folding chairs. Several of the cast and crew sat up front on the Aubusson carpet or to the sides on the harpsichord, on the grand piano, and the tables with their fantastic marquetry and clutter of porcelain figurines and clocks. Some smoked cigarettes or small cigars, others sipped wine, nibbled pastry or, arriving late and still in work clothes and boots, dined on huge sandwiches crammed with *pâté* and roast goose. The youngest of the cast ran rampant, a game of hide-and-seek. The older teenagers browsed, looked bored, held hands or slipped away to explore each other.

'The owners must be tearing their hair,' snorted Kohler, still searching for a sign of Juliette.

'Willi simply bought the place lock, stock and barrel. It was easier,' confided the Baroness. 'Besides, they were Jewish and he arranged things for them.'

Jewish, ah yes, the lucky ones. Passage to Tangier, Alexandria or Tel Aviv, perhaps even New York. Anything was possible if connections suddenly opened up and the price was paid.

Juliette had not come downstairs, not yet, a worry, thought Kohler.

Taking him by the hand, Marina von Strade guided him through the crowd until they reached the far side of the room and could see at a glance where her husband sat in the middle, smoking a cigar. With von Strade were the two directors, one French and the other German, the two lead cameramen, lighting men, casting directors, story and film editors.

'Lascaux,' she said. 'Can you not feel the sense of anticipation? It is like the prelude to orgasm, yes? Everything builds, everything must be perfect or all is lost. There is that exquisite tension, that mounting which then suddenly bursts with revelation which both overawes and overcomes. Never have they worked so hard and on a film of such importance.'

The lights were dimmed, the projector's lamp came on. A hush settled. One couple left off kissing to stare at the screen. A glass of the red toppled over, too late to be saved.

Flickering, the film's leader ran through a series of letters and numbers. *Moment of Discovery, Scene Twenty, Take One . . .*

A clapperboard arm crashed down on the chalked slate and suddenly the hush became a gasp as the screen filled with colour—deep red, brownish red, rusty brown, yellow and dark sooty black. In outline after outline, with some of the figures filled in, giant aurochs roamed beside reindeer and shaggy ponies across the white roof and walls of the cave.

Back-lit so as to give the effect of the animals rushing to overwhelm the viewer, the figures were life-sized and sometimes much larger, and often they overlapped. A red ochre aurochs bull with sharply curved horns preceded a black bison. Shaggy black or red ponies galloped in succession while deep red reindeer with huge spreads of antlers looked on and one had to seek out and follow every line. There was so much, they were so beautiful.

There was still no sign of Juliette, ah *merde.* . . . 'Fantastic,' sighed Kohler. 'Oh *mein Gott,* Louis has to see this.'

It thrilled her to hear him say so. 'The Chamber of Bulls we are calling it,' confided Marina with a whisper whose warm breath caressed his ear. 'This part of the Lascaux Cave is more than seventeen metres long but there are two other passages, you will see.'

She squeezed his fingers and pressed her hip against his.

About a metre and a half from the floor, the paintings began where the walls and roof had been naturally coated with a fine white crystalline deposit of calcite. Again and again the camera moved in for detail, sucking up colour and silhouette to reveal dusty spots of black or red beneath and within some of the ponies. Each rise and fall of the rock had been used to emphasize some feature, a powerful shoulder, a stampede-driven eye, the swollen belly of a pregnant mare, the figures moving with each contour, so much so that in some the artist could not have seen the head while drawing the hindquarters, yet the thing was perfect.

'Very simple, very stylistic and yet so full of life you feel you are standing in the midst of them. There is a sense of uplifting, godlike purity that is hard to define.'

Kohler could not help but feel humbled and said so.

The cameras panned the walls, came in close or stood well back and used changes of lighting so that very quickly, within perhaps two minutes, the viewer realized the silhouettes could not have been executed unaided. The walls and roof were simply too high. The passage narrowed to half a metre at floor level but broadened upwards. It twisted through the dark grey limestone until, distant now as one approached, one saw a light all but hidden around a corner. Softer, more amber and flickering. Shadows on the wall. A man . . . a woman. . . .

Using a primitive scaffold of poles that had, in places, been driven into natural openings, Danielle Arthaud stood on high with a hand braced against the black mane of a cave lion. There was a primitive stone lamp in her other hand and this she held up for the artist, so that one first saw her from the side, all but naked, slim, lithe, pert and primitive next to her tall, blond, muscular, blue-eyed mate whose hammer-hard buttocks few women could refuse to look at and linger over, ah yes.

'They are using a paste of goose fat and ground pyrolusite. That is a flint burin, an engraving tool, in his hand but he really doesn't scrape the rock or damage the figures in any way—we're not so thoughtless. Once the animal was outlined, the ancients then filled the scratches in with colours similar to those she will pass to him on the palettes. Woman is seen as the helpmate always.'

Danielle Arthaud's auburn hair was loose and uncombed. There were smears of grease and ashes on her flanks and arms, her face too. Around her slender waist there was a leather thong and from this hung a skin pouch of tools. Killing tools? wondered Kohler, suddenly taken aback and worrying all the more about Juliette. The actress wasn't wearing anything else but a strand of bone beads and primitive tattoos of dark blue dots on her breasts and cheeks. These items were zoomed in on so that one saw the beads and the dots very clearly.

Two naked children crouched beside the fire. The boy was grinding the pyrolusite, while the girl heated some over the fire perhaps to further darken it.

The first take came to an end. Take Two came up but apparently it lacked spontaneity, though he could see no difference. 'We'll go with the first,' said the film's German director. There was little argument from his French counterpart. Even so, von Strade, the pacifier, called out, 'Rerun the damned thing. They want another look at her ass.'

'*Nacktkultur*,' breathed Kohler. 'The nudist movement that is now such a part of Nazi ideology.'

'The cult of the body, yes,' confided the Baroness, 'but always the nakedness is seen as striving towards the perfection of a higher ideal than the self, in this case, the art of the cave and a record that has not only survived countless millennia but traces our ideology and ancestry right back to the beginnings of time.'

Goebbels would love it. The Führer also, of course, and Herr

Himmler, the ex-pimp, ex-chicken farmer and now head of the SS, but where the hell was Juliette?

'Why do they need Lascaux?' he asked.

They were rerunning the takes. She would press her lips to his ear again. 'To work out the techniques of lighting, filming and sound pick-up. To gain stock footage we can use and to offer a parallel to our cave which goes back in time so much further.'

'But the paintings at the Discovery Cave are similar?'

'Better.'

'Though done a lot earlier?'

She shook her head and placed the flat of a hand lightly on his chest. 'There the paintings are of the same age as these and Cro-Magnon in origin, but the amulet and the figurines are much older. They are Neanderthal, yes? So what we find very faintly among the paintings at the Discovery Cave, we find on the amulet also and thus our cave encompasses the whole of prehistory and is positive proof.'

'Do you mean to tell me there are swastikas among the Discovery cave paintings?'

'Yes. It's remarkable. It's fantastic. It is everything the Führer could have hoped for.'

Ah *merde*. . . . 'Why no clothes?'

Was he always such a doubter? 'The beasts are perfect specimens and they wear no clothes. Therefore it is thought to show perfection existed also among those who drew the animals and hunted them. One is surprised and shocked a little—it is unexpected, yes—but one is also fascinated by what is going on. There is that sense of mystery, that sense of body worship which glorifies perfection not for itself but for a higher ideal.'

'The State, the Party and the swastika.'

'Very few of the scenes have total nudity. Lascaux was a religious site, was it not? There perfection was worshipped and we must show this.'

She really believed it. The kids in the film came up again and Kohler felt a tug at his sleeve. 'That's me,' whispered a bright-eyed girl of seven, searching for praise he had to give.

'I'm impressed,' he said and grinned. 'Hey, I like it.'

'*Gut*,' said the Baroness harshly, 'then what you are about to see will not trouble you.'

There were takes of domesticity too, outside the Lascaux Cave and under the pines. Of Danielle and other women in skins cracking walnuts, then butchering a fresh-killed deer. Her bloodied hand gripped a flint knife to slit the skin and work deeply into the flesh until, arm buried up to the elbow, she drew out the guts. Blood on her knees and thighs, blood on her breasts, shoulders, neck and face. Using a handaxe, she expertly chopped meat from a bone and placed it on the embers to roast.

The heart, the liver and kidneys she offered up on her knees with dripping hands to her mate, the embodiment of Teutonic master race.

Ah *Gott im Himmel*, Louis, thought Kohler grimly, her eyes, they're so bright, so feverish she has to be on something. Cocaine . . . was it cocaine?

End of take. End of trailer. End of black letters and numbers . . .

'Who taught her to do that?'

'Professor Courtet perhaps, though he is not nearly so proficient. She was with us at the cave on the Friday. She couldn't wait to see it but when we got there, it was as though Danielle had known of it all along. She was the first to enter, the first to pause, the first to cry out in wonder and the last to leave.'

And now you've told me not only that you suspect her, and have let her get her hands on Juliette, but that you hate her. Is your Willi screwing the hell out of her? wondered Kohler. For a price of course. But who is her lover, who does she go to time and again no matter what? That big buck discus thrower in the film or someone else, someone you want all for yourself. Or is it simply cocaine?

'Look, I'd better find Madame Jouvet, eh? I'd better call my partner to let him know where I am. Is there a telephone?'

'Of course. Willi couldn't function without one and neither could the others.'

*   *   *

The jangling of an unanswered telephone was unnerving but St-Cyr let it ring until it stopped. He had to search the house of Madame Fillioux thoroughly. He had to be certain the woman hadn't hidden the postcards elsewhere and perhaps counted on waiting until later to tell her daughter.

'These old Renaissance houses,' he muttered. 'The poorer the owner, the greater the number and craftiness of the hiding-places.'

Shaking his pocket torch and saying, 'Ah damn the lousy batteries these days!' he went into the room at the head of the stairs to play it on the open drawer at the bottom of the armoire and ask again, 'Who else could have known of this other than the daughter?'

He was down on his hands and knees and reaching well under the other side of the armoire when the telephone started up again. He waited. He searched. Straining, he muttered, 'Ah *merde*, why don't you go away? The woman's been dead for a week tomorrow!'

As if in answer, it stopped. The wood was rough in places. There was no dust. There were no cobwebs, even though Madame Fillioux had not been an exemplary housekeeper. 'Too busy but . . . ,' he said and, heaving on the thing, moved the armoire from the wall sufficiently to shine the torch behind it. The floorboards were clean and bare and in short lengths. He moved the armoire a little more. The first round wooden peg came out so easily, he felt a rush of elation. The second, third and fourth were no different.

Stacking the boards, he played the light on Madame Fillioux's little treasures. There were the letters from Henri-Georges the woman had used as proof to obtain her marriage certificate, it also. Both wire cages and corks from those first bottles of Moët-et-Chandon were there, as were a fine silver necklace and a diamond pin.

Twelve louis d'or represented the savings of a lifetime. The 10,000 francs was missing but had it been spent?

In bundle on top of bundle, there were four sets of post-cards. Gingerly he took them up. Some were from a year ago and more—he could see this at a glance for they were of the printed message kind, the sender being able only to fill in the blank spaces here and there and cross out the unwanted words. Others were fully written out and more recent. Some were from the parents of the husband—requests for help that began in that first desperate winter of 1940–41. He'd read them later. No time now, no time. Others were from Professor Courtet—yes, yes—and still others from Danielle Arthaud, but. . . .

Caught unwares, he was startled by the jangling of the telephone and hissed, '*Ah, go away and leave me to it!*'

There were four rolls of tracing paper, of that heavy grey-white sort artists often use for rough sketching. Each was bound by an elastic band. Not all of the rolls were of the same width or length, but from beneath their outermost layers, inner colourings gave haunting shapes of animals in brick red, ochrous yellow and sooty black.

Unrolling the widest of them, and holding it to the light, he sucked in a breath and said, 'Ah *nom de Dieu*, has she been to Lascaux to copy the cave art there so as to then repeat it in the Discovery Cave?'

In silhouette, and sometimes only in outline, bison and shaggy black ponies raced across the paper with reindeer and sharp-horned aurochs. There were others too. The woolly rhinoceros, mammoth, musk oxen and giant elk—but had these been among the animals portrayed at Lascaux? He didn't think so. Red deer, wolf, badger, fox and rabbit also appeared on the tracing paper, salmon too.

Each pigment had been worked into the paper with a finger-tip where necessary, the woman using the technique to quickly flesh out colour and give shadings so as to emphasize line and form and highlight shadow, imparting life to the sketches.

With a start, he realized he had opened two of the other rolls yet had no recollection of having done so.

Test patches of natural pigments were displayed on the narrowest roll and he could see that the woman had experimented with them, adding clay, then water, for ease of spraying through a tube or for working into the rock face with thumb and finger.

Tucked inside this roll was another. Here a succession of handprints had been traced from a rock wall but try as he did, he could not recall any mention of such in the news reports of the Lascaux discovery.

'Two sets of handprints,' he said softly as he unrolled the thing further. 'One larger and far stronger than the other. A man, then, and a woman.'

From across the ages they seemed to cry out to him, but then a blown pigment spray of reddish-brown ochre outlined a third set. Below these last handprints Madame Fillioux had written her name, and he could see that she had not only tested the technique on herself but had juxtaposed her own prints with those of the past, if indeed they really were of the past.

Again the telephone rang. Again, startled half out of his wits, he jumped.

Stuffing things into his pockets and setting the rolls of tracing paper aside, he anxiously replaced the boards and heaved at the armoire until it was back in place.

Then he took everything upstairs to the attic to find a carpetbag and to empty her bedside drawer.

Again the telephone rang but so softly was it heard, he had to run down the stairs that now were all but in darkness, the beam of his torch bouncing from the walls and railing.

'*Allô . . . ? Allô . . . ?* Is that Beaulieu-sur-Dordogne?'

'Yes . . . Yes. . . .' He was out of breath and impatient.

'Give me the Chief Inspector Jean-Louis St-Cyr, please.'

'It's me.'

'Pardon?'

'*Me*, madame. Now connect us.'

'A moment . . . *Ne quittez pas*, monsieur.'

'Ah *nom de Jésus-Christ*, madame, you are giving me a fatal heart attack!'

'Bad-mouthing an operator is an offence against the law, monsieur. I shall disconnect you as of this moment!'

'Ah, no . . . no, madame. Forgive me. A case of two murders. Much work still to be done and obstacles to be overcome.'

'Obstacles?' she asked.

Ah *merde*. 'Just a few.' She'd be certain to listen in.

'Louis, it's me. Where the hell have you been?'

'Enjoying my dinner and a *digestif.*'

'I thought so. You're giving me a hernia. You know that, don't you?'

'Hermann, just tell me what you want.'

'I'm at Château d'Aimeric—it's named after one of their troubadors, I think.'

'Cut the travelogue, please.'

'It's to the east of the Sarlat road and about half-way between Lascaux and that other hole in the ground. I think the weather's fine.'

'Good for fishing?' Good for Hermann.

'The best. At least a river pike. A big one.'

'Have you a gaff?'

'Ah, no, not yet. Maybe I can borrow one from the sparrow. It's possible.'

Madame Jouvet must be with him. '*Don't argue*, then. *Don't agree* either. Just *do* it *again.*'

D.A., thought Kohler. 'Okay, Chief. I think I've got it.'

'Paris, four, fifteen, seven, five *place première* and still quite comfortable if jaded. Our second-in-command this year. A goose perhaps.'

'Good. Yes, that's very good, Chief. Hey, I think you'll like the fishing. I'll check it out for you.'

Danielle Arthaud had been sent a parcel by sous-facteur Auger on the 15th of April to Number seven place des Vosges, apartment five. 'Hey, Louis, I almost forgot. Your horoscope tells me there's likely to be snow and a shooting star tonight. Have you got your helmet?'

'Snow . . . ? My helmet . . . ? Ah, yes, I'll . . . I'll be sure to wear it.'

'You'd better. The first will make you do things you shouldn't; the second will bash your head in if you're not careful.'

They rang off and for a moment St-Cyr remained lost in thought and worried. Danielle Arthaud was at the château with Hermann who had evidence enough not only to suspect her but to suggest she was on cocaine. Herr Oelmann, 'the shooting star', was not there.

One always had to speak in code these days, especially in the North where the Gestapo, with all-too-avid French assistance, monitored everything. Regrettably no calls were allowed to cross the Demarcation Line unless to the SS of the avenue Foch or to Gestapo HQ in the Sûreté's former building on the rue des Saussaies. One could still call London from here. He could call New York, Lisbon, Zurich or Buenos Aires if he wanted and hear those voices from freedom so far away, but he could not call Marianne and Philippe to let them know he had been detained.

Perhaps she'd understand, perhaps she wouldn't think, as she had so often of late, that life was passing her by and he had simply forgotten them.

When he heard a car rolling softly up to the house, he silently cursed his luck. Had he left the lock off the door?

For the life of him he could not remember.

Juliette Jouvet was silent and uneasy as the last of the *truffes sous la cendre* was delicately divided in half with a thin and beautifully worked blade of grey-blue flint.

Danielle Arthaud heaved a contented sigh as she sat looking at the pieces. 'These things,' she said of the truffles, 'they fill my soul and make me feel like a lover condemned to a longing which can never be satisfied.'

The actress took another sip of the Monbazillac and let that sweet, golden wine trickle down her lovely throat before reverently placing one half of the truffle in a palm to pass it to her guest, her little charge, her schoolteacher, mother and battered housewife who still appeared so shy and timid.

'That blade is Magdalenian—Cro-Magnon,' said Juliette tightly. 'Where, please, did you get it?'

'Ah, don't take such offence. I borrowed it.'

'It's from the cave of my father.'

'Is that so bad? You were there. Ah, please don't deny it. You saw the paintings on Sunday, yes? Paintings like you had never seen before. Me, I saw them on the Friday as Marina will most certainly have told your detective by now. They filled me with rapture. I wanted to lie naked on the floor in supplication before them. Naked under an aurochs, madame, and with my legs spread to take the release of his little burden.'

Did such a thought embarrass her? wondered Danielle, having said it just to see what would happen. It must, for that little bird said harshly and in confusion, 'As the deposits of the *gisement* become younger, the tools become better and far more skilfully worked. One also finds flints from distant places, mademoiselle. These flints indicate trade between groups. That flint you still have in your hand, it is not native to my father's cave but is blue like those from the valley of the Seine.'

'Are you denying that you saw the paintings or merely avoiding the issue?'

'I . . . I don't know what you mean? I . . . I went in only to the *gisement*.'

And you are lying, said Danielle to herself, but lies are told only to hide other matters. They weren't getting on. For a start, the richness of the bedroom had made the schoolteacher ashamed of her poverty and ignorance of such things, the silks, the brocades of gold and silver, the clothes too. Clothes that were scattered all over the room as if, worn once, then dropped without a care until picked up by someone else.

Silk underwear clung to the canopied roof of a magnificent

Louis XIV bed. A pale rose brassière dangled from the arm of a Renaissance chair whose dark and deeply carved arms only further embarrassed the schoolteacher since she sensed, ah yes, that the chair, it had been used for more than one purpose. What purpose, please? demanded Danielle silently only to say, 'Relax,' and give a generous grin with lips that were as wide and fine as the schoolteacher's, were hers not so broken. 'I'm here to be your friend. You've had two terrible shocks. Then there is the little matter of your dress, your husband,' she said, nibbling delicately at her share of the truffle and giving the battered housewife the fullness of big brown eyes whose irises were so deep and wide and disconcerting.

'Herr Oelmann,' said Juliette, colouring rapidly. 'I think you mean him.'

Ah! the schoolteacher's expression was fiercely accusing. 'Franz, yes. Did he make you tell him things?'

'Such as?' she demanded hotly.

It would be best to give a little shrug. 'Such as, did you know where your mother hid the postcards I sent her?'

There was a sense of daring, of recklessness and yet of confidence in the look the actress gave. The flint blade was unconsciously fingered as if in its touch there was guilt.

When no answer was forthcoming, Danielle said, 'Your father's parents, Juliette. They are old friends of my family. Since your mother refused to answer them, they asked if I would write to her on their behalf and I did. They. . . .' Abruptly the flint blade was put down as if best left alone. 'They are reduced, poor things, to living in two rooms of their former villa which has been requisitioned by the Germans. A General Hans-Johann von Juenger currently resides there in splendour while they must come and go through a back door so as never to be seen. Always they must search for food. They are old. . . . They are not well.'

'Mother . . . mother could not have known of this. She . . . she was not an unkind woman. Yes, she refused all their requests for help. She had her reasons but then, suddenly, she decided to send things.'

'But *why?*'

'I . . . I do not know. How could I? She never told me.'

'But did you tell Franz where the postcards were hidden?'

Postcards . . . postcards . . . 'I . . . He. . . .'

'Tell me, damn you!'

'*No! No, I did not tell him!* They . . . they were stolen. Oh for sure, how would I know who took them?'

'Stolen . . . ? Ah no.'

The transformation was so sudden one was taken aback. From daring to despair, from complete self-assurance to tears. The glass was drained, the bottle seized and petulantly flung aside as if the actress couldn't believe it dared to be empty.

'*Why* did you have to tell me that? *Me*, for God's sake? *Two* murders. A few postcards—ah! those detectives of yours, they will suspect me. *Me*, damn you. *Me!*'

Realizing she had said too much, the actress got up to pace irritably back and forth. She touched a figurine, a vase, a button, picked up things and put them down, demanded a cigarette and when she had it, threw it down and said, 'Some wine. I must have a little more.'

Abruptly she left the room, left the doors wide open but once in the corridor, encountered a couple, kissed each of them, brushed a cheek and, her voice echoing gaily after them, said, 'It's early yet. Ah! you're so anxious, Marie. Go and enjoy each other's bodies, then come back to us refreshed.'

Alone, uncertain and not liking things, Juliette began hesitantly to take from an armoire a clean, simple dress of soft white cotton. Belted at the waist, its skirt was flared a little, its collar high, and with the half-sleeves and pockets, it fitted perfectly. So perfectly she felt ashamed that, unbidden, a little surge of pleasure had crept into her life. Paris . . . in spite of the severe shortages and the rationing, the dress was a Schiaparelli.

Looking for something to hide her bruises, she found the

dressing table in chaos. Things were open. No cap or lid had been replaced. Tissues were everywhere. Some stained with lipstick, some simply used to wipe a nose that ran—'An allergy to moulds,' the actress had said.

Uncovered, the skin pouch and leather thong lay in a drawer amongst deep blue glass beads and pearls, rings, bracelets and ear-rings.

Taking it out of the drawer, she set the pouch on the dressing table only to see herself in the mirror, suddenly so afraid.

Almond-shaped and chunky, the handaxe was Mousterian—Neanderthal and of the Middle Palaeolithic. Much older than the paintings at Lascaux and Discovery. Perhaps seventy thousand or more years old and from the lower layers of the *gisement*. It was pointed at one end, and had been flaked by coarsely chipping away the flint, but opposing edges had been sharpened with smaller, denticulate spalls. It came to raised centres on both sides and from these, the larger spalls appeared to radiate. Bare, unflaked surfaces fit into the hand.

In tears she blurted softly, '*Maman*, is this what killed you?' A sickness came, a memory, the flesh discoloured and bloated, the stench terrible, the flies . . . the flies. . . .

Shutting her eyes to stop herself, she managed to put the handaxe down.

A crudely worked auger had a point with which holes could be drilled in bone and wood by twisting the tool rapidly back and forth while pressing. There were knives and scrapers and one long knife with a serrated blade—blades to cut a breast in half and scrape the flesh from the skin? Blades to hack at her throat, her. . . .

'Those are from the film.'

'Ah! I . . . I was looking for something to hide my bruises.'

'*Then these are what you want!*' A jar of face cream and one of powder were snatched up and slammed down in front of her.

'Please, I did not mean to pry.'

'*You did*! So search. Go on, *look*. See if I care that the friend I open my heart to suspects me!'

Trembling, Danielle Arthaud turned away to find a glass and fill it to the brim. With difficulty the tools were returned to the pouch and the drawstring tightened but one had to say something after such an outburst. 'Those tools aren't correct if your part in the film has anything to do with the date of the paintings. The tools are Neanderthal and those people, they did not make the paintings at either Lascaux or the cave of my father.'

'You think they're fakes, don't you?' said Danielle emptily.

'The tools? Ah no, they are very real.'

'The paintings, idiot!'

It was almost a scream. The actress was shaking and in tears again. So beautiful, so self-assured and now so . . . so shattered she didn't realize her nose was deluging.

Caution was necessary. 'I do not know about the authenticity of those paintings Professor Courtet claims he discovered. I am not certain either of the amulet I saw today. It's the one from the trunk, yes, of course, but me, I have to ask, has it been tampered with.'

The fists were clenched, the face tightened. 'You little fool. How dare you say such a thing in a place like this? Everyone's future depends on *Moment of Discovery*. Their lives!'

'I . . . I didn't know,' Juliette said and blanched.

The eyebrows arched, the nose was hurriedly wiped. 'You didn't know. Even after Franz had played with you in the woods at that farm? *He* took me to that place, madame. He showed it to me. We walked all over it.'

'Ah no. . . .'

'We saw your mother's house too. He knows the roads. He drove you straight there, didn't he, and only at the last did you become lost because he let you lie to him.'

Herr Oelmann knew, said Juliette desperately to herself. *He knew where Monsieur Auger lived but never once let on.*

 IT WAS STRANGE TO HEAR THE RIVER UNDER moonlight. Beneath the sound of cicadas and crickets, it gave to the village of Beaulieu-sur-Dordogne a sense of peace, a hush like no other.

Perched precariously on the tiled roof in the shadow of its tower room, St-Cyr waited apprehensively. For some time now Herr Oelmann and André Jouvet had said nothing.

Each was known to the other. Both were used to things like this. Both knew beyond a shadow of doubt that he had left the door open and that he would not have done so unless still within the house.

Oelmann had a pistol. Jouvet had one too, a Luger. By easing the carpet-bag towards the crown of the roof, St-Cyr could pull himself up a little. The tiles were hard and warped. The nearest dormer was shuttered and not two metres from him. The heavy tiles were loose and unco-operative. One broke away and he had to lunge for it, had to pray to God and strain for it all in one breath.

God didn't care about such things. God had the universe to tend. By an act of sheer desperation, he managed to stop the tile and to lift it back. An honest, hard-working detective, he cried out inwardly to the heavens. Two brutal, savage murders and a massive case of fraud—is it that? he demanded. Everything was heading that way like a shooting star. Ah yes.

When the shutters opened, he was astride the dormer with knees tucked up, hugging his precious bag containing the things Herr Oelmann desperately wanted. Two torches shone out over the tiles to probe the recesses where moon-shadow hid so little.

'Try the other side,' said Oelmann, his voice a whisper. 'He has to be here.'

'Maybe he's above us. Maybe he's up on the crown of the roof.'

The shutters on the opposite side of the roof opened. There, too, lights played, and from the crown, its tiles loose, St-Cyr desperately watched the circus of those beams. They would find him. They would try to take the carpet-bag so as to have all the answers while he and Hermann . . . Hermann. . . .

The telephone jangled. Its sound was soft and distant, yet the cicadas stopped their mating chorus while the torches went out.

Again and again the sound came. Incessantly demanding, painfully stubborn as only a certain Bavarian could be until at last the switchboard operator in Argentat, ignoring the caller's pleas, disconnected the line.

Oelmann and Jouvet were arguing about the possibility of one of them climbing out on to the roof for a final look. Jouvet was insistent that his leg and hand would be useless to him. As always, they spoke German.

'When I get that bitch of a wife of mine alone, I will break her, Herr Obersturmführer. I'll teach her to hide things from us. She prayed I would be killed in Russia. She had confessed this to me when I broke her wrist before I went away to training camp. I beat her so hard, blood ran from her nose but she doesn't learn. She'll never learn.'

Oelmann leaned well out of the dormer and, straining, pulled himself up until the beam of his torch touched the distant crown of the roof and began to move along it.

'You will kill her. The film is far too critical. She might say things we can't have.'

Fraud . . . was it really a case of fraud?

They recrossed the attic to repeat the process. St-Cyr tried to stay out of sight. Spread-eagled now, he clung to the crown by his fingertips just waiting for the tiles to come loose. The torch beam passed over his fingers. It went on to its limits. Old tiles, thick tiles, tiles whose boards underneath smelled of mould and age.

'When the filming is done here, you will set fire to the house and make certain it burns to the ground. There may still be things St-Cyr has missed. We can't have him finding them.'

A fifteenth-century house, a small, if impoverished treasure in itself. Ah *merde*. . . .

'But . . . but if I do that, I inherit nothing.'

'That is not my concern. Your time will come. There will be other uses for you and your friends.'

Down on the cobbled street behind and far below St-Cyr, a cat paused in the moonlight to lick its paws while the Sûreté awkwardly clung to the crown of the roof.

A shooting star fell from the skies just as Hermann had said it would.

'Her mother was going to poison me, Herr Obersturmführer. The facteur in Domme listened in to the telephone call. He distinctly heard her saying to Juliette, "I will take care of them".'

'So you took care of her. You did it, didn't you?'

A tile began its long journey, interrupting the answer. Taking its time, it scraped against others, was caught on an ancient ripple and began to slowly turn. Moonlight showed it up so clearly. It was right there not a metre from St-Cyr but now . . . now the cat, that damned cat, was playing with it. *Ah nom de Jésus-Christ, Hermann where the hell are you when most needed?*

* * *

Kohler let his gaze sift over the room where a dozen of the film's executives were gathered for the mandatory post-rush conference. Gold was everywhere: in Meissen clocks, Sèvres porcelain, in the chandeliers and the delicate rococo panelling. It was in a desk by André-Charles Boulle, in commodes by Baumhauer and Delorme and sconces by Jacques Caffiéri. It was also in the frames of wall-mirrors that, though huge, exquisitely complemented everything including the Old Masters the château's former owners had collected.

'This is Willi's room,' confided Marina von Strade. 'He keeps it for himself.' She touched his arm to prevent his saying anything. 'Shh,' she whispered. 'It's time.'

The wireless crackled. Filling one of the Louis XIV armchairs, von Strade swirled cognac in silent contemplation, his gaze lost to its own crystal ball. Hans-Dieter Eisner, the Number One prehistorian from Hamburg, tapped cigarette ash into the jardinière at his elbow. Professor Courtet sniffed in distaste at such crudity.

Eisner was young, Courtet middle-aged. Where the first wore dark, horn-rimmed, very manly eyeglasses, the second wore gold-rimmed spectacles that gave him the look now not of a professor but of an apothecary in distress at having inadvertently poisoned a customer.

'*This is the BBC London calling. Here is the evening news,*' and never mind tuning in to Berlin for the truth. '*It is with deep regret that we must report Tobruk has fallen to the desert army of General Erwin Rommel. Heavy casualties have been sustained, as well as the loss of all remaining stocks of arms, ammunition and fuel. Considerable numbers of prisoners of war have been taken by the enemy.*'

'The blitzkrieg for Egypt's on,' said someone—Herr Richter, thought Kohler. The German half of the directing team.

Von Strade was short with him. 'I don't pay you to give proclamations about the war's progress, my dear Otto. If you want to work for the Propaganda Staffel please consult our friend Oelmann. If that one has any free time left these days, he might give you an interview.'

'Turning now to Russia, we report that all but one of the fortifications defending Sevastopol has been overrun. The summer offensive has begun.'

'They'll be in Moscow by Christmas,' said René Bresson, the lead French cameraman. There was an uncomfortable sense of awe in his voice, as if, having backed the right horse, he still could not quite believe it was a winner and was afraid.

In the Philippines all effective resistance to the armies of Imperial Japan had ceased. Now virtually every island in the Western Pacific was under the flag of the Rising Sun, as well as Burma, Thailand, Manchuria and other mainland territories. Clearly, Australia and New Zealand were next.

Lesser statistics about fighter aircraft and bombers shot down over London were followed by the sinkings of enemy submarines along the North Atlantic convoy routes. Having heard enough, von Strade switched off the wireless but remained lost to his cognac. The RAF had destroyed much of Köln with incendiaries on the night of 30-31 May and the glow from the firestorms had been seen from more than two hundred and fifty kilometres, a fine old city in ruins. The SS-Oberstgruppen-führer and Gauleiter of Bohemia-Moravia, Reinhard Heydrich had been assassinated by Czech partisans. The Imperial Japanese Navy had just been dealt a death blow at Midway in the greatest naval battle of the Pacific war.

'The Americans are determined,' said von Strade, not looking around at the others. 'That man they have in the Pacific isn't going to go away nor will Mr Winston Churchill. We have, my dear Kohler, no other choice but to complete *Moment of Discovery* on schedule and to personally deliver it in its commemorative can to the Führer. Tell us what you've found out about our cave. If it's a forgery, we in this room had better know.'

'Baron, it's no forgery. I'd stake my. . . .'

'Hans, spare me your precious prehistoric vanity. Don't any of you leave. *Well?*' he asked. 'Two murders, Herr Kohler.

Both with stones, or so I hear. The rumours fly, my friend, and I must stop them, yes? So, please, give us the benefit of your opinion. The French film industry is in the throes of a massive boom and we at Continentale would like to continue helping them.'

Ah yes, of course.

'Never before have our people had such opportunities,' interjected Christian Dussart, the French director. 'The war stopped the American and British films from flooding us out of business. Now we are at last getting a chance.'

'A chance that can't be stopped because some stupid woman decided to fart around with us,' said someone.

'The film-Jews,' said the German director. 'They've all been kicked out or have fled the country. *Kaput. Fini!* as the French are so fond of saying, Herr Kohler. It's been like a breath of fresh air. New and far better talent has now been allowed to come forward.'

'How tiresome of you,' said von Strade. 'I thought I asked Herr Kohler to fill us in. He's only too aware that the Reich lost virtually all of its film industry and France a good deal of its finest talent. No matter their race or whatever, let us not forget that we have a vacuum to fill and fill it we must.'

He was really worried, thought Kohler, not liking it one bit. 'As to the authenticity of things. . . .'

'Please don't use such big words. Did that dead woman do a job on us or not?'

'It's too early to say. Louis might have something.'

Must Kohler be so evasive? 'Sturmbannführer Boemelburg, your superior officer and Head of Section IV, the Gestapo in France, tells me you are difficult. A realist, yes, but not entirely unmalleable when it comes to women, money and such other necessities. Your partner, though, is a hard-line patriot who refuses to take anything for his personal comfort and seeks only the truth, as you do yourself, regardless of the consequences, and consequences there will be.'

An uncomfortable silence settled over the room. Distantly

the start-up dialogue of the night's screening could be heard but everyone ignored it.

'Boemelburg?' bleated Kohler.

'Yes. I spoke to him not three hours ago. I felt I had to do so.'

'Ah *Gott im Himmel*, then the SS of the avenue Foch will already know of it.' Would it bring Oelmann the troops he needed?

'That possibility did occur to me,' said von Strade drily. 'As in life, so in business, Kohler, one has to take chances. Herr Boemelburg has said you are to stick to crime and to leave pre-history to itself and our experts.'

'Is fraud not a crime?'

'Don't be impertinent. You know it will only get back to your boss.'

Courtet and Eisner exchanged worried glances. Christian Dussart, the French film director, asked, 'When can we start work at the house in Beaulieu-sur-Dordogne?'

'As soon as my partner and sous-préfet Deveaux are finished with it.'

Von Strade drained his glass. 'Deveaux is on his way right now, having given up his beauty sleep. He'll have the necessary men with him. We start work at 1800 hours tomorrow.'

'1800 hours but. . . .'

'No buts, Herr Kohler. Sturmbannführer Boemelburg is looking forward to previewing *Moment of Discovery* with you and St-Cyr even if your leg-irons and handcuffs get in the way. That little order, my friend, comes straight from Herr Himmler.'

'Ah *merde*, Berlin . . . ?'

'Unless Herr Himmler is in Bohemia still executing reprisals for Herr Heydrich's untimely demise. A village has been razed and all one hundred and ninety-one of its adult males given the rope or the bullet. That is in addition to the one hundred and thirty-one who were executed right on the spot of the murder. All the women and children of the village have been sent to concentration camps—let's not deny they exist. The children to one, their mothers to another.'

'I'll talk to Louis.'

'You do that. You take a leaf from our book. Find your stonekiller if you must, but keep the story line so simple even an ignoramus can grasp what you have to say. Titillate the masses with a few tasteful glimpses of our Danielle's beautiful posterior and you will have millions in your pockets and millions, my friend, are what is at stake. Marina, see that he gets everything he needs and enjoys himself. Your Toto is, I gather, busy elsewhere.'

'He's watching the rerun of *The Wizard of Oz* because I told him to.'

'Good. That should keep his mind busy. It's the rest of him you'll have to watch.'

'His cock, Willi?'

'My dear, when you get angry it only makes you more beautiful. Oh by the way, Danielle was not at the rushes. Remind her that attendance is mandatory and cast in stone in her contract.'

'Why not remind her yourself, darling?'

'Because tonight I'm busy. You can tell her that too. Tell her she's being punished and that from now on she had best behave herself.'

'She'll only come begging.'

'Then let her. That is exactly what I want.'

Danielle Arthaud had drunk most of the latest bottle of Monbazillac but still Herr Kohler had not come to find them. Still Juliette waited and prayed for him to release her from this . . . this torment.

Far from helping things, the wine had only made the actress more irritable. She constantly muttered, *'Willi, how can you do this to me? I need it, damn you.'* Now up, now down, now pacing about or glancing at her wrist-watch, she would hurriedly wipe her nose with the back of a hand. The deep brown eyes were no longer lovely and wide but the pupils hard and constricted. The lips were no longer generous but tight and uncertain.

'You refuse to tell me anything,' accused the woman

petulantly. 'I give you things; you give me nothing. The *coup de grâce*, eh, schoolteacher? Why, please, did your father come back?'

'He *didn't!*'

'He *did!*'

'He's dead. He died on the Marne.'

'Your mother . . . those postcards. . . . Are you certain he did not write to her? *Certain*, do you hear?'

'Stop it! Just stop it! I know nothing. A flask . . . his initials. *His* flask. It . . . it was found near the stream. Mother's . . . mother's blood had been washed off.'

Danielle sucked in a breath. 'So, evidence was carelessly left and yet you still doubt his return from the dead? Was there anything else?'

Kohler . . . where the hell was he? 'Two bottles of champagne, the 1889.'

And you hate to tell me anything, thought Danielle, because you are so afraid of what I might do to you with my stone tools. Ah yes, my battered little housewife, if I touched you now, you would jump. 'Listed as missing in action does not have to mean being blown to pieces or cut to ribbons by machine-gun fire.'

She was not smiling. She really meant it. 'If . . . if he has come back, I wouldn't know what he looked like. He could walk right past me and I . . . I would never know.'

'Then you do believe he *has* come back. Admit it!'

Ah damn the woman! 'Perhaps. I . . . I really do not know.'

And now you are trembling, schoolteacher. You are thinking—yes, I can see it in your eyes as you sit there at my dressing-table—that your father and I might have done the killings. 'There are photographs, paintings—the portrait the parents Fillioux commissioned of their son in uniform. I could get them for you. He was very handsome. Your mother must have loved him dearly. I would have yielded, too, to such a one but in that cave, I think. Yes, in that cave.'

With the tip of a forefinger, Danielle extracted a droplet of wine from her glass and, reaching out, made the sign of the cross on Juliette's brow. Abruptly it was wiped away.

'Tell me something, schoolteacher. Did that mother of yours ever visit the cave at Lascaux?'

The blue eyes leapt. 'So as to copy the paintings? No! Mother . . . Mother would have told me of such a visit. She wanted very much to see them, yes, of course, but the war, the Occupation in the North, the uncertainties. . . . It was not so easy to escape one's responsibilities at such times, or at any other for that matter.' She gave a shrug.

And now you are lying, thought Danielle, and your eyes, they duck away from me rather than face the matter squarely. 'But if she had gone there, what would she have done?'

Ah damn her anyway! 'Lighted a candle and stood in awe of the paintings. Wished with all her heart that my father had been with her.'

The mother had been to Lascaux but had the daughter not known of all of the visits? It was possible, thought Danielle, shrewdly looking her over, wanting to shake the life out of her.

In a whisper, she asked, 'Did your husband know we were to make a film of their discovery?'

'André . . . ? It's possible. I . . . I really don't know. Mother didn't tell me so he . . . he would have had to find out in . . . in some other way. Ah no, mademoiselle, did you . . . ?'

You poor thing, said Danielle to herself. You're so pretty in that dress of mine but are you even aware of it now? 'Then if he did find out, would your husband not have seen money in it for himself?'

Had they paid André for information? Had Danielle been the go-between? 'To understand him, Mademoiselle Arthaud, you must realize my husband hates everything around him, not just myself. The school, his humdrum life, the pittance of a salary he was paid and will be paid, the lack of all promotion. The war, it was passing him by. Talk . . . all he talked about was killing Communists, so the Germans, they let him.'

The glass was drained. Some bureau drawers were desperately searched and then those of the dressing-table. Again the muttering came for Willi von Strade to help her. And then she stood so close they all but touched.

'Women. . . . Did your husband do things to the women he and his comrades took prisoner? Did he not boast of how he could use the stone tools he had with him as objects of interest to set himself apart from the others?'

Ah no . . . 'Who . . . Who has suggested such a thing to you? Who?'

When no answer came, the schoolteacher dropped her eyes and blurted, 'It was André. You've been getting him to tell you about mother and her visits.'

One could take her by the shoulders now and she would not resist. One could slap her hard and all she would do was dissolve into tears. 'But if not me,' said Danielle, moving in closer still, 'then your father. Is that not so, my little one? He could have met and talked with that husband of yours and you . . . you would be none the wiser.'

She must smile up at her bravely through her tears, thought Juliette. She must give her the answer such a statement deserved. 'André would have told me my father had returned. He would have laughed in my face, mademoiselle, and would have shouted that my mother had been crazy to have waited all her adult life for a man who had neglected to tell her he was still alive.'

'*And* already married? Have you not thought of this, too, schoolteacher?'

'*No!*'

'But if he is alive, and if he did write to her and then kill her or get that husband of yours to do it for him, you can see why he would want to steal the postcards and kill the sous-facteur also. And you must ask, What will you do? Help him or help to convict him?'

The schoolteacher's hair was soft, and when Danielle ran her fingers through it, the woman did not resist but simply bowed her head and wept. 'I'll kill myself. I'll do it this time because if he's alive, mother meant to kill him and I . . . I said nothing to anyone about it. I'm so ashamed.'

'Good. Then go and kill yourself. Give him what he most needs, the silence of the only one who can speak out against him. Trade your pathetic life for his and let him get on with the research he has had to neglect for so long. It's what your mother would have wanted, madame, had she not meant to kill him. Now get out of here. I've got things to do.'

Sous-préfet Deveaux, his jacket cast aside in deference to a fireman's duties, refilled the tin cup with brandy and slid it carefully across the table in Madame Fillioux's kitchen. 'Another, Jean-Louis. It's not every night I have to pluck a burglar from the roof of a house in this little village.'

'A burglar . . . ah yes, the carpet-bag. I should have known better. So should the cat.'

Merde, what a night! The cat had trapped the tile. The torch beams of Oelmann and Jouvet had homed in on the creature. The neighbours, awakened in any case and secretly watching the proceedings, had seen the cat release the tile to hear it shatter on the cobblestones.

No sooner had Oelmann and Jouvet left in the car, than the citizens of the lower village had come out in force. Nightgowns, nightcaps, brooms, sticks and lanterns, men, women and boys . . . eager boys with sharp stones. Ah *nom de Dieu*. Long ladders had been placed at every corner of that wretched roof and others fast carried up to be laid on the tiles as in a fire drill. They had refused to let him climb down. An officer of the law on a murder case.

'The carpet-bag, they expected me to give it up before they would let me even *think* of using one of their ladders!'

Deveaux coughed cigarette smoke and wheezed in as the tears came. 'Ah, don't sound so wounded. A small miracle, eh?

Gendarmes from Sarlat in the nick of time. In Paris, the tenants would have dragged you free and let you chase after that tile just to see if you would sprout wings and play the harp.'

They would have, some of them. Deveaux had sent five of his best men out to Auger's farm to begin work there. Two others were dusting for fingerprints in the attic, while still others had the unenviable task of opening every last one of the parcels and of disposing of the contents after making suitable notations. The commissariat in Domme had been alerted and a magistrate's warrant restraining Jouvet would be sought. The husband had to be stopped.

'Jean-Louis, this thing, eh? It's getting a little bigger than either of us would wish. Heads will roll if that cave is a forgery and we proclaim it to the world. Vichy have informed me that I am to have the orchestra play softly so as not to awaken the snorers.'

'Ah yes, Berlin. Herr Goebbels invests 50,000 marks to show the world that the swastika owes its origins not just to the humble Cro-Magnon cave-dwellers of the ancestral Dordogne but to those from some fifty or a hundred thousand years ago. Presumably under all that Neanderthal body hair, pure Aryans existed. But to use that to lay claim to the whole of France? To legitimatize the conquest . . . ? Ah! as a patriot, I find that impossible to swallow.'

Deveaux refilled the cup and gave him the look of a priest at confession. 'Whether or not the Neanderthals wiped themselves with swastika leaves or prayed to that symbol is no concern of ours. Let history take care of itself and let Herr Goebbels claim whatever idiocy he wishes since he, and the others, have the muscle, eh?' Effusively he threw out his hands. 'Those prehistorians, Jean-Louis, they're like old women. Insidiously jealous of one another, insanely so and envious to the point of greed. Ah! so they want to warp history a little to gain prestige and power for themselves, others will come along to correct their mistakes and show us all what idiots came before them. You know that, I know it too. A year, two years—this war can't last for ever, can it? Time sorts out all things. God waits only for the bell of truth and so must the rest of us since He's the ringer.'

'You're trying to tell me something, Odilon. Since it isn't a request to see what I have in this bag, why not enlighten me?'

Ah *nom de Dieu*, must Jean-Louis be so stubborn? 'That bag, I could ask you to open it but I'm close enough to retirement to want my pension. André Jouvet was in Sarlat on the Monday from noon until the four o'clock bus. Several reliable sources have confirmed this. He *can't* be the killer of Madame Fillioux though one of his friends might have done it. We are still working on this.'

'And what else, Odilon?'

Regrettably it would have to be said. 'That woman paid three visits to Lascaux.'

Curses were heard from among the parcels, footsteps in the room above. 'Three visits?'

'Yes. The first was in the late fall of 1940 when the country was still on its knees and trying to wake up to the Defeat and partition. The cave at Lascaux was closed, of course, but Madame Fillioux, their only visitor in nearly two months, paid to have it opened and spent several hours inside alone. Like others who are passionately interested in such things, she just had to see the paintings. There was a sketchbook with her and some chalks, a pencil too.'

'And the other visits?'

'Have more brandy. You're still looking too pale. Last summer, in early August, from the 4th until the 7th, an extensive visit, again spending hours alone sketching the paintings. This time on tracing paper. "A scientific study," she said. "Research for her husband." '

'Her husband?'

'Ah yes, that is what the owner has told me. "I remember her well," he has said. "Her sketches, they were magnificent. That one has a real feel for those times." '

Merde . . . 'And the third visit?'

'Mid-November, after she and Professor Courtet had paid the

Discovery Cave a visit. A few hours was all she could spare. Sous-facteur Auger would have known of the three visits but did Juliette? The first visit, yes most certainly but the others . . . ah, that might not be so.

'And Herr Oelmann, does he know of the visits?'

The sous-préfet reached across the table for the top of his thermos and drained it. 'He was at Lascaux during the filming and will have looked through the guestbook the owner keeps. When one visits, one prints their name and address and gives the signature, then later adds a comment on leaving. If I can look, so could he. Besides, because of the Occupation, not many have visited that cave.'

'Then you would have seen if Juliette had paid it a visit?'

'So as to duplicate the paintings, eh? Ah *merde*, you're serious!' Deveaux pinched his nose in thought. 'Perhaps it is that Juliette has used another's name. For me she's not that kind of woman but. . . .' He paused. 'But I have to tell myself that no checks are ever made of any visitor's identity card.'

'Who else visited Lascaux?'

They had come to the crux of it at last. 'Danielle Arthaud "and friend." 25 May 1941, a Sunday, and not quite three weeks before Madame Fillioux's annual visit to the Discovery Cave.'

'Would our victim have read through the names?'

'Most probably since the entry was on the same page as her visit in August.'

'And Courtet?'

'The Professor? Ah! I have forgotten. Six visits at various times, some in the company of other prehistorians—one with Herr Eisner, of course, and two visits all by himself. "A most welcome guest." Herr Eisner has also paid visits without Courtet.'

'So, we are left with Danielle Arthaud "and friend." '

'A stonekiller.'

The initial postcard from Danielle Arthaud to Ernestine Fillioux was dated Sunday, 25 May 1941, the very same day

Danielle "and friend" had been at Lascaux, a worry to be sure. Ah *nom de Dieu*, what was this?

Alone at last in a room at the hotel in Beaulieu-sur-Dordogne, St-Cyr had set the four bundles of cards before him on the bed. In keeping with the law, since the 30th of September 1940 until the end of 1941, only those cards with printed messages had been in use. One filled in the blank spaces, a word for each, and crossed out the others where necessary. Making sense of a tragedy or some urgent problem was all but impossible but one did not stray from the printed words and spaces. If one did, the card was simply torn in half but not destroyed, ah no, they did not do things like that, the Gestapo and the French Gestapo or the Vichy police of the postal system. The card was saved, the sender questioned and then the recipient, who might not know a thing, was forced to give a very thorough account of themselves or else.

Sunday, 25 May, 1941

Fillioux parents DEAD, DYING, ⸺ WOUNDED, very ILL, WELL, REPATRIATED ⸺ PRISONER OF WAR AT ⸺ Have no NEWS OF you REQUIRES, ⸺, money, CLOTHING, FUEL, FOOD, desperately LEAVES, SENDS ⸺, BAGGAGE AT Am WHILE, returning TO, FROM see TO them WILL BE, IS LIVING, WORKING AT TO today HOSPITAL ⸺ SCHOOL FOR ⸺ BAPTISM, WEDDING OF ⸺ FUNERAL ⸺ WILL BE ⸺ TO, WHEN ⸺ ARE ⸺ 7 place des Vosges, apartment 5,

Paris,

France, zone occupée.

SALUTATIONS AND KIND REGARDS,

(signed) Danielle Arthaud

From among the others he chose the first card from the smallest bundle. It was dated 10 October 1941.

Am not DEAD, ~~DYING~~ though WOUNDED badly ~~ILL~~,
~~WELL~~, ~~REPATRIATED~~ 1914 ~~PRISONER OF WAR AT~~
missing action amnesia ~~NEWS OF~~ I ~~REQUIRES~~ beg your
~~CLOTHING, FUEL, FOOD~~, loving ~~LEAVES, SENDS~~ for-
giveness, ~~BAGGAGE AT~~ and ~~WHILE~~ understanding ~~TO~~,
~~FROM~~ Am TO ——— ~~WILL BE IS LIVING~~, WORKING
~~AT TO~~ on ~~HOSPITAL~~ ——— ~~SCHOOL FOR~~ film, ~~BAP-
TISM, WEDDING OF~~ ——— ~~FUNERAL~~ ——— ~~WILL
BE~~ ——— ~~TO, WHEN~~ ——— ~~ARE~~ ———
36 rue de Paris,
Monfort-l'Amaury,
France, zone occupée.

> SALUTATIONS AND KIND REGARDS,
> (signed) Henri-Georges Fillioux

Hermann . . . Hermann, he said and, reaching for his pipe
and tobacco pouch, threw everything back into the carpet-bag.
Deveaux would have to give him a lift. Death caps and fly
agaric. . . . No wonder Madame Fillioux had picked her mushrooms and hidden the postcards. Danielle Arthaud's 'friend'
must be Henri-Georges.

Juliette Jouvet had not yet rejoined him, a worry to be sure,
thought Kohler, and one from which the Baroness constantly
sought to divert him. It was as if she could not let him leave but
had to lead him down a path of her own, ah *merde*. . . .

The screen was filled with colour. The girl with the dog and
the pigtails was long-legged, purposeful and spunky to say
nothing of her eyes, her lips and voice.

'I like it,' he said, grinning appreciatively in spite of his worrying. The film was being shown in the château's *Salon Bleu*, a
sumptuously gorgeous room whose mirrors and chandeliers
added touches of psychedelic wonder to the young, the not-so-
young and old alike. The one hundred or so gathered were
spellbound. Since the dialogue was in English few could
understand, cue cards were being held up over on the far side of

the screen but few cared to read them. As Willi von Strade had said, keep the story simple. A tin woodman, a scarecrow and a lion were with the girl and her dog on a yellow brick road through a forest whose celluloid leaves trembled whenever the girl sang, and sing she could.

There was a witch, of course. One had to have that. 'The British Board of Censors have ruled the film suitable only for adults,' snorted the Baroness. 'Apparently those antiquated octogenarians feel it is not good to show a young virgin all alone in a forest with three men.'

'But that lion . . . he looks like a Neanderthal who has just awakened from his cave.'

'A Neanderthal. Who's to say what they really looked like?' she said, searching the crowd for her Toto. 'The British Censors also ruled *Snow White* forbidden to the under-sixteens. Again it was a young virgin in a forest but in that film she was asleep on a bed of leaves, having been discovered by seven lonely dwarfs who longed to awaken her when only her prince could do so.'

The sudden kiss was fiercely warm, wet and hungry. Pressed against the wall and trapped, Kohler had to succumb. Through half-shut eyes he saw Toto Lemieux sitting between two teenagers, pretty things with bright, shining eyes and soft lips. The nearest girl had her hand secretively on something she shouldn't have but watched the film so raptly no one would have guessed.

'*More*,' grated the Baroness. 'Let that bastard see that I have taken a new lover, yes? It's good for my ego. Besides, Toto has to be taught a lesson.'

'Just like Danielle?'

She pulled away to pout and stare across the audience at her dog. She pressed her seat against his hand and, catching it fiercely, held it to her thigh. 'Toto can sustain an erection for nearly forty minutes if I give him just enough. Did you know that such a thing was possible? Neanderthal's bones were massive—far thicker and heavier than our own—but what about the rest of him? Perhaps they died out long ago without a trace, as most prehistorians think. Perhaps, though, as Courtet and Herr Eisner now believe, thanks to the work of Henri-Georges Fillioux, they inter-mated with the Cro-Magnons and we are the result of both. That would have been the case, wouldn't it, if our cave goes right back to the beginnings of time? But no matter. I like to think that just as they were so very strong, they, too, could sustain themselves and bring joy to their women.'

Ah *merde* again. . . . 'Look, I've got to find Madame Jouvet. She might. . . .'

'Need you? Is it that you fear for her safety in our Danielle's hands?'

'You tell me.' He had no interest at all in her or in why Toto could sustain an erection for so long and yet not climax.

'Go and find her then. See if I care.'

So Lemieux was also on cocaine, but as an aphrodisiac. 'Look, I've got a job to do.'

'And so have I.'

He left her then, but watched through one of the french doors as she, too, slipped away. When he reached the wine cellar, there was no sign of her, yet he swore she had led him to it.

Mould and cobwebs were everywhere and the racks of bottles yielded up the ages on labels, some almost too stained to read. *Mercier . . . Bollinger . . . Krug* and *Heidsieck . . . Moët-et-Chandon,* ah *Gott im Himmel.*

Crouching, Kohler wiped off a label. The 1912. He found another and then another.

When he found the 1889, there was only one bottle left but places where two had lain were free of dust.

The château's silhouette stood above the trees against the night sky, its turrets and walls darker than the steeply pitched roofs and chimneys. Though far from the bombing routes, the black-out ordinance was being strictly obeyed as it was throughout the whole of France. Not a chink of light showed but because of this the place appeared all the more menacing.

Sous-préfet Deveaux reluctantly brought the Peugeot to a stop on a gentle rise before switching off the ignition. 'Jean-Louis, listen to me. Go easy, eh? Herr Himmler and Herr Goebbels? Who wants to have breakfast with them if your chin is resting on a silver platter and a waiter has his thumb at the back of your head?'

'Odilon, my partner's in there and so is Madame Jouvet.'

'Yes, yes, that's just what I'm saying. That bag of yours—ah! you know I can't keep it in the car for you. It's my neck if I do. Postcards Herr Oelmann wants? Sketches of cave paintings that woman may have subsequently forged? Do you still refuse to understand what you're dealing with?'

Damn the weakness of the civil servant! 'Is there still something you should tell me?'

Ah Paris, why the hell did he have to be so difficult? 'That place, there are rooms and rooms, staircases few will know of, bolt holes and secret panels behind which are hidden passages because that's the way the people that built it had to live.'

'Fillioux won't know of them. How could he?'

A call to the *préfecture* in Sarlat had established no one of that name had registered among the cast and crew. 'It's not just him that worries me. These old places. Lovely, of course. Quite splendid if you can heat them and do the repairs but steeped in history and deceit.'

'Just tell me, Odilon. Prepare me.'

'Good! Yes, it's good you should ask! Its first owner, the Duc de Montignac, was murdered by his youngest daughter. A beautiful child, a princess who loved to listen to their troubador on into the night. She drove a nail through her father's eye—you know the kind I mean. They normally put them through the timbers of their gates. He was drunk and asleep on one of the dining tables and probably didn't feel a thing but to avoid her mother's wrath, the child thought it best to kill herself by leaping from the roof.'

'A happy household but nothing out of the ordinary.'

A hand was tossed. 'No, of course not. Now, with the most

recent of past owners, ah there is a slightly different story. Jews, a wealthy banker, an old and much respected family. Yes, yes, of course. Passage to Morocco via the Vieux Port de Marseille. What could be cleaner, eh? First the wife disappears while doing a little last-minute shopping with her two daughters, lovely girls, very capable musicians. One played the harp, I think, the other the flute or was it the cello? All three were found in an abandoned warehouse, the girls both naked, bound, gagged and violated, their throats slit, the mother forced to watch but dead and missing all the jewellery she so stupidly thought best to carry with her.'

'And the father?' he hazarded, not liking this new development.

'The father, ah yes, you will have wondered why I was cognizant of the filming at Lascaux and touring around with the Baroness and her friends when we arrived in Domme the other day. The father was found dead of knife wounds near a brothel in the Vieux Port, stripped of everything including his underwear and left to kiss the cobblestones as was the couple's only son. Perhaps their baggage was sent on, perhaps it simply disappeared. One thing is certain, my friend, no trace of the money he was paid for that place was ever found and no blame can ever come back to rest on the new owner. I've tried. I've had to think it all through and wonder if I had missed something but Marseille is satisfied and so is the Vichy Sûreté. Enjoy yourself. I only tell you this for your own good. Don't cross von Strade. You're a long way from Paris and I have only so many men at my disposal.'

'Is the Baroness aware of what he did?'

'Perhaps. Though she hates von Strade's philandering, she's intensely loyal to him.'

'And Herr Oelmann?'

'I'm sure he knows or suspects but will say nothing. The rest probably don't even bother to question the matter since it little concerns them.'

'And Danielle Arthaud?'

'That actress? It's hard to say. She's a strange one. Very knowledgeable with the stone tools. An expert.'

'Is she on cocaine?'

Merde, what was this? 'Yes . . . yes, I believe she must be.'

'Will you get that restraining order on Jouvet? It's necessary.'

Ah! Jean-Louis would still not take the hint. 'Don't be a Neanderthal, eh? I'll ask—yes, yes, of course. It's my duty. As soon as I get back to Sarlat I will visit the magistrate between his meals but old Lantôt, he's going to want some proof.'

'The word of a police officer is not enough?'

'You know what he's like. He will still remember the last time you applied to him and yes, certainly you were right, but to Lantôt it was a slap in the face.'

'That was five years ago.'

'Please don't sound so dismayed. Five is not enough and you know it.'

'Thanks. Thanks a lot! Hey, I'll try to remember it when someone is attempting to slice my jugular in the dark with a wedge of flint!'

'Just don't get hit on the head. I wouldn't want to have to pick up the pieces.'

Hermann . . . Where the hell was Hermann? Eating, drinking and playing around with the girls or simply looking out for trouble?

Softly the sounds of swimming came to Kohler in the cellars of the château and he cursed the Baroness for playing games with him because he absolutely had to find Juliette and had left it too long. The woman was down at the end of a narrow passage in pitch darkness—she had taken the fuses from the electrical switch-box on the wall. Back and forth she went, the water dripping from her arms as she did the breaststroke but used the scissors kick so as to make less noise.

When he found her clothes, they were in a tidy mound above her high heels on the rocky platform that surrounded the pool.

A natural cavern? he wondered. The spring-fed water was ice cold; she was a real *Nacktkultur* addict then, the naked body taut with goose pimples, the mind alert.

Arching herself, she went over backwards, he thought, to gracefully touch her heels and surface smiling near to him, only to then swim away.

Though she said absolutely nothing, he crouched and waited, heard her roll over to do the backstroke, heard her dive right to the bottom probably. Naked ... naked like some beautiful siren calling out to him through her bubbles, beckoning ... beckoning. ...

When no further sound came, he hazarded anxiously, 'Baroness?'

Hurriedly he found two matches and in their lonely light saw the stalactites hanging from the roof above, the grey of limestone walls that curved, the pool. 'Baroness?' he asked again and cursed as the matches burnt his fingers and plunged him back into darkness. 'Baroness, two brutal murders have been committed. I'd just as soon there wasn't another.'

Myself? she seemed to say though she was gone from him.

The fuses were in the toes of her shoes. Under overhead lights that shone among the stalactites, he could see the bottom clearly now, the water emerald green and with round, white pebbles on the floor of an ancient channel perhaps three metres down. No sign of her anywhere. Where ... where the hell is she? he wondered, seeing her in his mind's eye caught on something, her mouth open, her body floating face up, no movement now. ...

When he saw a rocky ledge just above the bottom at the far end of the pool, he followed the channel below it back to the pebbles and understood. She was challenging him to join her. She wanted him to swim under that ledge to find the channel and then the cavern she must now be in.

You fool, he said. To swim alone in such a place, in darkness, is not wise. Had she things to tell him that demanded such privacy or was she simply trying to seduce him?

'Both,' he said but did not grin. 'Be careful, Baroness. Where one can swim, so can two but the next time the visitor might not be myself.'

The door was of massive oak with iron drift pins and a lock that must be three centuries old. Kohler knocked but there was no answer. He pounded, and the sound of his fist splintered the air. A girl giggled, another too, but the door and walls were far too thick for sounds like that to escape.

When he glanced over a shoulder, he saw two naked teenagers clutching flimsy shawls of silk that webbed their nubile breasts but left the rest exposed. 'Monsieur, are you joining the party?' asked one, whose dark red hair brushed loosely over pale white, freckled shoulders.

'The party?' he bleated.

'Yes,' whispered the other one, a brunette, her breath warm on his lips as she lightly explored them.

'Ah no, I've work to do. Juliette Jouvet, the school-teacher. . . .'

Both tossed their heads to indicate the staircase at the far end of the corridor. Both flicked their shawls away to coil their arms about the giant's neck and whisper, '*Couchez avec moi, mon grand détective.*' Fuck me.

'A *partouse,*' whispered the redhead. An orgy. 'There are six of us girls tonight. Toto Lemieux and a few others are coming. In there,' she said. 'You have only to knock once, yes? It is the signal.'

'I'll try to remember.'

They left him then and he stood out in the corridor like the Tin bloody Woodsman gaping through the now open doorway into a haze of tobacco smoke and naked female flesh, wondering if Juliette was still alive.

'Don't keep us waiting,' breathed the brunette, beginning to close the door. 'One knock, that is all it takes to experience everything.'

'All urges,' confided the other one, 'until they are satisfied even for those who do not wish to participate and come only to watch.'

Ah *nom de Dieu, de Dieu*, von Strade? he wondered. Von Strade.

When he found Juliette, she was on her knees frantically going through the trunk Courtet had guarded so jealously. The espadrilles were her own. The grey flannel trousers rolled above the ankles, and pin-stripe shirt, indicated she had helped herself to the Professor's wardrobe. Cast aside was the borrowed dress she would never wear again.

From time to time she irritably brushed a tear away and when, with a frightened gasp, she turned to look up at him, her blue eyes registered fear, not relief. 'What's happened?' he asked.

She swallowed hard. 'My father's come back! He's alive. Everything fits. The death caps, the champagne, that . . . that flask of his. Her. . . .'

'Not suspecting he would harm her.'

'The blow, the . . . the slashings, the. . . .'

Kohler went down on his knees to wrap his arms about her. 'Hey, easy, eh? Easy.' She buried her face against his shoulder and wept, 'That bitch Danielle has indicated to me my father is alive. He'll kill me, Inspector. I'm next. Don't you see, she's right? He must! I'm the only one who can prove those paintings are a forgery.'

A forgery . . . ah *merde*, so it was true.

Clumsily he searched his pockets for a handkerchief and, finding none, got up to look in one of the Professor's dresser drawers and found instead a loaded .455-calibre Mark VI Webley, ex-British Army revolver. 'Dunkirk,' he said as if struck.

Through her tears she saw the gun and was sickened because it could only mean the Professor was afraid of her father too. 'My father despised Courtet who hated him in return. Each was very jealous of the other and many times his student colleague tried to get at the contents of this trunk until now . . . now, finally, he has it.'

Her agitated fingers hurriedly wiped the tears from her cheeks. A shirt-sleeve was yanked out in which to blow the nose and dry the eyes, then rolled above the elbow. 'Excuse me,' she said and tried to smile. 'I'm a wreck and freely admit it.'

Herr Kohler gave her a few seconds. The emptiness that had so often been in his eyes was not there. He turned to rummage in the top drawer of the dresser and when he had it, emptied a packet of cartridges into a pocket. 'Mademoiselle Arthaud,' he said, and she knew by his look that there was more trouble. 'Danielle was in contact with your mother. A parcel in April to Paris. The sous-facteur Auger's name was on the return address.'

Ah no, *maman*, she cried inwardly, what is this he is saying? 'Mademoiselle Arthaud is not very nice, Inspector. Brilliant perhaps but cruel and demanding and utterly selfish. André should have her. They deserve each other. He would be so mentally outclassed, she would kill him with a little something from her bag of stone tools, and if not that, her bitchiness would make him hit her once too often.'

Herr Kohler asked about the stone tools and she told him they were supposedly from the film, and that André had probably been secretly meeting Danielle or Henri-Georges. 'But I have to ask myself, were the tools not also used on my mother?'

'There'll be postcards from Mademoiselle Arthaud . . . ,' he said, his voice trailing off in thought.

'She has asked for them. When I told her they had been stolen, she was very upset—unreasonably so.'

Still lost in thought, he said, 'We saw no evidence of there being two assailants at the murder of your mother.'

'But at that of the sous-facteur Auger, monsieur? Were there not two perhaps? This is what your eyes, they are telling me.'

'Come on, we'd best leave here while we can.'

She reached out to him. 'A moment, please. First you must see the journals of my father. It is what I have been after. There is not one mention of the paintings, nor is there a complete description of the cave. *That* is also missing.'

In page after page and sketch after sketch, Henry-Georges Fillioux had demonstrated not only where the tools had been found among the layers of the *gisement,* but how each had been made and used.

'There . . . there is also not one mention of my mother,' she said, holding back the tears. 'It is as if the father I worshipped as a child had done it all—found the cave, seen the light and expounded on the brilliance of *his* theories when many of his ideas were hers. *Hers!* He . . . he has even listed among his accounts the cost of the two bottles of champagne and has marked them down to *necessity.* A mere forty-five francs? But . . . but I must ask myself, are these journals not where Mademoiselle Arthaud learned so well how to use the tools?'

'The Baroness says Courtet may have taught her.'

'The Professor, ah yes. But Danielle has visited my father's parents at their house in Paris. She knows all about what has happened to them since the Defeat. Is she not the one who encouraged them to sell the trunk after first learning everything from it, or is it that she did not learn from these journals at all but directly from my father?'

'And not from Courtet?'

'No, not from that one. But if you like, I will ask him to fashion for us a stone tool even of the simplest kind. My thought is he cannot do it but we shall see.'

8 Moonlight lit the well-treed grounds of the château as St-Cyr heard beyond the symphony of insects, the muted whispers of an urgent love. 'Come in me, darling. In me now, *please.*'

Ah *nom de Dieu* . . .

'I can't find my rubber.'

'Then shoot the stork in flight before it lands. Jump from the train while it is still in motion. Don't stop now. Please don't. Just keep going, Erik. I *don't* want to lose it.'

Breathless in their tangle, the couple went at it and he stood not two metres from them. Pale white, all arms, legs, buttocks and breasts, they gave to the dewy grass a primordiality that made him uncomfortable. Their grunts and groans, their sighs grew until they filled the night and he had to move away to stand under an oak whose spreading limbs all but hid the moon.

Am not dead, wrote Fillioux. *Wounded 1914 missing action amnesia. I beg your loving forgiveness and understanding. Am to work on film.*

The postcard had been dated 10 October 1941. Five days later Madame Fillioux visited the cave with Professor Courtet who had then returned to find the second chamber and its paintings.

A mortar and some lumps of pyrolusite had been taken from the cave by the daughter on the day before the woman's death, the Sunday and the very same day the sous-facteur had been killed. Auger hadn't been aware of the danger nor had Madame Fillioux. Fools . . . had she been so foolish as to trust completely?

She had intended to poison that husband of hers as well as the son-in-law.

Rolls of tracing paper held the sketches she had made at Lascaux on at least two of her three visits, the last of which had been in mid-November, presumably after the Professor's discovery.

Animals other than those at Lascaux had been included, as were three sets of handprints—tracings of a man's and a woman's hands most probably—and her own sprayed imprints as well for contrast or proof positive.

10,000 francs were missing. Postcards from the parents, from Fillioux, from Courtet and from Danielle Arthaud might settle everything but for now they would have to wait. He had to warn Hermann and Madame Jouvet. He could not lose the contents of the carpet-bag. Without it, there was nothing.

Steps sounded on the gravel drive as someone hurried through the gates. A muffled male voice said in German, 'She's in there with Kohler. That makes things much easier.'

Ah *nom de Jésus-Christ*, it was Oelmann and Jouvet!

'What do you want me to do?' asked the husband.

'Stay out here. Get that wife of yours away from Kohler and kill her. Do it with a stone. Open her up just like her mother but do it where she won't be found for a while. The stables—yes, that would be best. They're over there.'

'What if they don't come out?' hazarded Jouvet tensely.

'They will. They'll have to. I'll make certain they do.'

'Don't you want me to question her first?'

Oelmann sucked in an impatient breath. 'Just kill her, *dummkopf*. Kohler doesn't have a gun.'

Again there were steps on the gravel. The moon hid itself and for a time Jouvet stood alone looking towards the gates, waiting until instinct drove him to pivot swiftly on that bad leg of his and demand, '*Who's there? Come out now or I'll fire.*'

Ah *merde*, Hermann ... Hermann, why must things be so difficult? 'Monsieur, it is only me, St-Cyr.'

Gilded swans craned their necks into staircase railings that lost themselves among the hanging tapestries and chandeliers of the floors above. From somewhere distant came the sound of a piano—Chopin perhaps—and then, elsewhere, that of a girl running her voice through its range for no other reason than that she felt like it at 2:00 a.m. and the tower she was in resonated beautifully.

In room after room members of the cast and crew slept, sometimes four to a bed or on the carpets, in chairs, anywhere they could doss down

Kohler cursed their luck. They were lost and Oelmann, having caught sight of them on the main staircase, was right behind them.

'The stables must be this way,' he said, only to see Madame Jouvet falter in doubt. He had thought the stables best for a speedy exit. *Verdammt!*

'That way?' he asked. The château was huge.

'We have come too far. We should have turned off back there.'

'That narrow corridor?'

'Please don't let him get me. *Please!*'

She started back and when Kohler caught up with her, he ran with her to the corridor and then darted down it into darkness. 'Look, this isn't it,' he said, convinced. 'It's a dead end.'

Panelled walls enclosed them on three sides. Anxiously she ran her hands over them even as steps in the other corridor signalled Herr Oelmann's approach. 'Why is there no door?' she whispered. 'There has to be one.'

'It's a laundry chute, that's why,' he said and she heard him opening its doors even as the girl with the voice ran through her scales and the piano player rippled the keys.

Kohler put the woman behind him and cocked the Webley. Shooting an SS, even if a member of the Propaganda Staffel, wasn't such a good idea, but. . . .

The steps went on to vanish in some other corridor or into one of the rooms. 'Come on. Don't wait.'

Running, they made it to the swan-staircase and went up it and along a mirrored corridor past vases of white silk lilies to stand uncertainly between two life-sized sculptures of Aphrodite.

'A bath,' said Madame Jouvet in despair.

Gently Kohler pulled her aside to ease the door open and then to softly close it behind them.

There was water on the floor in little pools, bare footprints too, and towels, a white robe, another and another but only the first of them was a man's. So vast was the room, so tall its fluted columns, the marble tub with its gold taps was all but lost on a dais behind a flimsy curtain.

'No one,' he breathed. 'Bath oil, soap, sponges, wine and biscuits. Three glasses but where the hell did they go? Wait here.'

'No. Please. . . .'

'Stay close then.' Oelmann must have beaten them to it and, seeing who the occupants were, had panicked and emptied the tub but had not yet pulled the plug.

There was no one in the adjoining room. Pyjamas hung on pegs. 'Boys', ' he breathed. 'Ah *merde* . . . A pair of specs.' He held them up to the light.

'Herr Eisner,' she said sadly, a whisper. They'd be naked, those two boys and this man. They would be hiding in some secret passage or cupboard from Herr Oelmann. Why could he not leave her alone? Not now, she said bitterly. Never now. I know too much and this . . . this business here is only one more thing he cannot allow.

Sickened by what they had stumbled into and trying to steady herself, she felt a clothes hook beneath her hand and let it take some of her weight. She was exhausted. Her children would be so worried about her. . . .

Softly the panel opened. Wet footprints on the parquet floor led down a darkened corridor no wider than her shoulders.

One after the other, they came out into what must, at one time, have been the bedroom of a concubine.

But it, too, was in darkness.

Under lights, in total silence now, vans, lorries, mounds and orderly stacks of equipment, wardrobe trunks—all the plethora of the film trade—were jammed into the stables where once horses and livestock had been kept and a carriage or two remained.

Jouvet made St-Cyr thread his way among the coils of electrical cable and spare generators, motion-picture cameras in aluminium cases and past tall stagings of boards atop which camera and cameraman would be seated in better times.

For St Cyr, a consummate lover of the cinema, it was a Herculean downfall, a policeman's disgrace.

Tossing the carpet-bag with its load into a corner of the stall Jouvet had forced him into, St-Cyr turned and said, 'Now look, my friend, interfering with a police officer in the course of his duties is most unwise since he is the only one who can save you.'

'Pardon?'

The walking stick was in his left hand and this Jouvet leaned on. The Luger was in the hand that, though badly scarred, was still far too useful. 'You were under suspicion of murder but . . . ah but, there is now perhaps sufficient evidence to suggest you may not have done it after all.'

Sufficient evidence . . . Had he time to listen? wondered

Jouvet. The Obersturmführer would want him out there watching for Juliette and Kohler. . . .

'First,' said St-Cyr, 'Madame Fillioux, on seeing who had come to meet her, would have tried to save herself if it had been you. Admit it, though, you were only too aware she intended to poison you.'

'The bitch. Always bellyaching, always listening to that daughter of hers.'

'She deserved to die, didn't she?'

The grin was broken. 'What if she did deserve everything she got? I didn't kill her.'

'Perhaps, but you see,' said the Sûreté, tossing a dismissive hand, 'my partner firmly believes you did.' This was not true — at least, he didn't think it was — but useful. Besides, Hermann could not yet know of Jouvet's having been in Sarlat at the time of the killing.

'I'm waiting for the other reason.'

The dark brown eyes held nothing but emptiness.

'The second reason is more difficult and that is why I cannot let you see the contents of that bag.'

The Luger came up. The shot shattered the silence, terrifying some pigeons among the rafters. Madly they flapped about up there. Feathers . . . feathers were falling so slowly, but then something plummeted to the ground at St-Cyr's feet and he saw the plump little body with blood all over its breast.

'Don't tempt me, Inspector,' said Jouvet tightly.

'It's Chief Inspector, Captain.'

'Just tease the words from your lips as a whore sucks juice from a fig or urine from a helmet.'

Ah *merde* . . . 'Henri-Georges Fillioux has returned from the dead.'

The Luger jerked. Life came momentarily into the eyes only to vanish as the lips spread into a wolfish grin. 'Returned,' sighed the veteran. 'So she meant to kill the two of us but he got to her first. She always swore he hadn't been killed. What did he do? Hide out in Belgium?'

'That we do not yet know.'

'But he's definitely back?'

'So it seems.'

Jouvet thought a moment, then said, 'They've been paying me. The one called von Strade. Yes, yes, *Chief* Inspector, I am an adviser on this film of theirs. She was only going to cause them trouble. I warned them. I told them she would stop at nothing to protect her lover's reputation. Her lover? Hah! Does Juliette know her father has returned?'

'Perhaps.'

Jouvet's eyes narrowed. 'Her father and mother were in contact, weren't they, but Juliette did not know of it because that bitch was too afraid to tell her.'

'You knew she would poison you if she could but you failed to realize there was someone else. Fillioux, my friend. *Henri-Georges Fillioux!*'

The filthy black beret jerked, the shot splintered the oak panelling above his left shoulder, the carpet-bag came up and was ripped open and dumped out. '*Look* for yourself then. *Read* if you can!' shouted St-Cyr.

Stone tools, photographs of the young man that ... that woman had married, lay among rolls of tracing paper and bundles of postcards, a scattering of louis d'or and some other things. Letters and bits of jewellery.

'Show me.'

'Of course.'

One room led to another, from darkness into a chamber holding back-lit figures who stood in a row in front of an overturned lamp between two complete skeletons, the one of a massively-boned, furrow-browed Neanderthal, the other of a Cro-Magnon who was quite like present-day humans. Tables held stone tools seen only out of the corner of the eye.

'None of these are very good specimens, are they?' said Oelmann, his tone of voice betraying how much he despised what he had stumbled into.

The Radom moved slightly to indicate the others but returned to Madame Jouvet. He'd kill her. Kohler knew this.

The two boys, of ten or twelve years, were naked and so terrified at having been found out, they shivered uncontrollably in tears. Herr Eisner was between them and looking decidedly uncomfortable. Stripped of even a hastily grabbed towel, the prehistorian from Hamburg was wet and worried and not without good reason. His life, liberty and career were up for grabs. Homosexuality of any kind was officially a no-no with the Nazis.

'I didn't mean to . . . ,' he stammered. 'We were only sharing a bath.'

'Of course,' said Kohler, 'but you see, I've two boys in Russia, my friend, with von Paulus and the Sixth. As a father I have to take exception to people like yourself; as a detective. . . . Well, what can I say, eh? but that it's interesting von Strade should want to give you everything just to keep you quiet about that cave of his.'

Oelmann teased the Webley from his hand. Juliette Jouvet sighed with anguish.

'So, what now?' quipped Kohler. 'Am I allowed to ask our friend a few things . . . things that might perhaps clarify that SS mind of yours?'

'Such as?' snapped Oelmann, backing away until he found a chair half-way between the visitors and the others.

'Such as why the Professor Courtet thought it necessary to keep a loaded gun in his room.'

'Fillioux . . . my father,' blurted Madame Jouvet. 'He has returned and the professor is afraid of him. Danielle. . . .'

'Is Fillioux's daughter,' said Eisner.

'His daughter? Please, what is this you are saying, monsieur?' She blanched. 'That my father, he was married when he met *maman*? That he had already had a daughter to call his own?'

'A child and a wife. Courtet was well aware of it and told me.'

'A child . . . Ah no, this . . . this I cannot believe. Why Arthaud, please?'

She was going to pieces and couldn't stop herself.

'The child's mother applied for a divorce, madame, but by then your father had been declared missing in action and presumed dead. Three years later she remarried. The parents refused to accept the new marriage and disinherited their former daughter-in-law and Danielle. They wanted her to remain a war widow but she refused because your father was going to leave her for another. Arthaud was the new husband's name and Danielle took it. She was only six years old at the time and had little choice.'

'What do you mean, they disinherited Danielle?' asked Kohler.

'Just that. She's bankrupt. She gets nothing.'

'And now?' he asked. Eisner would sing to save himself and Oelmann would have to listen because . . . ah yes, because the bastard should have known all about it long ago if he had been doing his job.

'Now Danielle is perfect for the part she plays and an excellent instructress for the others. I don't think anyone else is aware of who her real father was Willi might be. It's possible. But none of the others, apart from Courtet, of course.'

'Please let the boys go to their rooms,' said Madame Jouvet. 'They are so little. Not much older than my son.'

'Photograph them first. There is a Graflex and flash on Herr Eisner's desk. Use it, Kohler. Become a Press photographer.'

He found the camera but had to ask how to use it. He fiddled with the film pack and finally got it in. Focusing on the group, he told Madame Jouvet to move the lamp from behind them. 'Back-lighting will only spoil the shot.'

'Don't even think of trying anything,' snorted Oelmann. 'Madame, do as he says and then come to kneel on the carpet before me.'

Ah *Gott im Himmel*, could nothing go right? Blinded by the flash, Oelmann would have been at a decided disadvantage.

Juliette picked up the lamp by its standard but lost the shade and had to go back for it. Tears filled her eyes . . . Her father *married* and not telling *maman* a thing about it! A girl of seventeen and so in love with him, she would spend the rest of her life waiting and would remember every word he had said, every smile, every tenderness.

Kohler saw her accidentally swing the lamp towards him from behind the naked figures and when Eisner leapt as the hot glass touched him, he tripped the flash at Oelmann and threw the camera.

There was a shriek from one of the boys. Plunged into darkness, blinded momentarily, Oelmann fired. Flashes stabbed the darkness. The chair went over backwards. He fought to get away from Kohler . . . Kohler. . . . The back of his head hit the floor. '*Once, twice . . . a third time and out!* OUT, YOU SON OF A BITCH!'

The boys wept, the woman held her breath. The stench of urine and cordite filled the room. 'So, okay, everybody?' he breathed.

'Okay, I think,' hazarded Juliette.

'Okay,' said Eisner. 'Look, I really was only sharing the bath.'

'Save it for the tribunal back home, eh? Madame please try to find us a light.'

Oelmann lay on the carpet with his head under a table. Eyes shut, mouth open and bleeding. 'Christ, have I killed him?'

She shook her head and through her tears, saw Herr Kohler grin. 'It's been quite a day,' he said. 'Tired, are you? Here . . . Here, wait a minute. I've got just the thing. Find us something to drink and we'll each take three or four of these.'

Her questioning look made him say, 'Messerschmitt benzedrine. The fighter pilots use it to stay awake and alive.'

They sat Herr Oelmann up and brought him round with brandy and a cold compress. The boys she released with a warning to say nothing. Herr Eisner she told to get dressed.

Then they sat down, the four of them, at one of the tables now cleared of its stone tools and watched over only by the two skeletons. With his black, horn-rimmed glasses, short, crinkly dark brown hair, blue eyes and compressed lips, Herr Eisner looked not like a molester of young boys but the professor in trouble that he was.

'Ask what you wish and I will tell you what I know.'

Oelmann swore under his breath that he would see justice done. Kohler kept the Webley in his right hand, cocked and pointing at the Propaganda Staffel. The Radom had disappeared into a corner. 'How did you become involved? Let's start with that.'

'Quite unexpectedly. Eugene Courtet discovered the trunk in an antique shop last year and wrote to me of its significance. He had by then already applied for a research grant from the Friends of Culture and, as one of its jurists, I saw that he received a grant of 250,000 marks.'

'5,000,000 francs,' said Kohler. It was enough for murder.

'The swastika and the amulet, the figurines and my father's journals,' said Madame Jouvet, lost in thought only to have Herr Kohler shake his head. It's not the time—she knew this was what he meant, yet she wanted so much to settle the matter now.

'Who suggested the film?'

'I did. I saw its potential and called on the Reichsführer-SS Himmler myself. Herr Himmler was ecstatic and immediately authorized me to go ahead.'

'So, von Strade and Continentale were brought in and work began on *Moment of Discovery*. Who suggested the story line?'

'Courtet . . . from memory. He told me of his student days with Fillioux and the young prehistorian's love affair. Fillioux's parents were adamant, madame, that your father not leave his wife and daughter to take up with your mother. He rebelled. He wrote to her from the battlefields, three letters I believe. Letters she subsequently used to support her claim for a marriage certificate which, incidentally, could then be granted after the divorce and remarriage had gone through.'

Four years it had taken. Four years.

'So, he went missing in action and the former wife remarried,' said Oelmann, not taking his eyes from the revolver in Kohler's hand.

'And now the one daughter is an actress who has been dispossessed,' said Juliette sadly, 'while the other, who did not even know she had a half-sister, has had her mother butchered and the man whom she always called a friend brutally murdered. Why is it, please, that Mademoiselle Arthaud did not tell me we shared a father?'

Eisner looked questioningly to Oelmann and then to Kohler before saying, 'Perhaps because she knows her father is alive and that the two of them are working together.'

In spite of Jouvet's shots, no one had come to investigate and now it was again quiet in the stables, the stall its own kind of prison.

The bloodied body of the pigeon lay among the scattered treasures from Madame Fillioux's little hiding-place and near a superb black flint Mousterian handaxe, one too far away to reach.

The Luger, always steady, was still pointed at St-Cyr. Ah *nom de Dieu, de Dieu,* where the hell was Hermann?

' "Am to work on film . . ." ' muttered Jouvet, reading the postcard. 'But . . . but others would know of this? His papers, his *carte d'identité* and . . . and the *laissez-passer* he would have needed to cross the Demarcation Line?'

The shrug must be diffident and helplessly lost so as to augment Jouvet's worry. 'It's what he has said, Captain, but I have to wonder was Henri-Georges Fillioux so badly wounded few would now recognize him? Age would help, of course, but disfigurement also.'

'The papers would be false but she'd still have recognized him.'

'Exactly, but. . . .' A diffident hand was tossed.

'But *what,* damn you?' The walking-stick slipped, the gun wavered.

The helpless look, the wince, the shrug were given. 'But she did not back away, Captain. She knew her killer and though she planned to murder that person, must have smiled forgivingly so as to allay suspicion. Who, please, was your contact with von Strade?'

He would grin widely at this *flic* from the Paris Sûreté and then he would kill him. 'A girl . . . a woman . . . very nice, very pretty, and very persuasive but promiscuous, I think.'

'Danielle Arthaud?'

'Yes. She said von Strade needed certain information and that he would pay handsomely.'

'Did she tell you to go to Sarlat on the Monday?'

'So as to be out of the way?' snorted Jouvet. 'Inspector, what do you think?'

Ah *merde*, the Luger. . . . 'Monsieur, a moment, please.'

'It's Captain to you.'

'Does it not trouble you that there is proof that Henri-Georges is out there somewhere? That the day before her mother's murder, your wife felt someone was watching her as she went into that cave?'

'Fillioux . . . Fillioux,' he said. 'Why should I care if he's back?'

The trigger finger tightened, the grip of a wasted hand caused pain to join that of a bullet-shattered leg.

'FILLIOUX, AH *MERDE*!' cried St-Cyr, looking past him as the gun fired and he leapt to grab the bastard's crippled hand and to crush it . . . crush it. . . . They went over. They rolled about and tried to get at each other. Sharp fingernails tore at his eyes, his nose . . . the gun . . . the gun . . . the salty taste of blood . . . blood. . . . Must kill him . . . kill him . . . NOW . . . NOW . . . Smash him . . . smash him. . . .

Jouvet's head went back, the gun went off, his throat came up, the flesh began to tear, to. . . .

'Ah, no . . . No!'

The handaxe was in St-Cyr's hand. Instinctively he had picked it up in the melee and had used it. 'Ah *nom de Dieu, de Dieu*, he gasped, breathlessly straddling the bastard.

Blood trickled from Jouvet's right temple where now the bone was broken. It beaded from fissures to sweat away among the greasy hairs; it poured from the throat.

Dropping the handaxe in revulsion at what it had betrayed—

that primitive, hidden urge to kill that was in everyone—St-Cyr tried to get up but bowed his head. Ah *merde . . . merde*, it had happened so quickly. There had been no time to think. Of course he had killed before as a soldier and in self-defence as a detective but this . . . this was quite different. A moment of passion, one so savagely intense, it had reached far back to primordial instincts and all else had been forgotten.

'We needed you, damn it. There were things only you could have told us.'

Even in death was there a use for Jouvet. Exhausted, desperately in need of sleep, St-Cyr heaved the body into the front seat of Herr Oelmann's touring car so that the head slumped on to the steering wheel.

'There, I give you Henri-Georges Fillioux, my friends,' he said to the night and the château's darkened silhouette. 'Let us see what this brings.'

Pulling off the stained coveralls and bulky sweater he had borrowed, he tossed them into the wheelbarrow and tidied himself. Then, trundling the barrow back to the stables, he cleaned the stall, checked the Luger and collected the carpet-bag and its contents.

The sweater and coveralls went into a corner out of sight, the handaxe was washed. When he reached the great hall, he walked hesitantly among the tables with their piles of dirty dishes, the knives and forks, the half-eaten rubbish, empty wine bottles and bowls of salad et cetera, et cetera, a Lupercalian feast perhaps, but with the fertility rites now long passed into exhaustion and sleep.

Like a visiting abbot of old arriving late for the feast, he stood beneath a chandelier in the *grand salon*, seeing himself in the mirrors, shabby, pale and forlorn, a traveller down murder's lane. He would have to get himself cleaned up, a shave at least, a haircut. A new fedora . . . could one be found?

'Inspector . . .'

'Baroness . . . Ah, forgive me. I seem to be lost.' She was sitting all alone beside a film projector.

'I thought you were in Beaulieu-sur-Dordogne looking for things?' Her voice trembled just a little. Was she dismayed to find him here with this bag in hand?

'Yes, yes, of course I was there but I couldn't sleep. Some villagers. You know how they are at times. Hermann, Baroness? Have you seen my partner?'

'Not in several hours. I wanted him to swim with me but . . . but he was too modest, I think.'

'Can't you sleep?'

'Can't you?'

'Pastis or brandy . . . I need a little something,' he said and she could tell by his tone of voice he was unsettled.

'Too bad, then. All I have is this.'

She indicated a bottle and when he joined her, he saw that she had been crying but was not drunk.

'Danielle,' she said, ignoring the carpet-bag which he dumped at his feet. 'Our princess has a passion for this wine, Inspector, so much so, my Willi allows her the key to his wine cellar and she comes and goes as she pleases and drinks all she needs but often carelessly leaves the cellars open to others. They have no shame.'

He found himself a chair. 'Then I take it Danielle was recently here watching that film?'

'The rushes, yes. She was being punished for not having attended the evening's mandatory viewing but has now taken herself back upstairs.' To beg, she said to herself, to be fucked and used in other ways if necessary until she gets what she so earnestly desires, a little more cocaine.

The wine was warm and he judged she had been holding the bottle in her lap for some time.

'It's too sweet for me,' she said, and he caught again the faint quaver in her voice, 'but Danielle is a slave to it.'

And to other things? he thought and let her see this. 'The

rushes, Baroness. I'm a great lover of the cinema, starved of course these days for so many of the great films are denied us. Please, take no offence. I didn't mean to say that.'

'You did. Willi would agree. He has a fantastic collection. Everything from the Lumière brothers' first attempts to *The Jazz Singer* and *The Wizard of Oz*.'

'*Charlie Chan in Shanghai? Modern Times? Captain Blood?*'

From cops and robbers in China Town to Chaplin and the wheels of industry to pirates, all released in 1936. 'Yes, of course,' she said and could not help but smile faintly. 'Are there others you like?'

'*Carnet de Bal*—it's not as good as *Pépé le Moko* but Duvivier still stands out as a great director, another Jean Renoir perhaps. That's hard to match but . . . but, ah I go on. Please, your rushes. I would like very much to see them.'

'Then see them you shall.'

In frame after frame he saw the paintings at Lascaux then, like all the others, was fascinated by the sight of Danielle and her Cro-Magnon 'husband' on that primitive scaffold.

'She's very beautiful, isn't she?' said Marina von Strade tightly. 'Watch how she disembowels a doe.'

Ah *merde* . . . blood . . . blood on her thighs and arms, her breasts, neck and face.

'Danielle, Inspector. Danielle is the one you want.'

When Kohler and Madame Jouvet found it quite by chance, the room was in darkness but then Danielle came along the corridor in a hurry, swearing softly in French, crying, wiping away the tears perhaps and saying more loudly, 'Bastard . . . that bastard . . . Oh *mon cul, mon pauvre cul. . . .*'

She tripped, she cried out, 'Ah no!' and went down on her hands and knees to grope about the carpet and beg God to give it to her until at last she had it.

A light on the dressing-table went on. Behind the heavy drapes, Kohler clasped a hand over Juliette Jouvet's lips to smother her gasp, then eased his hand away.

Naked but for a leather thong about her slender waist and her skin bag of stone tools, Danielle Arthaud stood a moment to calm herself. A lower drawer was opened and a silver disc, perhaps ten centimetres in diameter, was taken out.

The disc was polished and held up to the mirror. Trembling, she searched for the flint blade with which she had so carefully divided the *truffes sous la cendre* and when she had it, licked it and used a crumpled blouse to dry it.

From a cigarette case, she took a straw of cobalt-blue glass and for a moment, delicately fingered this as if in the waiting there was heightened excitement.

Two halves of a walnut shell, the thing she had dropped, were carefully prised open and again Danielle sat there looking as if temptation's call was only enhanced by waiting. 'I can still stop myself,' she said and sighed. 'I'm still not a slave to it.'

Cocaine was dipped out of the walnut shell with the point of the flint blade and carefully tapped onto the centre of the disc. Spreading the snow-white powder, she smoothed it into a square that was divided into ten lines. She waited again for so long it seemed she really might be able to stop herself.

Two lines were taken, drawn through the tube and into each nostril, the head thrown back each time, the eyes shut, lips parted in a gasp, then a grin and a slow smile that grew until the lips parted in another sudden gasp.

Blood pounding, she sat there and, fingering the glass tube, held it to the light and watched herself in the mirror.

Grinning, she took some more and then a little more. '*It's enough!*' she said. Enough for what? wondered Kohler. Enough to kill?

Everything was packed away. Worth far more than gold these days, the rest of the cocaine was carefully returned and the halves of the walnut shell closed to safely hold their little treasure.

Von Strade . . . said Kohler to himself. The giver of all gifts.

'Toto . . . I'll fix him,' breathed Danielle. 'He enjoyed doing that to me while the others watched and Willi . . . Willi sat in that goddamned chair of his and made me beg. *Me* to whom he owes so much!'

Ah *merde*. . . .

The road was dark, the wind was in her hair and it felt so good to be leaving that place Juliette wanted to shout for joy but found only despair. Herr Kohler was ahead of her; St-Cyr behind. Caught between the two of them, they would ride through the rest of the night until, at last, they could walk the bicycles up through the woods and into that little valley to leave them by the stream and climb to the cave.

It all made sense. Everything. The trunk coming to light after all these years, the film, the visit of Courtet, the payment of 10,000 francs and André's . . . André's working for Danielle Arthaud and telling her things and then . . . then for Herr Oelmann . . . Herr Oelmann. . . .

André would kill her. He would relish the beating he would first hand out. Her face, her lips, her eyes and nose, and why . . . why is it, please, that he felt such a need to take out all of his bitterness on her?

Her father had come back. *Maman* had wanted her kept out of it and that is why she had told her nothing. Nothing of the paintings, the forgery. Nothing of what she had been up to, the unexpected, the impossible, in a cave she knew so well. Ah yes.

The tears were brushed away. The road went downhill and she hurried to catch up only to realize she was alone . . . alone.

Apprehensively her heart hammered. Disturbed, upset that the detectives had not told her to stop, she stood astride the bicycle Herr Kohler had stolen for her from the château and waited—listened—tried hard to find them.

Nothing . . . only silence and then . . . then that feeling of closeness, of his caring she had experienced, now the loss of it . . . the loss. He had really cared about her, she said. He had!

Her spirit was wounded and, yes, it hurt to know they still did not trust her completely. Hesitantly she began to walk the bicycle back up the hill.

A cigarette was being shared. Dark against the night sky, the two detectives had paused just on the other side of the hill so as to be alone, and when in dismay she called out to them, they stopped talking and waited for her to join them. Did they sigh inwardly with impatience?

'Your husband, madame,' began St-Cyr and it was clear that they had been discussing André and her father. Were they working together, was that it, eh, messieurs? Has André been telling Henri-Georges all about *maman* and her annual visits, visits that never changed until the last? And all about the daughter who secretly dreaded each of her mother's visits to the house afterwards yet had to show the brave front and the bruises, the smashed lips, the shame of a marriage that had gone so wrong?

'Your husband, madame. Hermann and I were simply discussing how best to protect you and return you safely to your children.'

'André is dead, madame. Louis had to kill him.'

'Dead . . . ? Please, what is this you are saying?'

St-Cyr told her then and in the silence of the night, they heard her suck in a breath and say, 'A stone. . . . Killed with a stone.'

Kohler reached out to her. 'Oelmann,' he said. 'He'll realize where we've gone. He may feel he has to get help this time from the Périgord *Sonderkommando*. Louis and me, we . . . we were wondering if it might not be best for you to go home to Mayor Pialat, madame. He'll do his best to hide you. Think about it, eh? The two of us could ride on together and then I could come back to help Louis.'

She squeezed the hand that had taken hers. She said, 'You both are kind. *Merci* but, please, you will need me at the cave, yes? The paintings? The second chamber Professor Courtet claims to have found all by himself. The postcards, too, I think.'

'They'll come after us, Louis. They'll have to,' said Hermann grimly. 'Oelmann won't be able to leave things now.'

She rode on ahead, but on the downhill slope they soon

caught up with her and she felt first one put a comforting hand on her shoulder and then the other, and she laughed aloud because she had to tell them how relieved she was to know they trusted her.

But at the bridge over the stream that would, some fifteen or twenty kilometers to the south, find its little waterfall, they again stopped to listen to the night.

Its stillness was of that other time and she knew they each listened as Neanderthal would have done, wondering why it was that just before dawn the night was always at its darkest. 'I love you both for the way you have made me feel,' she said. 'Just give me a handaxe and I will show you what I can do with it.'

 **9** It was like something out of *Toto and the Seven Dwarfs* or *Snow White and the Yellow Brick Road*, thought Kohler. It was not real—oh *mein Gott*, no. It was weird and horrific.

'*Nom de Jésus-Christ*, Louis. Look what the hell they've done to our valley.'

The dawn had broken and through its soft, primordial blush, cranes, ladders, platforms and towers stood stock-still, while straight up the right side of the valley, over brush and rock alike, a primitive wooden set of rails carried a cart and camera pylon.

The cinematographer in Louis was intrigued. 'As the Baroness and her prehistorian climb to the cave, assistants wind the trolley slowly up the slope so that the camera can record their progress for posterity.'

Juliette Jouvet was silent. Staging went up only so far, then the trolley took over. But right at the entrance to the cave, and on the same side, a platform had been built. Now an open parasol of unbleached Egyptian cotton stirred forlornly in the breeze as if waiting for something to happen. High above it, a honey buzzard circled. The hawk was so beautiful and majestic. How many times as a girl had she and *maman* watched one so similar would come away from the cave filled with thoughts of it?

'It's his valley, isn't it?' said Kohler, nodding at the hawk.

'Or hers. To me the hawk has always been a male, but now I wonder if I was right. Is that not my mother up there watching me?'

The film's set crews had done their job with blitzkrieg speed, even to somehow hauling in two huge, camouflaged electrical generators with banks of storage batteries, all courtesy of the Wehrmacht. Heavy black cables were strung here, there. Sometimes hidden, most often not, they were dabbed with yellow paint to warn people not to trip. Lights ... some big, some small, were even mounted in the trees whose interfering branches had been ruthlessly broken and left to hang or brutally decapitated and dragged away.

'They've completely taken over,' murmured the passionate naturalist and lover of prehistory in Louis. 'What was once so beautiful has been ravaged.'

Sections had been roped off—a portion of the stream where Marina von Strade and her prehistorian would pop the corks and toast their discovery; the picnic site where they would feed each other sweet cherries or mushrooms perhaps; parts of the path to the waterfall where the two would strip for a healthy bathe before a severely academic romp in the cave and doe-eyed glances under those of the aurochs or whatever, thought Kohler. But even in these locations there was change. Potted trees had been brought in and, still in their pots, planted where none had existed before. Leaves and branches had been carefully trimmed so as not to intrude. Pine needles had been scattered over the sharp husks of chestnuts from years ago so as to soften the lovers' picnic site and bugger that crap about audiences knowing one tree from another. When you've got the screen filled with a woman who liked to bathe in the buff or have her bottom polished, who would care?

Shabby in a dirty grey cloak with staff and beret, a scraggly-bearded shepherd came to stand at the very edge of the cliff, just above the dark entrance of the cave. As his flock gathered about him, they, too, peered curiously down at the scene below.

A stone fell to clatter and bounce until its sound was no more. The shepherd raised a hand in greeting and called out to them. He asked about the crane and platform hoist he had seen mounted up the valley by the waterfall. 'It is not safe, I think,' he said. 'More stones are needed to weight the base of it down.'

Down . . . down . . . stones . . . stones, the echoes came, his patois harsh and broken like the rocks from which it had sprung.

He moved his staff to point out the location. Frightened, one of the lambs bolted into space. 'Ah, no,' gasped Juliette. The thing hit a slab of rock and broke its head, bouncing and flying through the air before coming to rest. Hind legs twitching . . . twitching until at last they were still.

Ruefully the shepherd surveyed the loss and for a moment glared at them in silence. '*Idiots!*' he shrieked. '*See what you have made me do.*' Do . . . do. . . . '*A Christian gesture, one of goodness of the heart and you . . . you . . . I hope you all bash your shitty heads to pieces and give your blood to the stones.*' The stones. . . .

Ah *merde.* . . . 'Pay no attention, madame,' said Kohler gently. 'That's a month's wages. Anyone would have said the same. He didn't mean it.'

'He did. He has come to this little valley like that since a boy. It was always his special moment and even then *maman* and I intruded, though we fed him sometimes and tried to get to know him.'

The honey buzzard was feasting on the eyes and offal, and when they drew near it in their climb, intestines were being dragged out to glisten in the early morning sunlight. Blood red against the grey-white of the stones, the intestines momentarily became still under the fiercely glaring eyes of the hawk whose rights had also been intruded upon, ah yes.

'It is not good,' she murmured. 'It is an omen I must heed even as my ancestors would have done at the dawn of time.'

They were hungry and tired, and she wished the detectives would go to sleep but there was no time. Did they always run on Messerschmitt benzedrine? she wondered. Herr Kohler's hand shook. Jean-Louis said, 'This is positively the last time, Hermann. The heart, yes? You cannot go on like this. Crush them up, madame, and sprinkle them on the *pâté* and bread our illustrious Bavarian Gestapo has fortuitously stolen for us from a certain château. Then you must show us the second chamber and the paintings.'

'The paintings, yes,' she managed. 'Messieurs, there . . . there is something I must tell you. When Herr Kohler found me in . . .'

'It's Hermann. Please, it'll be easier.'

'*Merci*. When Hermann, he . . . he has found me in the Professor's room, I was going through my father's journals. I . . . I was certain then that . . . that the page where he had described the cave in depth was missing—carefully cut out with a razor blade or flint knife.'

'By Courtet or by Danielle?' breathed St-Cyr.

'Or by my father, yes?' she said sadly. 'Like Lascaux and lots of other caves in the Dordogne, there are often chambers with passages between. Here, at the back of this chamber, there are two passages. The one continues out to the east to end on the surface in an entrance big enough only to slither through. This one, the Professor has called a ventilation shaft, a chimney for the fires. The other passage, it . . . it does not go out to the surface and has troubled me very much, you understand. Mother spoke of it on her visit last year. She asked if I remembered her warning me not to enter it.'

They waited for her to continue and at last she said, 'Inside the cave, this passage, it is about three metres to the north-west of where the ventilation shaft opens. It is narrow, too, but soon it becomes a long chamber whose roof, though not so high as this, wanders in the rock for some distance. Because there were shafts in the floor and some loose rocks, my mother never let me explore it but she and my father did when they first came here. I'm certain of it. Certain, too, that there were then no paintings. Cro-Magnon was not fool enough to have used that chamber.'

'No paintings, Louis,' said Kohler. 'A forgery like I told you she said.'

She touched his hand in apology. 'Please understand that . . . that I had to find things out first for myself. When I came here on that Sunday just before she died, I crawled into this passage Professor Courtet claims to have discovered but which was, I think, sealed off so as to let him find it. It is not safe in there. It's really very dangerous but . . . but there are paintings now as . . . as good as any.'

'Madame, is there something else you wish to tell us?' asked Louis, causing her to start and hazard, 'No . . . no, there is nothing, Inspector.'

Wires led to lights. The set crew had even discreetly mounted switch panels at the entrance to the main chamber and at that of the second.

The storage batteries worked. All at once the cave lit up and, blinking, Kohler saw Juliette standing, ashen, beside Louis.

'Me first,' she managed, prising off her espadrilles. 'The bare feet, they are surer, messieurs.'

At once she hoisted herself up into the hole and disappeared from sight.

'You next, Louis.'

'The shoes, Hermann. Please tuck them out of sight. The carpet-bag, it must not leave our hands.'

'And the schoolteacher?'

'Let us keep a careful eye on her.'

On a white crystalline background of calcite, shaggy black and black-spotted ponies raced amid charging brown-red aurochs and yellowish brown to rusty red reindeer. Antlers and horns were all but interlocked, the figures often overlapping in an endless panorama, some filled in, some only in outline, the colours rich and earthy, the animals startlingly alive but of the distant past and haunting.

'Ah *mon Dieu*,' breathed St-Cry, 'they're magnificent.'

'But they can't be real,' snorted Kohler, 'unless we say they are.'

As at Lascaux, so also here, the chamber followed the channel of an ancient underground stream and opened upwards to an irregularly arched and pitted roof some three to four metres above them.

'Here,' said Juliette anxiously. 'The first of the shafts in the floor. Please be careful.'

The wretched thing plunged straight down into an uncomfortable darkness. The rock was grey nearest the floor and had a velvety texture Kohler didn't like because it crumbled when touched.

Cave bear and cave lion stared down at them from above in outlines of black and yellowish red with dusty spots of black to which sprayed red-ochre handprints had been added beneath the figures. 'A moment, my friends,' gasped St-Cyr breathlessly. 'A moment.'

Unrolling the tracing paper, he smoothed it over the handprints while Juliette and Hermann looked on and match was made for match. One set larger, one smaller and then ... then. . . .

'Your mother, madame, she has shown us that her handprints are not the same as these.'

'She has made a record of them to prove she had nothing to do with ... with any of this. She must have known what was happening to the cave last year when she came to visit us.'

'A forgery,' sighed Kohler, 'but is it one Courtet is all too aware of, or was he sucked in just like the rest of them?'

'Perhaps but then. . . . It is too early for us to say, Hermann, but could the man's handprints have been made by using a glove?'

'Made by a woman, then ...? Ah *merde*, it's possible,'

hazarded Kohler, catching the drift and not liking it. 'Madame, your hand. . . . Would you put it over the smaller of these?'

'The . . . the scratches on the walls, messieurs,' she stammered, abruptly moving on ahead to deftly point them out. 'Engraved by a flint burin. They are hardly visible, yes? beneath the salmon here and the head of the bison up there but . . . but in the beard of the woolly mammoth too, I think. Here . . . along here, please. No! *Be careful.* That shaft—ah it is so big and deep, messieurs. *Watch out!*'

A stone fell and they didn't hear it hit bottom. Sickened by her refusal to match her handprints with those on the wall and by the gaping hole in the floor, Kohler looked doubtfully up at the roof.

The engravings she had pointed out were very faint and overlain by pigment spray in rusty red, sooty black and ochrous yellow but how the hell did she know so much about them unless she had made them? Ah *merde* . . .

'The amulet,' sighed St-Cyr, looking at her closely.

'Ah! I have it here,' she said, avoiding his gaze. 'I . . . I have forgotten to return it to its little compartment in the trunk. Professor Courtet, he . . . he will never forgive me.'

'Nor us,' muttered Kohler acidly as she dragged the thing from around her neck and handed it to Louis.

'Incisions have been added to those that were already there,' she said, a whisper. 'Again, I should have told you but . . . but what was I really to do?'

A forgery. . . .

In line for stone-cut line those on the walls and roof were a match to those of the amulet and out of nothing but a jumble of faint scratches came swastikas.

Down through the long irregularities of the chamber there was nothing else to suggest a forgery, so cleverly had the paintings been done.

'The mortar and the lumps of pyrolusite, madame. Is it that your mother was prepared to let the forgery she had discovered continue so she could poison your father before exposing what he did, or is it that she merely wanted further proof she had had nothing to do with any of this?'

His gaze could not now be avoided and she knew then that he still did not trust her and that she should have matched her hands with those on the walls. But Danielle and I, Inspector, she said to herself, we are of the same size, the same build, so the handprints, they would be the same. Ah yes, the same.

'Well, madame, can we have your answer?'

'Mother . . . I think she knew what had happened here and that my father had come back to betray all they had believed in and worked so hard to preserve and record.'

'Then your father made the forgeries with, as the handprints suggest, the assistance of a woman and there was no need for the use of gloves to give the impression of his having been here?'

Ah damn, he still did not trust her. 'Yes . . . Yes, that is how it must have been. Revenge . . . my father wanted only revenge against Professor Courtet and . . . and mother must have threatened to tell everyone what he was up to.'

When the lights suddenly went out, both of them heard her gasp, 'Ah no, my father. . . .'

For several seconds there was nothing but the hollow sound of quietly moving air and then that of their breathing.

'HELMUTT, YOU'VE LEFT THE FUCKING LIGHTS ON AGAIN!' came a distant shout, echoing in the chamber. 'HOW MANY TIMES MUST I TELL YOU THE BATTERIES WILL ONLY BLEED DOWN?'

Down . . . Down. . . 'Messieurs,' called out the Sûreté. 'This chamber, it is occupied.'

Occupied . . . Occupied . . . 'Detectives, *mein Herr*, on a murder investigation.'

'And under orders,' sang out Kohler.

There were whispers and then, '*Verdammt*, it's those two from Paris, Helmutt. They've got no business being in there. Christ, we ought to leave them to fall through the floor!'

'Ah, no . . . no, *mein Herr*, that would be most unwise of you,' said Louis. 'The paintings are far too precious. Another Sistine Chapel, yes? but far, far better, I think, than Lascaux and exactly as the Baron von Strade has said.'

It was wiser to leave the valley in haste than to hang around and, though they walked the bicycles along the railway line towards Sarlat, the memory of the cave paintings endured but more than this, far more, thought St-Cyr ruefully, was that of the handprints and the holes in the floor, of loose rocks just waiting to collapse from the roof. Whoever had done the paintings had been desperate.

'The *Amanita phalloides*,' he said, causing the others to pause. 'The death cap, madame. It's a puzzle, for its symptoms, they are delayed from twelve to twenty-four hours. But why, please, did your mother choose also to use the fly agaric whose symptoms are much more rapid, though the poison is far less dangerous?'

'Louis. . . .'

'Hermann, we are presented with a case whose solution appears quite simple—a straightforward but very brutal and demented killing apparently done by your father, madame, since your husband was in Sarlat on the Monday and could not have done it.'

Juliette hesitated. Though he already knew what her answer must be, she would have to tell him. 'Mother . . . mother would have wanted insurance, yes? If the one didn't work, the other would.'

'And?' asked Louis.

'She . . . she would have wanted both my husband and . . . and my father to suffer a little but then to . . . to experience relief only to discover later on exactly what she had done to them.'

There, she had said it and now they would see how cruel *maman* could be, how willing to seek revenge herself. 'Had she not been killed, she would have had the postcards as proof of my father's involvement, also her sketches and the handprints of Danielle—they must be hers, yes?—and his, too, while I . . . I would have had the stone mortar they had used and . . . and the lumps of pyrolusite.'

'The postcards, Louis,' said Hermann.

'Yes, yes, we will get to them. Madame, a place for us to lie up, please. Somewhere out of the way. Even if hunger and thirst gnaw at us, sleep will be a benefit.'

And you want to read the postcards in private without my seeing them, she said to herself, dismayed that he still did not trust her. 'The farm, then, of my mother's uncle, Inspector. The place where she and my father stayed in the spring and summer of 1912 and '13.'

'Louis, is that wise? Fillioux. . . .'

'Wise or not, Hermann, even I can see that the last benzedrine you took has failed to work.'

The farmhouse was on a hill where overgrown pasture, now intruded upon by young poplars, had once fed a few cows and an old horse. Half the roof had fallen in and as they entered the cellars where the stables had been, sunlight broke through gaps in the floorboards above. 'It'll have to do,' said Kohler, finding hay to scatter. Fresh hay. . . . *'Fresh*, Louis?' he managed.

'My father,' said Juliette. 'He has lain up here.'

Ah *merde.* . . .

The ashes of a cold fire held her as she crouched over them.

'Sleep,' said Kohler. 'Louis and you first, then myself.'

She tried to smile and look at him but found she couldn't force herself to do so.

'Let me take the first watch, Hermann.'

'You sure?'

'Yes. It will give me time to think.'

The air was still, the sun too bright, and all about the ruined farmhouse, the swallows held dominion.

A fly stirred. Awakening, St-Cyr shook his head and breathed,

'Ah *merde* . . . *merde*,' when he realized what had happened. Four hours . . . five . . . had he been asleep that long?

Driven from the farmhouse by Hermann's snoring, which Madame Jouvet had apparently slept soundly through, the Sûreté's thinker-watchman had succumbed to the heat of a sun which was now well past its zenith.

Scattered postcards revealed the infrequent gropings of guilt-ridden hands and the black-printed words of the past leapt at him from among the tall and sometimes trampled grass.

20 June, 1941

Fillioux parents ~~DEAD~~ ~~DYING~~ seriously ~~WOUNDED~~ ~~——~~ ILL ~~WELL~~, ~~REPATRIATED~~ forced ~~PRISONER~~ ~~OF WAR~~ ~~AT~~ to sell trunk ~~NEWS~~ ~~OF~~ to ~~REQUIRES~~ Professor Courtet.

Danielle Arthaud had thought it best to tell Madame Fillioux the trunk had not only been put up for sale but had been bought by a person the woman would most certainly have hated. A man who had ridiculed her husband's work but now had taken it for his own.

Yet how is it, please, he asked, that Danielle learned who had purchased the trunk? Three days lie between the time Courtet supposedly stumbled upon it in that shop and her postcard. A telephone call from the shop perhaps? The money was needed. . . . Yes, yes, it is quite possible Danielle was only looking after the matter for the parents — her grandparents — but was that the case? Did she not also tip off Courtet as to the whereabouts of the trunk?

Another card drew his attention — this one from the professor and dated 13 July, 1941.

No NEWS OF you ~~REQUIRES~~ The Filliouxs need ~~CLOTHING~~, FUEL, FOOD . . . 'Yes, yes,' he said. ~~BAGGAGE~~ ~~AT~~ Trunk ~~WHILE~~ excites ~~TO~~ ~~FROM~~ me TO work

~~WILL BE IS LIVING WORKING AT TO~~ <u>on</u> ~~HOSPITAL~~ <u>cave</u> ~~SCHOOL~~ . . .

Courtet, having discovered the long-coveted trunk on 17 June 1941, had finally let her know of this, a first approach. He could not have known Danielle had already written to tell her of it.

<u>25 July, 1941</u> . . . Courtet requests a reply from Madame Fillioux and then again on 9 August.

<u>Still</u> <u>no</u> NEWS OF <u>you.</u>

'On the 10th of September, 1941, he tells her he has just visited the parents.'

<u>Am</u> ~~LIVING~~ WORKING ~~AT TO~~ <u>on</u> ~~HOSPITAL~~ <u>careful</u> ~~SCHOOL FOR~~ <u>examination</u> ~~BAPTISM WEDDING OF~~ <u>returning</u> ~~FUNERAL~~ <u>cave</u> ~~WILL BE~~ <u>on</u> ~~TO WHEN~~ <u>following</u> ~~ARE~~ <u>day.</u>

St-Cyr reached for his pipe and tobacco only to look uphill towards the house. 'It is so silent,' he said. 'Are they all right?'

Not a sound came to him, save that of foraging swallows.

'On the 11th of September, then, the Professor paid a visit to the Discovery Cave, a visit that he has so far failed to mention.'

Rapidly he picked through the cards until he had what he wanted. 'On the 5th of October, 1941, Courtet writes to inform Madame Fillioux that he will be arriving in Beaulieu-sur-Dordogne on the 15th. On the 12th he again writes—he is worried she hasn't received his previous card. Then on the 20th of November they are getting along so much better, he writes to ask if she has visited Lascaux as promised but . . . but we now know that Madame Fillioux had already paid that cave two visits. The first in November 1940, then again in August 1941, from the 4th to the 7th. What was it Deveaux said of that second visit? That she had told the owner she was doing "a scientific study. Research for her husband." '

Again he looked questioningly uphill towards the house. Should he not check on them? Fillioux? he asked. Had Fillioux returned to find them there? Were Juliette and her father not now working together?

Guiltily he ignored the necessity of stopping his thoughts and thumbed another of the cards. 'Then on the 17th of December, 1941, the Professor sends his last postcard.'

Lascaux is ~~DEAD~~ ~~DYING~~ slightly ~~WOUNDED~~ less ~~ILL~~ ~~WELL~~ ~~REPATRIATED~~ perfect ~~PRISONER~~ ~~OF~~ ~~WAR~~ ~~AT~~ as you agree NEWS OF Danielle ~~REQUIRES~~ have none ~~CLOTHING~~, ~~FUEL~~, FOOD money ~~LEAVES~~ SEND Filliouxs ~~BAGGAGE~~ ~~AT~~ Am ~~WHILE~~ returning TO ~~FROM~~ Berlin ~~TO~~ on ~~WILL~~ ~~BE~~ ~~IS~~ ~~LIVING~~ ~~WORKING~~ ~~AT~~ ~~TO~~ 22nd.

Madame Fillioux must have written to tell him she believed the Discovery paintings to be genuine and better even than those at Lascaux, yet she would have known only too well they were a forgery.

Except for those postcards Fillioux himself had sent, none of the cards mentioned him by name or even implied that he was alive. Fillioux could have returned after the Defeat of 1940 from hiding out in Belgium, as Jouvet had suggested. There had been hordes of refugees on the roads. No one would have noticed that he had slipped through to hole up in the family's country house but surely his parents and Danielle would have been aware of this, surely they would have been told much earlier on that he was alive?

Yet, there was not even a hint of this. Instead, Danielle had told Juliette their father had returned.

Courtet had kept a loaded gun in his room. He, too, had been convinced.

'Fillioux . . .' said St-Cyr to himself. 'Fillioux, ah damn.'

Gathering the cards, he strode up to the house to find the daughter absent and Hermann still asleep. Ah *merde*, had

Fillioux come to get her, had she left quite willingly? Surely Hermann would have awakened?

Behind the house there was a small orchard, much overgrown and let go to ruin. A shed of bleached, warm yellow stone was at the far end, visible through a leafy tunnel between two rows of plum trees.

Juliette Jouvet was bathing at a well. Naked, she stood under the deluge from an overturned bucket she had lifted high above her head, and he saw her through the shade in strong sunlight. No fear . . . no fear at all of her father coming to kill her. Eyes closed, she gasped as the shock of the water struck her. She wiped it from her face with a hand and squeezed it from her hair. Taking up another bucket, she repeated the process and he had to think of her in that little valley on that Sunday, standing naked then, too, beneath the waterfall.

She had sensed someone had been watching her when she had entered the cave to retrieve the things for her mother—'I kept my hammer ready,' she had said, but then the watcher had gone away and she had sensed this too.

She had then said of the valley and of someone's watching her, 'I often got those feelings even as a child. It's that kind of place.'

Lowering the bucket into the well, she drew it up to repeat the bathe. Wringing the water from her hair, she went over to the stone wall to lean back against it and lift her face to the sun. Eyes closed again and she so lovely. . . .

'*Nom de Dieu*, I didn't know you were a voyeur, Louis. Wait till your boss hears about this!'

'*Hermann, where is Fillioux?*'

'Not here, I think, but how would we know, eh, since we're both too busy looking at her? Nice . . . she's really nice, Louis. Oh *mon Dieu, mon Dieu* . . . .'

'*Please shut up, idiot!*'

She turned to let the sun dry her back. She reached straight up high to clutch the stones and press herself against the wall and only then did they realize she was crying.

'Louis, what the hell's the matter now?'

'The postcards from her father, I think. She believes he has named her in them and that this then proves beyond a shadow of doubt that she was a party to the forgery.'

'And does he?'

'Read them for yourself. Tear your eyes away from the pulchritude long enough!'

' *"10 October, 1941: Am not dead though wounded 1914 missing action amnesia. I beg your loving forgiveness and understanding. Am to work on film."* '

'On the 15th, Hermann, Madame Fillioux was to meet Professor Courtet *knowing* her long-lost husband had finally returned, yet Courtet apparently senses none of this and on 20th of November he is asking her if she has visited Lascaux as promised. Go on. Look . . . look.'

'At Juliette?'

'Ah *nom de Jésus-Christ*, at the next postcard!'

'Oh. *"12 November, 1941: Daughter Juliette lovely but worried about her husband. News of him unavailable. Children well. Am returning Monfort-l'Amaury tomorrow."* Hey, Louis, this thing was posted from the Marais. The place des Vosges, eh?'

'Ah yes, the link to Danielle Arthaud.'

In January of 1942 the printed messages had been done away with. Though still limited to a few lines, more freedom had been allowed.

' *"29 January, 1942: Am looking forward very much to seeing you again after all these years. What will I find? Will it be the same? We've so much to talk about, chérie. Lascaux . . . the cave paintings there are magnificent. Have you seen them? You must. Juliette was such a help to me, such a tower of strength. Throughout the fall we worked together tirelessly at the cave on several weekends. A neighbour took care of the children . . ."* Verdammt, Louis. Working at the cave?'

'Read on and curse yourself for being such a fool as to have trusted her.'

' "*She is every bit the assistant you once were. She has that eye for detail I so admired in you, that quickness of mind and deftness of hand.*" '

A forger . . . ah *merde*.

Juliette had now turned around to rest her seat against her hands and lean back against the wall. She had seen them deep in the orchard yet could not seem to bring herself to move.

Pinned to the wall, she waited.

'There are two other cards from him, Hermann, but they are more of the same until you get to the last one on 25th March, 1942.'

' "*Regrettably it is impossible for me to visit with you on 17th June without financial assistance.*" '

'Now read this one from Danielle. It's dated 25th April, 1942.'

' "*Parcel has arrived with stuffing intact.*" '

'The 10,000 francs Courtet paid Madame Fillioux.'

'Stuffed into a goose,' sighed Kohler.

'But to be handed over to her father who would then give it to a *passeur* who would guide Fillioux across the Demarcation Line between the *zone occupée* and the *zone libre* without any questions being asked. Presumably all his other visits to the cave had been accomplished this way.'

Such things happened all the time. For a fee, one got to walk through a vineyard or across a field at night and in the rain preferably, since the Wehrmacht patrols and the Vichy goons preferred to remain dry, ah yes. 'Why send the 10,000 francs to Danielle, Louis, instead of to him at the Monfort-l'Amaury address?'

'Why indeed? To signal to Danielle that our victim knew only too well what was going on or thought she did and that she had the sous-facteur Auger to call on if needed. That she was not alone.'

Juliette began to put her clothes on. First the leather thong with its amulet, as she looked towards them. Then the trousers she had borrowed from Courtet's room, the shirt also, and finally, having tucked the shirt in, the espadrilles.

They watched her walk towards them. Condemned, she didn't avoid their gaze but made straight for them with strides so strong they each could not help but envisage her naked as a savage of old.

'Messieurs, what . . . what is it, please? The postcards of my father, have they. . . . '

'Named you, madame?' asked Louis. Sleep had cleared the blue eyes Fillioux had given her. Tears had misted them — yes, yes, but she was indeed 'lovely.'

'Please let me see them,' she said.

Though cruel and harsh, he had to say it. 'Later, madame. For now we must leave this place before your father returns.'

Ah damn him, why could he not understand that she had to see those cards, that she had to put an end to her agony? My father, she cried out inwardly. My father . . . a handaxe, a stonekiller. 'It is not right of you to think such things of me! I *loved* my mother dearly.'

'But she brought you up to worship your father, madame. Your father.'

They were on the road to Sarlat now and she knew they would leave her at the *préfecture* and that there was nothing she could do about it unless she could somehow get away from them. Instead of that carefree happiness, there was silence. Instead of racing each other down the hill, they rode with her between them, unsmiling, having again relegated her to the position of a suspect.

The next hill was steep but not so high. She would try to lag behind a little. She would let them reach the crown and perhaps start over it before she turned to escape. The woods . . . she must run into the woods.

Her heart sank as an ugly black car came over the hill to abruptly stop. A door was flung open at the sound of brakes. The sous-préfet Deveaux clambered out. Wiping sweat from his brow and wheezing painfully, he started downhill towards them. 'Jean-Louis . . . ah *mon Dieu*, where the hell have you three been? I've been searching everywhere!'

'Sous-préfet . . . ?' began Louis.

'It's Odilon, my friend. *Odilon* and you had better listen to me. Madame,' he said, dragging in a tortured breath. 'Madame, a moment, please. Your husband. . . . First the Chief Inspector, yes, also Herr Kohler since I may yet be able to save their lives.'

'Ah *merde*, Louis . . . ,' began Hermann only to hear his partner say, 'Herr Oelmann, I think.'

'Then think again,' wheezed Deveaux, hauling out his cigarettes and lighter and pausing to fill his lungs with smoke. 'Try the *Sonderkommando* of the Périgord, eh?' He winced and coughed. 'Try all eventualities and try to think what *they* might do because, my friends, I have it on the best authority—ah yes, I have my sources—that the *Sonderkommando* has been activated as of early this morning.'

'Activated . . . ,' began Kohler.

'Please don't look so ill, Inspector. Vomiting on the roads is frowned on during the tourist season. The accusations of a forgery, you idiots. Herr Goebbels, Herr Himmler, Herr Hitler. . . . What the hell did you expect *them* to do?'

'But . . . but we haven't said the paintings are a forgery?' tried Louis. 'In fact, I said the opposite to the men who were checking things over at the cave.'

'Perhaps, but perhaps not. Ah, it does not matter. It's enough for them to fear such a thing.'

'And Herr Oelmann?' hazarded Louis.

Deveaux stabbed the air with his cigarette. 'Found that one's husband in his car and called in the troops.'

'Louis, you should have asked me before you. . . .'

'*Hermann*, be quiet!'

'It's all your fault. *Verdammt!* a fucking *Sonderkommando*. Oelmann must know the paintings are a forgery.'

Sparks flew as Hermann's chest was stabbed. 'He's just not

taking any chances, my friend. A stonekiller on the loose? The prehistorian Henri-Georges Fillioux? The Professor Courtet, he keeps a loaded revolver in his room—why . . . why, please, does he do such a thing unless . . . ah, unless he also knows the paintings are a forgery and that his former colleague and sworn enemy has suddenly decided to come back from the dead without his wings and feathers.'

Deveaux sucked in a breath and tore the top two buttons of his shirt open so as to allow his chest more room to expand. 'Madame, my condolences. It appears that your father has used a handaxe to rip out the throat of your husband and save the world a whole lot of trouble. One could have wished for something a little more refined but . . . ,' he shrugged, 'the result, it would be the same. Dead for at least . . .' he counted the hours off on stumpy fingers, 'for at least ten or perhaps twelve hours. My men are, of course, out in full force sweeping the countryside at the request of the Baron whose wife, it appears, is missing; the bit-player Toto Lemieux also. Filming is to begin in Beaulieu-sur-Dordogne late this afternoon, so you can understand the urgency of things.'

Kohler thought of the swimming pool at the château. Had the Baroness gone for another deep dive and taken her Toto with her, or had the stonekiller got to them?

'No one has seen either of them since you three left the château last night but I am certain the Baroness found the body in Herr Oelmann's car. Bloodied fingerprints were smeared on the leather upholstery of the passenger seat next the corpse. Her handkerchief was found on the floor. Blood on it also.'

'Good,' said Louis with that curt little nod Kohler knew so well, that shaking of the head too. *Shh, idiot! Don't tell him I killed Jouvet. Not yet.*

'Good?' exclaimed Deveaux. 'What's so good about it?'

Odilon was really upset but not without due cause. 'The Baroness will have gone to the cave with her Toto to have another look at the paintings.'

'Ah *merde*, Louis . . . Fillioux may be there.'

'I will drive you,' said Deveaux. 'It will be faster, yes? and together we can take him. Leave the bicycles. Someone will steal them, of course, but . . . ,' he shrugged, 'there is nothing we can do about it.'

'The bicycles, Louis. . . .'

'Madame Jouvet, Hermann.'

'The carpet-bag. She's got it in her carrier basket.'

'Ah no, madame,' began Deveaux. 'The chest . . . the breath. Please, I cannot run after you.'

She reached the top of the next hill to leap off the bicycle and leave it lying in the road as she caught up the carpet-bag and raced for the cover of the nearby woods. 'Gone,' swore Kohler. 'Ah *nom de Jésus-Christ!* Louis, she's vanished.'

St-Cyr let go of him and calmed his voice. 'Follow her. You will see where her trail is. Find her, Hermann, and bring her back for her sake as much as for our own. Odilon will return to meet you here.'

'And you?' asked Kohler, worrying about him.

'The cave, I think. The Baroness and her dog.'

An hour . . . two hours . . . Had it taken so long? wondered Kohler apprehensively. Downslope of him, moss-covered rectangular slabs and blocks of damp, grey limestone lay among oak and chestnut trees whose trunks were dark in the leafy shade.

There was still no sight of Juliette but he felt he had at last run her to ground. A twisted ankle—an espadrille had lain on a boulder—then the other one had been found and then the impressions of her bare feet in the moss. Limping . . . really limping.

She would have to hole up. Fillioux? he asked anxiously. Had she been heading for a rendezvous only the two of them knew?

Gingerly he took a step up onto a slab. Now he could catch a glimpse of the stream they had crossed and recrossed so many times. She had been following it, forcing him to struggle through the rubble of the ages.

The mossy smell of decay came to him and then the sight of twigs and saplings she had deliberately broken so that he would see them. Ah *merde*, what the hell had she in mind? The place was too still. Not a breath of air stirred, not the sound of a bird came, only the gentle murmuring of the water . . . the water.

The stream must eventually spill over the edge of the escarpment. Discovery Cave was not far now. A hundred metres, two hundred. . . . Would the lip of the waterfall be that far, a leap of a hundred metres or so to the rocks below?

She had wanted to kill herself in that abandoned mill at Domme. She had argued with herself, a woman in despair. 'My children,' she had said. They alone had stopped her.

Some thirty metres downstream, on the other side, a shelf of limestone jutted out. Was she hiding under it, in some cave only she and that mother of hers had found? She and her father too, or was she waiting for this detective at the very edge of the waterfall for a leap together into death?

Gingerly he crossed the stream. Louis would be down there in that little valley. Louis. . . .

When he saw the shirt she had worn, Kohler shuddered. It was hanging from a limb. There had been stone tools in that carpet-bag, tools the mother had had beside her bed. Tools the daughter had been forced to use to skin and butcher rabbits . . . Ah *nom de Jésus-Christ!* where the hell was she?

Naked, madame? Is that it, eh? he demanded. Naked and with a handaxe?

The trousers hung on another branch, the carpet-bag lay on the ground and up from them, only the darkened maw of a narrow cave entrance stared at him from the edge of the shelf.

Like a savage, a trapped animal, she had retreated in there to draw him in and kill him.

Louis, he said. Louis . . . but there was no answer because Louis couldn't hear his silent call and as for Henri-Georges Fillioux, there was as yet no sign of him.

*   *   *

Fillioux, wondered St-Cyr. Everything centred around him. The wife, the daughter—how could any woman force her own flesh and blood to revere a dead father so much, the poor child had had to write letters to a man she had never seen and had no possibility of ever seeing because he was dead to her, dead. Letters he would never read until ... until perhaps he'd stolen them from the mother's house during a desperate search for a small handful of postcards.

Fillioux had been married when he had met the sixteen-year-old daughter of a village innkeeper. He had had a daughter, Danielle Arthaud, whose mother had sued for divorce and so had known of the mischief in the Dordogne and that all had not been 'research' of the prehistoric kind.

That wife must have instilled in Danielle a hatred of the man who had deserted her. His parents had disinherited the child. The inheritance had been clipped by the Germans requisitioning the house in Paris but still, if the parents wished to sell it, the Germans would pay handsomely. A fortune, particularly if invested wisely.

Two daughters, then. The one, a schoolteacher, had not known of the other who had been all too aware of her half-sister's existence. Both schooled in the use of stone tools, the one by her mother, the other from the notebooks and specimens in the trunk of her father and a long-dead abbot, or from the father himself, ah yes, but after a reconciliation of some sort or an agreement.

Two daughters who, had the one not been disinherited, could quite possibly have shared the inheritance equally, a thing Danielle would most certainly not want.

But was the father really dead, or was he alive, and had Juliette really been working with him on the forgery?

Wiping sweat from his brow, he glanced up through the trees past the stagings and towers of a celluloid world to the mouth of the Discovery Cave.

Toto Lemieux and the Baroness had obviously had a picnic beside the stream where she and her 'prehistorian' would soon be filmed drinking champagne to toast their success. Like many great but temperamental actresses—was she great? He did not know—Marina von Strade had patently ignored the crisis, the time and the necessity for her to be in Beaulieu-sur-Dordogne to shoot the poverty scenes. The others—all the set crew, the cast, the cameramen, the directors and the producer could wait and to hell with them. She had had to come here.

Totally without fear of Fillioux or anyone else, the couple had bathed under the waterfall and had laughed and caressed until, naked still, the Baroness had led her Toto up to the cave.

He started out. By using the hoist rope the crew had strung to one side, he found the climb much easier but even so, his heart was pounding, his sweat blinding.

Darkness soon enveloped him.

'Toto . . . Toto, darling,' came the urgent whisper. '*Bitte, liebchen. Bitte.* You enjoyed Danielle, didn't you?'

Danielle . . . Danielle . . . her voice echoed.

'Damn you, Marina, he made me do it.'

'Willi?' she asked, her voice grating.

Willi . . . Willi. . . .

'You know he did.'

'But you enjoyed her all the same?' came the accusation, harsh and cruel . . . so cruel.

Ah *merde*, they were in the second chamber. Like the neck of a funnel, the narrow passage Courtet had found would have revealed the light of their candles. Juliette must have stood here on that Thursday, hearing the sounds of their lovemaking just as he did but knowing the inner chamber to be very dangerous.

She had come to collect the things for her mother but had not been able to enter the cave beyond the *gisement*, she had said.

Not, madame? he asked as if she was here beside him. And where, please, is this cache only you and your mother knew of?

It had to be in the main chamber and away from the *gisement*, for only here would it have been safe, so why, then, did she have to return on that Sunday when she could so easily have taken the things on that Thursday?

To see the paintings for herself . . . was that it, then? Or to see that nothing had been done to spoil them?

'Toto . . . Toto,' came the earthy demand so softly there was no echo, only shadows on the walls and roof that flickered and fled across the tapestry of animals.

When the Baroness cried out in ecstasy, St-Cyr turned away until the couple began to talk earnestly in whispers.

The handaxe was on the ground before Kohler, and Juliette was sitting demurely on a mossy shelf with arms clasped about her knees and her chin resting on them.

'There,' she said. 'Now are you convinced I did not want to kill you or anyone else?'

Ah *Gott im Himmel*, she was like a softly tanned forest nymph. 'You could have told me,' said Kohler earnestly. 'You scared the hell out of me.'

'*Good!*'

The cave, such as it was, had soon broken through to ground level above and that is where he had found her.

'I only wanted to see the postcards of my father because you both were blaming me for everything. Admit it, please. You thought I was the stonekiller! He has named me in those post-cards—yes, I can see this. What did he say, that I had helped him? If so, it's a lie. It's all lies, I think. That part of the cave, the paintings, the ages of the figurines the abbé found and this . . . this,' she said, plucking at the amulet and inadvertently letting him see a breast she quickly hid.

Chin again on her knees and arms, she said, 'Well, what is it to be, Inspector? The bracelets for my wrists so that Herr Oel-mann can perhaps question me again, or yourself as my friend and protector?'

She was putting it right on the line. 'Where is your father?'

'My father,' she said. 'The stonekiller. Perhaps you had best ask my half-sister for I, poor simple thing, do not know. Mother went to meet him, yes. She must have believed firmly that he would be there. She had no fear. Finally after all those years, what she had waited so long for had come true. They would meet again and make love perhaps but this time she would kill him. She didn't tell me anything, Inspector, only that she would take care of them. Of my husband and my father.'

'I'll get your clothes.'

'Does the sight of my nakedness offend you so much?'

'I'm only trying to help.'

'Then I will get my clothes myself and leave you to pick up the handaxe I did not use to kill you though I could have, couldn't I?'

Ah *merde*, there was not a thing wrong with either of her ankles. Not a thing!

'Toto . . . Toto, darling, you must say nothing. Oh for sure you know things, yes? but just keep everyone believing you are simply my stud, my *grand godemiche* whose stiffness lasts for as long as any woman could ever want. With a little help, of course.'

'Damn you, Marina. What makes you say things like that?'

'Your cock and the white angel that feeds it. Now listen to me. Willi is in trouble—trouble like he has never had before so we must help him.'

'Three murders . . . Fillioux, was it really him, eh, Marina?'

'I did not hear that, Toto. I really didn't.'

'Fillioux could be out there somewhere.'

'Yes, that's it exactly! Danielle and her father, they are working together. She was so anxious to visit the cave to see the paintings on the Friday before that woman's death, she led us to them. She behaved *exactly* as she would have had she been here many times before.'

'They're fakes. They're all fakes.'

'And that is why my Willi needs our help and your continued silence.'

'Danielle,' he said. 'Why did he make me do that to her in front of the others?'

'To teach her a lesson she must never forget. To break my

heart—yes, he's done it lots of times. You and she, how could he have been so cruel? Now make love to me again. It may be the last time we have the animals to watch us. I like to see them up there when you're in me. It makes me feel so powerful, Toto. Supreme. An earth goddess of fertility.'

'And the daughter, the schoolteacher, what of her?'

'Let us hope her father finds her.'

Night had been turned into day in Beaulieu-sur-Dordogne, shadows banished where not wanted. Arc lights brought the sun at noon to windows still leaded in spite of the centuries of wear and the poverty of an *auberge-épicerie* and PTT which could not possibly have replaced them. Giant fans produced a gentle breeze to stir the grape leaves and the potted geraniums of the balcony railing while songbirds chorused from hidden cages on the floor at Marina von Strade's feet and doves roosted on the shabby tower where not so long ago St-Cyr had been trapped on the roof.

Apparently everyone was here—Herr Oelmann looking grim and worried, the cast, the crew, the villagers who stood well back like sheep at a hanging. Would the cinema ever be the same for them or for himself?

He searched the crowd as Hermann and Madame Jouvet did. Film personnel came and went or stood in earnest discussion as sound booms, reflectors and screens were positioned for the take and a silk-screened blue and puff-cloud sky was raised above the roof. It would look so real on film.

Generators softly throbbed in the distance, cables were strung. Two tall wooden towers, looking as if left over from a Roman invasion, held the massive arc lights which could instantly plunge the set into darkness or blind the eyes if one was not careful. The first, second and third cameras would film from the ground, the side and above. Distance shots, pans to this and that, then close-ups to automatically engender empathy in the audience, then shots of the visitor, the actor-prehistorian, the second camera moving in and staying with him as he walked towards the inn and gave a wave, a smile, the sound of his voice. . . .

'Louis, I can't find Lemieux.'

'Maybe the rutting has tired him out. Maybe the season is over for him.'

Oh-oh. 'Odilon might have something. He's playing co-producer with von Strade.'

Lorries and vans filled the narrow streets behind the Baron. In surrealistic semi-darkness, dressing-rooms, make-up, hairdressers and costumiers competed for space with a mobile canteen. Everything that could foreseeably be needed was there and if not available, then readily made on the spot in the workshops.

'That one, he is like a voyeur driven out of madness to watch the behaviour of others,' said Juliette bitterly of von Strade. 'He pulls the strings and they all dance because they have to but I will not dance for him or for anyone else. Not now. Not ever again.'

'Stay with Hermann, madame. Don't let him out of your sight.'

'A forgery,' she said. 'All this has been mounted to perpetrate an untruth. Two hundred, three hundred—five hundred must be gathered here but at a signal, the whole place will shut up and no one—absolutely no one—will move until the clapper-board comes down.'

'The Professor will want his amulet returned, madame.

Please let me have it for safe-keeping. I want to hear what he has to say.'

'And Danielle?' she asked hotly.

Would such a sharpness not lead her into trouble? 'Mademoiselle Arthaud also, yes, and Toto. Both have much to tell us, as do the Baroness and her husband and your father, madame. Your father.'

'I ... I would not recognize him if he was standing right where you are.'

'But this is the world of film and anything is possible.'

'Even a mature thirty-five-year-old Austrian with the mind of a *fille de joie* playing a sixteen-year-old *périgourdine* virgin who airs the bedding as she greets the prehistorian who's about to come into her life,' snorted Kohler. 'From Essen of all places and bearing rucksack and hammer, no loose change, and holes not only in his pockets but in his socks!'

'It's magnificent, Hermann, and exactly as I had imagined it would be. Ah some changes, yes, since the days of the silents but mere refinements.'

'As in war, so in film, my friend. Most of the time people are simply standing around wondering what the hell to do. Then whoosh, eh? Lights, action and camera and it's all over in about thirty seconds or else two hours. The story of our miserable lives. She looks the part, doesn't she?'

'Ah yes, she does.'

Side by side, and dangling from their leather thongs, the two amulets, the real and the replica, were identical to the untrained eye. And certainly the deerhorn of the one was a trifle darker, a touch more of that deep bluish cast old bone often acquired, a few more of the hairline cracks, but really the match was quite remarkable. Line for line, the short, sharp, seemingly randomly arranged incisions of the flint engraving burin were so similar one could even see where it had first been pressed into the bone and then forced away or drawn towards the artist.

'I worked largely from photographs and detailed drawings,' said the propsman-cum-carpenter he had found all alone in the cluttered workshop where the smells of sawdust, paint and resin were pungent.

'I commend you, *mein Herr*,' enthused St-Cyr in *deutsch*. 'Even Professor Courtet will be hard pressed to tell the difference.'

The man grinned and accepted a cigarette of thanks. 'Take two,' urged the Sûreté. 'The Baron forgot and left the package at the château. He won't mind.'

They lit up. Though young, the man had seen enough of life to shrewdly give him the once-over.

'The Baron doesn't forget anything, Inspector. Is the cave really a forgery?'

'A forgery?' came the startled reply.

'Rumours . . . there are rumours circulating that we're all to be let go and blacklisted if we say anything.'

Ah *merde* . . . 'Until we find the stonekiller, the authenticity of the paintings must remain in question, though who are my partner and I to care so long as we apprehend the killer? Ours is not the task of patiently defining prehistory but of uncovering the identity of the murderer.'

'But that was why the woman was killed, wasn't it? She thought the paintings were fake and he couldn't have her saying that. She'd have only made trouble for him.'

'Perhaps, but then, perhaps not. Two persons may have been involved in the killing of the assistant postmaster but only one in that of the woman.'

'And of Jouvet, the husband of the daughter?' hazarded the man.

'One most definitely. A small struggle perhaps and then the throat viciously opened with the stone. A handaxe, I believe.'

'We could have faked those paintings easily. Danielle showed us how they were done. She's really very good at it.'

'Yes, she is, isn't she?'

'While she was at the university she used to work in props. That's how she got into acting.'

'And the stone tools, how is it she learned so well how to use them?'

So it was Danielle who was under suspicion. 'She was a student at the Sorbonne. Courtet was one of her professors. She was working towards her final degree in prehistory but had to give it up. Too broke, I guess. It's odd, though. Really it is. Courtet doesn't know as much about the tools as she does. If you ask me, I don't think he has ever made one. Experimented with them of course, but that's not quite the same thing, is it?'

'No . . . No, it isn't, is it?' Was Courtet held in suspicion by the crew and cast or did they simply not like him? Too arrogant, too demanding and covetous of his precious trunk. 'My thanks. You've been most helpful. Please . . .' St-Cyr indicated the amulets. 'I would like to deliver these to the Professor. I know how anxious he must be to get them.'

'Then I'd better come with you.'

'Ah, no. No, that would be most unwise. Stay here. Have that other cigarette and consider yourself lucky.'

'I've not done anything.'

'Of course you haven't. It's just that we are dealing with a particularly desperate killer and it would be safest if you were not seen in my company.'

'Is it her father?'

'Whose?'

'Danielle's.'

'What do you think?'

'I'm asking.'

'Perhaps but then, ah then, either he has come back from the dead as everyone has been led to believe, or he hasn't. Now, please, I have much to do. Will they continue all night with the filming?'

'We work straight through until we're finished, then go to the cave until the film is in the can.'

St-Cyr was at the door when the man stopped him. 'Here, you'd better take these too. The figurines the Professor wanted. The Adam and Eve.'

'Ah! yes, the couple. Cro-Magnon, I believe.'

'Neanderthal . . . the professors say they are at least from fifty to seventy thousand years old.'

'But these have only just been made so they could not possibly be of that age. Imagine it though. Lovemaking at the very dawn of prehistory. Kissing and doing all manner of things in a cave whose paintings look down on the couple as a child is conceived. Wild, yes, and like the animals above but also tender and caring when required or demanded. It's a miracle the swastika was ever thought of.'

Toto and the Baroness, was that it then? wondered the propsman. They'd been screwing in that cave and everyone knew it too. Screwing when she should have been working. No sign of Toto, though. No sign of him at all.

'A swastika. Yes, it's a miracle. Who would ever have thought it possible?'

'Only a student or a professor,' said St-Cyr with the toss of farewell. 'Someone with an eye for it and a damned good reason.'

Von Strade and sous-préfet Deveaux sat in canvas deck chairs with a bottle of the *vin paille* between them. And the street, with its half-shadows and its overcast light from the arc lamps, was a clutter of cables and dressing rooms that bore the names of Marina von Strade, her prehistorian, and that of Danielle Arthaud and others.

'Baron, where is Toto Lemieux?'

'Herr Kohler, how good of you to join us. Madame,' said von Strade, offering her his glass and letting her quickly shake her head. 'Madame, you keep good company in such difficult times but I would not place too high a value on it.'

Amen, was that it, eh? wondered Kohler.

'Inspector,' said Deveaux uncomfortably, 'it would be wise to listen. Herr Oelmann, he . . . he has a little something in mind for you and Jean-Louis and you, also, madame. Please, I . . . I cannot make the warning any plainer since I could not possibly know of the existence of a *Sonderkommando* in our midst. One with explosives in its possession and perhaps highly trained assassins.'

'I want the postcards,' said von Strade, taking out a cigar. 'Everything that partner of yours found. I'm willing to pay—yes, of course. It's what I do best, but we can't have rumours and we can't have trouble. Find the stonekiller if you must and bring him to justice, but let us finish *Moment of Discovery* in peace. Let us say 100,000 marks between the two of you with another 50,000 for you, madame. None of you are experts in prehistory and none of you could ever gain the upper hand by trying to prove those paintings a forgery. If you cry foul, we will only cry all the louder and our voice, well, what can one say but that it is so infinitely greater.'

'The postcards,' said Deveaux. Would Kohler not be reasonable? 'That's not possible, Baron.'

Was Kohler really so foolish? 'Oh, and why is that, please?'

'Louis hid them in a cache and until we have the stonekiller, that's where they will remain.'

'A cache . . . ?' asked von Strade, startled and looking to Deveaux who had the good sense to shrug.

'It . . . it is a place only my mother and father knew of, monsieur.'

'And yourself, if I understood that husband of yours correctly, madame. To hide the postcards there, with your father presumably having returned, cannot have been wise of St-Cyr but it really doesn't matter, does it?'

'The paintings are a forgery and you know it!' she said. 'This . . . this whole business is a sham.'

'And you?' asked von Strade. 'What will your children say when you fail to return to them? That you did the right thing by exposing this . . . this forgery, as you say, or by listening to reason and removing for ever all chance of want from their lives? Make no mistake, 50,000 marks is 1,000,000 francs. You need never work another day. They can go to the best schools and on to the university. They can study music, painting, medicine, whatever they wish. You could even take up residence in

Paris. That, too, can be included with all the necessary papers thrown in for good measure.'

'I . . . I cannot accept. I . . . I must do as mother would have wanted.'

'Then that's settled and I leave you both to the stonekiller and to Herr Oelmann.'

'Baron. . . .'

'No, Herr Kohler. The lady has spoken. The Reichsführer-SS Himmler, the Reichsminister Dr Goebbels and the Führer will doubtless hear whispers of your insubordination but, as in film so in life, truth is in the eye of the beholder. The people will believe what they want to because it makes them proud and happy and we will tell them that they have a heritage so great and grand it extends well back into Neanderthal times. And who is to say differently when you are gone? Think about it. Don't make nuisances of yourselves like that woman did.'

Danielle Arthaud was distraught. She got up, sat down, fiddled with a copy of the replica of *Vogue* magazine the Germans produced in Paris, then grabbed the cinema pages from *Aujourd'hui, Paris-Soir* and several of the other Paris dailies and threw them down opened at bad or not so bad reviews of her last film.

'Toto . . . Toto isn't here. Look, I don't know where the hell he is. How should I? Maybe he's fucking some little thing down by the river, maybe he has simply gone for a walk. Neither of us are in on this shoot though Willi always makes us come along. We're his, can't you see? *His!'*

Kohler crowded into the tiny dressing room and, closing the door behind himself and Juliette, put the bolt on. 'A few small questions. Nothing difficult.'

'*I can't tell you anything!*' she shrieked and stamped a foot. 'I can't, I can't!' Willi, she begged. Willi, please help me.

'I think you had better answer, mademoiselle. Postcards to tip off Madame Fillioux that. . . .'

She gestured dismissively. 'She was never anything to him. Just a foolish girl he had to fuck and use in other ways.'

'Ah, no . . . no, mademoiselle. Though our father did not mention my mother in his journals or give her credit for helping him, I still believe he fell very much in love with her. So much so, he told your mother of the relationship and she then demanded a divorce.'

'He killed her, didn't he?' snorted Danielle. 'He cut her to ribbons. Slashed her breasts, peeled back the skin, carved her buttocks, her mons, her . . . Ah no, no . . . I did not mean to say that.'

Merde, merde . . . 'I think you did, Mademoiselle Arthaud,' breathed Kohler. 'Tell us what she said to you in that little glade. She was expecting to meet her husband after all those years of loneliness but instead of him, you turned up, high on cocaine.'

Ah no . . . 'I . . . I found her after it had happened. I . . . I was in the cave. I really was. She . . . she couldn't have cried out. You must believe me. *You must!*'

Then why the tears of remorse, why the agitation of betrayal and a need so desperate only von Strade can help? 'But you were there at the cave?' he asked, to pin her down.

'Yes.'

Kohler dragged out his little black notebook. 'Your timing's impeccable, mademoiselle. On the 25th of May of last year you wrote to Madame Fillioux telling her the parents Fillioux were very ill and had had no news of her. The couple needed food and money desperately. You stated very clearly that you were returning to see them that day.'

'I . . . Yes. Yes, I went to see them that afternoon.' Would he let her have a cigarette?

'Good, because my partner and me, we're puzzled. You see, your name and "friend" appears in the visitors' book at Lascaux on the same day the card was posted.'

'That . . . that is a lie. I . . . I was never there. I was in Paris, I

tell you. *Paris!* Until we began filming, I had never visited
Lascaux.'

'But you had visited the Discovery Cave?'

She ducked her head. 'Only during the filming at Lascaux
and not before it.'

A lie of course. Inwardly she was begging von Strade to help
her. Kohler was certain of it. 'Then let's talk about the murder
of Madame Fillioux. Take it right back to your first postcard.'

Ah damn that stupid woman! 'I . . . I have nothing to say to
you or to anyone except that I am innocent. I only tried to help
my grandparents who are old and sick and not so well-off any
more since they failed to declare the contents of their safety
deposit boxes and these the Occupier has confiscated as well as
their bank accounts. All they have left now are two houses—oh
for sure it's lots, yes, if either was sold, but they cannot dispose
of even the smallest item of the furnishings in Paris and are constantly being watched. One more mistake for them and they
will lose everything.'

She was really bitter about it and not without good reason. So
many had failed to declare things, the SS and the Gestapo had
had a field day, but could she be trusted to remain here in her
dressing room? Of course not.

Kohler dragged out his handcuffs. 'Let's try these on for size.'

'And the stonekiller, Inspector?' she shrilled. 'Our father,
what of him?'

'These will help you to stay put so that you don't have to
worry about him.'

'*Bâtard!*' She snatched at something and swung. Juliette
shrieked, 'A handaxe. . . .'

The thing fell to the floor at their feet. Blanching, Danielle
said, 'It . . . it's not what you think. I. . . .'

'Save it for later, eh? Now turn around and give me your
wrists. Madame, that chair with the iron back. The one at the
dressing table. Turn it so that she can sit and not get too tired.'

'He'll kill me, don't you see?' pleaded Danielle. 'I had to tell him things. I had to help him. He knows the village and has been watching us. He can come and go as he pleases.'

'She's right,' said Juliette. 'Please let me stay with her. We'll be safe enough if you give me the Professor's gun.'

Ah yes, madame, said Danielle to herself, the Professor, we must not forget him. A loaded revolver from Dunkirk. Why, please, did he believe it to be necessary?

'Are you sure you can handle this?' asked Kohler doubtfully. 'I've got to find Lemieux.'

'I'll manage. André . . . my husband. In his lighter moments he used to stick the barrel of just such a gun into my mouth and pull the trigger. He didn't just have a Luger, Inspector. He had one of those and others brought back not just from Russia but bought also on the black market.'

Ah *merde*, was she telling him Jouvet could have sold the gun to Danielle?

She saw him thinking this and nodded. She tried to smile and said, 'When you found it in the Professor's room, my mind was too preoccupied with other things but now I'm certain of it.'

'There are two positions, the half and the full cock.'

'Two clicks. I remember them well.'

It was his turn to nod and he did so but reached out to brush three fingers against her cheek. 'I'll be back. Don't worry.' Louis . . . where the hell was Louis?

The village's café had never seen business like this. Only with difficulty was it possible to push a way through to Courtet and Eisner, two very worried prehistorians whose eyes leapt at the Sûreté's approach.

Courtet's glass went over. The hand that had hit it ignored the spill. 'Inspector, why haven't you apprehended Henri-Georges? He hates me. He's going to kill me. A stonekiller. . . .'

'Professor, please try to calm yourself.'

'*He's killed again! This time the husband of that woman's daughter. The throat . . . a savage cut.* Cognac . . . more cognac, please,' he gasped at Eisner, and tossed it off. *'Merci.* You see the state I'm in.'

'Good. Now perhaps you would be so kind as to tell me why you failed to alert my partner and myself to the danger?'

Alert . . . alert . . . danger . . . danger, ran the whispers, electrifying the café into silence while Herr Eisner fastidiously tried to avoid the spill which had found its way to his edge of the table.

'I . . . I did not know for sure,' confessed Courtet, his gold-rimmed spectacles winking in the naked light. 'I worried—yes, yes, of course. Unlike that foolish Fillioux woman, I had thought him dead long ago but now the cave, the paintings, the. . . .'

'These?' asked the Sûreté, dangling the amulets in front of him while Herr Eisner watched at the ready perhaps, to sacrifice his fellow prehistorian.

'That Jouvet woman stole the real one from the trunk,' seethed Courtet. 'Why, please, did she do such a thing? Is she working with that father of hers? Is she, Inspector? Ah damn, you do not even know!'

The amulets were swept into a decisive fist, the accusations ignored. 'A chair,' said the Sûreté, and when one was shoved into place, he sat down firmly opposite the two of them.

Opening his fist, he made a great show of indecision. 'They are so perfect, I cannot remember which was which. No, please, Herr Eisner, I want the Professor to choose.'

If I can, is that it? wondered Courtet acidly. Ah damn the Sûreté.

'A forgery, Professor,' said St-Cyr. 'A few more engraved lines made with a flint stylus—yes, yes, most certainly. But why question the matter too closely when Herr Eisner here held the purse strings and the Reichsführer Himmler was so determined to prove the claims of Aryan conquest extended back into the earliest of times? Fillioux did not note the presence of a swastika in his journals, Professor, though it would have been well known to him even then, nor did he indicate there were paintings in that second chamber but when the trunk became available, it was too good an opportunity for you to miss.'

'He's alive. He's come back. She said he would.'

'Madame Fillioux?'

Courtet gave a nod, a swallow but continued to stare at his hands. 'I . . . I thought the engravings genuine. I found the paintings. I really did. The wall was closed, there was no opening into that chamber but then, there it was. At first I could not believe Henri-Georges had been so stupid and arrogant as to have missed such a thing but . . . but . . . a major discovery. My moment at last.'

'So you fell for the forgery. You believed it absolutely.'

'If it is one, Inspector,' interjected Eisner, 'you will have a very hard time proving it.'

'Please don't be tiresome. Confine your tongue to silence lest you become an accessory to murder.'

'I did not kill her,' mumbled Courtet, still staring at his hands which now opened and closed and felt so useless. 'We met at the house here and I drove her to the railway line near the cave. The leaves were turning. The truffle hunt was starting. We came across only one hunter with his sows but she did not know him. "He's new," she said. "Since the war, things have changed so much."'

'Go on, Professor,' urged the Sûreté.

'She . . . she was a little nervous—unsettled. Yes, yes, that's how she was but I thought it due only to my presence. Here I was taking over the work she had tried so hard to keep for Fillioux. I . . . I told her she had nothing to fear from me and that due credit would be given. A bronze plaque with their names.'

One must go very carefully now. 'Did she ask how you had come by the trunk?'

'Yes. I told her I had received a telephone call from a dealer I frequented in Saint-Ouen. When I saw it, I realized right away what I had stumbled upon.'

A fortuitous discovery, was that it, eh? Hardly. 'And the amulet?' asked St-Cyr gently.

'It's that one and you must not handle it so carelessly. When . . . when I had it under my microscope and had done the tracing, I could not believe what I had found and for days I kept the secret to myself. I had to see the cave. At last, all those years of wondering what Henri-Georges had discovered were over and it was all mine.'

'And you had no hint that he was alive?'

'Only Madame Fillioux's firm belief.'

'Then why, please, did you think it necessary to keep a loaded gun at the château?'

Ah damn the Sûreté. 'You had no right to take it.'

'We had every right. A weapon from Dunkirk, Professor? How, please, did you come by it?'

'Danielle, damn you. Danielle thought it best for me to have it. Suggestions in that woman's hesitation to respond to my post-cards and requests led us to believe he could well have returned and now we find he has. First she and her sous-facteur are mur-dered and then Jouvet. It's too much to deny. The evidence is clear.'

'Danielle . . . ah yes. So now we are getting somewhere at last. Your former student, the daughter of your former col-league, a cave painter *par excellence* and a stone-user of note—ah, please do not think I said stonekiller yet, Professor. Or yourself either, Herr Eisner. A forgery, a lot of money, a research grant worth—how much was it, please?'

'250,000 marks,' said Eisner.

'5,000,000 francs.'

'And a film,' said Franz Oelmann coming to join them. 'You put Jouvet's body in my car, Inspector, so as to make us all believe Fillioux had really returned.'

There were two men with Oelmann. Tough-looking, grim and brutal. Still, he would have to say it and hope Hermann was near. 'But Fillioux hasn't returned, has he, Herr Oelmann? Henri-Georges has been dead for years. Madame Fillioux refused to believe it. Very early on in this Occupation, postcards began arriving from the parents but all they ever mentioned was food and money, then Danielle added her pleas and soon was writing to tell that poor woman the trunk had not only been sold, Professor, but to yourself.'

'Danielle . . . ?' stammered Courtet, caught unawares and sickened by the news.

'Yes! She warned Madame Fillioux it was you who had the trunk.'

Ah no . . . 'But . . . but that's not possible! Danielle said she would keep in the background. All I wanted her to do was to convince the parents to put the trunk up for sale. 5,000 francs — I paid her that much, and another 2,000 to the shop.'

St-Cyr let out a sigh. 'And she took you and everyone else for a ride. An amulet like this, a cave whose paintings surpassed even those of Lascaux. Swastikas at the dawn of prehistory and then, as her crowning touch, the return of the dead husband.'

'*Danielle*,' swore Oelmann. '*Get Danielle.*'

'Ah no, monsieur, a moment please. Jouvet's Luger, it is loaded.'

The crowd vanished. People dived for cover. Chairs fell, tables were tipped on to their sides. There was a mad rush for the door, the sound of breaking glass, a scream, a plea to get out.

Then silence. Ah *nom de Dieu, de Dieu,* two Schmeissers were facing him in addition to the Radom pistol Herr Oelmann had reacquired. 'All right, you win. The cave isn't a forgery.'

At a toss of Oelmann's head, St-Cyr put the Luger carefully down on the table and raised his hands. Hermann had not come to the rescue. Hermann must be busy elsewhere.

Moving diagonally away through the crowd, Kohler tried to keep out from under the arc lights. The German director was shouting in *deutsch* through a megaphone to Marina von Strade up on the balcony. A little more of her cleavage, more of a winsome smile. 'You're an ignorant peasant wench, Marina. Christ, you're going to want to seduce him, eh? Tease the bastard!' Her prehistorian.

Kohler ran. Clinging to the periphery of the set, he made it to the first camera, tripped over a cable, pulled the bloody thing down, was up and away to shouts and curses. Got to keep going, he told himself. Got to get Louis out of their clutches. First have to get Juliette and Danielle away before it's too late . . . too late. . . .

The street was nowhere dark enough, the lorries and vans looked as if just waiting for him. He could hear the *Sonderkommando* rushing through the crowd behind him.

When he got to the dressing room, it was empty. The handcuffs had been shot free. Ah *merde*.

He ran. He reached the river and went up it until all he heard was the sound of the current. 'Juliette . . . ?' he ventured but she did not answer. Where . . . where the hell had the two of them gone?

They were standing calf-deep in the river, in darkness beneath some overhanging branches. As Juliette pressed the muzzle of the gun into Danielle's back, figures darted along the bank, while over the lower village, with its cluster of Renaissance houses, the capsule dome of light formed a bubble under the sky.

Muffled, urgent voices were now heard. Lights . . . would they use their torches? she wondered.

'He'll kill you, madame,' breathed Danielle. 'Our Franz won't waste any time on you now.'

'Don't you dare try anything! I'm warning. I'll shoot.'

Surrounded by water, they waited until at last she said more calmly, 'We'll go upriver to the farm. Maybe then you will find the courage to tell me what happened. You were there when Monsieur Auger was killed, mademoiselle. Shards from one of those little tubes you love so much were found in the sand. Did you break it when you realized there wasn't enough?'

Ah damn her. 'I did not kill him. I only heard him die.'

The gun was jabbed into the small of her back. 'I don't believe you. *Now move!* Walk out farther. Feel your way with your feet. Take off your shoes.'

'And walk naked, is that how I did it, schoolteacher? Naked and with my little bag of stone tools? If so, please tell me who drove him towards me since I did not kill him?'

Danielle was only trying to agitate her so as to escape. 'You know our father did it. Only he could have walked right up to Monsieur Auger.'

And now you believe it, snorted Danielle inwardly. 'And what will you do when we three meet? Beg him to tell you the truth, or try to buy your life by letting Herr Oelmann have him?'

They were quite some distance from the shore. The water was getting deep. 'Mother didn't deserve to die and neither did Monsieur Auger.'

Were there tears now? wondered Danielle, her hands still held aloft. 'Beware, schoolteacher. You mingle with the darkness of Cro-Magnon times or was it from the Neanderthal the amulet and the figurines came?' she taunted. 'The Abbé Brûlé made a mistake that father you worshipped so much failed to see in his eagerness and inexperience. And that, my dear half-sister, made him believe the Neanderthal capable of feelings for each other which I'm certain they had.' She tossed her hands for emphasis. 'Love and sex, eh? Tenderness and nurturing, and even a belief in the hereafter, since they often buried their dead in the fetal position with dustings of red ochre, tools, and food for their journeys.'

A sadness came. It could not be avoided. 'The amulet and the Adam and Eve are Cro-Magnon, aren't they?'

'Of course. Even Courtet could tell you that but he's a nothing. He's no match for our father who hated him so much he refused to let him see the contents of that trunk and made our grandparents swear they would never release it.'

'Then how did you convince them to do so?' she asked sharply.

'Me? Hah! by simply getting the Germans to move it. Our grandparents were very upset at the loss but what could they do since it had been sold? The Professor wanted it so badly, and I made certain he got it because, my dear half-sister, that was what our father wanted. *Revenge* for having lost the bet that forced him to go to war. *Revenge* for having had his career terminated. So Henri-Georges created, with my help, a cave so beautiful it would rival Lascaux. A swastika was thrown in for good measure—it was his idea—and what do you think happened, eh? A professor from the Sorbonne who should have known better, made a terrible mistake and became an utter fool. A failure the Germans must now punish.'

They were well out in the river and it was dark, so dark. 'But mother found out what you were doing, and when she went to meet our father, she refused to wait until the film had been made, refused to go along with any of it, so he . . . he killed her. It's true then. *True!*'

And now you stupid, stupid cow, you have yet to realize in your grief that I am no longer your prisoner and will kill you to save myself.

Kohler cursed their luck. He was soaked right through and damned tired yet still there was no sign of Juliette and Danielle, and he knew he had let Louis down.

Wading in to the bank, he grabbed a branch to steady himself while he drained his shoes and stuffed his stocking feet back into them. He was upriver a good piece and perhaps not far from Auger's farm. Would they have made for the cottage? Was it worth a try? Hours . . . it had been hours since Louis had been taken. Ah *merde*, what was he to do? The stars were fading. The damp, sweet smell of hay came to him and then, as he moved inland, that of the mare.

He stopped. He was in the middle of the pasture now. No sign of the mare, no sound of the geese. Someone must have taken them away. . . .

The cottage was nestled among walnut trees whose dark silhouette all but hid it.

When he reached the door, he knew he was not alone. When he softly hazarded, 'Madame,' she fired.

*   *   *

One by one they had returned to the café. Now there were four of the *Sonderkommando* with Herr Oelmann. The handcuffs, St-Cyr's own, were too tight, his arms were aching. The chair, it was too hard, and he had had nothing to wet his throat in hours. Not a sip of the *vin paille*, not a taste of his beloved pastis.

When Juliette was flung into the café to lie bleeding from the forehead on the floor at his feet, despair swept through him. The cut was ragged, about six centimetres long and above the left eye. A handaxe? he said to himself. A handaxe.

'Hermann . . . what has happened to Hermann, madame?'

She gave no answer. She was dragged up and thrown into a chair. She was slapped hard and spat blood when they demanded to know what had happened. 'I tell you *nothing*, messieurs. Nothing!'

Ah *nom de Jésus-Christ!* 'A moment, messieurs. A moment,' he urged. 'Bathe her face and dress that wound. Can't you see she's terrified of you?'

She was soaked right through. There was mud on her bare feet. A toenail had broken in half. The toe was bleeding. . . . 'Messieurs, I beg you,' he said. 'Please, I need to know where my partner is.'

'He's dead. *Dead!*' she cried and sucked in a breath. 'Danielle . . . she got away from me. Hermann, he came to Monsieur Auger's cottage. He did not know she was in there, that for hours she had been hunting me. *Me!* I had lost the gun, Jean-Louis. *She* had it! He. . . .'

Hermann . . . Hermann, he said to himself, what have I done by getting off that train when Deveaux asked us and you wanted only to continue on to Paris to see your new girlfriend?

The dawn had not yet come, the night was very dark. Cold ashes met fingertips that felt so stealthily they hardly moved.

Verdammt, where was she? wondered Kohler. The cottage was small—just this one room. A table, two benches, stoneware crocks, a bed with big drawers beneath it, a plain armoire, both doors closed and walnuts scattered all over the floor in a desperate but futile search for cocaine.

When he felt the ladder, he felt the smoothness of peeled poplar and the steepness of it. An attic, had she gone up there? Was she now on the roof or only leading him to think this?

Danielle Arthaud, he said and realized in that instant where she was.

The Webley would be with her but had she managed to pick up the handaxe that had fallen to her feet in her dressing-room? he wondered. Had Juliette not seen this happen? Was the schoolteacher now lying dead out there or drifting slowly downstream to catch on a gravel bar and swing lazily back and forth in the current?

He heard Danielle sigh. He knew she was desperate. She hadn't hit him with that one shot of hers. He'd been through that sort of thing countless times and had known better than to stand in the doorway.

When his fingers touched the soaking wet cloth of her skirt, they found the hem and then the zipper at the back and he had to wonder why the two were so close together.

He heard the hammer fall. Even as he grabbed her wrist and tried to force the gun aside, the sound was there. The metal of the handcuff bit into him. A blinding flash of white-hot light was followed by a deafening bang but then he saw her swing the handaxe. She cried out. She screamed and kicked and bit and fought to kill him . . . kill him. . . .

Kohler clutched the gun and the hand that gripped the stone. 'Bâtard!' she shrilled and tried to bite him. He was forcing her back. . . . 'My arms . . . my arms,' she cried.

As she hit the floor, the gun went off and she pulled him with her, wrapped her legs around him. Together they rolled about, banging into things.

He gave a ragged gasp. Her chest heaved. He was so big, so heavy and strong and he had pinned her to the floor. Ah no.

The gun came free only with difficulty and he slid it as far away as he could. The handaxe was next and that, too, he removed.

She would bite her lower lip to stop herself from shaking, would bite right through it if necessary.

Kohler felt her relax. Every muscle seemed to let go all at once. Then she said, '*Couchez avec moi*,' and he heard her catch a breath. 'You can if you want. I'm naked below the waist. Naked, monsieur. Just give me a little. Please, I beg it of you.'

When he refused, she spat at him and hissed, '*Had I had it, nothing would have stopped me. Nothing!*'

Continentale's doctor finished putting the last of the sutures in Juliette's brow then ran a thumb over the wound. Using the Sûreté as interpreter, he said, 'A scar is inevitable, madame, but you've no concussion. Your eyes are clear, the pupils good. Give it five or six days and come back to see me, yes? I would like to take the sutures out then and check you over once again just to be sure.'

The doctor had insisted on Juliette's hands being freed. He had as much as cursed the *Sonderkommando* for their rough handling. A silent but conscientious objector, he had found refuge under von Strade's wing yet appeared untainted by it. 'I've warned you, Baron,' he said. 'Release them. Those hand-cuffs are cutting into the detective's wrists.'

'Ah, Ernst, my good man, it's just not possible yet but a deal has been struck with Herr Oelmann and his associates and I have it on record that their freedom has been guaranteed. You've no need to worry.'

Von Strade gave the doctor's arm a fatherly pat. 'When Danielle arrives, take care of her for me. A little something just to sooth her nerves and give her back that confidence we like so much to see. You know how she is. She's like a Stradi-varius with a string that might break right in the middle of a magnificent concert. We wouldn't want that to happen, now would we?'

Or else the Russian Front, thought St-Cyr grimly. Ah *merde*, what was the deal?

The doctor threw Juliette a frantic look and in that one gesture, St-Cyr saw only too clearly it was the end for them.

Courtet had reluctantly come into the café to morosely nurse a mug of *café noir* and smoke a cigarette down to its very last. There was still no sign of Toto Lemieux. No one seemed to know where he was. The Baroness was still shooting the trunk scenes in the attic but Courtet was not needed since Herr Eisner could handle everything.

All others, unless directly concerned with the murders or the *Sonderkommando*, had been excluded.

A deal . . . Exactly what had they in mind? Odilon fidgeted uncomfortably. Caught in the middle, he worried about his pension, fussed over duty and knew he ought to say something.

A forgery. Could they not have been more discreet? This, too, was written all over the sous-préfet because now he, too, was involved and yet he was not sure if his fate had been included in the deal.

'Cocaine,' said von Strade, lost in thought to the grandjean he had taken from a pocket. 'The favourite stimulant of the avant-garde, the artist, actor and writer. In small doses it produces intense well-being and great self-confidence, a sense of invincibility, of never getting caught. Inhibitions decrease. Sexual drive is often enhanced as a result, and in a young and vibrant woman like Danielle, her need often leads her to do anything to get more.'

He put the grandjean down on the table between them and looked to Juliette as if to say, Don't ever try it, madame. 'Had I known the addiction would lead to such vicious murders, Inspector, I would most certainly have been far more temperate in my judgement. Please be reasonable. We're both men of the world. Let us finish *Moment of Discovery*, then make whatever arrests you deem necessary.'

So Danielle was the killer, was that it, eh? Was it that simple? 'And the forgery, Baron?' he asked.

'Forget about it. Don't be troublesome.'

'But isn't forgery a crime?'

'Jean-Louis. . . .'

'Odilon, please let me handle this.'

'Then don't be so foolish, Inspector,' snapped von Strade angrily. 'Do you think I don't know what's been going on?'

'Good! It is just as I have thought, Baron. Danielle's addiction forced her to tell you everything. That makes you an accessory to murder and I welcome the opportunity to see that you are charged!'

'You fool, do you think you can say that to me?'

'*I say it even if my wrists are shackled, Baron!* You *knew* and so did the Baroness!'

A purist, Deveaux had said of St-Cyr, a stickler for the truth. 'Then take the platform you so desire, Inspector. Let me see how well you do. Audition, please. Don't stint yourself.'

'A cigarette . . . My pipe. . . .'

'Nothing. Such things are impossible.'

So be it then. All anger must be suppressed, the impassive faces and weapons of the *Sonderkommando* ignored. 'At the end, Madame Fillioux had to be stopped, Baron. Certainly she let the Professor think she would go along with things but she had her own reasons, her own plans. A forgery, a betrayal and denial of all she had struggled so hard to protect.'

'She would kill my father and then my husband,' said Juliette sadly. 'She would expose the forgery for what it was. A monstrosity.'

St-Cyr let sympathy register as he looked at her. 'But he did not come back, madame. Though we will never be certain of its location, he probably lies in an unmarked grave along the Marne like so many others.'

'Not alive . . . ?' she blurted. '*Dead*, Inspector? But . . . but. . . .'

'Please, it is a shock, yes, and were I able to comfort you, I would. As in film, madame, so, too, in murder, illusion is so often necessary. Your mother had to believe emphatically that your father had returned, otherwise she would not have kept silent for a whole year the knowledge that the paintings were a forgery. Remember, please, that she was unsettled after last year's visit. Things were happening then. The cave, it was not right.'

'The postcards had been arriving from my grandparents and then later from Danielle and . . . and then from the Professor and . . . and at last from my father.'

He turned to von Strade. 'Juliette did not help her father as the postcards from him claimed but . . . ah, but his words must have struck fear into your mother, madame, and doubly she resisted telling you anything.'

'It was clever . . . so clever. Had I known, I would have done something to help her,' said Juliette. 'She must have thought I was involved even when she asked me to visit the cave and get the things for her. Even then she wanted to keep me out of it.'

Courtet was staring sourly at the dregs of his *café noir*. 'It was necessary also,' went on the Sûreté, 'that everyone else believe Fillioux had returned, and so successful was the illusion, even my partner and I believed it for a time. But . . . ah but he never showed up. Two killings, so vastly different, the one as if in a demented frenzy, the other simply a crushing of the skull. The Baroness had no fear of him, Baron, though it was she who discovered the body of Jouvet in Herr Oelmann's car. She led my partner to your wine cellar—two bottles of the Moët-et-Chandon were missing. We had found them in the stream. After I had viewed the rushes, she told me Danielle was the one I wanted. A postcard was mailed from the Marais in Paris by Fillioux. Mademoiselle Arthaud was daring to the point of foolishness. She even had one mailed from there while at Lascaux with her "friend", knowing full well that Madame Fillioux would see the entry in the visitors' book.'

'So, no Fillioux, Inspector, and two murders,' said von Strade, signalling for a glass and bottle of wine. 'If Fillioux could not have done it, who could our stonekiller possibly be?'

'Baron, never mock the Sûreté. It is not wise.'

How close the room was, how still. 'The Professor, Inspector?' asked von Strade.

Courtet leapt. 'I had nothing to do with the forgery. *Nothing*, do you hear? I only found the paintings.'

Dregs of *café noir* shot across the flagstone floor as the mug shattered.

'Of course, Professor. That is exactly it,' said St-Cyr. 'You did what you were supposed to do. Mademoiselle Arthaud was the cave artist and she had you right where she wanted you.'

Desperately Courtet looked to the Baron for help. 'This is crazy. I did not kill that woman.'

'My dear Eugene, no one has said you did,' offered von Strade blandly.

Courtet clenched his fists in anger. 'Apart from a postcard or two, and one visit, I had no further contact with that woman. I had what I wanted from her and needed nothing else she could possibly provide.'

'YOU KILLED HER!' shouted Danielle, causing them to turn as she and Hermann, with wrists bound tightly behind their backs, were brutally shoved into the café by Herr Oelmann and some others.

'A *grâce à Dieu*,' began St-Cyr. '*Mon vieux*. . . .'

Herman wasn't happy. He was furious. '*She tried to kill me, Louis! A handaxe, damn it!* She's confessed to having been at the scenes of both crimes.'

'I DIDN'T KILL EITHER OF THEM, DAMN YOU!' she shrieked and tried to kick him. 'I WAS THERE, YES! BUT . . . but I . . . I could not stop things from happening. I really couldn't. Please, you must believe me. *Willi* . . . *Willi, can't you see I need a little? Just a little?*'

She was distraught but best ignored for the moment. 'And you, Professor?' asked the Sûreté as she was thrust into a chair by two of the *Sonderkommando* and held down. 'What have you to say now?'

'I didn't kill anyone. It's preposterous of you to even think such a thing. I'm a professor of prehistory, a holder of the. . . .'

'Professor, *please*,' said St-Cyr. 'Had I a free hand with which to caution you, I would. Two killings . . . ?'

'Each so vastly different, Louis.'

'Ah yes, Hermann. Auger's skull is crushed. There are no signs of the demented slashings, the experimental cuts, the disembowelling, but for a time there was the possibility of two assailants. The one to stalk, chase and make the kill, the other to leap out at the last minute so as to distract the quarry.'

'*Fillioux*,' hissed Danielle. '*He* did it!'

'But he's been dead for years, hasn't he, Louis?' said Kohler, straining at his handcuffs. 'Toto Lemieux offered a faint possibility but. . . .'

'There were last-minute touches, Hermann. Suggestions of daring, of defiance too, an attitude of catch-me-if-you-can.'

They were all looking at her now and through the tears she could not stop, their images were blurred. 'What touches, please?' managed Danielle.

Things must fall as they would, sighed St-Cyr inwardly. 'The Professor is another suspect, yes, but he had no reason to kill the sous-facteur, mademoiselle. He did not even know Madame Fillioux had sent you the 10,000 francs her husband would need to make the final visit. But you knew. You could not let Monsieur Auger live and the Baron made certain you understood this.'

'You did it all by your little lonesome,' said Kohler, breathing in deeply, 'and afterwards, on impulse perhaps and still high on cocaine, you cut the fishing-line and freed the worms from their prison.'

'But had, beforehand, found only enough cocaine for one or two hits,' said Louis. 'Admit it, Baron. You had Mademoiselle Arthaud dancing on the end of your string.'

It was time for a sip of wine, for a cigar and the careful study of these two from Paris Central who were from so vastly different backgrounds yet got along so well. 'What of that infernal nuisance, Inspectors? Our Madame Fillioux? Please don't stint yourselves. Is our Danielle correct or did she commit that killing too?'

'She was at the cave, Louis.'

'Yes, but not, I think, in on the killing. You see, Professor, your former student had no fear of Henri-Georges Fillioux. As creator of the illusion, she could by then only wait to see what you would do. Certainly she had originally intended to kill Madame Fillioux—there was no other choice, was there, mademoiselle?'

'He *hated* my father,' spat Danielle. 'He *gloated* over that trunk. He had everything now. It was *all* his at last!'

'A grant of 5,000,000 francs, Professor,' sighed Louis, 'for which Herr Eisner, ever mindful of Herr Himmler's desires, exacted but one thing in return.'

'A film,' breathed Kohler. 'A swastika at the very start of pre-history even though it was perhaps most professionally doubtful. Cave paintings like no others.'

'Madame Fillioux did not run,' said Louis. 'She knew you from your former visit and from the past, Professor. Admit it, you were afraid to deal with her but once you had the trunk, you took a chance. She paused, she realized that Henri-Georges was not coming, and then she strode out into that little glade to tell you exactly what she was going to do.'

'Destroy you,' said Kohler. 'Admit it.'

Moisture filled Courtet's eyes. Perhaps the Baron would intervene. 'For years the location of that cave eluded me. The Dordogne is full of caves and that woman would never tell anyone exactly where it was. There were the casual visitors she objected to, but never once did she disclose the location. We at the Museum of Culture and the University all thought the cave was near this village and she let us think that until she got what she wanted from us. I . . . I couldn't believe Henri-Georges had missed seeing such things yet . . . yet I was certain he had.'

'*You were a fool!*' hissed Danielle, struggling to lean forward. 'Even after all those years you were still so eager to get the better of him. I saw it in your lousy lectures, in your conceit. I had *no* trouble sucking you in. *None*. Just like a prostitute with her client, Professor, I finished you off in about ten seconds!'

'Ah damn you,' swore Courtet. 'Damn you for doing this to me.'

'YOU DID IT!' she shouted. 'YOU KILLED HER!'

Not a flicker of emotion registered in the faces of Oelmann and the others. 'You got caught up in the butchering,' sighed Kohler. 'You believed Fillioux was alive and that he and his wife had tricked you. You couldn't let her expose you to ridicule and failure, Professor. Not with the Occupier so keen on the film and Herr Himmler and Dr Goebbels lurking in the background.'

'You experimented,' said St-Cyr sadly. 'You tried to show Fillioux that you, too, could butcher an animal and you knew that others would believe he had betrayed his wife and that the couple must have fought.'

'The flask, Louis.'

'Another touch of daring you left for us, Mademoiselle Arthaud. You planned to kill her if the Professor didn't but . . . ah but he did. The illusion you had created had taken the turn you wanted most and there, suddenly, it was done. Why, she did not even scream or try to run away.'

'Why, please, the illusion?' asked Danielle, defiantly throwing back her shoulders.

'Why, indeed.'

'The houses in Paris and in Monfort-l'Amaury, Louis.'

'And their furnishings. Your grandparents, mademoiselle, they had disinherited you long ago but did they not perhaps make out a new will or say they were going to? Please, for such an illusion, such careful planning, artistry and skill, there has to be a deeper reason than merely your hatred of the Professor or desire to further your film career.'

'I have nothing further to say.'

'And the Baroness?' asked von Strade, raising his glass in a farewell toast perhaps.

'Very well, Baron,' said the Sûreté. 'Please ask her to join us.'

'That's not possible. We must finish the shooting here. She's distracted enough as it is.'

'And lonely, Baron,' he asked. 'A lover lost is always a distraction particularly if he posed the threat of saying too much and had to be removed. They made love in that second chamber but afterwards I am very afraid the Baroness did something for you she must now regret. I did not hear him fall down one of those shafts in the floor, Baron, since I had left the cave after her last orgasm.'

'*How dare you?*'

'Ah, please don't look so offended. We're both men of the world. No doubt her Toto was putting on his shorts or tying a shoelace. An accident . . . I'm sure your wife will tell that convincingly enough to the magistrate, and when you are both safely back in the Reich with your film, perhaps then you will treat her more kindly.'

'A deal?'

'Freedom and safety for Madame Jouvet—she has had to suffer far too much. My partner and I to return to Paris to file our reports after first conducting Professor Courtet to Vichy to face justice and the guillotine.'

It was a good attempt. 'And Danielle?' asked von Strade.

The Sûreté let him have it. 'Will, unfortunately, have to stand trial for murder, conspiracy to murder, and for forgery also.'

'Then it's no deal.'

'No deal at all, Baron,' said St-Cyr. 'The Sûreté and the Kripo of this flying squad never cut deals with anyone, particularly criminals such as yourself.'

'Ah *merde*, Louis. . . .'

'Hermann, for once, just for once, please let me have the last word. My pride demands it.'

'And your life?' asked sous-préfet Deveaux only to be silenced.

* * *

A week had passed and it had not been pleasant because Paris Central had refused absolutely to say anything on their behalf. Sturmbannführer Walter Boemelburg, an old acquaintance from before the war, an associate from the IKPK, the international police organization, had maintained an icy silence.

'Perhaps your boss wants to teach us a lesson, Hermann.'

The filming was over, the scaffolding had been removed. Everything in the little valley was as it had been on that first day. Even the honey buzzard soared high above them.

Kohler dropped his eyes to the darkened mouth of the cave and swallowed hard. What the hell were they going to do now? Juliette and Odilon Deveaux had been taken in there some time ago.

The charges were in place, the delays had been set. An hour . . . a half hour . . . the bastards of the *Sonderkommando* were going to blow the cave. 'They'll blame it on the terrorists, Louis, on a *Résistance* that has yet to find its members. Himmler will be incensed, Goebbels will have a field day—a major prehistoric site wantonly destroyed by French partisans. The Führer will scream for the total occupation of the country.'

'It's perfect for them. They will have their film, their *Moment of Discovery* and no one will say a thing against it because we and the cave will no longer exist!'

'Are you still certain Courtet killed Madame Fillioux?'

They had spent the week arguing. 'Yes, for the last time.'

'Then just remember, Danielle is an actress and she could have done both killings all by herself. You should have insisted that he sign a statement. I backed you up, but I had my doubts.'

How pious! Hermann had a thing about Danielle. Recurring nightmares in which he was assaulted with a handaxe by a naked savage who bore a striking resemblance to her. He had even started his partner dreaming of it.

A cigarette was lighted and shoved between Kohler's lips. 'Hey, what about my partner?' he asked his countryman.

'Tobacco shouldn't be wasted on scum.'

Ah *merde* . . . could he make the cigarette last? wondered Kohler. Could he stall for time? Something . . . there had to be something they could do to stop things.

Brutally they were hustled up to the cave—forced to climb at a run, to fall, to hit the rocks and bruise the knees, a shoulder, an arm . . . hands tied behind their backs.

Already *Moment of Discovery* was in Berlin, in its final stages of editing. Already Herr Oelmann was back in Paris, the Baron and the Baroness having a little rest at their home in Vienna, and the château had been emptied and closed.

Herr Eisner had returned to Hamburg. Of the film's personnel only Professor Courtet and Danielle Arthaud were to witness the final proceedings.

'They'll shoot them, Louis. Courtet's and Danielle's bodies will be found in that little glade riddled by bursts from their Schmeissers. One dead actress and one dead prehistorian in the wake of the terrorists.'

'Danielle will have realized there is only one thing she can do.'

'Hit you on the head with a handaxe, eh?' snorted Kohler only to be clubbed into silence.

At the entrance, the *gisement* was at its thickest, exposed in benches where Fillioux and the Abbé Brûlé before him had opened the deposits to study them. Rusty sardine cans, cast-off espadrilles and worn-out work gloves—the refuse of two-legged badgers—were strewn about . A rucksack, a broken wine bottle, innumerable shards of black flint, a litter of old bones. . . .

'Inspectors. . . .' Pale and shivering, Danielle came out of the darkness in tears between two of the *Sonderkommando*. 'The parents Fillioux were going to leave everything to that woman if she helped them. A goose, a chicken, some butter—if only she would forgive their long rejection of her, she would have it all but she did not know this and I . . . why I could not let it happen, may God forgive me. Now you know.'

'But you did not kill Madame Fillioux,' said Louis, shaking off the *Sonderkommando* who held him.

She flicked a glance at Hermann. 'No, but I intended to—it

would all have been blamed on my father, yes?—and I was going to if I had to, just as you have said.'

'And the postcards, mademoiselle? The things I left in the cave?'

'Juliette told them where to find the cache in the wall near the ventilation shaft. They . . . they have burned every last scrap of the drawings and the postcards, and have stolen the louis d'or and the jewellery.'

'And Juliette?' asked the Sûreté.

Would he condemn her right to the end? 'We have kissed and I have held my half-sister as I should have done long ago.'

'Then it's finished for us, Hermann, and we had best go in and get it over with. Goodbye, mademoiselle. *Bonne chance.*'

'You also.'

In the flickering light from two candles, a lunging aurochs charged, and as they sat on the floor of the second chamber, bound hand and foot, they heard, in imagination only, the sound of its hooves as it thundered over terrain long gone to join stampeding ponies.

The leader of the *Sonderkommando* gave them the once over and nodded curtly. 'So now we will leave you,' he said. 'Enjoy yourselves.'

Six men had gloated over their predicament for the past week. Deveaux was wheezing badly and near to death simply from the loss of breath. Juliette sat next to him with her knees up and her back and hands against the wall. Then there was a shaft, the chasm in the floor Toto Lemieux had fallen down, and then Hermann and himself. Ah *nom de Dieu, de Dieu,* why must things be so difficult for them?

'Louis, they're using cyclonite mixed with a plasticizer. Diesel fuel, crankcase oil and sawdust, maybe. Something to make it pliable like margarine. You can smell the bitter almonds but it's not nearly so strong as with Nobel 808 or even straight old dynamite.'

'And the detonators, Hermann?'

'Time pencils. Acid bulbs that are crushed by pressing a ridge on the side of the pencil. Wires of varying thickness give delays as the acid eats away at them.'

'Until the wire inside the pencil is gone and the spring it held back is released.'

'And the detonator is struck.'

'The pencils are coded red, I think,' said Juliette, squirming a little.

'Red for ten minutes or a half-hour?' swore Kohler. There were six satchels on niches along the length of the chamber, God alone knew what else out there and at the entrance to the cave.

Again Juliette squirmed and again. Falling over on to her side, she lay there staring across the hole in the floor at them. 'Danielle . . . ,' she said. 'Danielle has given me a flint.'

Her wrists came free. She sat up and began at once to cut the rope that bound her ankles. Hurry . . . they prayed. Hurry.

'Hermann, madame. Release him first.' Time . . . would there be time?

The aurochs watched, the ponies too, the cave bear and cave lion as shadows moved across the walls and roof, racing now . . . racing.

Must do it, shouted Kohler to himself. Have to . . . Have to. . . .

'RED, LOUIS! RED, DAMN IT! GET OUT, *MON VIEUX*. KISS GISELLE FOR ME. THE RUE DANTON, EH? THE HOUSE OF MADAME CHABOT.'

His new girlfriend.

They scrambled. They got Deveaux freed at last and tried to push, drag and coax him along the narrow tunnel that led to the first chamber. 'My lungs. It is no use, Jean-Louis. Leave me . . . Save yourselves.'

'Ten minutes, Louis. *Ten!*' shouted Kohler to hurry them up. A kilo of plastic to the satchel. First one and then another and another was checked and time pencils were not to be fooled with once their bulbs had been crushed. Not before either. The fucking things were always temperamental.

'Louis, I can't remove any of them. Those bastards will wait until the cave has been blown.'

'Leave it then. Hurry, Hermann. Juliette says that if we try, perhaps we can make it out through the ventilation conduit.'

They were lying among the scrub, sheltering themselves, when the charges went off. Debris and flame shot out over them. The ground lifted and fell, then shuddered as passages far beneath them collapsed and dust and smoke rose up into the air.

The sharp staccato of Schmeissers followed—two short, sharp, lonely bursts, then silence crept in as they shook the dust from themselves and checked for cuts and abrasions.

'Odilon is dead, Hermann. The heart, the lungs, it was too much for him.'

'Let's go then. We've a job to do.'

Pardon? wondered Juliette apprehensively. 'Messieurs . . . ,' she began but Hermann had taken her by the hand and was leading her away from the valley.

'We'll climb to the top of the escarpment and follow the stream back of the waterfall just as you did when you tried to get away from us with the carpet-bag.'

'We need to find the road to Sarlat, madame,' came the breathless urging of the Sûreté. 'They will have to walk out to the railway line and then along it to their car. Hurry . . . please hurry.'

'But what about Danielle and the Professor?'

'Nothing can help them now. It's ourselves we have to think of.'

Only then did she see the satchel in Hermann's hands and hear him say, 'In their haste to get the job done, one of them forgot to activate a time pencil. It happens all the time with cocky recruits. He should have had a taste of Russia.'

'And now?' she asked sharply.

'Now we're going to pay them back!'

Ah *merde*, these two, they were crazy. They each knew exactly what the other had in mind. They were desperate.

Boemelburg was brooding. The summers in Paris were always the shits. Hot, humid and far too often grey.

The storm would pass, the gutters would soon run dry to fill the sewers.

Well up in his sixties and close to retirement, he was as tall as Hermann and every bit as big. 'A rock-fall,' he said, not turning from windows streaked with the droppings of ungrateful pigeons too frightened by the shortages of food to roost anywhere other than the rue des Saussaies, the former headquarters of the Sûreté and now that of the Gestapo in France.

'A rock-fall, Walter,' offered Louis only to receive the cold shoulder of, 'It's Sturmbannführer to you.'

'Ah, yes, forgive me.'

The all but shaven dome of that grey and bristly head was irritably favoured by a meaty hand from which the sweat was then wiped. 'An accident. Tourists from the Reich on a little holiday in the Dordogne and what do I hear but that their car has gone off the road.'

'It must have blown a tire, Chief.'

'Don't "Chief" me, Herr Kohler. Just explain. A tire?' he asked.

Both Louis and he were dutifully sitting in front of the giant's desk. 'The left front. They were speeding. There was a bend in the road—you know how those roads are. A hay cart—who would have thought one would be sitting in the middle of that road?'

'Go on, I'm listening.'

Juliette Jouvet was safely with Mayor Pialat in Domme. She had hugged them both and had wished them well. 'The rockfall came down, the horse was frightened.'

Nordic blue eyes that were watery but not from sympathy surveyed them. 'Six men were in that automobile.'

'It went off the road and then it hit the entrance of a viaduct, Sturmbannführer.'

'And then, Hermann?'

'It skidded round and round into darkness, hitting the walls until it . . . it blew up.'

'*Explosives!*' thundered Boemelburg, clenching a fist. 'Time pencils in a box in the boot next to perhaps twenty kilos of plastic and seven hundred rounds of ammunition, to say nothing of the grenades. I'm surprised the horse wasn't hurt but it appears that someone had cut the traces.'

'We found it grazing beside the road, Sturmbannführer. The poor thing was nervous but I managed to calm it.'

The SS over on the avenue Foch were crying foul but was there proof? The Vichy police were making noises. They'd not been consulted. An actress and a prehistorian had been shot to pieces. A sous-préfet was dead.

'Gestapo Mueller wants a full inquiry but says *Moment of Discovery* is a triumph. Herr Himmler is delighted with the film but anxious for us to find those who blew up his cave.'

It was coming now and they both knew it. Boemelburg would have no other choice. Russia? wondered Kohler—he had not yet had time to see Giselle. They had come straight from the Gare d'Austerlitz. A car had been waiting for them.

'Monks,' said Boemelburg distastefully. 'Some little flea-bitten monastery where they make Calvados and raise bees. One of them has killed their abbot with a hatchet. You leave for Caen this afternoon—no, Louis, you do not even go home or call that wife of yours. You get out of Paris when I tell you to and you do not come back until I think it proper.'

'No chance of seeing Marianne? But . . . but. . . .'

'She'll leave you, Louis,' warned Kohler as they were hustled down the stairs and out into the courtyard to a waiting car. 'That wife of yours will find some blond, blue-eyed son of a bitch to take her mind off your absence.'

A surrogate papa for Philippe. A lover . . . ah *merde, merde,* why must God do this to him?

God had no answer. He never did. He believed firmly that

just as detectives should work things out for themselves so, too, should married couples.

In love, as in fighting crime, there were pitfalls.

'Giselle will miss me,' lamented Kohler, 'but, ah what the hell, Louis, it's better than having to face the SS over on the avenue Foch. Cheer up. You can send Marianne a postcard.'

'I can telephone her, *idiot!*'

'Not from the *zone interdite.*'

The Forbidden Zone, the Coastal Zone. Ah *merde* . . . a month? Had they been away that long this time? Three cases . . . three or was it four?

'Three,' said Kohler. 'But never mind. Absence always makes the heart grow fonder. It's that body of hers you're going to have to worry about. She's simply too good looking, Louis. You should have listened to her and let her go home to her parents in Brittany. You should have listened to your partner, but oh no, you had to keep her here in Paris. Wives are always best left at home on the farm with their parents. It's safer.'

'Unless there has been bomb damage to the tracks, there is a ten-minute stopover in Mantes. I'll telephone her from there and never mind telling me all about your own wife whom you haven't seen in years, Hermann. *Years!* You had better watch out yourself.'

But when he did telephone, there was no answer, though the switchboard operator let it ring and ring.